Kelley,
Just don't stop!
Charlie

By
Charles Martin Madigan

i

Disclaimer

This book is a work of fiction. Names, characters, accents and dialects, places, businesses, organizations, and events are either the product of the author's imagination or are used fictitiously. Any resemblance to an actual person, living or dead, events or locales is entirely coincidental.

Copyright © 2023

Dedication

This book is dedicated, first, to my wife Linda and my sons Eamon, Brian, and Conor, and then to the coal miners in my family, my father Gerald, his father Thomas and his father Martin, and to their 63 friends who died in the Sonman Mine Explosion in Portage, Pa. on July 15th, 1940.

About the Author

Charles Martin Madigan is the son, grandson, and great-grandson of bituminous miners from Cambria County, Pa. He is the first male in the Madigan line who never spent a day underground. Born in Altoona, Pa., in 1949, he attended parochial school and entered St. Columban's Seminary in Silver Creek, N.Y., where his intention was to become a missionary. He left there and finished high school in Altoona, Pa., then attended Pennsylvania State University. He dropped out in 1967 to take a reporting job at The Altoona Mirror, then moved to Harrisburg, Pa. to work for The Patriot-News. In 1970, he moved to United Press International in Philadelphia, where he was a writer and editor. He was transferred to UPI in the Soviet Union in 1976 and stayed there until 1979 when he joined The Chicago Tribune in Chicago. At The Tribune, he was a reporter, correspondent, national editor Perspective Editor, Washington news editor, and columnist. He received many writing and reporting awards, among them The Overseas Press Club honor for Human Rights Reporting for an investigation of war crimes in Kosovo. He was married in 1971 to Linda Kay Harbaugh. The couple has three sons, Eamon, Brian, and Conor. They live in Evanston, Ill. Mr. Madigan graduated with honors from Roosevelt University in 2005 and spent a decade there as Presidential Writer in Residence.

Contents

Preface: Deep in the Mine

Stanley Cornish sat at his table and waited for his wife to deliver the breakfast he had been smelling for half an hour; bacon, cornbread, eggs, coffee, enough of everything to hold him for the nine hours he would be working the coal face.

It was going to be a good day.

That fullness, that's what he was thinking about laying on his side two miles deep into Coalman Mine on a summer's Sunday morning, a day when no one was expected to work.

A great breakfast.

His wife was so good at that and always had been. She said if he was going to dig coal on a day when everyone else was off, he was going to work with a belly full of good food and a thermos of hot coffee with cream and a little sugar in it.

He and a couple of his pals always worked this way. Among a group of perhaps 90 men who spread out around Coalman on off days, generally, Sundays, when the 1,200 men who usually dug coal were off.

They were not supposed to be there. But they were miners, and coal meant money for them like it meant for everyone else attached to the bituminous industry. It was a workplace where people looked away a lot, which meant Sunday mining was fine for those who wanted to dig.

It made the place feel clear and clean, like working almost alone. He was undercutting bituminous, digging a long, flat chamber beneath the coal, about a foot high and as far back as he could reach. He stretched his right arm so the pick struck deeper and deeper into the vein of bituminous.

The undercut had to reach at least three feet under the coal face, so he spent much of his time stretched on his side, his freshly

1

sharpened pick biting chunks of coal with every swing. He would stop every 30 minutes or so to push the coal he had chipped away out of the gap. He knew this job well after 15 years at work. He knew how much he could put into it and how much he could take away. An extra $20 a week made all the difference for his family.

When he was done with the undercutting, he took a long auger and drilled a hole into the top of the coal face, then created a pathway through the coal that a squib, like a little firecracker, would follow, or a fuse if they were handy that morning, to set off the black powder charge he had made with a rolled up wet newspaper and a quarter pound of powder. He was happy to see fuses in the box because it saved time for him, and time in the coal mine was money.

When the charge went off, it broke away a whole slab of bituminous from the ceiling down to the trench he had cut beneath the coal. It was an old process, but it still worked well.

And the more you loaded, the more you got paid.

He was thinking of his daughters as he cut away, two of them headed for church school just that morning and a third still in the kitchen helping his wife bake bread. He loved that thought, the little blonde 3-year-old watching her mother and warming to the smell of baking bread in the kitchen. Even on his side chopping away at the undercut, it made him smile.

The Coalman mine was moving that morning.

He could hear the earth creaking and cracking in the worked-out section of the mine that had been "dangered off" with warning signs and a wood fence. There was coal there, and lots of it. Thick pillars of bituminous had been left standing to keep the ceiling in place. You could take one or two of them out without much risk. He ignored the "danger" and "Do Not Enter" signs, which were there to warn weekday miners to stay out of the "rooms" that had already been mined and were dangerous because of instability or high gas readings.

He had just wiggled out of his undercut and was standing out in one of the broader avenues so he could stretch out before he set his charges. He heard a loud whump, then felt a rush of air, then heat that grew more and more intense, then saw a wall of white light moving right at him.

It burned him to death almost instantly, turning his denims to ash and blistering every bit of exposed skin, which smoldered first and then broke into flame when the heat ignited the fat.

He would be dead before he realized what was happening.

That was a great blessing.

Sixty-two other men would die with him, but none of them as quickly. Some would be found without a mark on their bodies, killed by the gas. Some were blasted down where they stood and slain by the concussion. It took days to find all the bodies. Widows and children waited at the mouth of Coalman for any word about their loved ones. But nothing came out of that place that day but sad news and the occasional exhausted rescue worker carrying gear and nothing else.

Why it happened was anybody's guess.

It would take a good deal of time, long after the burials and even much of the grieving, to answer that question.

Chapter 1: Finn

Edward Finn began his day the way he began every workday, at his desk with strong black coffee and a few Lucky Strikes, and the latest edition of The Eagle. He could pick the paper up where he got his coffee at the stand run by Barry and Emma in the basement of The Pennsylvania Department of Commerce.

They were honest with their coffee.

Finn always had kind words for Barry, who had worn himself out digging anthracite coal near Scranton and ended up selling snacks and coffee and newspapers when his lungs were too far gone to be of any use underground. He got the job through a state legislator who wasn't much for writing laws but was very good at finding menial jobs for his voters.

Finn had seen hundreds of broken men in his years as a miner and mining inspector. He had worked with Barry in the anthracite mines near Scranton. Because of that, there was a bond welded by mutual respect for the skills of mining, for knowing the secrets of the earth and how it moved, the noises it made, and the warnings it sent.

Coal mining did not suffer fools, and to be sure, those people didn't last long. But the relationships that flowed from a life under the earth lasted and were dependable.

Not many other people could say that about their jobs, particularly there in the capitol building, where so much was based on politics and connections and influence.

Finn always tried to get a look at Barry from a little distance before he said anything, just to make sure he was okay.

Today, Barry looked comfortable and happy in his place behind the counter.

"You are looking good this morning, Barry," Finn said, with a warm smile attached to the greeting.

Barry said he was feeling good, happy about the weather being warmer, and having good fortune at his stand.

"I'm selling all the coffee I can make. People want all of it! It's a blessing. And I'm not so creaky when the weather warms up a bit. On the weekends, I can sit in the sun."

This was part of Finn's daily ritual.

Everyone has them, the pathways followed from life to job. Barry was like a milestone on the way, a half hour from home, a minute from his desk.

Finn admired Barry because he did not just stop and slump into a chair in his living room and wait for death, which he well could have done, given the shape of his lungs and heart.

He continued working, even at this diminished state job that paid him 20 cents an hour and whatever tips he could collect.

Sometimes he and Emma would walk away from the stand with $40 in tips on a good day. Around Christmas, people brought them gifts, tins of homemade cookies, and fruitcakes. Sometimes there were envelopes, too, with money in them. Barry was uncomfortable about this. He had worked his entire life for everything he got, and he didn't want people to view him as a charity case.

Finn put $1 in the coffee can with the 'TIPS' label pasted on the outside and saw it was half full. It was 10 a.m., an hour after the breakfast rush and an hour before the lunchtime crowd. That was a grand haul this early in the week.

The good coffee in a coffee wasteland was part of Barry's success story, moved along with eggshells to sweeten the water he used. But the other part of it was his plugging determination to get on despite the troubles in his lungs.

People loved it enough to walk past other coffee stands spread around the capitol just to fuel up on Barry's.

"My contribution to effective government," Barry joked.

Emma stuck with Barry through a nightmarish collection of medical procedures aimed at easing what was called miners asthma. She would report privately to Finn when she could.

"Slowing down a bit" could mean Barry was just tired or had picked up a cold or some other lung ailment. Sometimes Finn caught a tear in the corner of her eye. He would stand quietly, always looking at her, and listen to what she had to say. Sometimes all Barry could do was sit and wait for his breath to catch up. He would wheeze, cough, rest a bit and then nap and then come back, weakened, but there for whatever she wanted.

Whatever she needed.

Emma had scrubbed the coal dust from his back and his hair for so many years, cooked good meals, and raised two sons and a daughter while he was off mining.

The little coffee shop in the capitol was a point of pride for both of them, but in truth, it kept him alive and gave her a whole array of friends she could turn to for help of all kinds.

Barry was not so sure about some of them.

Monsignor Marty, the state house chaplain, would drop in for a blessing and the free donut he came to expect each morning, along with a hot cup of coffee. Barry saw him as a tarted-up religious parasite.

The priest gave everyone framed pictures of himself for Christmas. There was a halo of light around his head, suggesting impending sainthood.

"Can't come soon enough," Barry thought.

The monsignor's visits were more important for Emma. Her prayers with him were sincere, honest pleadings for God to bless them, to give her husband more time. To ease his pain.

To welcome the souls of the old miners who would be dying soon. When your job was watching your mate die, you took your help where you could find it.

That is what long marriages had become for so many miner's wives.

Finn knew that story well, and each time he reflected on it, he thanked God that he had left coal mining before any serious health problems developed.

He had moved to Harrisburg five years after he abandoned the hard coal region and used one of his connections in the legislature to get a job in Commerce in inspections and safety. In just three years, he was running the place, rising on the basis of his skills, experience, and the confident way he handled himself. His reputation was as an incorruptible man in a world that was plagued, besotted actually, with corruption at every level.

He was building a comfortable life, with a house with some land on the other side of the Susquehanna River. The topsoil was rich and deep and perfect for gardening. Angela, his wife, loved it, loved the location, and loved the fact that Finn had stopped working underground.

He was in a decent state job that required him to be as good a man as he could be, and she loved that part of his work, too.

Finn knew about everything a man could know about the economics, the profits, and the dangers of mining coal.

Reports about anything bad that happened in a coal mine eventually ended up on Finn's desk in a brown file with a label carrying the name of the particular disaster just to help keep them all in order. Fires, cave-ins, explosions, gas deaths, floods, they all demanded his attention. He had 345 of them by his latest count.

7

He had to decide which ones needed further investigation. They did not all land on this desk. By law, there had to be at least five deaths to elevate an accident to "reportable" status or a violation so egregious it could not be ignored.

Once a case presented five deaths, a formal record was added to the state files. Every dead miner was named, along with the number of years he had been working, whether a lack of English language was involved, and most sadly of all, a number reflecting those who survived him. It was far more attention than any state agency paid to a miner when he was alive and working.

Finn's case count, then, was at least 1,725 dead men and, perhaps, many more.

The meaning of this statistic rarely escaped him.

To his mind, the number five was a compromise in which the forces of good and the forces of evil had cut a deal. The evil people who wanted everything to be ignored lost their case, and so did the good people who wanted everything to be regulated.

After long arguments behind closed doors, the number five emerged as the solution. Less than that, there would be no formal record. More than that depended on the question, "How many more?"

Finn hated the consequences of that kind of choice.

It meant everything he was drawn into would be sad, bad, and hard to forget, even over a long time.

Fewer deaths than five and a newspaper clipping might eventually show up at his desk naming an unfortunate miner who fell into machinery or stood up and touched a 440-volt power line, but there would be no formal investigation.

That was done locally, usually by authorities who assumed coal mining was a fatal business anyhow, so death was inevitable, so why make a deal of it?

Finn saved the clips, now a yellowing batch of papers, in a growing envelope in his lower left desk drawer. They played no formal role in his job, which was to look for incidents and conditions in the mines that broke Pennsylvania mine safety laws and then to dispatch teams to investigate them. But they were perpetual reminders.

Compliance, he thought, was what it was about. Compliance and death.

He kept the clippings to remind him of the value of his job when he was in doubt. His simple, complicated mission was to save lives in an industry that was intent on stopping for nothing as long as the money was coming in.

The earth would roll, the walls would cave, the ceilings would collapse, the air would explode, and the miners would die. But the inevitable question at the site of the disaster was always the same:

"When can we get operating again?"

The answer from Finn and his team of inspectors was always the same: "When it's safer."

Much of his life was lived in the abstraction of badly written reports that would land on his desk because no one knew where else to send them. They recounted the many details, some of them quite gruesome, of how life ended underground.

"Mr. Salensky died when he was smashed betwixt two cars, and his innards were squirted against the back one. No attempt to revive him was made because he was completely dead and without innards to speak of."

He thought for a while that he would collect up these egregious violations of sense and tense and the other common rules of English and publish them as a darkly funny commentary on the way it went in coal mining, but he thought again about that, wary of anything that would reflect that he had anything but high respect for the people who worked with him.

9

They had sad, hard jobs for not much money and were safety and disaster investigators, after all, not authors. They didn't deserve shit from him on top of that. They could find the truth and then tell some widows, "We reported this to Harrisburg," and that might provide some consolation, an important part of the job, to Finn's mind.

Generally, Finn had teams in the field at all times because five death accidents were not a rarity and the big ones ate up manpower quite rapidly. If the accident was big enough, the gas explosion a few years back that killed 122 men outside of Pittsburgh, for example, he would go himself. He would call out his inspectors to comb the sites of the disasters, looking for clues about what had happened. He would also visit the site of the disaster and then examine the coal company's safety records, which were supposed to be kept under lock and key and never amended. But frequently, they were. Some of the records were so badly kept and sloppy that he could not tell what had happened over time. Gas readings would be conveniently smeared. Or missing. Some of them had fresh ink, a sign something had been changed in the wake of a disaster. These were clues he would carry with him through the investigation. They might lead to a question about the right person at the wrong time and an answer that explains why these men were so expendable.

He hated that part of his work, the pursuit of wrongdoing, but he knew he was the only person in the process who would do it aggressively. State fines for even egregious violations rarely exceeded $100 on individuals. Companies could face much bigger tabs, but they had more than enough money to pay the bill.

Coal, as long as it was moving, created money everywhere.

Finn's job was about presenting a story, an explanation people could grasp, to put death behind them and get on with their work.

Coal was simply too valuable to stop mining for any significant amount of time.

The bituminous industry was booming, and that's the way the state and the industry wanted to keep it. The railroads used coal. The steel industry used coal. The power plants used it. The homeowners with furnaces used it. Tens of thousands of men worked in the mines to feed their families. It was the backbone of the local economy in every coal town in Pennsylvania, and there were a lot of coal towns in Pennsylvania.

Finn's inspectors were almost always the first officials at the scene of explosions and an array of other disasters that happened with regularity in the mines, particularly in the bituminous mines in the western part of the state. Every mine manager had their names and their numbers and knew to call when the toll hit five. The inspectors in the field would then call Finn's office and get the investigation process underway.

The people who worked in Inspections and Safety in the Mining division had to know their work. In many cases, they would be explaining how miners died, with a good deal of specificity, assuming they could find that out. Because the accidents often led to legal actions, it was important to establish a clean, well-explained record of whatever happened.

It took a rare collection of skills to do that kind of work. Finn preferred former miners in those jobs because they knew the languages (Generally, most people in the underground part of the job were not speaking English), the conditions, the threats, and the dangers better than anyone else. Sadly, they were also comfortable with the idea of death, having witnessed so much of it.

But they also knew the aching these accidents caused and how to behave around the survivors. Speed was important. Inspectors could not work in a working mine, so the place had to be shut down, and they had to do their work quickly and move out of the way so the mining could continue.

Finn could not always control who got hired or fired because the governor's patronage office had the power to pluck people from the populace and plop them wherever the governor wanted or needed them. Not a lot of people wanted to be mine inspectors. They were not high-paying jobs, after all, but offered the security of state employment even in recessions and depressions, and, despite its regular boom periods, the coal industry was never very far from either of those economic realities.

You needed at least a little background or experience to get an inspector's job, but nothing like a real credential, like a mining engineering degree from a state school. Those men were snapped up by the industry, which was always in line after graduation to grab whomever it could find with the technical skill to operate a mine. The state required credentials for various levels of mining management. But the people who had them were rarely available.

Sometimes Finn had to reach all the way to eastern Europe, where there were hundreds of soft coal mines and lignite pits, to find the right people for the inspector's jobs.

The whole western end of Pennsylvania sat over rich bituminous coal deposits. There were mines everywhere owned and operated by some 200 holding companies. They used the state legislature the way a conductor uses an orchestra, louder here, softer there, faster, slower, but always under that firm control. Getting any regulation pushed into law was difficult, and safety regulations were the most difficult of them all.

Finn had few fantasies, but one of them was a system of penalties that matched the nature of the crime. The maximum individual fine of $100 was a pittance and an offense when the lives of miners were at risk.

And they were always at risk.

It was nearly impossible to identify all the ways people could be hurt in a mine, let alone codify and define them. The government was sitting directly in the center of the two competing forces in the business, the unions, and the owners, with the unions always emphasizing the very dangers the owners were trying to minimize.

They all ended up in the folders that would show up on Finn's desk each morning, carefully assembled by his unlikely deputy,

Valery Miller, the only woman in history to hold such a senior position in mine safety.

Chapter 2: Valery Miller

"Not V, not Val. It is Valery Miller or Miss Miller!" Finn told the inspectors who worked with him.

She was most diligent in her work and had a gift in that she made everyone who worked with her diligent, too. She lived in New Cumberland across the Susquehanna River with her mother and three sisters in a big house purchased with the money the United Mine Workers paid after her father, the famed organizer Michael Miller, was murdered in a labor dispute in Cambria County. That's how she got her job, union connections. The thought, the UMW felt, was that the loss of her father would make her an aggressive regulator.

And that was true. Valery didn't ask or tell.

She led by example and earned the respect of all of Finn's inspectors by being brilliant at her work and taking no shit from anyone. Ever.

She had her father's boldness and was just as likely to be found at the site of some disaster as she was to be found in the office. Either on the surface or piling through tablesful of documents, Valery Miller was often the mining inspector who made the cases.

She was that good at it.

The morning folders were a key part of her job. They would set the priorities for Finn's day, his week, and his month. From the accidents, he would review the people he might want to hire to the lists of new regulations that would show up, eventually, in the paper. It never hurt to know what was coming, and Valery was an expert in identifying what was coming.

She had graduated from Pennsylvania State University with an undergraduate degree in mining engineering, a rarity for a woman. The United Mine Workers picked up the tab. She had no intention of working underground or of spending her life in the coal industry.

She wanted to find the right state job at the right level, with just enough money and just enough responsibility.

Her father would come home every day and talk to her about mining, everything from the broad details to the specifics.

She would bring him his beer and put out his cigarettes, and brush the ashes from the arms of the overstuffed chair before her mother got a chance to see them. When the time came to decide about the future, she picked minerals and mining and Penn State as the place to learn about them.

She was an honors student from her first semester onward. For fun, she danced with her sisters, or sometimes alone, because she was the most graceful of the three and loved the motion of it.

"That girl, she had a knack," her father used to say, and he was right. He would walk with her up in the hills when she was small. She would collect rocks and then use a catalog back at home to identify them. The talks became more serious as she grew up. By the time he was murdered, she knew more about mining than most men who cut coal for a living.

She cried for a month when he was shot by people in Windber in Cambria County who were never caught. She prayed for him every day and expanded that prayer to include all the miners she met on the job, all the bodies she saw at accident sites, and all the survivors who wept at mine disasters.

It made her wise beyond her years, and it gave her a deep and abiding sadness that touched much of what she did.

With her intensity and the knowledge apparent to everyone who worked with her, Valery Miller made insecure men very uncomfortable.

Finn, who knew her as well as her mother and sisters knew her, was not among them.

At 56 years old, he had moved well beyond mid-life flirting and was secure and confident about the hard work he did. He knew

15

Angela would most likely kill any woman who tried to snare him and make him wish he was dead, too.

So, he never bothered with them.

Valery was like a daughter to him, and he had to be careful not to show too much pride in her intelligence and knowledge about coal mining, in which he had acted as a mentor. She was as comfortable with Angela as she was with her own mother and could talk for hours just about gardening and the insects that plagued it and how to combat them effectively.

But she got no edge on the job because of that. In Mining and Safety, no one played favorites. It was part of the tradition. It was one of Finn's unwritten workplace rules. You got what you got by being good at it!

She called him Mr. Finn, always.

The office had grown in importance even as coal became one of the biggest industries in the state. Finn was protective of the agency and proud of its track record, which was flawless in terms of knowing what it was that caused specific mine disasters. The first thing he said to any new employee was simple and chilling:

"This is serious business that decides who will live and who will die. Don't forget that."

He delivered this news from behind a heavy walnut desk that sat under a picture of the governor, which added gravitas to the moment. The second thing he said was, "This is my assistant, Valery. Valery Miller."

Everyone understood she carried almost as much weight in the office as Finn. She attended every important meeting in his place (because he hated meetings) and took detailed notes and boiled them down in her head, and reported quickly and clearly to Finn. She played a central role in most investigations, too, as an aggressive questioner with a deep knowledge of mining practices.

She looked completely comfortable, a little tilt on her state mining gear helmet in the green overalls with the state symbol on the back and the word "INSPECTOR" in reflective silver letters.

Because she walked like she danced, she added a strange taste of elegance to any disaster site. People who saw her talking with a handful of dirty, sweating, stumbling, damaged, and swearing miners from the mouth of some exploded pit did not forget it.

"Who the hell is that?" was the common response.

Her eyes were blue, not like the sky but like steel.

She knew how to use them. She was known as "that bitch from Finn" among the mining executives who would deal with Finn's office, but no one ever let Finn hear that.

Finn's assumption was that once people saw her in action, it would make them less likely to try to lie to her because nothing is more humiliating for a man than to be caught out by a woman in the middle of a lie, however fanciful.

She was an expert at reading people, lying eyes, cheating eyes, avoiding eyes, any of them, signs that more was going on than just the conversation. Finn made certain that he was present for all her interviews, not because he didn't trust her. It was because he trusted her completely. She had a nose for corruption, an intuition she could almost focus on anyone in front of her. She could tell who was lining his pockets, who was on the take, which could be corrupted by a few dollars. She was aggressive enough that sometimes she would need a defender. His presence, pen in hand and notebook in front of him, was all that was necessary. "That's enough," Finn would say, and the hostilities would end instantly. Finn didn't use that with any frequency. He wanted Valery Miller to have her own authority, and it was a challenge she met from her first days on the job.

"Morning, Mr. Finn."

It was how she started each day, walking into a dark office stale with the smoke from Luckies and the dirty ashtray and the faint but compelling smell of fresh coffee, with Finn reading files under his desk lamp.

Then she would turn on the light and open a big sliding window in the spring and summer, bathing the entire scene in the fresh air and incandescence that brought it to life.

They always had a little talk about starting the day.

Maybe something like, "I'm looking for regional accident reports today, particularly from Cambria County." Or something about what was coming in in the garden at home.

"Coalman?" she would ask, knowing full well that this was exactly what Finn was looking for.

He responded with one of those "hmm" sounds that might have been a yes, or a "no," or a "don't know."

Coalman Mine was down at the end of town in Portage. It was big, profitable, unstable, dangerous, and gassy, Finn knew, and it demanded as much attention as he could muster sitting at a distance in Harrisburg some 150 miles away. If he had his way, he would be living in Portage and visiting that mine each morning, taking gas readings himself and making the local fire bosses and crew chiefs toe the line. He would be determined to close it.

He talked to the locals each week, particularly to Tom Madden, the fire chief in town, as tough and honest as Finn but a bit older. Tom would tell him about the individual deaths, the roof falls, the small disasters, and things that claimed lives, but not on a big scale.

In mining, the truth always came out one way or another. It could be in the explanations for why the mine was shut down so many days of a given month when bituminous prices were soft or in the inspector or police notes about deaths on the job. He had been in mining for 30 years, and he knew that the ground always yields the truth given enough time.

It was all about reading.

Not between the lines.

Beneath the lines.

Soon enough, he knew, it would be Coalman's time. He trusted his own instincts. He had seen it hundreds of times in the files that landed on his desk. Each of them started with a problem and ended with death.

Roof falls were the most common killer in the bituminous mines in western Pennsylvania. Mostly, the earth claimed its victims one at a time. Finn would hear about it but not to investigate.

They came without warning. One minute he would be eating his sandwich and sharing some crumbs with the mice that gathered wherever anyone sat down. Then, the ceiling would break with a crack that sounded like a rifle shot, unleashing a slab of coal or rock that might weigh several thousand pounds. If one of those hit you, you would be dead before anyone knew it.

It happens hundreds of times a year.

The miner's union locals always blamed the disasters on management, and in cases in which the condition of the mine had been ignored, sometimes they were right.

But sometimes, a bigger cause, a physical cause, was involved.

The earth was always at work, always in motion struggling to fill in the holes men dug to extract their minerals. Roofs fell. Walls collapsed. Floors rose. Nothing was ever stable underground. A man might not be able to sense motion at all because those shifts were so subtle. But he could hear them if the mine was quiet enough, its machinery shut down.

19

Like fatal roof falls and explosions, economic problems were built into the business, too. The equipment was expensive. Manpower was mostly a marginal cost, but strikes could knock production to zero.

For as much tonnage as moved through the mines each week, they were so narrowly profitable that even the ethical operators, and there were a few, had to find ways to cut sharp corners to make money needed to keep the mines operating. This amounted to shaving pennies off the cost per ton of getting bituminous to the surface. The miners knew this, too, and they watched each load of coal closely as it went into the car and moved out of the mine. A coal boss could reject whole cars just because there was too much rock mixed in with the coal. It was in their interest to load as clean a car as they could. That way, there was no reason to stop it for an inspection.

There was an unspoken conspiracy at work, too, because the men made no money unless they were mining.

It was their choice, they reasoned, to work or not to work. Whether they might be injured or burned in a fire or crushed by a roof fall made no real difference.

They would be just as dead.

It's just that some ways were faster.

Finn carried his own dark thoughts about these realities, his "institutional memory," into just about every aspect of his job. Ghosts walked with him during every visit to Barry and Emma's, Finn's legacy of deep and long knowledge of the victims created by what happens down beneath the earth.

He had seen every bit of it, and it marked him.

When people got killed on the job, he did everything he could to find a way to get money for their survivors and identify any physical clue that might be repaired to prevent more deaths. It was a hopeless job. But Finn's quest for justice for these men was unyielding because he knew the process would never stop to create time for its victims.

It pressed on as quickly as it could.

There was money to be made.

To his mind, in every case that reached his office, somebody had to ask why. Those were the people he wanted with him, the people who pressed for the "why?"

The answers were down there in the mine or in the records, well or poorly kept.

These matters, weighty, irresolvable in some cases but always present, filled Finn's head most days.

All of that would all have to rest for today, though.

There was no disaster file on his desk. Nothing but "personnel" matters. He had six positions to fill and 40 applications for the job. An inspector made $2,200 a year, plus state benefits and limited expenses.

There were many other places in government offering easier work for the same amount of money. It always surprised Finn that his agency was so popular.

Perhaps it was Valery.

He smiled at that thought.

Everyone loved Valery when they first saw her. It took a few days for them to understand that it would not be returned.

She had many good men in her life, with her father being the best in the past, her two brothers close behind him, and now Finn first of all, although she kept her admiration and affection for Finn very close.

She set a high standard for anyone else to meet. It wasn't that she wasn't healthy or interested. It was simply that no one was good enough.

21

She was impossible to flatter, and many had tried.

Finn was thinking about his plan to try to promote her to a job in the governor's office as he thumbed through the folders Valery had placed on his desk. She screened the applicants. She was determined to weed out anyone who did not meet her standards.

The names were on tabs attached to the files.

On the top of the pile was a file labeled "Apostle, Anders." Valery had put a star next to that name.

He was special; she could tell, a perfect candidate.

He had sent only a brief description and told her what he could on the phone as he headed toward Harrisburg. She had jotted some of it down: "Miner, fluent in three/four languages, solid engineering degree with honors, father killed in the explosion, safety."

Chapter 3: Anders Apostle

Anders Apostle was not a regular at the Dark Castle Bar on a side street near the center of Vulcan, a favored spot for the men who toiled in the lignite mines a couple of miles from town. It could get wild at the Dark Castle on a Friday night, with the workweek behind, a pocketful of money, and lots of women to fight about. Anders was her prize, the only one of her sons to graduate from the institute for engineering in the first rank. His honors status meant he paid no tuition and had access to everything in the university, all the labs, all the libraries, and all the professors.

In no way was he a mama's boy, but he paid her respect because she deserved it, and he loved her. He always behaved well.

Since his father's death in the explosion at Vulcan, he had grown into his role as man of the house.

No charges were filed in the explosion of powder left behind in shot holes by an earlier work crew, and the company was excused from paying extra benefits because its role in the death was not clear.

Feeling badly about the loss of a head of household, they gave Anders preference for the next job, which was how he ended up at Vulcan despite his success as an academic, mathematician, and engineer. It could take an eternity he could not spend to get a job at the university. So, he went to the mines. Everyone was sorry for his loss. But they also noted that mining was dangerous. Anders took the job without complaint and worked diligently six days a week. People liked working with him. You were much less likely to be injured if Anders Apostle was at your side. He turned his pay over to his mother every week and heard the same warning, "You be careful at that."

At the Dark Castle, Anders drank only beer but never judged his friends, who would wash down shots of the brutally strong local sour cherry vodka until they could no longer stand up, long after they stopped making any sense at all, even to one another. He avoided the bar girls. It was customary to get drunk Friday nights and have a tumble with one of the girls, a celebration that marked making it through another week in a job that killed a dozen men a year through no fault of their own. They would be paid the equivalent of $5 a day for their mining, along with up to $10 more, depending on how much lignite they delivered at the end of the workday. Most of them could count on about $35 a week if conditions were right. At 24, Anders worked as a miner for just a year to save up the money he needed to leave Transylvania and head to America. That was why he was in this bar with his fellow miners.

It was his farewell.

Most of them were so deep into their vodka that by the time he made his announcement, they could only say, "Good luck," and offer a sloppy wave. Two of them kissed him on the cheek. There were some wobbly hugs.

He did not know what he would do in the United States, but he spoke good English in addition to an array of other Slavic languages and Russian, was qualified as a miner, had solid engineering degrees, and the conditions in America could not be worse than they were in the deep mine where he and his friends carved out their livings.

It was independent work but demanded a good deal of sophistication. Explosions were not unusual, but typically, they were small events set off by headlamps or sparks from the electric cars that pulled the carts of lignite out of the mine. Two hours before the start of the workday, the fire bosses would enter the mines and make a tour with long sticks with smoldering rags tied to the end. The thought was that the flame or sparks from the rag would set off any pockets of gas near the ceiling of the mine and make it safe for the remaining miners to come to work and wear their carbide headlamps. It was so dangerous that the custom was for the fire boss to soak a heavy wool coat and pants just to keep from catching fire on the job. Usually, it was old men who had been miners who did this work. The pockets of gas would flash and pop when the rag entered the area. If they did their jobs properly, there would be no lingering methane to cause trouble.

It worked well enough for everyone to make a pocketful of money every week, with extra cash for the old men who volunteered to be fire bosses. They were viewed as valiant beyond description and perhaps somewhat crazy, not to mention very dramatically scarred from bad choices.

Anders had been a particularly diligent student when it came to the world of mining. He knew, in fact, that he was the last of a generation to work in these mines and that the best avenue forward was into the sunlight and as far west as he could go.

His plan was to get a train into Germany, probably to Bremerhaven, and then ship out to New York as a deckhand in exchange for passage. His engineering degree gave him an edge in the competition for those jobs. Most of the candidates could not write simple sentences.

The train to Bremerhaven was almost full. Anders assumed these people, too, were looking for a way out. He had some advantages on the train. Fluent in Romanian and Hungarian and comfortable in Polish and Russian, he had no shortage of people to chat with as the train made its way through the mountains.

A red-haired girl and a man he assumed was her father sat across from Anders. He asked her father if he could give her one of his cookies. Permission granted, she seemed delighted with the little fennel-flavored biscuit. She told him her name was Minoo. She was 9, a student, and going to Bremerhaven to meet her cousin, who was coming back to stay with the family for the summer. She sipped a cold tea as she crunched away at the hard biscuit. She had a wonderful smile.

He felt as lonely as he had ever felt.

"Where are you heading?" the girls' father asked.

"America." Anders turned away from the window and replied.

"Job?" the man asked.

"Yes. But I don't know where."

"What did you do in Vulcan?" the man asked.

"Miner."

"Ah," the man said, nodding.

"Did you support the strikes there?"

Anders hesitated.

The man had a tiny red worker's union pin in his lapel, a sign he was sympathetic to the cause of labor and, perhaps, an organizer for the communists. But Romania remained conflicted about the strikes and the people who were involved. Anders did not want to deal with a secret police setup or arrest. So, he was careful.

"How could I not support the strikes?" he said.

The miners had been agitating for a 40-hour week and safer conditions for months. Who could argue with that? The strike had led to violence after the owners brought in some 80 members of the national guard and a large contingent of gendarmes. Twenty-two miners were slain, and another fifty were wounded in the incident. That was months ago now, but Anders felt he still had to be on his watch. You never knew.

He changed the subject.

"Where are you two going?"

"To see her mother in Bremerhaven and bring her cousin back home," the man said. She has been there staying with her sister for five months now, getting some sea air to help with her lungs. She was sick for almost two years, and it left her weak and in need of a change. I hope we can bring her home with us, too, but that's up to her doctors. We have missed her so much...

At that, the little girl looked up, and Anders saw tears welling up in her eyes.

"I'm sure she will be well, and I know she will be happy to see you," he said.

"Yes," she replied, shifting her gaze to the window.

"You were right, you know, to go on strike," the man said.

"Mining is hard, dangerous business and the people who own those places will squeeze everything they can out of you for the least amount of money they can pay."

He was happy to be leaving that world.

"Yes," he said to the man, dropping his guard. "It was a very hard life for not much money. I left most of what I had saved with my mother. I didn't...

The man interrupted.

"Then you'll have dinner with Minoo and me," he said.

"Anders was going to protest, but the little girl was smiling, and he wanted to hear more from her.

"The westbound train has a good dining car, and I will happily pay the tab so the three of us can talk. It will give Minoo a chance to work on her Romanian."

"Or maybe we can speak some English," Anders said, hopeful about the chance to work on what had been his third language at the university. Hungarian and Romanian were the first two.

"She doesn't know much," the man said of his daughter.

"Yes, I do," she replied in English with a heavy Romanian accent. She put her chin down and gave him a piercing look with her deep brown eyes.

The man smiled and nodded.

"We shall see," he said in English.

"I am Vladimir," he said.

"Professor Vladimir Kozinski."

"So, you are... Polish?" Anders asked.

"Yes," the man said, "from Lvov. I teach languages at the university there. Not a lot of English, but enough."

He explained that he would invite his daughter to sit in class with him all day.

"The future belongs to people who are prepared."

Anders liked that. It was familiar. His mother had her own way of saying the same thing.

"Your head is your luggage," she would say, "Pack your bags as though the world were your destination."

That, he took to heart.

A conductor came to their cabin to announce with much more formality than necessary that the table was ready for "Mr. Kozinski and guests."

They formed a short line, with Kozinski and the girl in the front and Anders following, walking down the long stretch of the Wagon Lits car with its thick wool carpeting past the sleeping rooms to the door that led to the dining car. Kozinski opened the door and held his daughter's hand as she stepped across the gap and through the door that led into the dining car, with Anders close behind. The conductor, now in a waiter's jacket, stepped from a side room at the end of the car and led them to their table midway down the dining car.

Anders told the man more about himself, about his mother's career singing folk music and dancing with a troupe of girls she had worked on stage with for 20 years.

The pate came first, with small good yellow butter crackers and a tiny bowl of capers and cornichons.

"May I?" Anders said to the girl.

"Please," she said.

He used the silver knife to cut the corner from the pate and spread it on a cracker for her, topping it with three capers he placed with the little knife and one of the little dill pickles.

"Thank you," she said after he plated the cracker and handed it to her. She nibbled it at first, then popped it in her mouth and crunched it up and swallowed and smiled.

"Do you have children?" she asked Anders.

"Not yet," he said.

"When I am married, I think I would like, perhaps, ten daughters and two sons."

"Oh, my," she said, her brown eyes opening wide.

He smiled to show he was joking about that.

But not completely. Anders delighted in children.

He was going to say that he missed his mother, but he didn't want to bring thoughts about her own ailing mother into the conversation. It had gone very well so far, and he wanted to keep it that way.

She offered her hand, and Anders shook it and lightly kissed it.

"I am delighted to meet you," he said. "Perhaps we will talk again later."

"Breakfast?" said Kozinski, so impressed with his daughter's command of basic English that he wanted to hear more.

"Fine," Anders said.

"Then it will be my treat! The dining car at 7:30?"

"Excellent!"

It snowed overnight in the mountains, which gave them a panoramic view of the last scenes of winter as they sat at their table for breakfast.

The conductor/waiter offered hard rolls, butter, marmalade, cold cuts, coffee, and hard-boiled eggs for not very much money. Kozinski ordered a glass of yogurt for his daughter, who was becoming excited about seeing her mother in only a few hours.

"Papa can Anders come with us to meet Mama?" she said.

Anders said he would be happy with that, but he could not. He had to visit the shipping line office to try to get a ship with work to America.

"What if you can't find it?" she asked.

"You just have to wait sometimes.

Chapter 4: Leviathan

The Hamburg-American Shipping line was in a tall, long white warehouse on the waterfront, its name freshly painted across the front of the building in big black letters. There were huge sliding doors on the front where trucks could unload, then walkways to the waterside and gangways up to ships. To the left, far down the side of the building, was a small office surrounded by glass windows. Two workers, an older man, and a young woman, were inside. With his bag over his shoulder, Anders walked to the room. Outside, there was a bulletin board with many notices about ships and jobs, and other opportunities, some of them in the United States. He tore a sheet from one of the notices, one for a mining inspector's job in Pennsylvania, and stuffed it in his pocket.

The next ship out at the end of the week would be Leviathan, the biggest and fastest in the Bremerhaven-American line, a ship that had 1,400 sleeping rooms, ballrooms, huge kitchens, and sophisticated new oil-fired engines that pushed four huge screws.

Anders walked in and drew a bright smile from the woman and a dismissive nod from the man.

"What do you want?" the man asked.

"A job for passage to the United States," Anders said.

"Not... since... the... war," said the man, never lifting his eyes from the invoices and shaking his head. "Karl" was embroidered on his jacket.

"Business runs on paying customers. The ship is booked for this trip, and there's no room, even in tourist class. There's nothing we can do."

"Is there anyone else I can talk to?" Anders asked.

"In about an hour, the ship's chief engineer and its designer will be here for an inspection. Maybe you can talk to one of them in a bit. But they have everyone they need, I can assure you."

Anders was familiar with the "impossible" response, which one heard just about everywhere in Eastern Europe after the war.

No one knew anything about him, about his engineering background, about his work in the mines, about his collection of skills, about his determination to get what he wanted and needed. It was easy for them to say "impossible" to Anders because they almost always dealt with people who heard that answer and hung their heads and walked away. It was the defining characteristic of people who lived in defeated, humbled nations, giving up so easily.

He was also familiar with people who gathered what authority they could and built it into an imaginary castle with fortifications and a moat so no one could enter. He ran into them at university.

And now, here.

Leviathan, silent save for some hissing steam, was docked beside the long shed.

The ship was at least 900 feet long, maybe 50 feet tall, and as white as snow on a mountainside, having just been painted. He had never seen such a beautiful ship. The brass rails, the mahogany rail caps, the bells, every piece of metal was shined and waxed. Some crew members walked the teak deck, inspecting fittings and doors, making certain the massive ship was ready for its inspection. Anders decided to walk the length of the ship to use up some time. Leviathan's official length, at 954 feet and six inches, made her the biggest ship in the Bremerhaven line, the flagship of a company that had fallen from prominence, just as Germany had fallen at the end of the war.

It retained its pride.

Portholes climbed from the waterline up the side of the ship from end to end, and each circled with a thick ring of brass on hinges. He walked all the way back to the ship's stern, where he could see the huge propellers that drove it through the ocean.

It was breathtaking.

The Germans had constructed her as the S.S. Vaterland in 1912, but she was taken-stolen in the view of the Germans who built her-

31

by the United States Navy at the outset of the war, repainted in "dazzle" camouflage, then renamed Leviathan and used to ferry American troops to Europe for the war.

When the war ended, she was handed over to the Hamburg-American line and refurbished once again at the cost of $6 million to provide first-class service in great luxury for transatlantic crossings. The ship had made some 350 crossings since it was first launched. It had never been attacked.

He was examining the waterline welds when he heard a voice behind him and turned to face Klaus Herrin, chief engineer of Leviathan, accompanied by a man in a suit who was never introduced and who, Anders assumed, had something to do with the refurbishing of the ship.

"Did you have to do much reinforcement when the ship was rebuilt after the war?" Anders asked before he even introduced himself. How was the hull, the rivets, the rust? Was it a huge job?" He peppered Herrin with questions about the repair of the ship, its useful life, its ownership, and command. Herrin just smiled at Anders and replied, "Huge enough." There was no problem with the ship, he said, but they had to replace the engine boilers with a new oil-fueled system. That led to a conversation about steam boilers, coal, and efficiency.

Herrin was so impressed he presented a job offer.

Anders could become his engineering assistant on Leviathan after he assured Herrin he could produce his credentials in a little time. The company would not only cover his transit but pay him $900 for his services. Herrin said he wanted him working out of his office, doing whatever he needed him to do, given his knowledge about boilers and his fluency in Hungarian and Romanian.

Anders didn't ask him about the details of the job. He had already told him about his engineering degree, his top grades, and his mine job. Leviathan sailed in two weeks. He was invited to stay on board in the interim in exchange for a little work, a big gift for a raw crew member. "Tomorrow morning, come to my office, and I will get you set up," Herrin said. "There will be plenty of work for you, getting familiar with the ship, its crew, all the small details. It will be good to have someone to talk to about…about…coal mines!"

Then he laughed.

Anders had liked him from the first bits of conversation, and that only grew stronger as the talking went on. He was given a tiny cabin down the hallway from Herrin's office, along with a brass key. The room contained a bed that folded down from the wall, a desk to work on with a light, and a sink. There was a bathroom down the hall. Like everything else he had seen, the room was efficiently set up and pristine. It was clear the line took the renovation seriously. The floor had new green wool carpeting. The woodwork was Circassian, with the wild color variations that were common in Russian walnut, freshly stained and varnished. He folded the bed down from the wall and settled in. It was comfortable. No one had scribbled on the woodwork above it. He was situated so he could feel the boat coming to life in the morning, especially when the crew fired the boilers to test the complex of controls that told the ship how to behave when to move when to stop, and so on. He was eager to get engineer Herrin's official tour of the ship the next morning.

In the interim, he would do some searching around on his own. He walked out of his berth and into the hallway that ran the length of the huge ship. He turned right and walked toward the bow of Leviathan.

A brightness signaled the end of the hallway, and when Anders reached that point, the entire deck opened up in a sunny room surrounded by windows that looked out on the bow. A big wheel defined the center of the room just behind a compass on a stand that included a brace of other dials that measured the health of Leviathan's huge engines, the amount of oil in the bunkers, the amount of available freshwater, the amount of gasoline to power an array of motors that served special purposes and a vast electrical panel that controlled lighting all over the ship.

"You shouldn't be up here by yourself," came a voice from behind him. Chief Engineer Herrin knew every rule that defined life aboard the ship, and this was one of the most important. The "bridge" was for the captain, his underlings, and his close associates and invited guests, never for casual visitors.

"There will be time enough for you to see how everything works after we get underway. You can be here then because I will be here then and you are my assistant. It won't be a problem. Let's take a walk away from here now."

Anders had not seen the small window at the top of the bulkhead at the back of the bridge. There was no light in the room at the moment. Klaus pointed up to the window and said, "That's the captain's cabin, and you have to always assume he is there, watching. Because he usually is."

"I'm sorry, Klaus," Anders said. "I was just exploring, and it led me to this bridge, and I could not resist the visit. Such an interesting place with all the gauges and dials and the like."

"Yes, it is an engineer's dream, and you will get to know every inch of it before we have been at sea for a day, so get ready to do your studying.

Then Klaus seemed like he was reading Anders' mind.

"Let's go look at the engines!"

The power plant that drove Leviathan was nine decks below the bridge and in the aft of the ship, a long walk from the high spot of the bridge. There was a sense that it was in another world, so far away and so isolated from the rest of the ship. That was intentional. Leviathan was set up, so some areas were blocked from access for anyone who didn't belong there. The engine room was one of them. That was for safety during the war, but even now, the captain insisted on keeping everyone in the right place. That helped explain why the ship was so rigidly structured and run. The captain, Edmund George, made certain to invite well-behaved sailors to the bridge while Leviathan was underway, just so they could see the process.

The complexity of the machine itself, its huge turbines and boilers, which took up much of the lower decks, was all but overwhelming for Anders, who had never seen anything to compare in size and complexity. Anders opened a door marked "Engine Room" and looked inside and down. The entire space was painted a stunning white enamel, and everything that might be polished fairly glittered in the incandescent light that illuminated the engine room. "Come on down," Herrin said as he walked down into the cavernous room, silent now but for some hissing valves and an occasional clank of wrench on steel. The ship still smelled clean, with just a hint of the scent of machine oil, which was used on valves. There were no grease spots in sight. Any drop of oil that landed on the deck was cleaned up immediately by the engine room crew. The men moved quickly down there, and even a drop of oil could lead to a fatal fall. There were signs everywhere reminding engine room people of their responsibility for keeping the place spotless.

"At speed, that engine generates 30,000 horsepower and can push this ship at 24 knots all day and all night," Herrin said, clearly proud of the ship. It generates electricity for 11,000 lightbulbs and a variety of devices that do everything from drying wet clothing to toasting bread in the morning. It's like a top-class hotel that floats! But this is the heart of it all, the place that generates the power to go from here to…to…anywhere." They climbed down six sets of stairs to the bottom of the engine room. Anders noted that the floor down there was as clean as the floor up above. Everything that could be buffed or polished was as clean as it could be. Nothing was even dented. He stopped listening to Herrin for a few minutes and listened only to the ship. Nothing. The engines were not running, so they made no noise. At a couple of points, he heard the clanking again of metal on metal, wrenches he assumed tightening some bolt someplace. He and the chief engineer were the only people he saw on the bottom of the ship. He was surprised by that but then realized they were two weeks from setting to sea, and there was no need for much of a crew anyplace at this point.

In a week, the 1,300 seamen who ran Leviathan and tended to its needs and the needs of its passengers would be coming aboard, bunking in their dormitory halls down on the lower decks or, for a few of them, their cabins (reserved for senior crew members). Anders walked past the huge valves that controlled the flow of fresh water and steam. Each of them had a clearly marked gauge that included a red warning zone and well-graduated scales to measure steam and water pressure. Whatever happened down there, he concluded, would be well-measured and closely watched.

The rebuild contract covered everything from the bolts on the bulkheads to the controls on the bridge. Everything on Leviathan was well in working order, down to every light switch, every lock, every handle on every porthole. Anders had never seen anything so marvelous. The Germans lost the war, but they did not lose their efficiency and attention to detail. He could not wait for the journey to New York to begin because he was fascinated by the ship; Anders's two weeks swept by like they were driven by an ocean wind. He met various members of the crew as they signed on but paid close attention only to those who would be working in the engine room, where he was likely to spend most of his time on the crossing.

Leviathan's departure from Bremerhaven, like the departure of most huge ships, involved an almost miraculous motion, soundless except for the blasting of the horn, and very little sense for those who were on board that anything was happening at all. If she rattled before the renovation, that was all removed with surgical precision before she was released from Newport News. Anders was in his berth at departure time. He did not meet the captain.

"Not necessary," Karen had said, making it clear that he was the most senior officer Anders was likely to be dealing with on the crossing. The huge ship simply slipped away from the pier and then turned out to sea. There were no tugs for pushing and not much noise to it at all. About the only noise he had heard all morning were the orders to cast off lines bow and aft, check on the big doors in the center of the ship that opened to the sea, and a few bells that signaled orders from the bridge to the engine room to get underway. There was little sense that the ship was even turning. It was just a big, sleek mass that moved out into the ocean.

Anders had no sense that the engines were even running until Leviathan reached the channel that led to the Atlantic. The ship pumped out some black smoke and, with another loud blast of the horn on the front smokestack, moved rapidly into the ocean and on its way. Anders walked all the way down the companionway to the stern of the ship, where he could see the U.S. flag snapping in the wind. Bremerhaven was all but gone a few minutes into the journey. On his way back, he opened the engine room doorway and was immediately bathed in the loudest noises he had ever heard. Levithan's engines were running at full tilt, the burners beneath the boilers hissing fuel oil that was in flame. Rods were being pushed and pulled, pistons thumping, and the thick iron axle that transmitted power to the screws that moved the ship was whizzing with almost no sound. He felt completely confident about Leviathan and its crew at that point, so much so that he went back to his cabin and had a brief nap. He would be manning his shift from 8 p.m. to 8 a.m., and he wanted to be in good form for his first night on the job. He would be watching and listing the numbers reflected by 18 separate gauges. They measured everything from oil consumption to elapsed time. It wasn't a hard job, but it demanded attention to detail. Anders knew he was very good at that, so he was comfortable in his job.

That would start in three hours.

It was the first time he had even a few minutes to think about what would be waiting on the other side of the ocean. He remembered the notice he had peeled from the bulletin board at Bremerhaven and found it in his jacket pocket, wrapped around a one-mark piece. He turned on this desk lamp and read it for the first time:

"The Commonwealth of Pennsylvania seeks degreed and experienced engineers to perform mine inspection duties. First consideration will be given to English-speaking men of at least 25 years of age with experience in European languages, Hungarian, Romanian, Polish, Italian, German, and Slovenian. The job requires 24-hour availability. Background working as a certified deep coal miner will give the candidate an advantage in this position. Salary, $2500 per annum. The job requires mine safety and disaster inspection work at various sites in Pennsylvania's bituminous and anthracite mines. Candidates should be experienced in all aspects of deep mining, with particular attention to safety and disaster issues. Must be able to summarize investigation results and reach defensible conclusions about various aspects of mine safety." At the bottom, it included a note to apply listing experience and education to "Edward Finn, director of inspection and safety, Pennsylvania Department of Commerce, Mining Division."

He didn't know how to approach the application. He could not get mail to the state office, of course, but he might be able to get a telegram to Mr. Finn and note he intended to come to apply for the job. But he would have to get the telegraph operator in the radio room to agree to do it, and he had not yet met him.

Now that the ship was underway, Karen was always busy pursuing his engineer's job, a big responsibility on a ship the size of Leviathan. He was not sure how he would approach him when he opened his cabin door and stepped into the hallway, and found himself face-to-face with Karen. "So, my friend, are you enjoying yourself so far?" Karen asked him. "You're shift begins in a few hours. Anything you want to know?"

"Actually, yes," Anders said. "Can I get some help with the radio operator to send a cable to Harrisburg? I'm applying for a job, and I need to let them know who I am and that I will be coming."

Karen's visage darkened.

"You already have a job here on Leviathan," he said. "What do you want to get another job for? There is nothing in Pennsylvania but woods and coal and a lot of wild Hunkies. No. You shouldn't do that. This is a great job on a boat that is like new, and you can do very well here...."

Anders had no idea of how he stacked up with women.

He had no girlfriends in Vulcan, which was a raw, rough Transylvanian backwater of peasant women with gaps in their teeth and bumpy skin and deep longings for farmer husbands. He had no interest in being married at that point in his life.

38

He never made advances, never tested them for interest. He was simply himself at all times. There were no concerns about whether he was misleading anyone.

He was somehow indescribably valuable in every circumstance, working or social; it didn't matter. If Anders was there, there would be a calm, accurate voice to describe everyone's experience. He always had what seemed to be the right answers, not the correct answers, the right answers, the ones that resolved not just a situation but feelings about a situation.

He was that valuable to his friends.

He got all that from his father and his mother, legendary in Vulcan for their dependability no matter the crisis.

"All you have in the mine is the person next to you," his father said. "It's the same for him. So, you both need to be the best people you can be all the time."

This Anders took to heart, perhaps more deeply than any other piece of advice his parents gave him.

His father told him just one thing about women:

"Find someone like your mother."

To his mind, he was overpaid for the $900 he would collect at the end of the voyage. Mostly, he watched gauges and fluid levels and listened closely to make certain nothing was making much noise at all.

If he found a noisy valve, he could call an engineering mechanic to inspect it and fix it if necessary. But nothing was much happening he had to worry about. He enjoyed writing the nightly reports he would hand to Karen each day. They were meticulously done, like ship logs, full of details, and each had its own narrative. Anders thought that was like high literature, particularly on a boat on which nothing bad was happening. He read the thick books closely, looking for signs of where trouble might present itself. But there was nothing. A few valves failed during the war, but with no injuries to the ship or its crew. There was a coal bunker fire, which could have ruined everything and sent Leviathan to the bottom of the sea, but it was extinguished.

The other pages of the reports reflected only the fact that Leviathan, back when it was launched as Vaterland, had been exceptionally well built. A few engineering notes chastised the U.S. Navy for stealing the ship while it was in port at the outset of the war. Anders understood Leviathan had been a war booty in that case. Besides, the Americans had obviously taken very good care of her.

The sailors and engineers who worked on Leviathan treated her as a living thing, a dependable friend and safe haven from the wilds of the North Atlantic, particularly in winter. He wished he could have read the captain's logs to compare the two sets of reminiscences, but that was not likely to happen.

Captain's logs were possessions of the captains and kept under lock and key, generally in the captain's quarters. They might be called out in the event of an incident to see what the captain was up to, but generally, they were for his eyes only. He also understood he was very close to the end of his time on the Leviathan and had already started to miss aspects of his temporary job.

He would be leaving the sailing life and entering a foreign life that had its own dangers and challenges.

He thought about that on deck as Leviathan steamed toward New York harbor. He admired Lady Liberty in the harbor, admired the skyline of the great metropolis, the likes of which he had never seen. When Leviathan sounded its final horn blast, it settled in the bottom of his stomach and almost made him laugh because it tickled him so much. He had one more task on Leviathan, and that was saying farewell to the man who had treated him so well since their meeting in Bremerhaven, Klaus Karen.

That they would do over the only lunch he actually had to buy on the ship in the 14-day crossing, and it was one he would remember for quite some time. He would finally be meeting Max Dorfman, the captain of Leviathan and a legend on the North Sea for his boldness and skill.

Klaus led him from his stateroom down the long hallway that led to the bridge of the boat, turned right at the end of the hall, and led him up the narrow stairs to a teak doorway with shining brass letters on it: "The Captain."

"Captain Dorfman," Karen said when Dorfman opened the door to his cabin, "Here is Anders Apostle, my assistant engineer. We both thank you for the invitation to lunch."

This was clearly about something more than lunch. Anders felt that in the pit of his stomach.

"Let me show you around my quarters," Captain Dorfman said, his hand on Ander's elbow. Anders wished he had worn some kind of suit. The captain was stunningly dressed in dark blue wool with the insignia of the line on his lapels and the captain's stripes on his sleeves. He wore a stiffly-starched white shirt with a formal collar and a pale blue tie with a tight Windsor knot at the neck. Everything about the man was as perfect as the ship he captained. They went together like they were born together. It made Anders want to salute, but he fought the impulse. He had no actual place in the hierarchy of Leviathan save for the humble space given to him by Karen. And that this instant, he knew it and felt it.

He was as lost as he had ever been.

"Would you like a drink Mr. Apostole?" the captain asked. "Beer, something stronger? Whatever you would like."

"No, thank you, sir," Anders said.

"Maybe a coffee?"

The captain turned to the steward, who had appeared mysteriously and took the place next to him.

"Bring Mr. Apostole a coffee, please," the captain said. He carried his politeness like a blessing. He was completely comfortable in the role. Anders made a note of that and thought, "I would like to be this way someday." He knew that was unlikely.

"Klaus?"

"Also, a coffee," Klaus said.

They moved to a table in the center of the captain's quarters. The walls were the same Circassian Anders had seen in the first-class lounges, with the same deep green wool carpeting. They all sat down at the same time. Anders was overwhelmed by a feeling of immense formality. He was starting to sweat. Not yet outside, but in his armpits, which were saturating his shirt and sending little rivulets down to his waistline.

Small talk ensued. As small as talk could get at a table where the captain of Leviathan was welcoming guests from below deck.

"That was a fine crossing," Klaus said, not directly to the captain, but that is where the comment landed.

"It was, indeed," Dorfman said.

"This is a good crew that knows the ship well."

The coffees came, and Dorfman sipped at his and leaned in toward the trio to tell stories, war stories actually."

"This ship has made 350 crossings since 1917, and no one has touched her in war or peace," the captain said. "I have had seven other commands, and nothing approaches her for comfort, speed, pure class."

Anders and Karen agreed, as one would, as the captain ran through a litany of praise for the big ocean liner. "Finest. Cleanest. Quickest. Best looking." The captain had them all lined up, ready to recite.

And then he turned to Anders.

"I want you to join us," he said. He handed him an envelope that had nine crisp $100 bills in it, along with a letter thanking him for his work.

"I want you to be on the engineering staff on Leviathan. You are well educated and know how to get along well with workers. That is valuable to us. It will pay you very well, take you from here to there and back again many times in great comfort, and give you enough money to take care of your family back in Vulcan. You will have the rank of lieutenant, along with the uniform and insignia."

42

"Thank you, sir...how did you know about my family in Vulcan?"

"We all come from someplace," the captain said.

"It wasn't hard to find out where you lived, what you did. You are a rarity at sea, a man with an honest background. I had people from the company check it all out.

"You don't have to answer right now. We will be leaving this ship in three days, so I would like to hear from you by then."

Lunch was plated and presented, salmon in a dill sauce, freshly baked bread, boiled potatoes, also with dill, and chocolate cake for dessert.

"We always do chocolate cake when we reach New York," the captain said, as though he were revealing a special secret.

They finished their lunch, gabbing all the way about the ship and how she handled and how sleek she seemed in the water despite her 900 feet and immense tonnage.

"The Germans built her very well," Dorfman said. The Americans rebuilt her very well. I don't think there is a vessel on either sea that can touch her. I have been her captain for six years, and we have had not a single problem with any aspect of the ship. I attribute that to having a solid, dependable crew. This is why I am talking to you, Mr. Apostole. But, later..."

With that, the captain rose from his chair, gave a polite bow, and headed down the steps toward the bridge.

Anders had some heavy thinking to do, so he went straight to his cabin for a nap.

He had a dream. It wasn't about the ocean, and it wasn't about Leviathan or even Capt. Dorfman. It was about coal mines in Pennsylvania. When he awoke, he knew what he had to do.

He went to his desk and found the little ad he had pulled from the board in Bremerhaven. He needed to leave Leviathan and find a way to get to Harrisburg as quickly as he could. He wanted to talk to Edward Finn.

43

He packed his bag and sat down to write a letter first. To the captain and then another to Engineer Klaus Karen.

"Dear Capt. Dorfman," he wrote, "First, thank you for the offer of a position of rank on your fine ship. I wish I could take it, but I must say no. I came all the way from Vulcan to start a new life in America, in mining in Pennsylvania. I intended to do that. So, I can't accept your offer. But you have my eternal thanks for the kindness I have been shown on Leviathan. I got an education from Klaus Karen that I could never have purchased, not to mention the advice from crew members and engineering mechanics. I wish you good fortune. Respectfully, Anders Apostle."

It was more difficult to say farewell to Klaus, who had been a good friend and a good boss on the crossing.

"Dear Klaus, I cannot thank you enough for the kindness you have shown and the expertise you have shared with me on this crossing. Leviathan is a great ship, and at least some of that greatness comes from you and the crew. I salute you. But I feel I have a different calling, as wonderful as the offer from the captain was. I need to go to Pennsylvania and work as a mining inspector. My father was killed in an explosion, and I still feel I owe it to my family to bring a sense of safety to this dangerous underground job. I will never forget my time on Leviathan and how well I was treated. I truly hope I can return that favor someday. I will keep in touch. I have already thanked the captain for his offer, but feel free to tell him how impressed I found him and how much I loved the time on his ship. Thank you for everything. Anders."

More than that, he could not say. He packed his few belongings, tucked his cash in his boot, and headed down the gangplank that led to the New York harbor. He was planning to go to Grand Central Station and catch the first train he could that would get him to Harrisburg. He pulled his hat down and kept his eyes on the sidewalk so he would not draw attention to himself. The waterfront was crawling with thieves. He had no intention of becoming a victim. He caught his own reflection in the windows of storefronts and was amazed at how well he fit into this big, loud city, so unlike where he grew up. It was like no one would know he had just crossed the ocean in Leviathan, just packed $900 into his boots, and was headed deep into the bituminous country in Pennsylvania, the heart of the

American coal industry. Life had its way of adding valuable layers to people. He had a plan but no idea of where it would carry him and whether it would work out.

But it would not be because he didn't try.

"You, lad!" he heard a scratchy voice behind him. "I need to talk to you!" He looked back and saw an elderly man in a dark blue suit with a vest and white shirt. "I need your help...."

"Nothing here for you, man," Anders said, hoping it would deter the well-dressed man now following him. He noticed the man was speeding up to approach him. Anders stopped and gathered himself. He knew how to appear intimidating despite his stature. The man asked if he could spare some change. Too well dressed to be a beggar, Anders thought, turning to face the man. The man had his hand in his coat pocket, which could have meant he had a gun or a knife. He checked his own pocket and found he had three quarters and a dime. It would be a worthy contribution if it got the man to stop following him. "Here," he said, handing the man the 85 cents.

"Thanks, but that's not enough," the man said. "I have a sick daughter who needs medicine, and it's going to cost me $10, and I need that; she needs that, or she might die." Anders thought for a few seconds and realized he could not give the man paper money without digging into his boot.

He said, "I have given you all I had. Let me alone now."

Then he made the second mistake.

"What is wrong with your daughter?" he asked.

The man drew very close, much closer than he had to come to talk. His breath smelled of alcohol, and Anders could see that his fine shirt and suit were very soiled, as though he had been sleeping on the street. His skin was florid, with broken blue capillaries like spider webs on his cheeks. He looked like he had had a rough time of it. Anders decided to be bold about the encounter.

"You don't have a sick daughter, and I don't know what you need the money for, but I suspect it's going to put you in an even deeper hole. What's going on with you? Tell me the truth!"

"I'm hungry," he said. "Very hungry."

"Let me buy you some food, and then you can be on your way. I have to catch the train at Grand Central, so I can't linger long."

A few doors up the street sat "The Seaman Delicatessen," with a lunch counter and booths with seats in them. "Let's go in there," Anders said.

They entered and sat at the counter.

"Give this man whatever he wants," Anders said, surprised at his own tone of authority. "He says he's hungry."

"A beer?"

"No, I said I would feed you. But I'm not buying beer or anything else with alcohol in it. You don't need it."

He ordered soup and bread, and while it was being served, Anders looked for the restroom so he could dig the wad of money from his boot and pay for the meal. It was in the back of the restaurant, down a little hallway. He was halfway to the room when he realized the man was following him. His heartbeat rose, and he felt his cheeks flush. He prepared to confront the man. There was a brass fire extinguisher on the wall, and in a move that was a tribute to his coordination, he turned and grabbed it at the same time.

"Get away from me, or I'll break your head with this," he said, brandishing the extinguisher. The man looked at him and seemed ready to shout but simply slumped to the floor and began to weep."

"I've ruined everything," he sobbed. "I'm broke. I'm alone. I'm hungry. I'm drunk. I'm...I'm...."

"Go back to the counter and wait for me," Anders said.

The man got up, honked his nose in a piece of linen he pulled from his pocket, and headed back toward the counter. Anders went into the men's room, peed, washed his hands, and then put his boot on the sink and fell down inside for his money. It was still there. He pulled the $900 out and took $10 from the wad. Then he put the rest of the money back into his boot and cursed himself for breaking his own rules this early in the trip. He would buy the man's meal, then give him $1 and send him on his way. He hoped that would get rid of him.

It was not a great bowl of soup. It was a watered-down version of yesterday's chili, which was a watered-down version of something else before it made its way onto the menu, called "goulash." Anders knew goulash, and this was not goulash. But the man was hungry. He dipped his thick white bread into the soup and slurped with a spoon, and consumed every drop in the white bowl. Four pieces of bread slathered with butter later, he was finished with the meal. He and Anders had coffee. He asked a few questions, which Anders did not answer.

"I can tell you are not from here. Where do you come from?"

Anders decided not to answer. In fact, he decided to have no further contact with this man.

"Go," Anders said.

Anders handed the dollar to him. He sat at the counter. The man said, "thanks," and got up and walked out the door.

The man behind the counter told Anders he had seen the man in the nice clothes before and that he came in for a meal two, sometimes three times a week. "I don't know who he is, but he has some money sometimes and knows how to dress up," he said. "I think he's a drunk or maybe a drug addict, but he's from a good family. That explains the suit and the fact that sometimes he presents himself very well. I think the booze, drugs, or something else is the problem. I see it a lot down here. Did he ask you for money for his kid?"

"Yes," Anders said.

"That's usually the pitch these guys use, some family problem that a couple of dollars will help. Then they take the money into the first bar they can find. It's an old racket that feeds itself on the kindness of strangers. But it's still an old racket."

Anders made a mental note of the counterman's story and determined in the future to help only himself as he made his way to the center of Pennsylvania. There were many lonely men on the streets near the docks, and they were all hungry for something.

Most of it, money could not buy.

That much Anders knew.

Chapter 5: Pennsylvania

Grand Central Station was 15 blocks west of the diner, and he was eager to get there to look at the train schedules. He was hoping to get a train direct to Harrisburg. That, as it turned out, would not be possible.

"Broadway Limited to Chicago," the man at the ticket counter told him. Leaves here at 4 p.m. and goes straight to Philadelphia, then heads west. Get you into Harrisburg sometime tomorrow afternoon, depending on what connection you make in Philadelphia. It's $17 or $25 if you want a cabin. If I had the money, I would take the cabin. At least you get some privacy at that level. Anders took his advice. He went to Track 23 and to car 14, climbed on board, and found his cabin, 3C. The Pennsylvania Railroad was not like the European lines. It was essentially practical transportation, nothing fancy. There was a dining car but also a snack car one car back that served coffee and sandwiches, and desserts. Anders put his bag in his cabin and left to visit the snack car.

He spent $1.20 on coffee and a turkey sandwich unlike any sandwich he had ever had (the bread was terrible, spongy with hardly any texture!) He stripped the bread from the sandwich and ate just the turkey. The waiter asked him if there was a problem. "The bread is bad," he said.

"What do you mean?"

"It's not like bread. It's…just bad."

"I'm sorry," the waiter said. He took the bill from Anders and tore it into two pieces. "No charge,' he said.

There was a woman across the aisle who leaned over to speak with him. "If you want good bread," she said, "Get it at home. You aren't going to find it out here."

"I wish I could be at home eating my mother's bread," Anders said to the woman, who was dressed in a long gray coat and wore a white bonnet. She was eating hard-boiled eggs from a basket. She offered him one, along with a cracker-like bread she was munching on. He thanked her and offered to pay.

"Absolutely NOT," she said.

"I would never take money for food. Our job is to take care of the hungry and sick, and you certainly look hungry to me, so I'm taking care of YOU!" She leaned in to jab him in the chest with her index finger when she said, "You!"

She said that as though it were a joke and laughed at the end.

"Anders," he said, introducing himself.

"Sister Frances Mary," she responded. He noticed she wore a cross on a chain. She wore a wedding ring, too, but was clearly traveling alone.

"I am a Sister of Mercy. I'm headed to Lancaster. We have a mission there."

Anders had heard of the Sisters of Mercy. They came from Ireland after an earthquake that wrecked half of Vulcan and left hundreds of people dead or injured. They worked tirelessly to help people survive. They cooked for them and cleaned for them and asked nothing in return.

He mentioned the disaster.

"I remember that," she said.

"I was in school then and too young to go. The people who came back told us all about Vulcan and Transylvania. They said it was beautiful, and they didn't believe the stories about vampires at all!"

"Vampires?"

Anders was confounded by the comment. There were a million things to talk about in Transylvania before you got to the legend about vampires. Vlad Tepes was a murderer for certain, but he didn't suck blood from the necks of his visitors. He used horses to stretch their bodies over sharpened sticks. They were impaled until they were dead.

He just killed other enemies (and some of his guests) in more traditional ways, knifings, hangings, and the like. He was also clearly not immortal. He was cut to bits by his enemies and planted in a hundred different places. At least, that is what Anders' mother told him. Since it happened hundreds of years ago, he didn't know whether it was true or not. Legend said garlic cloves grew over those burial sites. In the spring, you could find them by the thousands.

It was a handy legend to use on tourists. The young men would get them liquored up and then take them to the woods for a hike. They would tell the murderous Tepes story, with the ending of him being chopped up and planted. Then they would grab a handful of the wild garlic cloves and pull them up and let people smell them.

"See!"

Very effective.

In reality, Vlad Tepes was beheaded, and his head, preserved in honey, was sent to Hungary. Where they put it is unknown. The legends of vampires continued to grow, even though Anders knew because he had checked when he was in school there were no vampires mentioned anywhere in Romanian culture.

True, Vlad Tepes had a lovely castle on a mountain ridge that was at the top of the list of tourist attractions, and many people who worked to build it were impaled. That might have been where the myth came from. The people around Vulcan made great sport of foreign visitors, telling them wild stories about forest creatures and spirits from the graveyards. To be sure, the place had deep, dark forests and lots of graveyards, so it's not hard to see how people sometimes believed what they heard. But none of it was real. It was a good way to get people with handy money to buy drinks.

Stories and drinks go together, Anders had learned early in his working life.

51

But deaths in Vulcan were caused not by vampires or spirits.

They were caused by coal mines.

Just like everywhere else.

The train rattled on through New Jersey and the nun, rocked by its persistent rhythm, drifted off for a nap while Anders pondered the uniformly lovely terrain, pine forests and swamps and hardwoods, a big wilderness area with a railroad cutting through it. It reminded him a little of home. On occasion, the engineer would blow the whistle on the train, and they would pass through a grade crossing. Farm trucks and cars usually waited at the crossings. Anders, too, was lulled into a deep sleep.

When he woke up, the train was shifting through a set of switches in what appeared to be an industrial outskirt. He checked the time and concluded they were just about in Philadelphia. The train rattled on, now slowed down by congestion that seemed attached to factories on each side of the tracks. He could smell the smoke from the engine when the conductor opened the door from the next car and came to announce arrival at Philadelphia, the north station. Anders would be riding downtown on the train before he shifted to another one heading west to Harrisburg. The nun was awake and gathering her things. She offered him three hard-boiled eggs and a thick piece of bread with butter. "I'm not going to eat these, and I am going to change trains soon, so you should have them. God bless you and keep you in whatever you do."

With a satchel over her shoulder, she moved toward the door at the end of the car. Anders smiled, and she smiled right back. Somewhere, an interest stirred deep inside of him, but she shut it off with one thought, "It's a sin to want a nun," he told himself.

Then he settled back into the bench and waited for the train to stop. With an immense amount of squealing and squeaking and the smell of hot metal, it finally stopped at a station labeled "North Philadelphia." He watched as the nun left the train and walked down the platform. He waved at her from his window, but he didn't think she noticed. He was alone in his room now, but other passengers were preparing to board. He got up and walked to the door, and stepped down to the platform. He looked for a "Harrisburg" sign but didn't see one. So, he walked up to the ticket window and asked.

"That train has been delayed and won't be leaving here for another three hours," the ticket agent said. "You can buy your ticket now and get the best seat. It's going to be $4." He reached into his pocket and pulled out $5, then put the change back into his pocket. The ticket agent said there was a good restaurant on the first floor if he was hungry. He thought about the eggs and bread and concluded that would be just fine for him. So he walked into the cavernous waiting room, took a spot on one of the long walnut benches, and took out his eggs and bread. He realized he had not yet talked with Mr. Finn in Harrisburg and doubted the man would be at work at this hour. He got $2 in change and went to a payphone.

Finn's office phone rang four times and then answered. It was a woman.

"Valery Miller," she said. "The office is closed until tomorrow morning."

Anders introduced himself and said he was coming about one of the safety inspection jobs he found in an ad in Bremerhaven.

"My God," Valery said, "You have come a long way. Come in first thing in the morning. Mr. Finn will be here at 8:30 a.m." She hung up. Anders made a note that he liked her voice a lot. He gave her the short version of his life, then said he would see her in the morning.

With that, he ate his nun eggs and bread, went to a food window to buy some coffee, and settled in for the wait. The train was delayed two more times and would not be leaving until 11 p.m. That would give him a chance to sleep before he got to Harrisburg and clean himself up before he went to see Mr. Finn.

The train was showing its age when Anders climbed on at midnight for the five-hour trip to Harrisburg. It wasn't a long distance, but the Pennsylvania Railroad stopped at every town and village on the Main Line, so a lot of the five hours would be spent just sitting in stations. That would not have happened on a European train, and Anders took note of this, early proof that what he had heard about everything in America being better was, perhaps, wishful. It chugged on through the night and then pulled alongside a big river as it headed west. The Susquehanna, he was told by a man in his cabin, was "wide but shallow, just like the people in Harrisburg."

The train arrived in Harrisburg at 4 a.m., exactly in time to get to a place where nothing was open, no people were on the streets, and only lonely dogs passed their time outside the train station. He had finished his nun eggs on the long ride from Philadelphia and found himself hungry again when the train pulled into the station. He picked up his bags and got off the train. Down the platform, he could see that the sun was coming up, that a new day was beginning, and he delighted in the freshness of that thought. He had to find a place to clean himself up. He had one clean shirt left, clean underwear, and a change of socks. He needed a shower, but he didn't want to have to rent a hotel room to get one.

He walked past a building that had a "Salvation Army" sign outside and a note that overnight rooms were available "for transients." He decided he would try that. A man in a sharp dark blue wool uniform stood behind the counter just inside the door and eyed him closely, perhaps checking to see if he had been drinking. Anders met whatever standard the man was applying. He told Anders, "It's $2 for a night, but the night is over, so you can pay $2 and sleep here tonight, too." Anders asked if there were showers and the man said each floor had a shower room. He put him in a room on the second floor and handed him a thin, well-worn towel. "Thank you," Anders said. "God be with you," the uniformed man said. "It's safe here, but don't leave money laying out because, you know, you never know."

He climbed the steps, found his room, and, after hiding his money under a carpet and locking the door, walked down the hallway to the shower. It was clean, well-lit, and empty. He hung his clothes on a rack on the wall and took a long, hot shower. What felt like weeks of fatigue and grime washed down the drain. Now refreshed, he dried off, put his clothes back on, and returned to his room. The money was still where he had left it, under the carpet. His things had not been disturbed. The morning, he concluded, was going very well.

He went to the counter to ask the man how to get to the Department of Commerce, and the man said, "No, you have to attend morning services before you leave. It's required." Anders had never heard of such a thing, but it was a new country, a new place, and he figured he would go through whatever motions necessary to get to where he needed to be by 8:30. The man at the desk pointed him to a breakfast room at the end of a hall. He went in. There were perhaps 35 men there, some in very bad condition, waiting for breakfast and the service. He sat at the end of one of the rows of chairs.

One of the men leaned over and vomited, and the smell set off a round of gagging among the others, too. Anders was happy he had nothing in his stomach to throw up. He gagged a bit and then moved down the aisle, away from the mess. A Salvation Army worker in a blue coverall came in with a bucket and mop and cleaned up the mess. It was clear this kind of thing happened frequently. Anders surveyed the men in the room. A battered collection of troubled people, he concluded, and as good a model as any to help a person make a decision not to drink. He resolved to stick to beer. Truth be known, he had never enjoyed drinking so much he lost control, although most of his friends started their evenings with that objective. A man walked in another uniform, this one black with a roman collar, and stood behind a podium.

"Brothers," he said, "It is never too late to repent. To reform. To clean yourself and your head and your heart and move toward Jesus. We're here to help you. Please don't forget that. You will always find shelter here, but not if you are under the influence of liquor or drugs. It's all we ask, that you keep yourself straight. We will help you with that. Now let us pray.

He led the group in the Lord's Prayer. It ended, and the man in the collar walked out just as three other people rolled in steel carts with trays of scrambled eggs and bacon. There was toasted bread, too, and a big container of hot coffee and a pitcher of cold orange juice. The men lined up to pick up plates and coffee cups as women in uniforms and aprons dished out the food and smiled. It was good, and you could have as much of it as you wanted. Same with coffee. But at 7:15, the carts were rolled out, and cleanup began. The men filed out of the room and headed for the front door.

"I'm looking for the commerce department," Anders said to the man at the counter. The man surveyed Anders, his shirt, tie, and suit, and his clean shoes.

"Left out the front door. Three blocks down that street, make another left, and it sits right on the corner. You can't miss it. You are looking fine, sir, so good luck!

"Thank you," Anders said.

He headed out the door. It was beginning to warm up, the start of a great Spring day. Anders took in the air as deeply as he could and breathed it out through his nose. It all felt like a good day was shaping up.

Following the directions, he found the "Pennsylvania Department of Commerce" building sitting on the corner of an intersection. It was just a few years old, so the exterior was still clean. The "Commerce" identifier was in big gold letters, just beside a plaque shaped like a state.

The doors were brass, with clean handles and glass. He pulled one open and walked in. The place smelled official, soapy, maybe. A woman in a stern gray dress stood behind a welcoming counter at the top of the steps. He walked up.

"Hello," he said. "I'm looking for Mining and Safety Department, a Mr. Finn." The woman stared at him through her thick glasses and then looked down at a registry on the desk. Anders assumed she was new at the job.

"Ah, yes," she said. "Edward Finn, Mining Inspections and Safety. That would be downstairs toward the back of the building." Look for B-26 at the end of the hall. She pointed to a stairwell. Anders walked over and found his heart beating a little faster. He didn't know why perhaps excitement at the chance for a job interview.

He turned left at the bottom of the stairs and found himself in a long, dark hallway with doors on either side. They had frosted glass windows and names stenciled to describe what was inside. "Revenue," it said on one door. "Cashier" on another. "Reviews and Reconsiderations," all the way down the hall. Finally, he arrived at a B-26, which simply carried the word "Mining" on the glass.

He reached for the handle, but the door was still locked. It was not yet 8 a.m. There was no light on behind the glass. He decided he would wait on a wooden bench across from the doorway. He sat down and, despite his excitement, fell fast asleep. It was the first time in his journey he had a sense of how far he had traveled in such a short period of time. He was breathing deeply when he felt a hand pulling at the sleeve of his jacket.

He opened his eyes.

Valery Miller.

Blue suit. White blouse. Red lipstick on a full mouth. Cross on a gold chain around her neck. No other jewelry. "Wake up..." Mr. Finn will be here in about 20 minutes. Wake up!" He reached out his hand and said, "Anders Apostle."

"Valery Miller," she replied.

"I called yesterday about the Mine Inspector's job," he said. "Do you remember me?"

She did, indeed. She just did not know what to do with him for 20 minutes. Finn did not like strangers sitting in the waiting room. Neither did she. She set aside her concerns about sending the wrong message and asked Anders if he wanted a coffee and a donut. "Why, yes," he said. He did not know why because he had eaten well at the Salvation Army breakfast. Perhaps it was her gray eyes and red hair.

As they walked down the hallway to Barry and Emma's coffee stand, he told her about his journey, about his plan to join the corps of inspectors working for Mr. Finn, and about his family back in Vulcan.

She seemed very interested in his stories about Vulcan. He had no sense she had an interest in him. That would take more time.

She turned and looked him full in the face.

"Are there vampires in Vulcan?" she asked.

"No. There are no vampires anywhere in Romania. There may be no vampires anyplace. No vampires at all. It's a myth. I studied it in college literature. It persists, but it was never real. There are no vampires, even in the literature of Romania. Vlad Tepes liked to kill his enemies by sticking them on sharpened spikes. That's why they called him Vlad the Impaler, but that was never about vampires. He was just a very bad ruler. Romania is a lovely place, with thick forests and great people.

"But no vampires!"

He realized he had said a lot more than he intended to say, but he found Valery Miller very compelling.

She said she had seen a movie only a week ago with one of her girlfriends about the vampires of Transylvania.

"It was very frightening. I had nightmares for two days about men coming to suck blood from my neck."

"That would never happen," Anders said with a little chuckle.

"Your neck is much too beautiful for that!" He was turning red with embarrassment by the time they reached Barry and Emma's.

"I'm sorry I said that," he told her. "We don't know anything about one another. It was bold."

"Yes, it was," she said.

But she didn't think that at all.

Barry and Emma were fully engaged with coffee and donuts by the time Valery and Anders reached their stand. Quite politely, she introduced him as a job candidate and asked for a coffee and a plain donut. She handed them to Anders and paid with 50 cents from her pocket.

"Barry and Emma don't work for Mining, but they keep everything running here just the same," Valery said, a broad, warm smile across her face.

"Thank you," Anders said. "I'm very happy to meet you."

He took a bite of a donut and washed it down with some coffee. It had no cream or sugar in it, but it was still sweet. It was good, not like the swill that got served up in most places.

He was telling her more about Transylvania and what he did there when a middle-aged man in a brown suit and striped tie walked up to the stand. His hair was cropped short to his head. It was gray.

"How are you doing this morning, Barry, Emma? Are you both well?"

Barry said he was just fine, then he turned to Anders and said, "Anders, this is going to be your boss. Meet Mr. Finn."

Finn laughed and said, "Well, we'll see about that." Then he shook Anders's hand. Anders liked the feel of Finn's handshake.

"Let's go down to my office. I see you already met Miss Miller."

"Yes," Anders said.

"Did she tell you what she does," Finn asked.

"No," Anders said.

"She runs the place," he said.

"She knows more about coal mining than anyone I have ever met. She has spent plenty of time underground in accidents, which you can't tell now because she cleans up so very well. But I've seen her caked so thick with coal dust you could see nothing but teeth and eyes. She is the assistant director, and remember, the name we use for her is Miss Miller! Or Valery Miller."

"Okay," Anders said.

He did not know why Finn had said it that way, but he got the clear sense it was not just office talk, that she had authority attached to her job and knew how to use it and had earned Finn's respect.

Finn's desk was clean and well organized, with stacks of folders, a clean ashtray, a telephone, and a Coffee cup sitting near his ink blotter with a logo that said, 'Pennsylvania Fish Commission."

"Valery said you called yesterday, but I don't have an application from you," Finn said.

"Did you fill one out?"

Anders told the story of the crossing on Leviathan, of the captain's job offer, of how he had no chance even to send a message from the boat because they wanted him to stay on board as an officer.

"What kind of pay were they offering," Finn asked.

"I don't even know. I didn't want to find out. I told them I wanted to come here to work in mine safety."

Then he told him about his father's death in Vulcan and how he took the job in the lignite mine when it was offered because the family needed the money.

Everything he heard about Anders made him want to dispense with formalities and just add him to the team. But formalities were formalities for a reason. He asked if he had his degree and college records.

"No, but I can get them if you give me some time. I was an honors graduate and student in engineering and literature. My minor was in mathematics, but I haven't had to use anything I learned in that field, so you can think of it as fresh."

Finn laughed at that.

"Languages?

Anders said, "Romanian, Hungarian, German, some Russian, and of course, English."

They talked about mining in Vulcan, how the men depended on each other and how they owned their spaces, how they helped each other any way they could, and made certain no one took advantage.

"And how did you do that?" Finn asked, knowing full well that some miners would cut corners just to make an extra dollar a week.

"I think you would say by example," Anders said (again, the right answer.) "I would never lie, never steal, never cheat. My father taught me that, and I always believed, even after he died, that I owed him for that."

Finn heard everything he needed to hear.

"I want you to write a letter for me telling me how to get your academic and work records, and then we'll get it done. Welcome to Mine Safety and Inspection." Finn shook Anders's hand.

"This is a life and death business, Anders, so you must take it seriously, understand?"

"Yes, I do."

"Do you need money? It will take a month for your first paycheck to arrive. I can get...

"No," Anders said. "I have most of $900 from Leviathan in my boot. Is there a bank I can use nearby? I don't want to be carrying it with me."

Anders pointed him toward the Credit Union window down the hallway. "It's safe there, and you can have money deposited automatically. After a while, you can even get loans. It's a very good deal."

With that, Anders headed to the Credit Union and came back to find out where he should sit. He arranged to have half of each monthly paycheck held in savings. That would leave him with plenty of money for living, although he had no idea what that might be like in this strange new town.

He kept an eye out for Valery. But she was not to be seen for the rest of the day.

He got an office, which surprised him. It would have its own phone, its own typewriter, and its own filing system. It was six doors down from the door that led to the office Finn and Valery shared. It had a number 9 on the door in brass.

He felt honored.

Finn told him to take the day to find a place to live.

The area around the capitol in Harrisburg had plenty of apartments for rent.

After two blocks of walking, all the buildings looked the same, brick on the front with porches, front doors with three mailboxes.

Inside, the floor patterns were the same, too; a living room in the front, then a dining room, then a bedroom, then another room, and a kitchen in the back. The kitchen door led to a back porch with steps that went down to a cement walk to an alley.

All kinds of people lived in those apartments.

A saxophone player was practicing on the third floor, and Anders could hear it on the first floor. Not a good choice, he thought.

In another, a trio of young women was sharing a floor and playing loud music on a radio, which he could also hear on the first floor. He decided he had to pick someplace with quiet people on the second and third floors. Maybe retired people. He would like that. He was comfortable with older people, particularly older women who reminded him of his mother.

That is what he would be looking for.

He found it on his fourth stop at 435 Cameron Street. It would be an easy walk. Mrs. Estelle Johnson lived on the first floor, a widow whose husband had been a state police commander. She was 60, still quite handsome, and seemed very engaging.

On the second floor, an open apartment had been rented to a secretary who kept it clean and well-painted. It was $200 a month, a price he could well afford. On the third floor were a city policeman and his wife. ("Security!" Anders thought.) They had three children and a dog named Susquehanna. It was a hunting dog, black and gentle.

He took the second-floor apartment and paid three months' rent in advance. He viewed that as $600 well spent. He would have to do some painting and some work on the woodwork and find some furniture, but that didn't bother him.

He had to be at work on time the next day because that is when his training in mine safety investigation would begin.

Chapter 6: Life or Death

Anders arrived at the Commerce Department's Department of Mining at 8 a.m. and went to the stairwell to go down to meet Finn to begin his training.

There was no one else in the hallways on the basement floor. He flipped his jacket over his shoulder and walked down the hallway, past the No. 9 door that would be his office, and down the hallway to a door marked "Training." He knocked, and no one responded, so he went in. There was a long mahogany table, a big blackboard, and overhead lights. Windows toward the ceiling lined one side of the room, so it wasn't as dark as he thought it would be. There were a dozen filing folders on the table, full of papers, and a book called "The Coal Industry" by A.T. Shurick.

He picked it up and looked at the index. The book was broken into four sections: The CoalFields; Mining Methods; Distribution of Coal, and Economic and Sociological Conditions. It had dozens of illustrations, including a chart that projected coal production to the year 2055. The graphics alone told an interesting story, beginning with one that showed how coal once was carried in a basket with a forehead strap.

He was going to start looking at the various folders, too, when the door to the room opened, and Valery Miller walked in, smiling broadly and carrying a shoulder pouch full of documents. "Anders, hello," she said. "I'm going to be your instructor today in the process of mine disaster investigations. I've led seven of them in the past few years, so I know what is required and where to find it. But let's start with a coffee and a donut!"

They went down the long hallway past Finn's office and down to the friendly stand where Barry and Emma were already working. Anders said it would be his turn to buy this morning, returning the favor for yesterday's donut and coffee.

He reached for a chocolate-covered donut. She took a plain one. Barry drew coffee for both of them and asked if they wanted cream.

She said yes, and he said no.

It was served up.

"First day?" he said to Anders.

"Well, it's for training," Anders said.

"Valery is going to tell me how to investigate disasters. I'm looking forward to it." He was not kidding, and there was no hesitation in his voice. He seemed quite eager to hear what she had to say. They sat down at a small table to drink their coffee and eat their donuts.

Anders wondered if this would be a daily event. He wouldn't mind that, but he would not assume it, either. Barry said he heard Valery was a good teacher, particularly if you were a good student. Anders knew those kinds of relationships well, having excelled at them in college. He was intrigued. "Where did you complete your studies," he asked her.

"Penn State, School of Engineering with a specialty in bituminous coal mining," she said.

"That must have been hard for you," he said, realizing immediately he had made a mistake assuming that engineering would be hard for a woman.

"No," she said.

"My father was a miner. I knew when it came time for college what I wanted to do. Becoming an engineer made sense to me because it presented a lot of opportunities after graduation. Particularly if you wanted to work in state government."

She told him she could have gone to work in the Transportation Department building highways, or in the buildings department maintaining the stately old capitol, or in the office of the state engineer, where there was always lots of work and plenty of chances to succeed.

"So why did you end up in mining?" he asked.

"Seemed like it would have a good future," she said. "And I loved my dad's stories about the mines, about the kinds of things that happened underground. From my first day in school, it was what I really wanted to learn. I was the only girl…woman…in the class in the beginning. I got a lot of attention from men who assumed I would flunk out or quit because it was too hard. But I was an honors student from year one onward. I did very well in my classes. Left a lot of men in the dust.

They treated me like shit for that, but I always knew that would be coming. No one expects to see a woman in mining regulation."

At this, she blushed, which was very engaging to Anders's mind. He had never met an engineer who blushed before.

"I have a minor in education, which is why Mr. Finn thought I should teach these intro classes. I'm very good at research, so I know all about what happens when things go wrong in a coal mine."

"I see you were looking at Shurick's Coal Industry book. That's probably the best text you can find that covers just about everything you need to cover if you are going to investigate mine accidents. He knows his business, for sure. But he's a little bored about it. Mr. Finn views it as the bible of coal mining, so if you want to get along with him, you will know all about that book, chapter, and verse."

She finished her coffee and donut and stood up to head back down the hall. They both said hello to Mr. Finn, who was standing in his doorway when they walked by at 8:15.

They walked into the training room, and Anders sat on one side of the long table. A beam of sunlight was falling on him, and he liked the feeling of that. Valery went to the blackboard and, in white chalk, wrote:

"1. Life or Death." She waited for just an instant for that to sink in, then she turned toward Anders.

"It's not just a job," she said.

"If you do it right, you will literally be the difference between life and death for a lot of miners. When they are hurt or killed, it will be your job to find out why. If there is foul play involved, it will be your job to find out how that happened. She put her hand on the pile of files on the table.

"You are going to have to know these cases very well," she said. "They are like an encyclopedia of what goes wrong and what happens after that...."

Anders listened to her and watched her closely. She was not at all like the woman who bought him coffee and a donut when they first met. He had heard the phrase "all business" to describe professional women before, but this was the first time he had ever seen one up close, in action.

Her demeanor completely offset the fact she was beautiful. She became almost crystalline on the outside, hard, and difficult to penetrate. He didn't know whether he liked that in her, but he did admire it.

She was going to be a great teacher, he concluded.

The first case was the Darr Mine explosion at Pittsburgh in December 1907. He thought that was a dated even that would not have much modern application.

But he was wrong.

"This is perhaps the most revealing of the disaster files I will present to you, but I'm not going to tell you why. You are going to tell me why after you have had a chance to review it. We'll come back to it after lunch, and I will want to hear your conclusions about it then, but not until then.

"There are a lot of layers of responsibility in an accident this big, starting with the fire bosses and their jobs and climbing right up the ladder to the highest level of management at the mining company. There are lessons around every corner in this case, but the question is, what do they lead you to conclude about the event, and what it says about mining in general."

1907 was the worst year for accidents in the bituminous fields, with 3,000 miners killed in dozens of cases. But Darr was the worst of them all.

Some of the story was revealed in the records of the investigation, which focused the attention of 24 investigators on the site.

"Superintendent Black, who was in charge of the mine, had recently resigned, as did David Wingrove, the former fire boss, on account of the gaseous nature of the mine. It said they notified mine officials that the mine was unsafe for the men to work in. There are many such reports current here...."

Witnesses told investigators there were two explosions, the first of which shook the ground beneath the homes close to the mine. The second sent fire blasting from any opening, dragon-like. Between the two, some 220 men were slain, probably instantly. All of the stoppings, the temporary wood and canvas walls built to shift air down the shaft, were blasted away. Some more permanent structures were destroyed, too.

Two other mines were connected to Darr by drilled openings that allowed air to pass from each of the mines. Because the Darr mine is at a higher elevation than the other two mines, explosive gasses, lighter than air, naturally flowed through the openings, which were informal parts of the mine ventilation system, into Darr as they left the other two mines. It became a receptacle for the gases released in the other two mines. A huge volume of gas must have been building in the hours before the blast. If fire bosses were taking accurate readings, they would have known that long before the gas ignited and could have closed the mine down.

He understood the physics of the blast.

In explosions like the one that hit Darr, he knew, what frequently happened was the initial blast would fill the air with flammable coal dust, and then a spark or some other source, again maybe a miner's headlamp, would set off a secondary explosion. That would take all of the air out of the mine. Black damp, mostly carbon monoxide, would move in, a fatal condition for someone trapped underground.

Anders found himself making notes on a yellow legal pad as he read the report.

"Why weren't the warnings of the men who quit heeded?

"Why wasn't Darr adequately ventilated, especially receiving the gas from the other two mines?

"When were these three mines last inspected by the Department of Mining?

"Where are the records of fire boss reports of gas readings in the weeks before the explosion?

"Have the regional police been notified to determine whether criminal charges are warranted?"

The more Anders read, the more he felt he could have changed the outcome if he had only known the conditions. It was apparent to him that the mine should have been closed, and fans should have been used to evacuate the gasses before they reopened. Almost all of the victims were Hungarian.

Had any of their survivors been interviewed to find out what they knew about conditions in the mine? Had anyone interviewed the supervisor or the fire boss who quit? What had been done about their reports? Who was responsible for day-to-day operation in the mine? Was the miner's union on site, and did it raise any objections? The further he read into the investigation, the angrier he became. The men were working in a death trap. They apparently knew that but kept working anyhow.

Why?

By the time he reached the end of the report, Anders had written a full page of questions about conditions in the mine and responsibility in such an accident. He was becoming agitated at the very thought of it. Even in Vulcan, certainly no model, men would not have been allowed in such a gassy, dangerous place. Especially not men wearing carbide lamps with open flame.

"Jesus!" he whispered at the end of the report. "These people should be in prison."

Valery had left the room while he completed his reading of the accident report. He was surprised at the literacy of the effort. The handwriting was nearly perfect, and the language, too. These may have been stated mine inspectors, but they were educated at some point and took the job seriously.

He looked at Valery.

"Shocking," he said.

"Heartbreaking."

"Yes, indeed," she said.

"Let's go get lunch, and you can tell me why."

"Sure," Anders said, relieved to be stepping away from the ghastly file on the disaster.

Nickie's Little Ritz was just two blocks from the Commerce Department in an alley beside the Harrisburg Police Department. A sign on the door said it was off-limits to police officers until 9 p.m.

"All others welcome," the hand-written sign noted. It was signed by Nick himself. Inside it smelled like stale cigarette smoke, chili, beer, and women from last night.

Nick stood, as ever, behind the bar, his apron neatly wrapped and tied around his waist. He wore a purple shirt that was opened at the collar. He was a slight man but handsome, with a well-tended goatee. It was not warm in Nick's Little Ritz. It was not cold, either. It was a little skanky but not disgusting. Sitting at the bar, Anders and Valery were comfortable, despite the stickiness of the bar stools.

Nick, a slight man with a well-trimmed beard and mustache, eyed them up. There was a dark tint to his skin, something Italian, Anders concluded. He noticed a bulge under the back of his apron. Probably a pistol in this belt.

"Valery, I know," Nick said.

"But who are you?"

"Anders Apostle," he said.

"I'm a new mining inspector. I just got here from…from…He couldn't finish the sentence because the logistics of the past week would seem baffling even to him, and he was IN them. "From Vulcan… in Transylvania in Romania, then from Bremerhaven, Germany on the U.S. liner Leviathan. And then on the Pennsylvania railroad and now in my new apartment on Cameron Street."

Nick paused for a few seconds and eyed him up…

"Not of THE Vulcan Apostoles?" Nick said with mock surprise.

He held that thought for a moment until Anders recognized he was teasing.

"Well, yes," he said politely.

"Stop that. I'm just fucking with you," Nick said.

Anders glanced at Valery to see whether she had been disturbed by the vulgarity. She was not. That was good because he didn't know what he would do if she had been. He could speak English quite well, but the customs were still a little strange to him. It bounced off her like a rubber ball. He was happy to see that because, in his experience, there were few people as vulgar as coal miners.

71

"So," Anders said. "What is good for lunch?"

"Something back at home," Nick said.

"But I do have our eternal chili, which is always fresh because it gets added to every day. Today, green peppers!"

"Or maybe a hamburger, but the meat is starting to change colors and about due to become Chili…So, I would stick with the Chili. It comes with packs of saltines you can crunch up and make it into, like, a Mexican meat paste…."

Anders was learning quickly that Nick was not to be taken literally. But he was very entertaining and friendly despite the pistol, and there was always the chance that his chili would be tasty.

"Miss Miller?" he said.

"Chili," she said.

"Me, too.

"And two beers.

"No," she said, "Just a coke for me."

It was too late for him to change his mind. So, he determined he would sip the beer like a gentleman.

It was cold and in a clean beer glass, which was what he had hoped for.

The chili was in a white porcelain bowl. Her Coke was in a glass that said "COKE" on the side, as though it had to be identified. The crackers, wrapped in cellophane, were in a bowl Nick sat in front of them. It said "crackers" on the side.

"So are you enjoying America, Anders," Nick asked. Anders gave him a puzzled look, and Nick repeated the question, this time in perfect Polish. That made Anders smile broadly as he sipped some beer.

"Pretty nice so far," he answered in Polish. "I haven't seen much except for what you can see from a train."

"Then you've seen it all," Nick said. "If we got on a train and went to San Francisco, you would be surprised at how much of the next place looks just like the last place. But it's a good country."

"Nice people, I'm thinking," Anders said.

"So, how many of them have you met?" he asked. Anders went down the list, spending some time on the nun with her eggs and the drunk man in the nice suit in Manhattan."

"We have those here, too," Nick said.

"I mean nuns with eggs, not drunks in suits…Well, them too."

The chili was very good, not too spicy, but with enough bite; Anders was happy to have a small beer to cool the flames. Valery just sipped her Coke and smiled at everything Nick said. She rolled her eyes when Nick and Anders slipped into Polish but seemed to enjoy the show. Anders was worried she might think he was trying to show off.

But she didn't.

She was impressed with how easily he slipped from English to Polish without even the slightest hesitation. She made a note to let Finn know he was absolutely fluid with language, which would be a great asset in investigations.

"Ask him about the vampires," she said to Nick.

"There are no such things," Nick said.

"It's an old wife's tail, and everyone knows it. Right Anders?"

He was stuck on the phrase "Old wife's tale" and had an image in his head of a cranky old woman with a tail. He couldn't shake it.

"Well, you never know," he said.

73

It was another one of those English language expressions that filled in space without saying anything at all. It gave a person time to think in small conversations, like when women answered "Not really" when you asked if they wanted something, which left the issue undecided.

"Nichevo," Anders said in perfect Russian.

"Well, Valery said, now smiling broadly, "Back to work!"

Outside, she looked Anders straight in the eye and, in a frank and direct voice, said, "Don't think Nick is a friend. Nick is a criminal. He's a funny guy and very engaging, but essentially a thief."

"What?"

Yes, works here for the Philadelphia mob, and other than buying a number, you don't want anything to do with him. You should think of him as being armed and dangerous because he is armed and dangerous."

"But he makes good chili!"

"Why do you think he doesn't let cops in during the day? That's when he is doing his business. Don't make a habit of this place because it's the bottom of the barrel and a lot of sick fish end up here. You don't want to be associated with them."

"Okay," he said.

But he put that piece of information in his head in case he ever needed to find one of these "sick fish" (whatever that meant). Maybe Nick could help him. But he wouldn't tell Valery about it.

She was all business back at the office.

"What was the most important lesson no one learned from that explosion," she asked him.

"I would say they should have listened when the mine chief and the fire boss quit because they felt it was too dangerous. After all, they would have known because they had access to all the fire boss reports, all the incident reports, and, assuming they existed, the records of gas readings in the mine. That condition didn't just show up on the day of the explosion. The place was primed to blow up for a long time before that."

It was what she wanted to hear.

"So, if you were the lead investigator in that case, what would YOU have done?"

"I think I would have called the cops early on. There's half a dozen significant violations of mining laws, as I understand them, in the first ten pages of the report. This one should have led to charges and trials, and prison sentences. Why didn't it?"

Because that's not how things were handled in 1911, she said.

The big issue in that mine was its continued operation in the face of a lot of safety challenges. The miners knew that, and so did their bosses. But they decided to take the risk because they wanted the money; they ALL wanted the money from the guys at the top who sold and shipped the coal to the guys at the bottom who dug it. No one wanted the place to close.

"I've seen that in a dozen cases in the six years I have been here. Miners will do anything they can to keep moving coal. First, it's who they are and how they get their money. Second, no one benefits if the mine shuts down. It's in everyone's interest to turn their heads, from the fire bosses right up to the mine managers, just to keep the coal moving. Always remember that. The mine is like an animal that wants to keep running no matter what conditions. There are bodies all over these hills that tell that story. It's the most important reality you have to carry into each investigation that everyone is motivated by money, and that's not happening if the mine closes, even for a few days. It's why they are always so eager to get us out of there and get back to work. We can talk all we want about safety, but these are people who are digging coal and living on the margins. They think it's their risk to take, not yours. Upset their income, and there will always be hell to pay.

"Always!

"But a warning about these people, particularly these managers. They are also motivated by money, and if the mine closes, the money stops.

"They won't hesitate to try to bribe you to get a favorable outcome. No one wants the blame for the loss of life underground. They will do anything they can to shift the focus from them. They all know you make $2,500 a year. It's not hard for them to put $5000 on the table to get you to go in another direction. That's why bribery attempts are so common. Think of it this way, 'That way lies prison.' It's a sin to try to bribe a mine inspector, but it's also a crime. Take good notes with names, dates, incidents, and offers. You will need them if a county prosecutor wants to take a case like that to court on criminal charges.

"But those are very, very rare. I have never seen one that wasn't negotiated out beforehand and closed with a contribution to a miner's family fund, which is a bribe, too, but harder to prove as a bribe. We haven't had an inspector charged with accepting a bribe in the past 25 years, I am told, and Mr. Finn doesn't want that kind of a blotch on his record, I can assure you.

"It sounds stupid, but the best way to do your job is just to do your job and ignore everything else…that's why you are there. Find the cause. Find the culprits, Deliver.. a… measure of …justice…."

Her face was getting red as she lectured, and her volume rose. Anders thought he would never forget it because it had such passion behind it. He decided he would make the phrase "Deliver a measure of justice" his secret anthem.

It was just about noon, time for a break or for lunch. He didn't think it was appropriate to ask her again, and he was pondering that when she stood up and asked him. "Want lunch? There's another place I want you to see…."

"Let me go to the credit union and get some cash," he said. "I'll buy today."

He withdrew $30 from the Credit Union and hoped the lunch would not cost even half that much because he had determined to be careful with his money.

"We're going to "The Senate" for lunch. It's where the other half goes. It's a block from Nick's, but you would never know it."

Let's go. She grabbed her bag and put it over her shoulder, then headed out and turned left to go down the hallway. She moved quickly, so Anders had to hurry to keep up. On the steps in front of Commerce, she stopped and stood in the brilliant June sun for a little while, drinking it in like it was water, her face looking toward the heavens.

She said nothing.

Anders wondered if she did this every day, or whether it was a special gesture, or what. He did not know and did not want to ask. Sensing he was intrigued, she said, "I'm praying…I pray every day, for my father, for the miners, for Finn, and I will add you to my prayer list if you would like."

"That's okay," he said. "I think my whole family is praying for me back in Vulcan. It all goes to the same God, so I think I am well protected."

"Okay. Look, I'm offering to pray for you. You just have to accept that!" she said with a chuckle and hurried down the street with Anders, basically, in tow. She turned right at the first corner and crossed the street, entering a set of rolling hills that formed a park in front of the state capitol building. Secretaries and office workers, and legislators were coming from the building, all heading for a string of restaurants and bars across from the capitol. One on the corner had, in big silver letters, "The Senate" on the front. Valery said, "I know the owner very well. He'll have a place for us." They walked in and were met by a skinny, tall man in a dark suit with a white shirt and striped tie. He had a name tag on his jacket that said, "Immanual, Host."

"Hello, Valery," he said, smiling and bending forward to kiss her cheek. "How have you been?

"I'm just fine," she said. "This is my co-worker Anders Apostle. Is Jimmie around?"

"In the back. I'll get him."

Jimmy was the size of a small truck. He barely fit down the aisles of his own restaurant but obviously knew everyone who had been seated. He greeted the people at each table. Then he walked toward the host station and said, in a booming voice, "VALERY! Lovely as ever. And with a friend?"

"No, he's a co-worker Jimmie, a new mine inspector. I'm just showing him around, and I wanted him to see the best restaurant on the street!

"Thanks, Valery," Jimmy said.

"That will get you a good table and a drink if you want one."

Of course, she did not. They were well seated.

She turned her focus to the center of the big, horseshoe-shaped bar, to a man in a blue suit. He was drinking Martinis.

"Lawyer for the Senate Republicans," she said. "Not much help to the miners, but a direct pathway to the people who own the mines."

Down the other leg of the horseshoe sat a big man with a fluff of gray hair that was all but out of control and a rumpled, dark suit. You see, he's eating the biggest salad you have ever seen? It's that for lunch and fish for dinner. Never changes the menu. State CIO secretary. He also has direct access to the governor, mainly because he got him elected. He can walk right into the office. Make friends with him, and you have a direct pathway to the governor's ear.

"And there's one to avoid," she told Anders, glancing at a dark-haired man sitting on the last seat. He was drinking coffee and picking at lunch he was sharing with the woman sitting with him.

"That's Mario Carsello from Philadelphia. He heads a family of the mafia that has complete influence over the mayor of Philadelphia. There's nothing Carsello can do for you, but a lot he can do to you. Stay away from that type."

"So, where do you live, Valery?" he asked.

"Other side of the river with my mother," she said. It's called New Cumberland. She has a nice old house there, and I help her with it. My sisters live there, too. There were four of us in all. I, two teachers, and a nurse. I was the one who went in for the hard science stuff because of dad.

"He was a very good guy, a union man from the start with the United Mine Workers. He would have been great working in politics, but he had no time for that. He just wanted to organize everyone and cause big trouble for people with too much money!"

He thought she was joking.

She was not.

Martin Miller was a legend in the ranks of union organizers, fearless and creative, and most of all, very smart. He could pull a union crew out of a mine at a moment's notice and shut the place down, even blocking the railroad from collecting coal at the tipple.

His influence stretched beyond the Mine Workers and reached into the Brotherhood of Railroad Trainmen, the Teamsters, the Pipefitters, and all the important labor groups. They all knew and respected Miller because he was an unquestionably honest man. It could not be bought. It could not be rented. Could not be intimidated, even to the point at which, when guns were pulled, Martin had his own, always close at hand. He could use it, too. In his view, there were two kinds of people; workers were the most important. The rest didn't matter unless they abused workers, and then they mattered a lot.

"He was my favorite man of all time," Valery said. "A great dad, handsome, a great union man, a great leader. He had it all."

And where is he? Anders asked shyly.

"Heaven."

There was no uncertainty in her voice.

"Killed in Cambria County many years ago in a dispute with the people from Berwind-White in Windber. They ran that part of the county. A gang of thugs pulled him out of a bar and shot him in the head, and left him in the street to die. The police never found them. It could have been the Pinkertons because they were on the payroll at that point. But we didn't know and never found out. Goons probably. Even the State Police were baffled because the trails kept evaporating. Just when they thought they were on to something, it would zip…go away. They never arrested anyone. I was sick about it for years. I still have his gun, a little Owl .32 revolver. Maybe we can go up in the hills and shoot it someday.

"I have never fired a gun," Anders said.

"Those were for soldiers and criminals in Transylvania, and I was never either of them. I did have a slingshot when I was a kid. I could kill birds and squirrels with it, but then I realized I didn't like killing birds and squirrels. I didn't like killing anything…."

That moved Valery, another thing to like about Anders. If there was violence in him, it was deeply buried. So many American men carried their anger on the surface that she had come to expect that of all men. To find this very well-educated foreigner with a different kind of demeanor was refreshing. She enjoyed spending time with him.

She did not tell him that her intent was to find out who murdered her father and kill them with his pistol.

Then she remembered she was supposed to be teaching him.

"Back to class," she said. "Besides, Mr. Finn wants to see you at the end of the day."

The afternoon fairly zipped past, and before he knew it, Anders was sitting in Mr. Finn's office, waiting to talk to him. He reminded himself that Valery was to be referred to as Miss Miller and treated with great respect.

They moved through the formalities, and Anders sat across from Finn at his desk.

"Darr Creek," he said when Anders told him about the case he was reviewing. That was at the end of one of the worst years in the history of mining. What do you think was at work there?"

Anders gathered himself and moved into what he thought the problems were at Darr Mine. It wasn't just laxity in measuring the gas in the mine; he told Finn. Black powder was dangerous because it was too volatile and exploded with a flame, and the mine was filthy with coal dust, which English miners had identified as the likely source of secondary explosion in many shafts in the first part of the century. The explosion put all that black dust in the air, then the flame set off a secondary explosion, all the air was used up, and anyone in the area would suffocate. He then added his opinion that the explosions didn't have to happen if the mine had been better ventilated and the coal dust had wet down with clay powder. It was a tedious process that added costs to the operation, but it might have saved dozens, if not hundreds, of lives at the Darr Mine.

"We've been trying to get the governor's office to make dusting a requirement for all underground mines, but we haven't been able to get it into the legislature. It's that old problem. The profits are just not big enough for any kind of sophisticated safety systems, and dusting isn't sophisticated; it just makes sense."

He shifted focus and seemed, for a minute, to be transformed. He wasn't talking about mines anymore. He was talking about people.

"We do our jobs because it's the right thing," Finn said. "Families deserve an explanation when a father or a son dies. We're

81

not saying we can fix everything and make coal mining like a walk in the park. We can't. From the very first mines, it has been dangerous, and that's not going to stop."

"You need to hold that thought close to your heart," Finn said, looking straight into Anders's eyes. "We can't make this safe. We can only make it a little safer."

With that, his phone rang.

"Where?"

There had been an explosion at a mine in Wilkes Barre, Pennsylvania. Finn unfolded a sophisticated map on his desk and pinpointed the location.

"Don't worry; you will be getting one of these, too.

"Let's get Miss Miller and get out there."

Valery was in her office down the hall. Finn shouted out his door. "Valery, we have an explosion in Wilkes Barre. Check on the train schedules, or we can get a car."

Chapter 7: The Baltimore Shaft

Finn's department had access to a small fleet of Ford cars with "Bureau of Mines" stenciled on the side. They were fast, well-kept cars.

Finn called the garage to get a car.

"Okay, Finn," he heard the mechanic say on the phone. "It will be waiting when you get here."

They gathered in Finn's office. He was on the phone when Valery and Anders came in. It did not sound good.

"How many men, at least 80?

"Who's there now?

"Still burning? How many companies?

"Don't let the firemen all go down that hole. Send in teams of two at a time, but tethered, so you can drag them out if you have to…Tell them we are on the way."

He hung up the phone and then dialed his office in Wilkes-Barre. They reported they called in nine inspectors to meet them at the site. Finn told the man on the phone to send in the inspectors in teams of two until he arrived, too. "Wear tethers," he told them. They already knew why. It would take about four hours for Finn and Valery, and Anders to get there. They had an early description of what had happened. It was very clear to him that anyone on that train, or in that mine for that matter, would be dead. Black powder explosions were almost all the same, brutal and complete and full of smoke and fire. The concussion alone would kill almost anyone underground within 200 yards of the blast.

"The trip was moving down into the mine, and it had something like 150 men on it in 14 cars and a car in the center for carrying blasting powder. I don't know how many times you have to tell people not to do that. You can't have miners and blasting powder on the same trip. It's just too dangerous. So, somehow a tool, maybe a pick that was upended or something, came into contact with the power cable for the trip and broke it, or maybe the cable was sagging, one guy said, and it came in contact with the top of one of the power barrels and started sparking and landed on …Then…."

Valery and Anders knew where the story was going after that. Sparks from the power line set off the blasting powder, about 600 pounds in all, and it all went up at once. That blast then filled the remaining air in the tunnel with fine coal dust, which exploded from sparks from the first blast. Those who were not killed in the blast burned to death in the fire that followed it. Their remains would be cinders and strips of burned flesh. The scene, Finn knew, would be horrific.

There were not likely to be survivors.

When we get there, Anders, I want you to look for survivors outside the mine. Valery, find out where they keep their records and seal the area. I don't want anyone in there until we have seen what we need to see." He did not have to add, "Don't let them push you around," because he knew Valery was good at pushing back.

Finn drove like a madman, but it still seemed to take forever to get from Harrisburg to Wilkes-Barre. It was the middle of the night when they arrived at the Baltimore Shaft. Officials from the company that owned the mine, the Delaware and Hudson Coal Co., were outside drinking coffee and smoking when Finn and Valery, and Anders arrived.

None of the company officials would talk to Finn when they approached him other than to say hello and shake his hand. That didn't surprise him. No one knew what actually happened, and no one wanted to bear the responsibility of making an official guess because it was clear laws had been broken on a number of levels. There were many children among the victims, Finn had heard, and that was a clear violation of the law. The story about what happened was revealing, too. The first was that it was illegal to move miners and to blast powder on the same trips. The second would be the kinds of containers the powder was in. The more Finn looked at the catastrophe, the more the violations stacked up. After he talked to the local officials, he walked over to a group of firefighters and introduced himself, Valery and Anders.

He thanked him for their help and then began asking a series of simple questions. "When did you get called?" he asked. The man wearing a white hat that said "Chief Dzerzhinsky" on the front told him the story of the explosion as they found it. They were from a company that usually responded to fires at the mine. They were about a mile down the road. There was a phone call, the chief said, and the guy on the other end said, "bring all the firefighters and ambulances you can reach." He said there could be hundreds of dead and injured. They turned on the fire whistle, which would draw volunteers and trained firemen from all over the region, wrote the name of the mine on the blackboard with the word "EXPLOSION!" after it, and raced to the mine. "I also called all the hospitals and told them to expect serious injuries and to send whatever ambulances they could find." The hospitals contacted the Wilkes Barre fire department and pulled it into the disaster, too. It had trained firefighters and first aid specialists on hand, along with ambulances, stretchers, and emergency equipment.

"It was like hell when we got here," he said.

"Fire everywhere, white smoke, then another blast from deeper inside. We could hear it, but we didn't have anyone inside yet. The smell was terrible, burned flesh and sulfur. It made you want to vomit.

"We got about 150 feet down the shaft with our hoses and extinguished what we thought were spot fires. They were actually..." he had to stop for a minute...' Burning bodies. Everywhere. It was awful...."

Finn could see the chief was weeping, so he put his hand on his shoulder and thanked him for taking his men into the mine to save whomever they could find. The chief said they used stretchers and canvas bags to remove the remains. "Some of them, their skin, their flesh, just came off when you tried to move them. I've seen a lot of fires in my time, but nothing like this."

Finn asked whether the power was still on when they went into the mine.

"I don't think so. There were no lights, and I don't think any power to the cable above that trip. That stuff was all blown away when those kegs went up."

"Thank you," Finn told the chief, who walked away to rejoin a small clot of bewildered-looking firemen that had gathered near the mine opening. Finn noticed Anders was having an animated conversation with one of the few survivors. He walked over. They were speaking a language Finn did not recognize. It was Romanian. There was a lot of gesturing, and the man was reaching up into the sky as though he were trying to bring down stars.

"What was THAT about," Finn asked Anders.

"He was on the front of the train in the first car, so he was far away from the explosion. He crouched down in front of the first car, so the impact did not hit him. That saved his life. He was showing me how the fire just seemed to roll down the tunnel and kill everyone it touched in the cars. He was only 14 years old.

"He should not have been in that mine," Anders said. Finn added another mental note to the climbing list of violations he was assembling. Youngsters could pick boney outside the mine, but the days when the company would use children to open and close the air gates as the trips came were over. They were not to be inside the front opening of the mine under any condition. The legislature had just passed that law a year ago, and it was signed by the governor with a lot of fanfare, so it wasn't like they didn't know.

Finn called Anders and Valery aside and told them he would be assembling all of the inspectors in the mine headquarters building at 10:30 a.m. He told them to be there and to look for anyone in the green canvas Department of Mines jackets they were all required to wear at accident sites.

In all, 12 of his inspectors, Finn included, showed up at the meeting that morning. Valery (Whom Finn referred to as deputy Miller) would be running the actual session. She had already sealed the mining company's records and found they had not yet been disturbed, so there was a good chance she would be able to get the kind of detail she needed if the Mining Department had to build a case.

Even with so many deaths, it was not always possible to ascertain who was actually responsible for such a cataclysm. Certainly, the men who decided to load black power kegs on the man trip would face a variety of charges, but they were probably already dead. Who decided to continue to employ children in mining jobs so long after the governor signed the last banning the youngsters from mining? Finn knew the answer would be "their fathers" because that's almost always how kids ended up doing that kind of work. But it was likely their fathers were dead, too.

"Okay, let's get underway."

Valery stood at a podium in the front of the room, her canvas overalls opened for comfort and her notebook sitting on the podium. She had a safety hat on with the logo of the Commonwealth of Pennsylvania on the front. It had the words "Mining Inspector" on the back. She looked completely official, Anders thought.

How would she handle this?

"It's not a mystery how these men died," she said, "But it is a mystery why they died. You can all see the violations stacking up in front of you, from black powder on the man trip to very poorly kept electrical equipment. Kids in the mine. It surprises me that it took this long for something like this to happen in this place. But that's not why we are here. We are here to identify obvious, ongoing violations and decide what they tell us about modern mining methods and the dangers they bring to the people who use them.

She broke the group into subgroups of four men each. They would be looking at specific kinds of risks apparent in the mine. "A reminder. Write it all down in your notebooks. We have a camera if we need it, so don't hesitate to ask if you want photos.

"Anders, come up here…."

Anders walked to the front of the room.

"This is our newest inspector, Anders Apostle, from Vulcan in Transylvania. Introduce yourselves, please and welcome him. I'm sorry we could not meet under happier circumstances, but this is the work we do. So…Onward."

With that, she left the meeting room and headed to the company's records room to start her work there.

Anders smiled and met the men around him.

"So, vampires?"

"There are no vampires," Anders said. The same thing kills people there as it kills people here.

They all introduced themselves and then shifted into a rolling conversation about what they had seen in the mine.

"I've never seen death like that," said one of the inspectors. So many burned black, charred. I've seen people crushed, blown up, and electrocuted. But never burned like this on this scale.

"That's what black powder in that volume can do. That's why you are not allowed to move it into the mine on the man trips. That's criminal, I'll tell you…."

At that Anders spoke up.

"So, do we call the police if it's criminal?"

"Well…I don't think so. That just makes the whole thing a lot more complicated with lawyers and everything. I wouldn't call the police in…."

"But don't the people responsible for this have to pay for their crime?"

"Anders, things don't always work that way here. We'll all do our reports and see what happens later."

Anders left the room and went to find Finn.

"I'm confused about something," he said to Finn in the hallway outside the meeting room. "It's pretty clear the company broke the law by putting all that black powder on the same trip as the miners. So why aren't we calling in the police?"

"We are the police. We need to collect everything we can here, then take it to the county prosecutors and ask them to bring a case into court. That's how it has to work here. We have that kind of police authority under the mining laws. We can build our own cases or not, depending on the circumstances."

"So, we will build the case here?"

"Yeah," Finn said. "It's not something we hand off to other authorities. First, we lose control of the case if that happens, and second, our evidence leaves our control, and we have no idea what other people will do with it. I don't want to make you overly suspicious about the companies and the people who run them, but they aren't always interested in justice for anyone. They are interested in money for themselves. Get that firmly embedded in your brain because, in the United States, money still runs everything."

Anders turned away from Finn and saw Valery had walked into the back of the room through the back door. "Mr. Finn, I think we have a big problem. The records are terrible. No fire boss reports. No gas readings. Nothing. This place was making up its rule book as it moved along. The problem is we don't have records. I should be able to tell who issued that black powder and when and how often that happened. But they didn't even keep track of that. I think we have to take this place apart...."

"So, we will," Finn said.

"Miss Miller, I want you to take charge of building up an inventory of explosive lists; I want dates, shipments, how it was stored, everything you can find in the records. Anders, find the fire boss reports and catalog them so we can see what the mine has been telling us in the numbers. I don't know where they kept them. You may have to go down to the fire boss stations in the mine to get the morning reports on gas readings. Be careful. They are required by law to do that, so go down there and find them."

"Okay," he said. "Is there a map showing fire boss stations?"

"Make one if you have to."

There were sets of coveralls in the state car, so Anders went to retrieve one for himself. It was too big, so he rolled up the pantlegs and sleeves. Once it was buttoned up, he looked fine and felt covered. He pulled on a big pair of rubber boots, then sloshed through the muck of the fire to the mine opening. He had a bright flashlight with him, his notebook in his coat pocket, and some pencils.

It was only a few hours after the accident, so the mine was still hot from the fire. The bodies had not yet been retrieved, so he had to be careful about where he stepped. The floor of the mine was still covered with detritus from the fire. Every few yards, there was the blackened mound of a body of a miner nearly incinerated in the explosion. They had a terrible smell about them. He flashed his light down about 50 feet of the mine entranceway and saw what appeared to be a phone booth just on the other side of the track that was used by the trip. It was burned black on the outside.

Anders sloshed through the muck on the floor of the mine and made his way to the booth. On the outside, there was a sign: Fireboss 1. The door had been blasted in. Inside, everything was charred. There was a book that looked like a phone book resting on a shelf above a stand that once held a telephone, which was melted by the fire. He opened it. Charred paper and some barely visible writing, but he thought it could be important. He put the book in a satchel, labeled it, and stepped out of the booth to go deeper into the mine. The entrance now took a downward slope that followed the track for the trip. He counted off 300 steps and saw another booth, this one on the other side of the mine. He crossed over to it and found the same kind of book as in the first booth but with nothing written on any of its many pages. This book he also labeled this and put it into his satchel. Then he went back out into the slope and found himself going down again, another 350 steps or so, and there was another booth against the wall. "Fireboss Only!" this one said. It was scorched on the surface but had not been burned. Again, nothing was written in the book. That could mean a couple of things, Anders thought. The fire boss might not have registered his readings every day, or he may not have even taken them. That book he added to his collection, too. Then he ran into 9 bodies in a pile on the tracks. They were stacked up as though someone had put them there. It was clear the explosion that followed the fire reached this deep into the mine and killed these men. Their bodies were not as severely burned as the bodies he saw earlier in his search. But they were certainly just as dead. He leaned over to touch the hip of one of the bodies. It was cold as ice. He made a note in his notebook to make certain these bodies were retrieved. Then he moved further into the mine and found Fire Station No. 5. Again, nothing was written in the book, no gas readings, no observations, nothing. This book he also collected this and put it into his pouch. Even deeper, he found two more of the fire boss stations. Same story for both. Empty books with no signs of readings.

Anders turned and headed back out of the mine. He was happy to see sunlight after he had walked for about 40 minutes. Finn and Valery were waiting when he came out of the pit. He was covered with ash from the fire, and some blood, too, from bodies he brushed up against.

"What did you find?" Finn asked.

"I went in about three and a half miles. There are still lots of bodies in there. I found five fire stations with logs in them. I have them with me. Most of them don't reflect any measurement of anything. Some of the books from the fire stations deep into the mine are empty. I don't think they were taking readings on a regular basis. If they were, they were not recording them at the fire boss stations. It looks to me like the conditions in the mine didn't much matter to them. I know we have to do more work, but it's not good so far.

"Great, Anders," said Valery.

"Now we can take those books you collected and stack them up against the books in the offices. I didn't look into any of them, so we will get to them first thing tomorrow."

Finn said he would buy dinner downtown, where they could pick up hotel rooms for the night.

The William Penn Hotel was one of those faded glories that paid tribute to Wilkes-Barre's past when it was a successful place where people with a good deal of money came to visit or live.

Finn, Anders, and Valery parked the state car outside and walked into the lobby through the front door. The old men sitting in the lobby smoking and reading their newspapers stopped just to glance at Valery as she walked past in her state coveralls and boots.

"That will be $12 a night each. How many nights?" the man at the desk said. Finn suggested three but said they might be leaving before then, and the clerk said it would be no problem. Finn paid the $36 for the rooms, and the trio headed for the elevators. The rooms were all on the 9th floor.

Anders scrubbed himself up as well as he could and used a stick of deodorant already in the medicine closet in the bathroom. He smelled it. It was manly, which was all he required, and probably strong enough to push its way through his shirt. It was 7:25 p.m.

Valery reported first at dinner.

"Nothing at all about safety training, rules for moving explosives, nothing at all. I will ask tomorrow whether they keep those things in another area, but I'm not finding a lot of high-quality record-keeping at that place.'

"I have never seen a mine that didn't keep at least a basic chart of gas readings on site," Anders said. "How would they know whether it was safe over time? There was nothing like that at all in the fire boss stations."

"Maybe I can look for documents in the morning that will tell us about that," Valery said.

There was, of course, a budget for dinner, but Finn ignored it. "Get whatever you want," he told Anders and Valery. "We've earned a good dinner today, just based on what we have seen."

It was a very simple menu. Anders ordered fried liver and onions and roast potatoes. It was $2.50 and included pudding for dessert. Finn ordered a chopped steak and mashed potatoes, and Valery ordered a New York Strip steak, rare, with fried potatoes and a side order of greens.

Anders had water with his dinner. Finn had a local bottle of beer, as did Valery. Anders was happy to see she wasn't shy about drinking around her boss. She drained her first glass and ordered a second to drink with her steak. She looked very satisfied when she was done. She took a cigarette from her purse and smoked, quite contentedly, as the waiter brought fresh cups of coffee for everyone.

Anders noted Finn was smoking, too, and for an instant, he regretted it was one of the habits he had avoided, even though everyone in Vulcan smoked like they were issued cigarettes at birth. He never took up the habit and had no intention of starting now. They drank their coffee and formulated a game plan for the next day of the investigation. Anders would return to the mine to see whether there were any protocols underground for how fire bosses were to start the day. Those kinds of things would be somewhere in the booths along the mine entranceway. That meant he had to enter and pass those bodies again. It made him shudder to think of that.

Anders slept in his underwear, with his eyes closing the minute his head hit the pillow.

"This is what I wanted," he reminded himself. "This is what I have to do."

They were to meet in the restaurant at 7:15 a.m. Finn wanted to get to the mine headquarters before any of the local officials arrived. He already had his suspicions, and he didn't want them touching what he knew would be important evidence in a wrongful death investigation. Generally, mine officials who had that kind of intent started laundering records well before state inspectors arrived. There was no time in this one. Finn would have that rarest of experiences, a clean record of laying out, measuring, pondering, listen to what it told him. Valery had sealed off the room so that it was protected.

Finn had scrambled eggs and toast and bacon, "The holy trinity of breakfast," he joked, while Valery had a poached egg, one piece of toast, and half of a banana. Anders, still very new to American menus, ordered something called "oatmeal" and was delighted to find what they meant to say was "porridge." He put a spoonful of brown sugar on the mound in the bowl, then poured cream from a silver pitcher into it, added a lump of butter, and mixed it all up.

"Goodness," Valery said, "You certainly know your oatmeal."

"Where is the chicken skin?" he asked when he had finished. "All bowls of porridge included a chicken skin all over Europe! But not here!"

"Well, here, Anders, they generally throw them away or leave them on the bird when they fry it," Valery said. "It would be pretty upsetting to find a chicken skin on the bottom of your oatmeal."

"We need the fat!" he said, speaking to no one but sounding definitive about it.

Finn played with his eggs and smiled as the menu discussion spun out across from him. It was clear that Anders had not tried to sleep with Valery, even though no one would have minded or been surprised.

Anders had his thoughts, but he respected Valery, worked for her, and didn't want any of that to "slip off the rails, as some of the inspectors put it when they found something had gone wrong.

Anders was training himself to think in idiomatic expressions, not because he needed them but because everyone else seemed to speak an idiomatic version of English that could lose a foreigner quite rapidly.

He was determined to keep up.

They walked out of the hotel and to the state Ford to return to the site of the disaster. Anders had sent his clothing to be cleaned, and it was promised for the afternoon, so he felt confident he would not look like a bum at dinner, assuming they didn't just return to Harrisburg. "So, now," Finn said.

"To the scene of the crime...." Anders, of course, took that literally. It wasn't meant that way, but...

There was not much conversation on the half-hour ride to the mine. The countryside was quite different in the daylight. Everywhere there was a mine, there was a pile of mine waste, some of them huge. They were gray and red rocks mixed in together. The streams flowing from some of the mines were orange with Sulphur, so polluted they could support no life. Even the trees along the streams seemed stunted.

Soon a series of official-looking road signs warned of "dangerous conditions ahead," and Anders realized they were approaching the mines. There were some fire trucks and ambulances outside the entrance. Finn said they were probably still collecting bodies. A mass grave was being prepared nearby. Trucks had been brought in to collect the remains of the 240 dead miners. There were priests of every description at the scene, Roman Catholics with oils for last rights, Orthodox priests, including one Bishop with a huge black hat and gold cross around his neck, and even some nuns. The priests would anoint the bodies before they were put on the trucks, splashing holy water on them (and everyone else at the scene) as they tried to keep up with the tragedy of it.

Finn, Anders, and Valery got out of the car near the headquarters office of the mining company. She walked into the building while Finn and Anders headed for the mouth of the mine.

Anders stopped there to put on his coveralls and boots. It was still mucky, with detritus from the fire mixed with water from the fire trucks and the wreckage that had been dragged from the shaft. Nothing was burning. Finn told Anders to take gas checks and readings before he got too far into the shaft, and Anders opened a case and took out a safety lamp to help with the readings. It was a simple tool for an important job. Once the lamp was lit, its flame would continue to burn until the oxygen in the atmosphere dropped below 18 percent. The flame would flicker, and the miners would know to leave the mine. The biggest concern was black damp, mostly carbon monoxide, which could settle on miners and kill them in minutes. The safety lamp would always give them the warning they needed.

He took samples at each of the nine fire boss stations as he went back down into the mines.

He turned back at station 11, first because he was becoming light-headed and second because the flame was flickering on his safety lamp. By the time he reached the surface, he felt as though he would faint. The lamp was out.

"Anders," Finn called to him as Anders leaned up against one of the fire trucks. "Are you okay…You look…" with that, Anders went face-first to the ground. Finn and a couple of the other inspectors knelt beside him, slapping his cheeks and trying to revive him. After a minute or so, Anders revived and sat up.

"Weren't you watching your lamp, Anders," Finn asked him.

"I was. There was just not enough of a warning. The flame was flickering, and I turned and left the mine, but the minute I got into the fresh air, I fainted."

"But I got air samples from almost all of the fire boss stations I visited, so at least that part worked out okay."

Finn told Anders he would be taking him to the hospital for a check-up. He told him to get out of his gear and get into the car. "But I am okay, Mr. Finn," Anders said. "I can…." With that, Finn took him by the arm and forcefully moved him onto the front seat of the state car. Then he went to the other door, got in, and drove off. He told one of the other inspectors to tell Valery he was taking Finn to the emergency room.

"Tell her he is probably okay, but I just want to make certain."

He sped from the mine and headed back to Wilkes Barre to the hospital. He went straight to the emergency room door, helped Anders out, and took him to the first doctor he saw.

"Finn, from Harrisburg mining," he said.

"This is Anders Apostle, one of my inspectors. He went down into the mine and came out and fainted. Can we get him checked out?"

The doctor said, "Of course."

Anders found himself sitting on an emergency room table and surrounded by medical people.

They checked his eyes, his ears, his breathing, and his heart and took blood. Then they told Finn he seemed fine, that it might just have been exhaustion or "maybe some oxygen deprivation from the foul air in the mine." There were at least four gases to be careful about in the wake of a mine fire. Three of them could kill you in any volume, and the fourth, carbon dioxide, could make you faint. Three of the four were explosive gases, with hydrogen being the most threatening. There was nothing in Anders's blood to tell them he had been exposed to any of them.

Thanks, Finn said.

They were driving back to the mine.

"In almost every case, enough people have already died in the mines we're inspecting. I don't want my people added to that list! Mine gases after explosions can kill you, and you know that. I want you out of there at the first signs of trouble!" Finn said.

At first, Anders thought Finn was angry, but then he realized he was simply very worried.

"I'm not angry at you, Anders because you did the job I sent you to do. I just can't ever get used to sending people into dangerous situations. That's what you are hearing."

That settled him.

Valery was standing on the steps outside of the headquarters, her face up to the sun and her eyes closed. Anders assumed she was praying. She put her hand on his shoulder and, with the tiniest squeeze, said, "I am so happy to see you are well." Anders, once again, found himself blushing. "Praying for your father?" he asked.

"No," she said. "Praying for you."

Finn lighted a cigarette and stood on the steps of the headquarters.

"What did you find, Valery?"

"You're not going to like this at all," she said. "The fire boss records are complete in the office files. All the data, all the conditions, all as required." Anders injected himself into the discussion...

"No, there were no records in the stations. How could they have records up here when no one wrote anything down in the books at the stations?"

Chapter 8: Delaware & Hudson Co.

"That's what we need to find out," Finn said. He was not upset about it at all but very determined. Let's go in and talk to some folks about it."

In the office, they were met by a secretary who was still clearly upset about the disaster and the losses it caused. She said the officers of the company had not yet returned from a memorial service at the mass grave dug for the victims. She expected them within the hour.

The Delaware and Hudson executives stopped for lunch after the ceremony at the mass grave, which was in a relatively flat field about ten miles east of Wilkes-Barre. For the moment, everyone got a white cross with a date on it but no name and no explanation. Gravestones were to come much later.

It took them two more hours to get back to the office, and it was clear by the time they arrived that they had been drinking.

Finn introduced himself and let Valery and Anders speak for themselves.

"We have a number of questions about the mining records," Finn said.

"Questions," one of the executives said. "We ALL have questions, but we don't have a single goddamn answer…No answers at all."

"We sealed all your records when we arrived early this morning and returned to them at about 8:30 a.m. We can't find any record of conditions, gas levels, whatever, at the fire boss stations in the mine. Do any of you know anything about that?"

The trio of executives was silent.

"Do you have a list of fire bosses and schedules for their deployment?"

Again, silence.

"Do you have a roster to show us who was working where in the mine at the time of the explosion and fire?"

More silence. (But at least one of them shook his head).

"You are aware that it is illegal to carry miners and black powder on the same trip?"

More silence, then:

"Perhaps you could speak with our lawyers. They will be here directly," said the man who was clearly in charge of the others. He was, at least, somewhat sober.

"How about office managers? Are any of your office managers around?"

One of the men answered that the office managers were all at the ceremony for the miners and could be coming soon or not, depending on whether they stopped for lunch...."

"It's a hard time for us here, losing so many men under such violent conditions...we...."

With that, Finn raised his hand and said he would rather talk to the lawyers and the managers and any surviving fire bosses when they arrived. He said they would leave the mine now and return at 5 p.m., and the executive should have those people available for interviews.

"I need to warn you that this has now become a criminal investigation centering on violations of a variety of mining laws, particularly given the loss of so many lives," Finn said.

"You should tell your people we will be building a record, that they will be sworn and are required to answer our questions and that we are here as law enforcement representatives of the Commonwealth of Pennsylvania, the same as the State Police.

"They can have a lawyer present if they need to."

As they walked out of the building, Finn turned to Anders and Valery and told them they were going to the local state police barracks to pick up a trooper to stand as a witness to what the mining company people would testify when they returned.

"We don't have to do that, but it always helps to have a cop in uniform on the scene, and state troopers wear those uniforms very well," Finn said.

"People respect that up here. It will help us."

Susquehanna Troop headquarters was 10 miles from town on a side road off the northeast extension of the Pennsylvania Turnpike, a project that crossed the state from east to west and had branches north on either end of the state. It was a big red brick building, two stories, sitting back off the road. The Commonwealth flag flew from its roof. There were Green and Yellow state police cars lined up out front, 15 of them.

They parked and walked inside to a front desk where a trooper in a gray uniform with sergeant's stripes and a campaign hat with a broad brim was on watch. It had a black state insignia on the front. Finn showed his credentials, which included a silver badge with "Department of Mining" stamped on it, and asked the Sergeant who was in charge. He said he would call Lieutenant Franklin from upstairs.

"We had some troopers at the scene as the firemen were bringing up the bodies. What a terrible thing. We are so sorry about the losses. We don't have a list yet, but it's pretty certain that some of our troopers had relatives injured or killed. You all have our sympathies and any help we can give you for the investigation."

"Thank you, sergeant," Finn said.

Franklin came down in a minute or so, suit pants, a revolver in a holster on his shoulder, and a white shirt with a tie. He looked like a businessman but well built up to his shoulders and had no sign of a gut. "That comes later," Finn thought, glancing down at his own waist."

Because it was a state police barracks, there were sleeping quarters on the second floor, showers, and a small kitchen with a dining room. Troopers coming in from all-night shifts would have their coffee and breakfast there and clean up before they went home. The place had all the charm of an army barracks but was very clean.

Lt. Franklin asked how he could help, and Finn told him what they encountered at the mine and how it might be very helpful to have a uniformed trooper with them as they conducted their interviews. They anticipated drafting criminal charges, and the trooper would be a strong presence as a witness as the interviews proceeded. The lieutenant was pleased that Finn recognized the authority a trooper would bring to the process. They had all worked hard to develop that sense of presence.

"Do you have anyone we could have for a couple of days?" Finn asked.

"Can't say without checking the roster. He went into the desk and pulled out a clipboard with a sheaf of paper attached. "I have three extra men here now, two uniformed and one detective. Anders asked if any of them spoke Hungarian, and the lieutenant said "no," not much use for that when you're just following traffic."

The lieutenant walked away, and Finn pulled Anders aside.

"Hungarian?"

"I looked at the list of the dead. Most of those names were Hungarian. I thought it might be good to have someone who could talk to family members, things like that...."

"That would be YOU, Anders," Finn said.

"Anders smiled and said, 'of course.'"

A uniformed trooper came bounding down the stairs and through the doorway. The lieutenant introduced him as Trooper Howard Morgan and said he was training as a detective. He looked like an Irish boxer with a pug nose, big shoulders, and a jaw that seemed chiseled from granite. The skin on his hands was flushed red, with callouses on the knuckles. From his chin to his belt buckle, he was as flat as a board, all muscle, no doubt. Finn always wondered where the state police found these characters. Truth be known, they built them. Each barracks had its own gym, with weights and an array of workout machines Troopers would use to pass the time.

"We would be happy to lend him to you for a couple of days. No problem."

He told the trooper to wear his firearm and that his biggest job would be to represent the authority of the state police at the mining office. "Mr. Finn and his associates already have arresting powers and police powers, so you don't have to worry about any of that. Just be there and look as tough as you can."

They walked to Finn's state car. The lieutenant came out on the porch and told Trooper Morgan to take one of the patrol cars. "Don't be shy about it, Morgan. You're on-site to be a presence, so be a presence." Make sure the light is on when you drive on to the place so everyone can see. Probably not the siren…."

Trooper Morgan turned to Finn.

"So, what do you really need me to do?" he asked.

"I need you to stand there in your uniform with your badge showing and the authority of the state of Pennsylvania apparent to everyone in the room. You don't have to say anything. You are waving the flag for us, and that will be a big help, I think, with these people," Finn said.

"Okay!"

It seemed simple enough.

Finn made certain that Trooper Morgan would lead them back to the mine headquarters and enter the parking lot first. He knew the executives and a lot of the secretarial workers at the headquarters would be watching. He wanted them to understand that the cavalry had just arrived. He didn't have enough of force to overwhelm himself with numbers, so he had to let the images of authority work for him. A magnum revolver in a black leather Sam Brown holster and a trooper who looked like he was cut from rock worked well for that.

There were certainly some slick characters at the top of mining companies, but not all of them. Some people would be humbled to have state police on site. Finn had considered arming his mining inspectors but decided against it. They were simply too far-flung and too independent to control. He also didn't want to have to cope with the domestic violence and mayhem that would ensue should a "mining agent" shoot someone in a bar fight. A trooper was a good substitute for all of that.

Trooper Morgan was as solid a driver as anyone had ever seen, and when he turned into the parking lot of the coal company with his red roof light flashing, it drew everyone's attention.

Finn hoped he remembered to clip the cuffs on his belt. That always impressed people.

Morgan, Finn, Anders, and Valery climbed the front steps together and walked into the lobby. Finn asked the secretary where they would be meeting, and she stood and led him down the hallway to a long meeting room with a walnut table and comfortable chairs.

Four men in suits waited in the room. They were introduced as the treasurer, executive secretary, and operational directors of the company.

"Where are the books?" Finn asked.

"What books," one of the operational directors asked.

"We need to see the reports based on the fire boss records. Conditions in the mine on given dates. There were no records in those stations after the fire.

"There were!" said the man.

"I put those books there myself not two months ago."

"Not a word is written in most of them," Finn said. "The law requires fire bosses to register their air check results and cite conditions in the mine before the shifts enter in the morning. Then those results are supposed to be registered in a safe area away from the mine in a general log."

"This investigation is about the explosion,' right?"

"Yes," Finn said. "

"Then why do you want the general condition logs?"

Finn paused.

"...And whatever else we need it to be about. We need those books."

The men walked to the side of the room to consult with their attorneys.

"We'll be back," they said, all departing at the same time.

"Now it's going to get interesting," Finn said.

About 20 minutes later, the men came back with a cart loaded with ledger books; each had a month written on the front, with days and dates and station numbers clearly written on the insides. "Here you go," one of the men said. "Feel free to review whatever you want."

"And who fills out these reports?" Finn asked.

"It depends. Sometimes secretaries in the office here get the reports from the fire boss stations and use them to complete the records. They are diligent about it.

"We need to talk to them," Finn said.

"One of the lawyers stood up at that point and hinted that Finn would need a specific subpoena outlining what they were looking for."

"All of it," Finn said.

"All the reports from the fire bosses. We also need a few of the fire bosses here who were working in the weeks before the explosion."

"Mr. Finn, my understanding is that the Commonwealth is investigating the explosion of the kegs of black powder on the man trip. Is that correct?"

"Yes," Finn said. "But we also need to know why there were no records at the fire boss stations, and yet, they show up here in great detail in these logbooks...who filled them up and how?"

Finn knew well the dangers of reaching conclusions too early in an investigation, but he was just about certain that the people at this coal company were not taking readings at all and simply filling in the books with data that painted a healthy picture of what was going on in the mine. That would keep the coal moving without problems and provide cover for management in the event of an unfortunate accident. Finn had seen that before, but never to this degree that none of the fire bosses were keeping records, if there even were fire bosses. But not a lot of men stood in line to be the fire boss. It was one of the most dangerous jobs in the pit in those days. It had evolved. Nowadays, the men were basically assistant foremen responsible for keeping an eye on ventilation conditions in the mine, the placing of brattices, for example. They used a series of instruments to read air levels and recorded them on sheets. They would be carried to the main office, and any problems with conditions would be written into the overall logbook. Any potential high-risk problems would show up in that check, it was assumed.

Of course, no one wanted a mine to blow up.

That would stop everything.

"Who decided the seating order for the miners in the trips in the morning? Who would have decided to put casks of black powder on that trip?" Finn asked.

The men formed a little group and consulted. One stepped forward to report.

"Dead in the explosion," he said. And who was in charge of that man?"

Another consultation.

"Dead in the explosion…," the same man said.

"…And in charge of that man…?

"Also…dea…"

It was clear that "dead in the explosion" would be the answer to any questions about responsibility for putting the black powder on the mantrip.

"Do you have any surviving fire bosses?"

"Certainly," the executive answered.

"Have them here later in the afternoon, please."

"What about the subpoena?" one of the attorneys asked. Finn said he would have it later in the day.

He had called the county court before lunch and asked an assistant district attorney to draft as general a subpoena as they could for anything related to the blast. He realized that would probably be too broad a request, but the assistant DA seemed supportive, and Finn didn't mind taking the chance.

"I'll send someone over with it later in the day," the prosecutor said.

It arrived in an official-looking envelope as anyone at the courthouse could find. Inside, a simple document that said the court was looking for any information about the explosion of black powder...then the date and the time of the incident.

Finn and Valery read the document just after it arrived and then called a meeting just of the state crew, Finn, Anders, Valery, and now, Trooper Morgan.

"Okay, I need specific questions to ask in connection with this subpoena. I'm thinking we need work lists to show who was in the mine at what time, fire boss assignments, any reports over the past three months about conditions in the mines, any correspondences dealing with the transfer of the black powder from storage areas to the coal face and all points in between. None of that is going to tell us anything more than that this wasn't a coincidence, that this shifting of explosives was planned and ordered. We just need a couple of answers then we can proceed. But we can't base a homicide argument on this information. We can get them on violation of regulations that, essentially, were designed to have no teeth. The most we can get from it is a consent decree where they agree there was wrongdoing, but without any specific confessions."

"Wait," Anders said.

"We can't charge them with killing those miners?"

"No," Finn said. "That's not our purpose here. But we can create enough of a record that the county authorities can proceed with our help. Again, this is the frustration in this job. It aims to find violations that can be corrected. Not violations that should be prosecuted. We already have them for using and moving black powder on man trips. We have them for failing to keep proper records. But those kinds of things lead to fines, not to prosecutions. We need to gather what we can here and then get someplace away from it all and talk about what we can do."

At the very least, the Hudson and Delaware Mining Co. would have a hard time renewing its business license when the date came in the next year.

Not much satisfaction for so many deaths, Finn said, but that's what they could do, as much as they could possibly do. If they did all of that right, there could be a chance someone in the county government would be aggressive enough to prosecute.

From the corner of the room, Trooper Howard spoke up.

"I could follow up on this end to make sure it's not just dropped," he said. Finn turned toward him and, in an expression of true thanks, told him that would be a noble pursuit. There was a diligence to the trooper that was apparent to Finn and Valery.

Everyone gathered in the same room back at the mining headquarters. In addition to the lawyers and company officials, five men, apparently fire bosses, also showed up. They were dressed in mine coveralls, clean for the occasion but well worn.

"I'm going to ask just one question of all of you, and you can answer however you please," Finn said. "Has any of you ever checked to see that your fire boss information was correctly entered in the ledger?"

"No," was the response.

Finn showed them the ledgers that had been retrieved by the lawyers. "These books are supposed to show the information you wrote in your fire boss station reports every morning on your shift. We could not find any of those reports in the logs at the stations after the explosion. What happened to them?

The general response was, "Don't know." They all insisted they had filled out reports as required each morning before the working mine crews were allowed in the shaft. They said they didn't know what had happened to them.

"Weren't you required to deliver those reports to the office here at the end of your shifts or earlier if you found anything that would place anyone in danger?"

No one knew how to answer that question. Finn was not surprised. Ignorance of the law of responsibilities was common in the mining business. Not a single fire boss could describe the process used to deliver the reports to the office.

"Who was responsible for receiving the reports?" Valery asked, fixing a piercing gaze on the legal team as she delivered her question. "Secretarial staff here," was the answer.

"Name them," Anders said, surprising everyone with the aggression with how he delivered the question.

"We'll have to check," replied the attorneys.

"Do that," Finn said.

He said the team would report back in the morning.

With that, they packed up their things and walked out the door. No one said goodbye except the Trooper. Who said, "See you first thing in the morning."

On the way to the car, Finn invited the trooper to dine with his team and made it clear the primary purpose would not be food.

"I need to know what we all think about this," Finn said.

"And for our purposes, you can think of yourself as one of us."

"Thank you," said the Trooper.

Finn made a mental note to contact the governor's office when he got back to Harrisburg and commend Trooper Howard and also ask for a temporary reassignment to the mining safety and inspection crew. He was a solid young man with a good heart and a good head, and Finn was drawn to that.

They didn't want to draw attention to themselves, so Finn decided that William Penn would not be the right choice for dinner, especially with a conversation about what they were going to pursue. He asked the man at the desk whether there was a good bar or restaurant nearby where they might get a private room for dinner.

He also ordered up a room for the trooper and told him to get his uniform cleaned if he felt the need.

"Inn on the River," the man told him. "Very good food, good atmosphere, and privacy if you want it. I've sent lots of men over there for...mmmm...dinners if you know what I mean. Finn, of course, knew exactly what he meant and concluded the Inn on the River would be the perfect spot for their business. It was just a few blocks of walking.

In the lobby, he told Valery, Anders, and the trooper they were going to go to the Inn on the River for dinner and a talk. The Trooper knew the place and said it was good.

It was a brief walk, and it turned out the Inn on the River had just the spot for Finn's meeting, a second-floor dining room that looked out on the Susquehanna River, just a block west of the hotel. They climbed the stairs and walked into the room, which had regional oil color paintings on the walls; it was quietly lit and, once the doors were closed, almost completely private except for the entrance from the kitchen.

"Perfect," Finn said.

"Have a drink if you want to. I'll be back. I have to report in."

They gathered around a round table with a pot of cheddar cheese spread and crackers in the center. There was a little knife for spreading.

Valery ordered a Rolling Rock beer, which came in a small bottle. Anders ordered one from the menu called Dinkel Acher, which he knew from Germany, and the trooper ordered vodka straight up with water on the side.

"Now that's a man who likes his drinking," Valery thought.

Anders was excited to find a beer from Germany. He settled in with a cracker with some cheese on it and waited for his drink. Valery and the Trooper had cigarettes while they were waiting.

Chapter 9: Trooper Howard Morgan

"How long have you been on the force," Valery asked the trooper.

"This is my fifth year. I had to go through the police academy twice because I got sick in the middle of my first term. I think I caught something from one of the horses," he said.

"Horses," Anders said.

"Yes, we all had to be trained in riding at the State Police Academy. I'm not sure why because troopers haven't been on horse duty in 40 years. Anyhow, they had some horses that were not well, and I suspect I caught one of their horse diseases."

"What happened," Valery asked.

"Well, it's person...priva...Well, I had explosive shits for two weeks, lost a lot of weight, couldn't take in anything but water, and then got well. Miserable thing. It kept me from my classes on law enforcement, so I would have failed the academy. They gave me another chance because of the illness.

"Did you always want to be a trooper?" Valery asked.

"No," he said.

"I wanted to be a priest, but I could not get into any of the seminaries, so I just gave up and decided law enforcement would be a good substitute. At least I could be helping people."

"Do you have a girlfriend?" she asked, pushing one of those boundaries she promised to herself she would never push.

"Yes, I do. But she lives in Lock Haven down the river, and I don't get to see her much. She always worries about me, what with the Klu Klux Klan stuff in the center part of the state. Those guys are mainly bluffing, but they can get violent when they are in those big groups. I don't get that level of hatred for the Catholics," he said. "They think the Pope rules all of us around, that there's some kind of secret tunnel from Washington to the Vatican, and he can send Jesuits in to force people to do what he wants."

"Hmmm. That sounds completely crazy to me," Valery said. "I think they hate Negroes, too, and Italians and anyone else who looks like they were not descended from the Mayflower people. I hate that kind of thinking. In the work we do, we spend a lot of time with immigrants and their families. They are fine, fine people, always kind and so supportive of the kinds of things we do.

"So, Valery," the trooper asked, "Are you married? Do you have a boyfriend?

"No and no," she said. "I'm going to spend the next decade of my life working, then I'll think about getting married. Or maybe not. You can't say, you know?"

"Right," he said.

"Okay, Harrisburg is fine with us pursuing a plan that will nail this company for about $20,000 in fines, along with relaying what we find to the district attorney and state attorney general's office.

"Trooper Morgan," he said, 'I've asked my boss to ask your boss to extend your mission with us for a little longer. I'm thinking about six months if that's okay with you. Our guys make less money than your guys, so there's no problem with that. We'll give you an expense account and, of course, a clothing allowance. You're not going to wear your uniform on the job unless it's very helpful, like now. So, we'll dress you. Don't get excited. It won't be a lot of money. Probably get two suits and some sports jackets and shirts out of it, and ties, of course."

Morgan seemed stunned.

"Thank you, Mr. Finn," he said. "I'm honored you would ask."

113

Valery watched him closely. There was no sign of dishonesty in his reaction, nothing but acceptance. When he smiled, his whole face seemed to light up. She had not seen that when he was in uniform. She could see both kindness and toughness in him. A rare combination. He would be an asset, she concluded.

"An asset on our team."

She had never thought of what she was doing as part of a team. But Finn and Anders were very good company, smart and experienced, and this trooper could be a big asset in investigations, and that was what she was interested in now.

"So, a team has been formed," she thought.

"Let's see how it can work."

They had a great dinner of river perch with peaches and scalloped potatoes, a specialty at the Inn, and apple cobbler with ice cream for dessert. Anders was beginning to like life on the road. Good beer, good food, and, he thought, glancing at Valery, good company.

"Happy you all enjoyed your dinners," Finn said as they gathered around again when the table had been cleared. "But remember, we are here because more than 100 people were blasted or burned to death just yesterday morning, and we need to find what we can recommend that will prevent that from happening again.

"Tomorrow, we will have a chance to put the nail in one coffin, the one that shows those records in the office were fabrications. But we need to coordinate our plan. Valery, I want to you to plan to ask questions of the secretaries they present. Don't be meek about this. Be as aggressive as you would be with a man and see where that goes. Remember, we don't know, but we think that they have fabricated all of the fire boss reports in their central files. Keep that as your target.

"Anders, I want you to keep an eye on the room. Look for people who seem to need to say something but obviously, can't.

Write down the names. We can come back to them later. Trooper, just be the trooper, and you know what we mean by that!"

"I want us to be out of there by noon. Don't focus on what we didn't get. Focus on what we have.

"Questions?"

"What happens if they admit everything, basically spill the whole can of beans, the fabrications, the decision on the black power shipments, all of it?" Valery asked.

"That will all go into our report to the county prosecutors. They have the authority to follow it from there, and given all these deaths, all the reason to."

"Okay, have some more drinks in the Commonwealth of Pennsylvania, and then go to bed. See you in the morning."

"Trooper, could you please come with me?"

"Sure," he said.

They left the dining room and headed back to the William Penn Hotel for its bar. Standing there nursing a beer was one of the fire bosses who had been in the office earlier. One of the attorneys was with him."

"He left a note for me to see him after dinner in the bar," Finn said. "I want you here as a witness to what is said. "I don't know why the attorney is with him, but we'll find out."

"Hello," he said. "I'm Edward Finn, and this is Trooper Morgan.

"Stanley Branchonski," the man said.

"And I'm Leo Burckwick of Burwick and Candliss," the man in the nice suit said.

"How can I help you, Stanley?" Finn asked. There was no edge in his voice at all. It was soft and welcoming.

115

"Those reports you wanted," he said. "No one ever did them. Not at all. The company told us to ignore them. Even if the results were bad and the place should have been shut."

"Just a minute, Stanley," Finn said.

Turning to the attorney, he asked, "Whom do you represent."

"United Mine Workers Local 325," the attorney said. "You are not here representing the mining company, correct," Finn asked.

"Not in my lifetime," the lawyer said.

"Why were you at the office this morning?

"Representing the union."

'Fine, let's proceed.'

"Stanley, you said no one ever filled out fire boss reports?"

"Yes, sir," he said.

"We were told that would be taken care of in the office and that it was not our problem. So we just ignored them."

'What about your readings? Gas and air reading, ventilation readings?"

"Nope. We were told not to worry, that the office would take care of all of it," Stanley said.

"My oh my," Finn said. "This is pretty bad news."

"Yes, it is," the lawyer said. "But not bad news for Stanley, I hope. He was doing what he was told to do."

"I understand that," Finn said.

"We, meaning the UMWA, are prepared to help you with another matter should this item be resolved in Stanley's favor," he said.

116

Finn didn't want to barter away any important part of his case unless it was a worthy trade.

"What do you have?" he asked the attorney.

"Why they were hauling black powder on the man trip. Who ordered that? No maintenance on the high power line that set off the explosion. Which secretaries fabricated reports. I have it all written down here in an affidavit that I will give to you. Just give us a pass on Stanley and the other fire bosses."

"How many other fire bosses?" Finn asked.

"Six."

"Done," Finn said.

The attorney handed him the statement, and Finn looked at it. Signed and notarized, it itemized what he had promised and gave Finn the ammunition he needed to accuse the company of forging the documents and lying about conditions in the mine. The name of the man, Supervisor Emil Getner, who ordered black powder on the man's trip, was there, too.

"Thanks," Finn said. He did not finish his drink.

"See you in the morning, Trooper Morgan," he said.

He headed back to his room to prepare for the next morning.

Finn and Valery, and Trooper Morgan headed back to the company headquarters at 9 a.m. the next morning to finish the questioning. Anders stayed behind in the hotel lobby, waiting for a call from Finn that he planned to make at about 10:30 a.m. Stanley Branchonski was with him. They drank coffee and talked. He did not take notes. He did not ask questions about the explosion. He was

117

kind and supportive because he knew Stanley took a great risk in talking to Finn.

Anders knew Stanley would be a key witness if the county prosecutor in the deaths proceeded. He was basically with him to protect him. People have been slain for less serious disclosures, and coal mining was a particularly raw business when it came to revealing company secrets. Finn had the sworn statement in his pocket about the company's role in the failure to keep records and about who decided to put the black powder on the man's trip.

The questions were very simple and began with the three fire bosses who showed up.

"Did you ever record gas readings and mine conditions at your station?"

He asked the same question of each of the three fire bosses. They all said they had not, that they were told not to. Then they questioned the secretaries who were responsible for the logs. Valery was aggressive but well within bounds.

Laura Vickers was the secretary whose name was signed most frequently in the logs.

"Miss Vickers, I see your name on page 130 of the July/August ledger, and I see you reporting the oxygen level in the air was at about 80 percent. Where did you get that number? She asked.

"I don't know," the woman replied.

"Did you just make it up or what? Didn't you have the fire boss reports?"

"No, I didn't," the woman answered. "There were no fire boss reports."

"So you wrote in the report that the oxygen level in the air was fine, correct?

"Yes," she said.

"How did you know? How did you know it was safe?"

"They told me it was safe," she said.

"They told me all the numbers and said they were safe, so I put them in the books."

"Did you do this every day?" Valery asked.

"No, no. Of course not. We would wait for a week or so and then put them all in at the same time, so they would look uniform."

"And who told you they needed to look uniform," Valery asked.

"Mr. Getner, the supervisor," she said.

"Thank you. Thank you very much," Valery said.

Then it was time to ask the question they already knew the answer to:

"Where is Mr. Getner?"

The company attorneys conferred, and one of them stepped forward.

"We believe he is dead," he said. "We are not yet certain, but we believe he was on the second car of the trip as it entered the mine just before the explosion."

"We have been informed in a sworn affidavit that Mr. Getner was the man who decided to load the black powder onto the mantrip. Is that correct?" Finn asked.

"We believe it is," one of the attorneys answered.

"And he was the shift supervisor?" Finn asked.

"Yes."

"Thank you," Finn said. "This concludes the Commonwealth's questioning of company officials in this case.

"We will be writing a summary report that will charge Delaware and Hudson with violations of state mining codes in that it allowed the use of a single trip for men and explosives, that it failed to complete the daily fire boss station logs, that it fabricated the results of those logs for its summaries. This report will be forwarded to the County Prosecutor's office with a recommendation that criminal charges will be pursued in connection with these violations. The Commonwealth, of course, will make its dedicated witnesses available to the prosecutor to pursue this case. There are confidential informants who will not be called. This part of our investigation is over. We plan to recommend an array of fines for the violations we found."

The company officials had just one question in response:

"When can the mine reopen?"

Finn, Anders, and Valery exchanged glances. It was true.

It was all about the money.

Finn read the funeral notices on the bulletin board at the headquarters. Because most of the victims of the explosion were buried in a mass grave outside of town, there would be no formal funeral. But there was a memorial service planned for the next day. Finn suggested the team spend its last night in the hotel and then head to the service first thing in the morning to see whether anyone could cast more light on what happened and why.

Anders was eager to ask questions about what was happening just before the miners climbed aboard the trip for the ride down. He thought someone might have an idea for why the shift boss, now apparently dead, had loaded so much high explosives on a trip full of miners. Finn had his own plan. He wanted to talk to family members to hear what the men had been saying about the mine before the accident. Sometimes there could be revelations in those conversations that explained the conditions around an incident. He also wanted to know who lied. "Everybody," of course, was the answer, but he needed more specifics. If the county was going to follow up on this explosion, then it would need names for its own investigators to question. Finn knew he could save some time by identifying a handful of people with knowledge who could be interviewed. No better place to find them than at a memorial service. But just as the investigation had to follow a strategy, so would this part of the effort. Finn suggested another dinner at the riverside in down the street from the William Penn. They all agreed. They would meet there at 7 p.m. in the upper room.

There was beer on the table already when Finn arrived. Anders and Valery were sitting beside one another with a file between them. Trooper Morgan was sitting across from them. Anders nodded when Finn walked in, and the Trooper stood up as though an officer had entered the room. "Not necessary, Trooper," Finn said. "We're not military about this. But thanks for the gesture."

Finn ordered a beer, too, and the conversation began. "We've done pretty well with the investigation so far in that we know what happened. But our objective tomorrow morning will be to find out why. I doubt that any of the executives at the mine would tell us, would be able to tell us why it happened. But the miners will know it in their bones, and their survivors will have heard the story. We don't need this for evidence, so hearsay it just fine. We are talking to these people to get to a level of awareness the facts just can't present. Call it the truth; call it what you want. You all know how I feel about these things (Anders, of course, did not).

"We want this report to go straight to the right committees in the House and Senate so they can have a chance at creating a solution in law to what you saw in the devastation in the mine. Obviously, it won't do to make it "more" illegal to put black powder and miners together on the trip. Maybe we want to mandate better training in handling explosives, maybe require less volatility, or more specifics on what you can and can't do.

"But we're going to be talking to people who are deep in their grief of loss, so do be careful. Respect what they say, and don't push. I'm talking to YOU, Valery. Bring your sweetest self tomorrow morning because if we aren't at least kind to them, they will clamp up and tell us nothing, and it will take a lot of work to get them to open up again. Memorial services are perfect for this because they focus people on their losses and the question, "Why?" That's what we have to go for.

"Should we approach them as teams, so one can take notes while the other asks questions," the trooper asked.

"No. That's not the objective. In this kind of thing, we want to be there almost as family members. I don't know what we will find, but it would be something like what you could find if the dead spoke. Respect that, and these people will be happy to help us. You have to think of this as a conversation at a bar after a few drinks and some chat about what had happened. That might open some doors for us."

"Sounds complicated," Valery said.

"It is, but I know we can do this. You're all good people, I know, so let that goodness open doors for you. Don't be solicitous or fawning. Just show them how you feel about their losses and then listen to them."

It was time, again, to eat. Anders was beginning to think much of his life would be constructed around meals, given his experience on Leviathan and now, in the Inspection and Safety section of the Mining Department. He could not have been having a better time, given the realities of what he was looking at on the disaster site.

Based on a recommendation from Valery, Anders got something called "Shepherd's Pie," which had some stout, carrots, potatoes, peas, onions, sautéed lamb, and some other vegetables all served under a crust of baked, mashed potatoes with some light cheese sprinkled on the top. This they split because it came in a dish big enough to take a bath in.

Trooper Morgan got a steak the size of his foot. Finn, too. Mounds of mashed potatoes came on the side.

When the bill came, the waiter wouldn't take any money. "We all know what kind of work you have to do, so have the dinner on us," he said. Finn figured they had eaten about $50 worth of food, so he recommended they all put $5 each on the table as a tip so the waiter's efforts would be recognized. $20 was a very healthy tip for a waiter in Wilkes-Barre.

"Remember," Finn said, in reference to the memorial service, "We're not looking for anything other than the kind of information we can use to understand how people felt about that mine. Was it generally safe? How did the place respond to lesser accidents? And while you are doing this, remember everyone we are talking to lost someone, so treat them with respect, please."

No one said much in the car. They were all just thinking about how to talk to the survivors. It was in an old Catholic church that was constructed when the Catholics had all the money in town and gave it freely to the local pastors.

A priest read a prayer about coal miners, then a widow spoke about her love for her husband. She wept, and so did everyone else. She had nothing written down. She just spoke from her heart, which is why everyone was so touched by what she had to say.

"He went down in the hole six days a week to dig out some money so the boys and I could eat, be clothed, live in a nice house…have what you need in life. He never complained, even when he was injured or felt abused by the people at Delaware and Hudson. He was a good, good man, and he can never be replaced. I loved him with all my heart, and I will miss scrubbing him down after work each day and listening to his stories…and his songs."

When she was done, a young girl with an angel's voice sang "What a fellowship…", very unusual in a Catholic Church but a song everyone knew and related to. Some who knew the words sang along. "Leaning on the everlasting arms…" for some reason, drew a sigh and weeping. There would be coffee and cake after the ceremony in the social hall, the priest said.

Valery and Anders were the first in the social hall. Very quietly, Anders told the woman he was so sorry for her loss and the loss of everyone. She thanked him and shook his hand. Valery was next with a long, warm hug for her.

"Women are so good at this…." Anders thought.

She was starting a conversation with the woman when their attention was drawn by some commotion at the back of the room. "Those bastards killed those…" was what Anders heard. Finn was at the man's side in an instant.

"Calm yourself, friend," Finn said. "Now is the time for respect for the dead."

"What respect did they have for the dead?" the man said. "What respect did they have for the…." Then he started weeping.

"They just blew them up like they were rock," he said, still sobbing. "They knew better than to put that powder on that trip. We all knew better."

He was about 60 years old, tall, and thin. Finn put his arm around him to console him. The man didn't move, just sobbing and wiping his nose on a handkerchief he had pulled from his jacket pocket. He coughed a few times, then straightened himself up and regained his composure.

Finn introduced himself and asked what the man knew about why the powder and the men were going on the same trip. "I don't know," he said. "Somebody was taking it; I know that."

"Taking the powder?" Finn asked.

"Yes," he said. "I think they were selling it before they took it down below."

"Selling it? To who? What for?

"Independents. People running their own operations."

"Those casks should have been sealed; no way a wire could have sparked that explosion unless a lid was loose. That's the only way…."

"When do you think they were selling it," Finn asked.

"In the early morning, just after the kegs had been loaded from the armory to the man trip. Ask the supervisor about that. He was the one doing it. Bastard."

Valery and Anders, and the trooper made their way over to Finn to see what was going on. Finn just glanced at them and said, "This man tells me someone, the supervisor probably, was selling black powder from the kegs before they were taken below. That was supposed to happen at night with no men on the trips. Instead, he was doing sales in the morning, then loading the kegs to take them down to the bottom of the mine.

So, who wants black powder? Finn asked of no one in particular.

Trooper Moran stepped into the conversation.

"Criminals buy it and use it for blowing up safes, blowing up buildings, blowing up anything they need to blow up. It works pretty well for that. But it's very dangerous to move it that way, hauling it in the wrong kind of container. Any kind of spark can set off the black powder, you know. That's why people have to be so careful about it."

Finn asked the man to give him his name. He said it was Kaspar Vaychick, and he was one of the coalface bosses below. He didn't work on the day of the accident and was saved from the explosion, he said, but the whole thing made him wonder more about what the foreman was doing with the powder.

"Who was he selling it to?"

125

"We don't know. We may never know because everyone involved in the process, except the guy buying it, is probably dead."

Anders, in an attempt to console the man, began speaking in Hungarian, and the man's mood shifted. No longer at all shy, he was talking passionately and gesturing. They talked for about 10 minutes before the man said he had nothing more to say, then left the ceremony.

"Mr. Finn, Vaychick said there was a business being run during that shift by the supervisor. He not only sold powder, but he also sold everything from his car, from fresh meat to alcohol, to his workers, all stuff it would have been hard for them to find in the stores. Bread, too. He was like a rolling grocery store with explosives, too!"

Finn pulled out his black notebook and wrote that he needed to question the company people about this man to see what they could tell him about the "business" the supervisor, Mr. Getner, was running.

It would mean spending another day in Wilkes-Barre. Finn decided to send Anders and Valery back to Harrisburg in the state car. He would hitch a ride back with Trooper Morgan in the patrol car. Morgan said that would not be a problem at all. He and Morgan would spend one more night at the William Penn Hotel, then head south first thing in the morning after talking to the executives at Delaware and Hudson Coal.

Chapter 10: Explosions in the Night

Trooper Morgan Finn asked in the car, "would you call Harrisburg or Wilkes-Barre and see if anyone has any reports of unexplained explosions over the past two months or so? I don't know what we're looking for, so just make a general inquiry and see if anyone has literally heard anything."

Morgan made his call at the hotel.

There was nothing unexpected or unusual at headquarters that might explain why black powder was being sold at the mine in the morning. But there was one story, a very strange story to the trooper's mind, from rural Cambria County. People had called reporting hearing explosions in the night. In the morning, troopers were called to what was left of a mining company headquarters a few miles west of Portage. They found an industrial-sized safe sitting in the center of what remained of a mining company headquarters building. It had been destroyed in the explosions, which were, obviously, aimed at cracking the company safe two days before the payroll was to be distributed. Nothing had been turned up yet, but it was clear that black powder loaded into cans had been the source of the explosions.

There were no reports of black powder missing from company stores at the mining company or at any of the many mining companies in the area. Trooper Morgan had a thought he shared with Finn.

"What if they were buying black powder up here to replace the powder they stole down there to try to crack that safe? It's all the same kind of powder, so you could do that and, assuming you didn't blow yourself up in the process, no one would know anything was missing. The two places are, what, 250 miles apart, so people wouldn't think of it. They would have had to have a partner locally to do that, but that is not so unusual. That's why the man trip was carrying high explosives to the bottom of the mine. They needed to take some out early in the morning to ship to the west. That's what I would pursue in this kind of case. It's not really an insider kind of job. Lots of people, especially the shot firers, know how to use black powder."

The trooper called several other state police barracks in the southwestern part of the state to see whether they, too, had had reports of explosions. Two cars were destroyed by blasts that were believed to be connected to a battle between two union locals. One said a storefront was destroyed by a fire that started with a blast, and that one, too, had miner's union connections. The United Mine Workers had been involved in a struggle with another union, The National Miners Union, this one Communist based, for years. Violence was common in these struggles, but not usually with black powder stolen from a mining company. It was easy enough to get a variety of other explosives in the mining country. Lots of pistols, too.

Still, they might be connected, he thought.

He decided to write them all into a report he would give to Finn that night at the hotel. That way, there would at least be some record to pursue. Then he had another thought. What if this was all about the struggles between the National Miners, the leftist miner's union, heavily influenced by the American Communists, and the United Mine Workers?

Back at the William Penn, he sat down to gather his thoughts in a note to Finn.

"Mr. Finn, I'm having some thoughts based on what I found at PSP headquarters and in a call to the western part of the state. There have been three separate incidents involving explosions, two cars, and one storefront. This is happening as the National Miners Union and the United Mine Workers struggle for influence. The NMU is connected to the American Communist Party and gets its funding from them. The UMW is, as it has always been, an independent union made up of mine workers in bituminous and anthracite fields.

128

Given the fact that explosives are common in the mining operation, I checked to see whether there were reports of any missing in the wake of those incidents. There were not. The stores were as they should be, with not an ounce missing. My thought is this, though; what if the radical miners used black powder bought from supervisor Getner at Delaware and Hudson to replace the black powder used in those three explosions? It could take as much as 15 pounds of powder for those blasts, and that's a lot of powder to replace. But if you arranged to buy it and transport it regularly from Wilkes-Barre, it could be done. My thoughts are not yet clear on how this would happen, but I'm still thinking about it. Regards. Sgt. Howard, PSP."

To Finn's way of thinking, it was a very solid piece of deduction from Trooper Howard that made complete sense. It would not have been difficult for outsiders to find out Getner was running a private business from his supervisor's job at Delaware and Hudson. Once you know, he would sell bad meat and moldy bread to his own miners, making the leap to black powder wasn't so difficult. He decided he would put the trooper on the case in the morning after he had a chance to talk to the mining officials about the business their supervisor was running.

It was a bright, dry morning when Finn and the trooper finished their breakfasts and climbed into the state patrol car to head back to the mine headquarters for what Finn hoped would be the last time. He needed to find out more about Getner.

He told the trooper he would be giving him an assignment at the end of the morning that would help him develop his detective skills and help the team move on with the explanation of the cause of the explosion.

The Delaware and Hudson executives, accompanied this time by one of their attorneys, met Finn on the porch of the headquarters and only stepped aside when it was clear Trooper Howard was going to help Finn get entrance.

"It won't take long," Finn said. "Just a couple of last questions."

They went into the conference room and sat on opposite sides of the big table.

"Were you aware that your supervisor, Mr. Getner, was running a business in addition to the job he had here?

"What do you mean?"

"Well, he was selling just about anything the miners wanted at a decent profit and holding the mantrip overnight instead of using it to safely take the black powder to the bottom of the mine at night. We believe he might have been selling black powder as part of that scheme, which was why the tops were off the containers when they came into contact with the overhead power line, which, as you are well aware, caused the explosion.

"Did you know about that?"

There was a pause, then one of them said, "We knew he was selling some items to miners because, as you know, there are no company stores on our property, and they would sometimes need groceries and the like. It was a convenience for them. He didn't make a lot of money at it.

"And as for the powder?

"We have no knowledge of that," the attorney said.

"That would be illegal."

"Exactly," said Finn.

"We had hoped to close the investigation quickly because it seemed such an obvious tragedy, but this is a new development that causes a problem for all of us…We'll get back to you later about this. You know you need a license to sell black powder. In the interim, we need all your black powder inventory sheets for six weeks before the explosion."

"I don't know if…

"Try," Finn said. "It will help all of us."

Then the trooper put on this hat. Finn closed his briefcase, and they walked out to the state police car to head south.

"That might have put the fear of God into them," Finn said to Howard in the car.

"Let's hope."

It was a good day for a fast drive to Harrisburg, and no one stopped a speeding state police car, so off they went.

"Tell me what you are thinking about the black powder," Finn said.

"It's more than just about powder," Trooper Howard answered.

"You know as well as I do that the National Miners and the United Mine Workers have been battling for years to win control of a majority of the people who work in the hard coal region. You also know how rough those kinds of contests can be. I'm thinking that black powder was being used to substitute for the powder used to blow up those cars and that store. It would take, what, three pounds to do that? That's a lot of black powder if you have it in a container under your seat, but not so much black powder if you are looking at a company storeroom that has, maybe, 50 barrels of black powder in it. Unless they weigh the barrels every week or even monthly, it would not be missed, and I don't think anyone weighs black powder that closely. So it's the perfect opportunity for someone like Getner to unload a couple of hundred dollars worth of black powder in a month, and who is going to notice?

As a Supervisor of miners, he was paid, what, $250 a month, maximum. And he would be the guy responsible for weighing the powder. So we need to do a couple of things, 1. Check for connections between Getner and Western Pennsylvania; I'm thinking brothers or cousins, and 2. Check his finances to see whether he was getting lumps of money from someone to sell that powder, bigger lumps than he could get selling cheese and milk and stale bread to the miners.

131

"Well, why don't you just do that," Finn said.

"Take this part of the investigation over and do whatever you need to do to get the answers. I'm sure you will do a good job, and I do trust you, having watched you at work and talked to your superiors. What do you think about that?"

"So, it would be my own case to pursue?"

"Sure would. So, go get it."

Trooper Howard was impressed with Finn's decisiveness. It was a good chance for him. Besides, Finn had treated him very well and made him part of a tested team. He wanted to return that trust and was determined to be diligent in his pursuit. His mind was already cranking on how to connect Getner to Western Pennsylvania.

First, he would have to get the uncooperative people at Delaware and Hudson to give him Getner's personnel file so he could see where he came from. Then...

Howard looked up, and there was a huge buck on the road about 30 yards from his patrol car. He turned the wheel hard to the left, slammed on the brakes, and put his arm in front of Finn, all at the same time. They just missed the back side of the deer, stayed on the road, and regained control in an instant.

"Well, that's not going to do me much good in your eyes, killing us both on the body of a deer because I wasn't paying attention. Imagine that, "Trooper and state official killed by deer. That would be the headline."

"I'm willing to forgive that one. Damn, your reactions are like lightning Trooper Howard. Have you always been that quick?"

"Pretty much," he said.

Trooper Howard suggested returning to Wilkes-Barre to talk to the mining company people about Getner. Finn decided not to because, as he put it, "We've seen enough of each other these past few days. I don't want them to know us well enough to feel it's okay to lie. We'll talk about it in Harrisburg."

The trooper straightened his hat and decided to pay attention only to the road until they got back to Harrisburg.

Anders and Valery left the memorial service as soon as it had finished and started back to Harrisburg in Finn's car. It would take three hours to get back to Commerce, and it was already 11 a.m., so they would have to find a place for lunch.

"Are you okay, Anders," she asked after they had driven in silence for about half an hour. "Yes," Anders said. "I'm just thinking about how this might have all happened, the selling of the powder and everything else."

"Well," she said, "Things don't always work out the way we think they should. There's a lot we don't know about Mr. Getner and what he was up to. There's a lot we don't know about Delaware and Hudson Coal. A lot we don't know about…about everything."

"Investigations are always like peeling onions. You keep on going down through the layers, and sometimes you only get tears, and sometimes you get answers. But you have to peel down to find them…You have to ask the right questions."

Anders was silent for a few seconds, then said, "When my father was killed, no one asked any questions at all that I could determine. It was clear the last shift left those shot holes primed and ready for firing, but no one told anyone about that. I have thought about it a lot, and I always wondered whether someone did that on purpose…But I never found out."

"If I might ask, what was going on at the mine at that time," Valery said.

"A lot of times, you have to stand way back from an incident to see what was swirling around it before it happened. Was there turmoil in the mine, any kind of turmoil?

"Do you know anything about the explosion? Was it fired, or did it just blow? That can happen with a lot of different kinds of explosives; they just get agitated, and then a spark comes from someplace and sets it all off...."

"I understand that," Anders said.

"But the problem here was no one even wanted to look. No one was questioning anything at that point. Europe was just getting over war, and people were happy to be doing anything that didn't involve killing their neighbors over territory...."

With that, the conversation settled into a stone silence.

Valery didn't want to let it end with that.

"Sometimes, Anders, we just have to hold on to the memories we have of happier times and let go of what time has stolen from us. I know it's hard to do that, but even here, we sometimes find questions we simply can't answer."

They kept on driving in silence after that until they saw a sign for a turnoff to Lewisburg, a place on the Susquehanna where she suspected they could find an acceptable meal. They drove into the downtown part of the borough and found something called "Darr's Stopover."

A man in an apron came to their table and asked them what they wanted. "Well, a menu would be a good start," Valery said.

"No menu," the man said. "We have soup, sandwich, meat pie, bratwurst, and sauerkraut. What can I get you?"

"What soup," Anders asked.

"Oxtail with onions and dumplings. If you have never been here before, it's the local favorite."

"Soup for me," Valery said.

"Me, too," Anders chimed in.

Want drinks? He asked. Anders asked for any German beer they had. Valery, who was driving, said she would just have a soda.

Before they knew it, the man was back with a plate full of thick slices of homemade bread with butter in a crock for spreading and a relish made of pickles and onions.

"Try this," he said. "Also, a local favorite."

It was sweet and perfect for spreading on the buttered bread. They both covered the thick slices of white bread with the butter and relish and began eating.

"My God," Valery said, "This stuff is wonderful, and the bread is perfect!"

Anders, still continuing his search for acceptable bread, agreed.

"I guess I could come *here* to live," he said.

Valery laughed and said that would be fine until he got tired of the bread, "Which would happen, you know because men are never happy with anything for long. Then where would you be? Stuck up the river without a paddle, that's where!"

"Another saying to remember, Anders thought. "Up the river without a paddle!

His collection of idiomatic expressions was growing, although he didn't have the confidence to use them yet.

"So," Valery said, "What do you think of what we have found so far about this explosion?"

"It's not adding up for me," Anders said.

"It is presented as though it were an accident, but there are already too many questions for that to be the case. I'm not saying someone did this deliberately, but we need more answers before we can write a report about what happened and why."

Do you think it has something to do with the business the supervisor was running?

"Yes, but I don't know what?"

The oxtail soup arrived. It was a tomato broth with potatoes, sautéed onions, and rich pieces of deep burgundy-colored oxtail floating in a thin gravy, perfect for dipping such good bread. Anders and Valery could both see why it was a favored meal in Lewisburg.

They ate and then walked out on the porch of the restaurant to sit in the rocking chairs and talk more about the disaster. Valery had a cigarette and offered one to Anders, but he turned it down.

"Not a habit I need to pick up," he said.

"I can take it or leave it," she said.

"Just now, I'm taking it!"

He had already noticed that smoking was not a constant thing for her, and neither was drinking

"She makes her choices," he thought. "Her own choices."

While she sat in the sun on the porch, Anders shifted his thoughts back to the business Getner was running from his supervisor's job. The food he understood.

Miners worked long hours and rarely had time to break off to shop for anything. Some companies had their own stores, but these were not popular with union members and were generally a source of contention because of prices and the quality of the food they sold. Getner could step around those problems by buying better groceries and selling them at just a little profit. Anders realized he had to allow room in his formula for nothing being wrong in Getner's business.

Maybe it was just a business.

But there was no way the sale of the black powder could have been innocent. You needed a license for that and had to keep specific, itemized records of sales. Black powder was only good for a couple of narrow purposes, and if you were not running a mine, the most important one was off the table.

Why would you need to do that?

He had fixed his focus on a woodpecker in a copse of sugar maples across the street to think about this. Valery was finished and ready to go.

"Anders…Anders…Time to go," she said.

"Of course," Anders replied, putting his thoughts aside for later.

They got back into Finn's Ford, and Valery headed down the highway, which followed the Susquehanna, back to Harrisburg.

Fishermen in their flatboats were working the rock flats that spread like pancakes across parts of the river. They would float and cast down to the end of the rocks to deeper water. She could not see the bait they were using, but she suspected it would be earthworms or if they were bold enough to get them, hellgrammites. She saw one man pull a chain up from the back of his boat that was full of green-brown fish, the smallmouth bass, she suspected. They would bite on anything at this point in the season. She thought of her father and their occasional fishing trips to the river.

"We used to catch those by the dozens," she told Anders, gesturing toward the fishermen. "Smallmouth bass, great for frying for lunch. They were very clean fish and, at this time of the year, hungry for whatever you fed to them.

"Was that the only fish in the river?" he said.

"Oh, no," she replied.

"Perch, Pike, muskies, even some trout if you fished by one of the limestone streams that fed into the river. I loved those afternoons. My father would tell me coal mining stories and talk about my mother, on and on, for hours as long as the fish were biting."

"So, you and your father were very close?"

"Like peas in a pod," she said. (Anders found himself making yet another mental note, 'peas in a pod!')

"So, when it was time to eat the fish, we cleaned them very well, scraping away all the scales and cutting off the fins and the skin, then battered them in flour and water and salt and pepper and fried them in lard. Some freshwater fish taste, how should I put it, fishy? That's the oil in the skin, which is why you skin them. But not these. It was all in how you prepared them. You could do the same thing with the perch and, of course, the trout."

"Maybe we can fish up here someday with Finn, and you can show me," Anders said.

"Sure."

They drove for another 30 minutes without a word. Anders was thinking hard about Getner and his business. "I think I need to find Mrs. Getner and talk to her about her husband's business," Anders said.

"Careful. She's a new widow, and her feelings are likely to be right on the surface. Maybe I should go with you. I'm not the most gentle person I know, of course, but I can act that way if I have to, and I am very good at acting."

"That's a good idea. When we get back to Harrisburg, let me look her up."

"Fine," she said.

When they pulled into the Commerce Department Parking lot, the State Police car was already in Finn's parking space. Anders felt the hood. It was warm, so they had not been there long. Valery admired that, feeling the hood to check on how long the car had been sitting.

"Where did you learn that?" she asked Anders.

"On strike in Vulcan.

"Were you a troublemaker in Vulcan?" she asked.

"Yes, I was. Yes, we all were. You would have been too if you saw the conditions we were working in. We lost, what, two men a month in explosions and roof falls, and there were only 40 to 50 of us in the pit at one time, so the chances were strong you would know who was killed."

"No one does anything with lignite here," Valery said.

"There's a lot of it down in the southwest and along the Mexican border," she said. "There have been talks for years of turning it into briquettes after the other coals are depleted, but no one wants to get into that now.

Anders was astounded that a woman could talk so clearly about such a narrow aspect of coal mining, but then he realized she was the deputy director of the department and had strong degrees in geology and mining, so why not?

They walked to their offices after stopping for coffee. Barry and Emma said hello, but not much more. They were so busy. Finn was sitting in his office with his door open, so they both said hello.

"Trooper Howard is just three doors down on the west side," Finn said. "Drop in to let him know you know where he is, and tell him where you are, too. If this gets any more complicated, I'm going to have to draft a seating chart."

"I want us to meet after lunch to discuss what we have and where we are going with all of this. Trooper Howard is reaching out to find out whether Getner had a contact in western Pennsylvania.

"Anders wants to talk to his widow, so maybe Howard wants to be a part of that, too," Valery said. "I volunteered myself to add a "woman's touch" on this one. At that, Finn laughed, knowing full well Valery would just as soon whack someone with a stick as play the meek woman on an investigation.

But he knew she could play "meek" very well because he had seen her do it many times.

"Okay, let's meet in here at 1:30 p.m. and look for a future," Finn said.

"Tell the others."

There was an unusual energy in the room when the meeting began, a sense that everyone had something to add to the case.

Finn brought everyone up to speed. He told them he had assigned Trooper Howard to the western Pennsylvania connection to see if Getner, the supervisor in Wilkes-Barre, had contact out there and to locate them and find out what was happening. Anders would be working on questioning Getner's widow in Avoca, along with Valery. Finn would be drafting, essentially, an indictment of the company for its laxity in handling powder and work conditions to deliver to the county prosecutors and the mining company. Anders asked why he would give a copy of that report to Delaware and Hudson Mining Co.

"We're not trying to surprise them," Finn said.

"We want them to know everything we are doing because that's the kind of investigation this one is." Anders sat quietly and listened and said, "Thank you," when Finn gave his explanation.

Trooper Howard found a family in Western Pennsylvania with a clear connection to Getner, and he wanted to continue pursuing that. Anders found Getner's widow Lucille in a town near Wilkes-Barre called Avoca and was ready to reach out to make contact.

She was said to have a problem with alcohol.

Finn asked the Trooper to summarize what he knew about the political context of the disaster.

Howard was fairly shy about this but began rolling about 10 minutes in and did not stop for an hour. No one was bored by anything he had to say. It was like listening to a political science fairy tale.

"There has been hatred between the United Mine Workers and the National Miners Union forever, all of it based on the struggle to collect membership. The UMW has been winning this battle for years," he said.

They are backed by the International Lady Garment Workers Union in New York, a relationship they built between the ILGWU and the UMWA after the Triangle Shirtwaist Factory fire. The National Miners are connected to the American Communist Party and get their money from Moscow via the New York chapter.

"It has been a pretty bitter struggle over the years. You all know how tough it has been in the coalfields in Western Pennsylvania and how both sides have been pushing membership drives, particularly in Westmoreland and Cambria Counties, where there are a lot of coal company headquarters. They really hate each other. The police chief in Portage, Tom Madden, tossed the Communists into the street when they tried to interrupt the district UMWA session at a big theater in Portage. We had to go in to break up the fight that ensued. It took 20 troopers from Pittsburgh to do that. The troopers who were there were surprised no one was killed.

"We suspect there are lingering animosities there.

He summarized a few other coal field fist and stick fights between the two unions and then noted that the National Miners were not shy about using explosives. He told the story of the safe found in the destroyed mine headquarters outside of Portage and then noted cautiously, "We haven't yet established whether this was an actual attempt at a robbery or something more vile, a setup of the UMW people by the National Miners that somehow went wrong.

"It didn't stop there, either. A couple of the mining companies went out and brought in Pinkerton agents to subvert the union organizing on both sides, pitting the Reds against the UMW people. A couple of people got shot, including one of the Pinkertons. But no one died.

So, long and short, there are lots of reasons to buy black powder from Wilkes-Barre if you are stealing supplies in Western

Pennsylvania and need to refill those barrels before someone notices."

The trooper sat down, and it was all the others could do to keep from applauding he had done such a complete job.

Valery had a sheaf of documents from the company noting inventories of black powder in storage. There was no record of whether it was weighed regularly, but the company claimed there was nothing missing from its records. Finn could not resist the moment, "Like they would know!"

Howard was also ready to report on Getner's bank account.

Finn turned the meeting over to Valery at the outset and sat in the back of the room, taking detailed notes on what everyone was saying.

Trooper Howard went first.

"Getner's family has a whole branch that lives near Johnstown and works in Cambria Mines in bituminous coal. She doesn't have any connections to anything but short-order cooking.

Getner had an account at Wilkes Barre Bank & Trust, and it shows $870 in savings at the time of the blast. Most of the deposits were made in person and were for small amounts, with the biggest being $30. If he was making a lot of money selling stuff at the mine, he wasn't putting it there. We need to get a warrant to search his home. His wife is grieving and not very receptive to visits from authorities, and I don't know why yet.

Finn reported he had started to draft the letter to the Delaware and Hudson Coal Co. and said it would be very detailed in the charges it made about conditions in the mine, lax control over black powder, and the failure to keep consistent and accurate records.

Finn said he would call the county to get subpoenas to cover the search of the house.

"Trooper Howard, do you need anything else to pursue the connections out west?"

"No, sir," the Trooper said. "I think I know where I need to go from here."

Finn told Valery and Anders to make plans to go to Avoca and interview the widow and search for the house. He said he would tell the county to have the subpoena ready for them by Thursday.

"That's tomorrow," Valery said.

"Anders and I have to make some plans."

"Go do that," Finn said.

"The rest of you, thanks for your work."

Then he went off to try to pry the trooper from the state police. He would work through Dick Dorrance, who he knew well in the governor's office.

Dorrance had known Finn since the days he was still mining and had thought of him from the very first as a dependable friend. He was not in a position yet to help him when Finn was looking for his state job, but he knew some legislators he could ask, and they intervened on Finn's behalf. That was generally how things worked in Pennsylvania. You had to know someone, or someone had to know you.

Finn called Dorrance's office to set up a time to talk, and Dorrance said he would make time for Finn whenever he needed to see him. "I'm on my way right up," Finn said.

Dorrance's office was just off the reception room near the governor's office, a big open room with tall windows and paintings of historical events anywhere there was space. Finn announced himself to Dorrance's secretary, and she said, "He's waiting," and showed him inside. Dick Dorrance had an office made for meetings, and he used it as expertly as anyone ever had. As the governor's legislative secretary, he was the pathway for key patronage jobs and serious legislative proposals. Still, he was an engaging man with a friendly demeanor and a sense that he would do what he could to help. This he applied for everyone who came to see him, from Philadelphia criminals looking for gubernatorial pardons to nuns looking for help with institutions they ran.

"Finn," Dorrance said, "How's the world of mining treating you?"

It was the same question every time, and try though he might, Finn could never come up with a suitable smart-assy response. So he always said the same thing.

"Getting along!"

"What can I do for you?"

Finn explained the situation, how they had asked the state police substation in Wilkes-Barre for some help and how Trooper Howard came to be on the team investigating the Delaware and Hudson explosions.

"He's a really good man," Finn said. "The state police were lining him up to be a detective, and I think we could continue that process in the Mining Department. We could use a detective there all the time, and Trooper Howard is smart, aggressive, and famously engaging."

"Has he tried to fuck Valery yet?" Dorrance asked, smiling broadly.

"Now, Dick, you know I don't talk about things like that."

Which was quite true. Finn did not gossip, and Finn did not trade in rumors about shenanigans. He may have had a few of his own, but Dorrance never could find them, despite trying. He kept it all close to him, as close as he could in such a public job.

"How's he going to fit in there with your new Transylvanian…Anders. Right? Has HE tried to fuck Valery yet?"

Finn gave him the same expression and cut off that avenue of conversation by being very direct.

"So, Dick, can you get him for me?"

There was a moment's pause because Dorrance always wanted to play every situation for as much advantage as he could get. "Let me see what I can do. I'll call you about it tomorrow, okay?

"Perfect," Finn said. Then he got up and walked out. He didn't like it when Dorrance tried to inject sex into every discussion that even vaguely involved his deputy. He felt that was improper.

Dorrance always had the same reaction, "Gawwwwd…such a fucking Catholic!"

But he made the call to the State Police because he knew Finn was probably the most valued administrator he had in government, always diligent and always focused and, so far, anyhow, always right.

"Get me, Commander Jackson," he told his secretary. She called the state police and hooked Dorrance up with the chief of the state police.

"Michael," he said. "I need a favor. A personnel favor. You have a young trooper, Howard Morgan, who is on loan to the Department of Mining for a special investigation. Mining wants to give him the detective's title and add him to their staff. I'll give you two future draft picks for this one if you could just let me have him."

"What barracks was he from," the Commander asked.

"Wilkes-Barre," he replied.

"Yes, you can have him. I think we're up three people there, and there is no chance anyone else is going to be promoted or leave. Tell your man to make his plan. We can award the "detective" title at the same time in case he has to return. The salary, $2,500.00

annually, transfers over to Mining, please. Remember, now, you owe me!"

"You're on," Dorrance said.

He asked his secretary to call Finn.

Finn immediately called the State Police Commander and thanked him, then asked for a promotion letter to detective and the badge to go with it. No problem. There was only one coal inspector's badge, and he held that. Then he called Dorrance and told him he owed him, to which Dorrance replied, without a moment's hesitation, "I know that! And you have the cover the salary out of your budget."

All he needed to do now was tell the Trooper and get the paperwork underway. Valery could handle that. He called her.

"Great news for us," he said.

"We've now got our own detective. Trooper Morgan is being promoted to detective and transferred to us. Could we please get the paperwork going to add him to our staff? We don't have any detective positions, so get him in as an inspector with a couple of years of experience to get him $2,500 a year. That will work!

"Yes, Mr. Finn," Valery said.

"And now you owe Mr. Dorrance?" she asked.

"Of course!" he replied.

Chapter 11: The Communists

Trooper Howard was on the phone in his office working on the western Pennsylvania connection. Through the FBI in Pittsburgh, he learned that Getner was a secret member of the Communist Party and working in league with the National Miners Union despite his supervisory position at Delaware and Hudson Coal.

A Party cell in Pittsburgh met every month, and Getner had been there the last three times. The FBI couldn't figure it out. If he was in management, what was he doing working with the Communist Party's Union? Still, they followed him everywhere, intrigued by what the American Communists were up to. J. Edgar Hoover was perpetually interested in the communists and their attempts to overthrow the government. He had no idea what they were up to, but it was a constant in his annual address to the House and Senate Appropriations Committees. Nothing drew federal dollars like an emerging Red Scare!

So far, Getner had done nothing for the party other than to attend those meetings, which included miners and members from four western Pennsylvania counties. The rhetoric was classic "working man's revolt" stuff. Down with corporate parasites and up with workers. Destroy the status quo. Communism brings food to all the world's working peoples, solidarity forever, that kind of thing. Howard was careful with what he knew about Getner and the black powder. He knew the feds had a tendency to fire on warning, and he didn't want to wreck the investigation by having a dozen federal agents drop in on the despondent Lucille Getner and start questioning her about Soviet influences.

He passed all of this on to Anders in the form of a long note. (Howard was partial to long notes). He asked him to share it with Valery before they headed off to Avoca to interview the widow Getner.

Valery called her Wednesday afternoon to tell her they were coming.

"We have the subpoena to search your house," she said. "I hope you don't mind. We will probably be there early."

"Search my house! Why should I mind that? Have I done something wrong? Am I some kind of a criminal? I don't know anything about Mr. Getner's business. Maybe you should ask his girlfriend…."

"We'll see you tomorrow Mrs. Getner," Valery said. She had an early sense that it would not be easy for her to play the gentle cop with Lucille Getner. They would go early, hopefully before Mrs. Getner started to drink for the day.

Valery and Anders left Harrisburg that afternoon in one of the unmarked mining inspection cars. They zipped north to Avoca and headed into Wilkes-Barre to get a room. Anders told the desk clerk he and Valery were state investigators and needed rooms on the same floor.

"Sure," the clerk said with one of those knowing smiles that indicates a man thinks something else is going on. He gave them keys to rooms on the third floor, rooms 3C and 5C, which were connected by a door.

"We can talk about how to approach this at supper," Valery said. "I'm taking a nap. See you at, what, 6:30?

"Sure," he said. "I'll be in the bar."

He had a small steak. They split a bottle of the hotel's best wine, which was ghastly.

"So," Valery said, "How are we going to approach this woman? What do we want to find?"

"Well, as Howard told us, he was putting money someplace, so first, we need to do a thorough search with our warrant. Or maybe we should talk to her first and then do the search. I'm not sure which

148

would be best. Maybe you could make friends with her, and we can go from there. Maybe we should have a drink with her. I just don't know," Anders said.

"We do NOT want a drink with her," Valery said, noting they would be lucky if she wasn't already drinking when they arrived. She told Anders they had to focus on a couple of very clear questions and get answers before they began the search. Did she know he was running a business from his supervisor's job? Did she know anything about black blasting powder and where it might be kept? Did he have firearms? Pistols? Anyplace in the house, he told her to keep away from.

"Do you actually think she is going to answer those kinds of questions," Anders said.

"Never know," Valery said. "Sometimes you just have to ask them, so the person you are talking to knows you know what you want."

That made very good sense to him.

"She also said something about a girlfriend, so maybe we should find out about that...."

They had not settled on an approach before dinner arrived. They ate what was in front of them and finished with pie with ice cream on top and then decided to walk down to look at the Susquehanna. While they were on the path heading north and looking at the span of the big river, he found himself taking her hand. He told himself that was so she would not fall, but that was not why he did it. She squeezed his hand while they looked at the river.

He squeezed back.

"I have always loved this river," she said.

"I have seen it during floods when there was so much water in it the top looked like it was curved. I've seen houses float by, along with loose boats and chicken pens and cars. It's a very powerful thing."

Anders maintained a respectful silence while she talked about the river.

Then she surprised him. "Would you be holding my hand if Finn were with us?"

He let go of her hand and said, "Of course not. You are my boss. It would not be appropriate. She took his hand once again and said, "Anders, it's fine. It doesn't bother me. It wouldn't bother me if Finn were here, either. We both think very highly of you, Anders, so you don't have to be shy with me. At least when we are not at work."

Anders was happy to hear that because he felt drawn to Valery but was so unfamiliar with American courting that he literally did not know what to do. He decided he should probably tell her that.

"Ummmmm...Valery, I don't know how to court American girls," he said.

"The same way you would court girls in Transylvania, but without the neck biting," she joked.

Anders laughed at that and felt comfortable with the informality between them. He just didn't want it to become a point of contention in the office or on the job. They agreed there should be no hand-holding in the Commerce Department, no kisses of greeting, nothing anyone could interpret as romantic.

"But I really do want to be romantic with you, Valery," Anders said.

"Yeah, me too. But we have jobs to do, and they don't involve a lot of hanky-panky in the office.

"Hanky-panky?"

"What," he said, is this "Hanky panky?"

She grabbed him by his tie and pulled him toward her, pushed him back into a bush, and planted a big, wet kiss on his lips.

"That," she said, "is where hanky-panky starts."

"Okay," he said and made a mental note to always remember the feel of her lips and the smell of her breath, and the touch of her skin, but not so much that he had to be close to it whenever they were together at work.

This, he concluded, required a plan. But not now.

"Did you ever swim in this river?" Anders asked. "Oh, sure, she said. "But not up here. It's just too fast with too much current around the rocks. Have you ever gone river swimming, Anders?"

"Can't."

"Can't what?"

"Can't.... Ummm...swim. I can't swim."

"My God," she said. "We have to fix that this summer. We can go to the "Y" and use the pool, and I can teach you."

"Okay," he said, not knowing at all whether that would actually be okay.

They finished their walk and checked out of the hotel, and got into the car to head to Avoca to see Getner's wife. It was 1:30 p.m., and Valery knew where she was going, so she drove. Anders sat with his eyes closed. "Sleeping?"

"Thinking."

Nothing more was said.

Lucille Getner lived in a single-story home at the end of a street lined by houses and maple trees. It was a picture book neighborhood, every house well-tended. Lucille was sitting on the porch, drinking a coffee and waiting.

"Mrs. Getner?" Valery asked.

"Yes."

"Inspector Miller," she said.

Valery pulled out her ID with its official-looking symbol and said, "This is my colleague Anders Apostle, who is also investigating the explosion at Delaware and Hudson. We have a search warrant and some questions.

But before we get into that, please accept our condolences for the loss of your husband. We are sorry for it, and we regret it, along with the other deaths.

Valery showed her the search warrant, which was so vague and open-ended that they could look anywhere for just about anything.

Mrs. Getner did not seem at all like a woman who drank too much. She seemed to be quite ready to talk, too. She had a manila folder on her lap.

"Did your husband travel frequently to Western Pennsylvania?"

"Yes," she said.

"Do you know why?"

"I assume it was the girlfriend. I don't know."

"So where would he go?"

"I think Johnstown, the Johnstown area. As I understood it."

"Did he tell you he had a girlfriend or did you just figure it out yourself," Valery asked.

"I figured it out."

"What did he tell you he was going to Johnstown for?" Valery asked.

"Company business he said, but I don't know what that could have been about. There's no connection between Delaware and Hudson and Cambria Coal."

"Other than the girlfriend, did he have any other friends out west, particularly around Portage in Cambria County?"

"I don't know, but I do have this series of letters to show you from the government. I don't know why he got them or what they might mean.

She had three letters with their envelopes in the file. The return address was the same in each case, "Department of the Treasury, Bureau of Investigations." They were all sent in the same month, January of 1929.

"Mr. Getner," the first letter said, "It has come to our attention that you are associating with agitators from the American Communist Party who have been trying to infiltrate the National Miners Union. Any information you might be able to present on the ACP and its actions in Western Pennsylvania would be deeply appreciated by your government." It was signed "Agent Thomas Johnson."

"Mr. Getner," the second letter said, "It has been brought to the Treasury Department's attention that you have joined an organization called the National Miners Union, which we have reason to believe is affiliated with the American Communist Party. Any information you can provide about either of these organizations would be greatly appreciated. Agent Thomas Johnson.

"Mr. Getner," the third letter said, "An agent will be contacting you for an interview in connection with activities of the American Communist Party and the National Miners Union. Agent Thomas Johnson."

Mrs. Getner stopped there and looked up.

"I have no idea what he was involved in here. I thought his only interest in Western Pennsylvania was this girlfriend. Now I don't even know whether he had a girlfriend or what these questions were all about. He was in Management with Delaware and Hudson and would have had no interest in union membership whatsoever. What is this about? Why are YOU here now?"

153

Valery gathered herself.

"We want to know all about the business he was running from his supervisor's job. We know he was selling things to the miners, and we suspect he was selling black powder to people out west. That's why we are here. That is what we are investigating. We want to search for any powder he might have stored here and any money or firearms he might have hidden. I know this is a difficult time for you, and we don't want to complicate it. But we simply have to find what he was doing with the black powder and who was using it out in Western Pennsylvania."

"I...I don't know about powder or firearms," she said. "I don't know about what he was doing with any cash he got from that business. I just don't know much about him at all. He was very secretive about his work and his interests. That's why I thought it must be another woman, but now I just don't know. Am I in trouble? Am I going to be arrested?"

"No," Valery said.

"We are interested in what your husband was involved in and what role that might have played in the explosion. That is our main focus, what we are really concerned about now.

"Did the Treasury Department ever contact you or your husband?"

"No. No, they did not. But I don't know what I could have told them. My husband ran the business. He was very quiet about it, and now he's gone, so I don't know what to say about it."

"Here is the warrant again. We want to search the property," she said. "You can come with us or not. It's your choice."

Anders said he would start in the garage. There were two large wall cabinets, a workbench with drawers, and a collection of wood bins of various sizes stacked in the corner. He started in the wall cabinets.

Both were made of wood and had big doors that closed together in the center with a hasp latch to hold them shut. He opened the hasp and looked into the first cabinet. The top shelves were filled with old books about coal mining, no surprise there. He removed a few of the books because the shelves were deep with room behind them to store any number of items. He found a Smith & Wesson .357 magnum pistol, much like Trooper Howards, on the shelf pushed to the back. There were no bullets in the gun, and there was no other ammunition in the cabinet. There was a brown envelope that contained $1,400. He removed the gun and the envelope, tagged them and wrote the gun serial number down on a list, and put it in a box labeled "Removed from Getner property/garage."

The second shelf held a collection of dried-out old paint cans, long beyond saving, jars of screws, bolts, and nuts, and washers. Just what one would expect to find in a garage.

The third shelf held three small wood barrels, very well made with wood tops that fit tightly on the top. Anders cautiously removed one of the barrels and put it on top of the workbench. Using a screwdriver, he carefully pried the top off. Inside was about ten pounds of what appeared to be black powder. He took a small sample and put it in a paper bag with a label on the front. Then he put the lid back on the barrel, returned it to the shelf, and wrote "black powder in the wood barrel" on his inventory. There were three other barrels of the same style, all of which were filled to the top with the same black powder as the first barrel. Again, he took samples, carefully labeled them, and returned the lid, and added the cans to his inventory list.

In all, he estimated he had found 30 pounds of black powder in the cans, all ready for removal to someplace else and all protected against accidental explosion. Two of the barrels were sealed with wax around the edges. There was no identification on any of the barrels.

Ten pounds of black powder would be enough to cause quite a few significant explosions, he thought. That could well be enough to explain the explosion and robbery attempt at the mining office near

Portage. Clearly, to his mind, the intent was to use this collection of black powders to replace some that had been taken from mining company inventories. He just didn't know where. The cache of powder became more revealing when Anders checked on the bottom shelf in the cabinet, where he found a box of 100 electrically ignited blasting caps, each with wires in red, white, and black that would tell a shooter what he needed to do to make a safe electrical connection. On blasting job sites, these kinds of charges were often wired to explode in sequence, igniting a line of shot, for example, to open the face of a mountain. But they weren't of much use for anything else.

He was convinced he had solved the mystery of the theft of black powder from the Delaware and Hudson stores when he opened the second cabinet and found it full of the same kind of wood barrels that held the powder in the first cabinet. He went through the same sampling process, labeling each sample clearly and closing the lids tightly again. He did not unseal any barrel that had wax around the rim. That was plainly too dangerous.

He also realized he was looking on at perhaps 300 pounds of black power in a total of 40 smallish containers, about the same amount that exploded on the mantrip at Dayton and Hudson mining. Should it all explode at the same time, it would take out the garage, the house, and half the neighborhood. He could not leave it in the garage.

It would have to be moved.

He went inside to tell Valery, at the same time keeping close to a window so he could keep an eye on the garage.

"There's enough black powder in that garage to blast away half of Avoca," he told Valery.

"We have to find a place to put it where it will be safe. It can't stay in that garage any longer. I think we should call Finn and see what he thinks.

"Yes, that's a good idea," Valery said.

"I don't think Mrs. Getner knows anything about any of this. She's having a panic now about the federal authorities and what they were looking for with the communists and the National Miners Union.

"What do you think we should do with the powder?"

"Well, I have two thoughts, the first of which is that we can't leave here without having it removed from this property. The second is maybe we get Delaware and Hudson Coal and ask them to come and retrieve it and put it in safe storage since it was probably theirs in the first place."

"Let me ask Finn," she said.

She went to use Mrs. Getner's telephone. Still distraught, she had no problem with Valery making a phone call. "I think you should hear what we have to say on this call, so you know what is happening. There is a substantial amount of black blasting powder in your garage, more than enough to kill everyone on this end of town should it explode. That's what I need to call about."

She got Finn at his desk and told him about the powder Anders had found in the garage.

"Jesus Christ in a cracker!" Finn said.

"Stay out of there and tell Anders to stay out of there. Give me a minute to think."

She told him what Anders had suggested, getting the coal company to come in and pick it up and safely remove it. "That sounds like a good idea. I will call them, and then I will call you back at the Getner house. Give me the number. No one goes back into that garage! She gave him the number and then put the phone back on its rest.

"Mrs. Getner, I think we should take a trip downtown for a while until we can make sure this place is safe for everyone, okay? Do you have a favorite restaurant or hotel?

"Geeeeeezzzzz!" she said. "Geeeeeezze!"

The William Penn in Wilkes-Barre is the best hotel, and it has a good restaurant, she said.

"Okay," Valery said. "We know the place. We will go to William Penn in my car. Anders will stay here to guard the powder. Get some clothing, enough for two days, please, and then we can leave. We don't want to be here any longer than we have to."

Mrs. Getner filled a small suitcase with what she would need for two days, then left the key to the house with Anders. Valery was very surprised she was so cooperative, which made her suspicious. Either she was covering for her husband or really didn't know what was going on and was scared nearly witless by the process.

Just then, Finn called.

He said a team from Delaware and Hudson would be arriving in about an hour to take that powder out of there.

Valery asked Anders to join him in the kitchen and told him the plan. He was to guard the powder but not to go into the garage under any condition until the mining team arrived to remove the explosives. All that made sense to him.

She gave him a handshake and a hug before she and Mrs. Getner headed downtown.

"See you a little later," she said. "Get a receipt for the explosives. Be careful."

"Yes."

He watched her leave, her red hair blowing in the wind as she got into the car.

Valery and Mrs. Getner checked into the William Penn about an hour later. They took three rooms, one for each of them and one for Anders, then went downstairs for lunch. Mrs. Getner started with a Manhattan, then had two more before the food arrived and another after lunch. By 2:30, she was intoxicated, slurring her words and talking a little too loud for the room.

"Maybe we should have some coffee," Valery suggested.

"No, I'm comfortable just drinking these. I'm always comfortable drinking these.

"Why don't you have one?" she suggested.

"Well, I'm working," Valery said. "And they are too sweet for me. I generally drink gin or whiskey on the rocks. I get headaches from sweet drinks."

"Tell me about what you know about your husband's work," Valery said.

"Well, he left early in the morning and came home much later in the day and never had anything to say about it. He didn't like the Delaware and Hudson Company because he said they were cheap and never paid their managers enough for the work they expected them to do."

"Why was he riding on the mantrip with the miners when he was a supervisor? What was the point of that?"

"I don't know. I do know he would always head to work with the back of the car filled with groceries and a lot of other stuff to sell to them. He was like a company store without an actual storefront. I think he would walk down the mantrip in the morning and deliver the stuff, then ride down into the mine with them and collect his money after that, then come up on the trip once the powder had been unloaded down at the bottom. It took a couple of hours at the most in the morning. Everyone was happy with it.

"Did he ever say anything about the powder being taken down in the mine in the morning? I thought the plan was always for that to happen at night because the mine would basically be empty. Much safer, you know?"

"I don't think those people thought about safety at all. Or any other rules, for that matter. They put kids to work, spragging, opening and closing ventilation doors, all kinds of things that were usually done by older men. Then they put them outside to pick rock from the coal so it could be loaded clean. Their fingers would be so torn up that they would bleed through their gloves in the winter. That is all illegal. No one is supposed to be hiring kids to work underground at all. But they treated them as badly as they treated the adults."

"Did your husband ever try to intervene in that kind of thing? (Valery knew she was fishing, but it seemed like a good chance to expand the conversation.) Wasn't he bothered by any of it?"

"Look, Mr. Getner was there to make as much money as he could; however he could, just like everyone else in that mine. The salary was terrible, but his extra stuff made a good deal of money for us. The company knew it and looked the other way. It kept him coming to work and kept the men in supplies so they didn't leave early to shop.

"How much money do you think he made on his extra business?

"Well, it would more than cover the costs of what he had bought to take in in the morning, so I would guess he would get, say, $20 a day in profits. He wasn't piggy about it, but he knew how to make money and what the miners wanted. He would not sell them alcohol before they went into the mine, but he had no problem selling that when they came out at the end of the day.

"So he would make, like, $600 a month extra just selling food and alcohol to the miners? That's a lot of money."

The drinks had settled on Mrs. Getner, and she was becoming freer with her comments.

"Do you have a cigarette?" she asked. Valery gave her a Lucky and lit a match for her. She saw Mrs. Getner was starting to get very

shaky and boozy in that "I-could- fall- out- of- my-chair" way that hits people who drank a lot in the afternoon.

"Well, then there's... the powder money."

"The powder money?"

"Oh, yes, we made a lot of powder money. A whole lot of powder money. I would guess maybe $600 a month extra just on the sale of those little kegs. Very profitable business. He would fill them in the morning from the mining company stores, hide them in his car and bring them home and stack them on the shelves out there."

"Didn't you think that was dangerous," Valery asked.

"Of course. It was dangerous, but what the hell, he...we wanted the money, and he damn well found a way to get it. It's not like we were contracting to blow things up. He was just selling something he assumed the mining company would not miss. It was perfect because he was responsible for weighing in the powder and keeping the records. A couple of pounds a day wouldn't be missed because the company had tons of it. He was always very careful with it. An accident could kill us and bring an end to it for everyone. We didn't want that."

"Understood, but who was 'everyone'?"

"Well...I'm not...Nope. I'm not going to talk about that because then things become pretty dangerous for all of us. You included."

"I'm used to it," Valery said.

"Who was 'everyone'?"

"Yes," she said, ordering another Manhattan.

"He sold surplus black powder to people who needed it for other things. I don't know what they were using it for, but they wanted a lot of it. Those wooden barrels in the garage, they were all for sale. He would put them in his car when he headed west and deliver them to someone in Johnstown. I don't know who.

161

"You sure?" Valery asked.

"I don't know who. And I need to go lay down."

Okay, let me help you to your room. You can nap. When Anders gets here, we can make a supper plan.

"And have drinks, too?"

"We'll talk later."

Valery was as gentle as she could be with the now-intoxicated Mrs. Getner. She was also convinced Mrs. Getner's earlier claim of knowing nothing about anything was not true. The deeper she dove into the Manhattans, the more she had to say about her husband's "business," much of which involved stealing explosives from his employer and selling them to who knows who and for what in Western Pennsylvania.

She was certain Mrs. Getner was sound asleep when she began rifling the contents of her purse. She was not surprised to find a substantial amount of cash. She was surprised to find a .32 caliber revolver. There was an address book, too. She looked under "P" for Pittsburgh and found one number, then "J" for Johnstown, and found many more, including one for the National Miners Union office just outside of Ebensburg. She wrote that one down. Then she thought for a moment about stealing the entire address book but realized that could backfire later if a criminal case flowed from their investigation. She could take it under the terms of the search warrant, but then Mrs. Getner would know it was gone. It might be better for her to have Mrs. Getner, not knowing she found it.

Mrs. Getner was out, for the time being, so Valery went back to her room to call Finn to report.

"She's shit-faced, loose-lipped, whatever you want to call it. She's also up to her eyes in this stuff, whatever this stuff turns out to be. Her husband was making regular trips to Western Pennsylvania with dozens of little barrels of black powder in the back of his car. He was always very careful. He was responsible for keeping track of the inventory, which made him the perfect thief. I think we have found an explanation for what happened here, although it doesn't explain the accident itself. His business was to take what he could from the miners in Wilkes-Barre and sell as much powder as he could steal to the Reds in Western Pennsylvania so they could resupply what they had stolen to cause mayhem across the region.

Trooper Howard, it seemed, had it absolutely right.

Finn asked after Anders and the garage full of black powder. "I haven't heard any explosion, so I assume it's working out," she said, trying to defuse the tension with a little humor.

That swept past Finn like a cold wind.

"I just don't want any of you to get hurt," he said. "Oh," Valery said, just about to announce that the woman had armed herself when she thought better of it. Finn already had enough to worry about. "Nothing…never mind."

"I don't want anyone to get away with anything. So far, Delaware and Hudson have been able to blame everything on a bunch of miners who were blasted or burned to death. But this takes us out of the mine and into a living world of criminals. We have to continue our pursuit, but we have to be very careful about it."

"Agreed," Valery said. "And so noted."

She said she had to check and see if Mrs. Getner was out of bed yet.

"Probably have to hold her hair over the toilet. My guess is this isn't going to sit well with her. It would certainly not sit well with me if I had that much to drink in such a short time."

She hung up the phone, perked herself up a bit in the bathroom, and headed to Mrs. Getner's room. She ate two breath mints so she would not smell sour and prepared herself for what would likely be a very sour-smelling Mrs. Getner.

But when she knocked, Mrs. Getner, revived by her nap, answered the door and then went back to brushing her hair in front of the big oval dressing mirror on the dresser.

"Are you okay," Valery asked.

"Never better," she said. "The nap was good for me."

"I'm happy to hear that. I was worried you would be...ummmmm...

"Vomiting? Never going to happen, Ms. Miller. I know how to drink, and I know how to hold my liquor. I always stop one drink short of my absolute limit. That way, I have a good time, and nobody, particularly me, gets hurt. I burned up a lot of good nights learning that one...

It was the first time Valery allowed herself to think of Mrs. Getner as good-looking, but she was. Broad shoulders led to a narrow waist and lovely legs, not at all skinny or muscular. Her skin was clear, and her hair perfectly framed her face, which was well sculpted with a sharp jawline, but a soft chin. Clearly, she had taken care of her look. She put her face on with Anders watching, glossed her lips and turned toward the door, and said, "Okay, let's go downstairs."

She was, of course, thirsty.

In the elevator, Anders reported that the transfer of the powder was without incident. He gave Valery the receipt for the 30 10-pound casks.

"Thanks, Anders," Valery said. I'm sorry I left you alone with all that powder. But it worked out just fine. Finn will be happy to hear that.

"And who is this Finn?" said Mrs. Getner.

"Head of mining," Valery said. "Our boss and an expert in what can go wrong in a coal mine."

"Does he do marriages, too?" Mrs. Getner asked, with a little chuckle at the end.

They laughed, not quite comfortably, at that line.

Her husband was dead, and as yet, she had shown no sadness, no remorse.

"So your husband of how many years is dead, and you don't even show the smallest sign of sadness.

"Why not?"

Chapter 12: Emil

"It wasn't much of a marriage," Lucille said.

"He was always at work or away, and I was always at home and alone. That is how it has gone for these past ten years or so. I'm sad he was blown up, but I'm not that sad he was blown up. He wasn't much of a husband. At least he was a good provider."

"So, did he have a girlfriend in Johnstown?" Valery asked. "You mentioned that earlier… then you seemed to change your mind about it. He can't hear you anymore, so say what you have to. Explain this to us."

"Well…"

She ordered another Manhattan, her sixth for the day. When it arrived, she talked.

"Okay. Mr. Getner was always more interested in men than in women, you know? I think he could find that kind of life away from home, so he worked hard at getting to it and maintaining it. He could never get away with that up here."

"So, his love interest was a man?" Valery asked.

"He had a man as a lover?"

"Yeah, that's what it was. His man lover."

"Do you know his name?"

"Yes," she said.

"Tell us."

"No way. This is already as complicated as I need it to be. I don't want to drag anyone else into this mess."

"You need to understand that if I had my way, I would have torched the garage and blown up this entire end of town and just run away. That's how much I had come to hate the lives we were living."

"I need another drink."

It came with her steak.

Anders decided it was time to question her more about her husband's business.

"So, who were these people out west that your husband was connected to? Were they in mining, in unions, what?"

She was becoming much more revealing with this new drink.

"Basically, they were communists working out of New York City. They set up business in Johnstown because it was a union town, and they thought they could take advantage of the situation there. Every time there was a strike, and that would happen once a week or so in some mine someplace, they would show up and start agitating. They were trying to turn miners against the United Mine Workers, who they viewed as fools, and promised more aggression in the National Miners Union. They had tried to do it from the inside, but they could never get past John Lewis...so they decided to try from the outside."

"When did things start blowing up, the cars, the storefront, the other places we have identified? Who was behind that?"

"That wasn't directly about the unions, as I understand it. There was a very aggressive criminal element in the Johnstown area, lots of people who came from Sicily, black hand types, and their business was extortion and protection and, later, bootlegging. They would pick their targets, blow them up and then provide protection to other businesses by telling them they were going to be attacked, too, unless they paid them a certain amount every week. It was a crude business, but they knew how to do it."

"How did you find out about all of this?" Anders asked.

"Mr. Getner told me about most of it. He was proud he could bring home so much money just by selling little kegs of black powder he had stolen. He didn't care who they went to. Just so they sold. The criminals would blow something up. There would be a story in the paper. He would brag about knowing who they were and what they were up to. I thought that was fun at first, but after a couple of people were killed in the explosions, I felt a lot less comfortable about it."

Anders was relieved to hear that.

Mrs. Getner most certainly was an alcoholic and a criminal, but she had some standards and drew the line at murders that were not just accidents.

Still, they were murders.

He and Valery talked over what they had learned from Mrs. Getner and concluded there was a lot more investigating to do in the Johnstown area in connection with the National Miners Union and its ties to the New York Communists. They wrote up a few pages of notes and then prepared to call Finn to fill him in on what they found, what they needed to pursue, and how to do it.

Valery decided she would not tell Anders about Mrs. Getner's pistol in her purse unless he was planning to see her alone, which she didn't think would be happening as long as she was making the decision. Anders was a good man and had the potential to be a fine investigator, but not until he had a little more experience with wrongdoing and the many masks it wore. She was always learning herself, not the latest experience, which was the lesson from Mrs. Getner.

"In vino veritas," she was thinking.

"Use what you can," Valery told herself, a good rule for an investigator.

She and Anders returned to William Penn and went to Anders's room to call Finn. They had their papers with them. They were going to recommend a trip to western Pennsylvania to find the National Miners Union and see what it was about.

With both of them talking into the receiver, they told Finn what they had learned, the black powder from the mining company was actually fueling organized crime attacks many miles away in Western Pennsylvania. They started out looking for the cause of a coal mine disaster and, along the way, uncovered a criminal conspiracy complete with an organized crime connection that stretched all the way across Ohio and into Illinois.

"It's clear from what she told us that Mr. Getner was up to his eyes in some pretty shady business in western Pennsylvania," Valery said. "We think the possibility of a Communist connection is valid, even though those people have put most of their focus into the hard coal regions and organizing there. There is enough conflict within the UMW to open the way for that kind of influence. We think, at the very least, Trooper Morgan should look into that while he is out there and check with any sources he has in the Justice Department."

"Pretty clearly," Anders said, "Getner had become the source for black powder for all kinds of people all over the western part of the state. It wasn't just thieves trying to refill the stuff they stole from their own companies, although that's part of it. It was criminals, too. We don't know what they did with it, but we can try to find out. We think there may be some "black hand" influences involved in the Italian Community in Johnstown, but that would be in a specific part of the community, not general."

Finn was silent for a little while. "I'm thinking," he said.

Then he surprised them.

"Our mission, as you both well know, is to improve mine safety, so people don't get killed in accidents. What you have hit on goes far beyond that, and into whole other areas of criminal activity, lots of it covered by federal law that we are not equipped to investigate. Even with Trooper Howard on board, we still don't have the trained personnel to pursue this kind of criminal case. Getner's sale of black powder without a license is a federal offense the U.S.

Attorney in Pittsburgh is going to want to pursue. I think I need to go to the attorney general's office and talk to them about it and see what the state wants to do. Don't go any further into it on your end. Tap Mrs. Getner for whatever you can find out about her husband's business. But stop at that. This could get dangerous very quickly, and I don't want to move any further until I talk to the Attorney General. Okay?

"Yes," they said in unison. They resolved to wrap up their work with Mrs. Getner the next day and head back to Harrisburg to await further orders.

"Mr. Finn," Valery said. "We're not in trouble for this, are we?"

"Absolutely not, Valery. You have done excellent work, both of you, and I am not surprised. Let's get focused again on the Delaware and Hudson blast and go from there. See You."

Anders put the phone back on its receiver and looked at Valery.

"What have we got ourselves into now?" he said.

"I don't know. But I think I need a drink."

They went to the bar in the lobby of the hotel. Anders had a beer, and Valery had a glass of whiskey over ice. She sipped at it very slowly while she talked about the case with Anders.

"I think we have accidentally stepped into a hornet's nest," she said (which left Anders adding another item to his growing list of metaphors). We've discovered something that goes beyond what the Mining Department is supposed to do. Now we need to decide, basically as friends here, how aggressive we want to be in pursing this. Finn is going to talk to the Attorney General, and his inclination is to form task forces to go after various issues. This could be a task force. They are likely to be looking for investigators to borrow from other parts of the government to make it work. So, you need to think about whether you are ready to step away from Mining Inspection and Safety before you have even started and rushed down this rat hole of shit toward who knows what. I think I want to just stay where I am and look out for mining safety issues. I don't need to be part of a team chasing Italian black hand killers and black powder thieves. But let's see what Finn tells us after he talks to The General."

"The General."

What a man.

He was a hero in World War One, a hero in post-war famine efforts, and a hero in everything he touched after the war. He was the first cabinet member the new governor named when he took office two years ago, confirmed without a single negative vote and perceived, probably correctly, as a grown-up Boy Scout with no lust, no corruption, not a single hint of trouble anywhere near him.

He knew his weaknesses and did what he could to protect himself and the state from the mistakes he might make, given his own way.

They would be well-intentioned. But their consequences could be disastrous in so many ways. He was saved by the true fact that all of his intentions were good. No one could ever say something bad happened because he planned something bad to happen. Still, plenty of bad things happened under the command of The General. People who worked in government knew this. He was the last person you wanted to entrust with anything perilous. Finn was very surprised he was sitting in this waiting room. He was, after all, here to discuss a conspiracy of such complexity and potential for the damage he was thinking over and over about exactly what he should say. He concluded it would be best to keep it short and sweet. Describe the situation. Ask for help. Say thanks.

"Edward Finn!" the General said, arm extended, as he walked through the walnut doorway that led from his office to the anteroom. "Damned good to see you! How is everything in the coal industry? That's big business, I am told, big business for Pennsylvania and its people, and big business for the nation, too!"

"This is Mr. Reese. He will be sitting in on your meeting if you don't mind."

"Not at all," Finn said.

Come in here to talk to me. Coffee? Something stronger? Want a cookie or a piece of cake? Whatever you need to make you comfortable. Happy to help."

"Well, general, I…."

The general interrupted for some social mixing.

"How's the wife? Still, digging up the yard over in New Cumberland? Get any vegetables yet?"

Finn politely interrupted.

"We have found a ring of criminals out west who are using black powder stolen from mines in the hard coal region to intimidate people they are trying to shake down. That and union problems, too. We really need some help with this investigation, detectives, specialists in unions, and special investigators."

"Black powder? What would they do with something like that?" The General asked.

"Blow up cars, stores, houses, people…"

"Why would they do something like that?"

"They have their own reasons," Finn explained, avoiding any detail that might spark more unrelated questions from The General.

"How many houses have they blown up?" The General asked. "Have people been killed or hurt? Men? Women? Children?"

"Yes, in all cases," Finn said.

"What cars do they blow up? Do they blow up new cars or old cars? I've seen old cars blown up in movies, but not new cars. Too expensive. What kind of cars? Fords? Dodges? Chevrolets? Chryslers…"

"Yes," Finn answered as directly as he could.

"These are very bad people," The General said.

172

"Yes," Finn said.

"All Italians?" The General Asked.

"No. Not at all. Italians are not bad. These people are criminals who just happened to have come from Italy a while ago. They are bad, and they were bad in the old country, but not all Italians are that way."

Finn feared a standard "General" overreaction, police raids at Italian social clubs all over Western Pennsylvania, and street arrests of people who looked like Italians. It would all be bad and futile.

"What kind of special investigators do you want, Finn?"

The General asked. "Specialists in unions, detectives...."

"People who know how to follow leads, who know coal mining business, who know black hand business, who know how to track the behavior of criminals. That's what we need."

"Of course, Finn. Black hand. Bad business. How many and for how long?"

"Damn," Finn thought, "I didn't realize it would be this easy."

He had no idea how many to ask for.

"I think we could use 10 people for 10 months and see how that goes. They would have to be attached to my agency but keep all their police powers."

"Why sure, Finn. I think we can do that."

Mr. Reese was quietly shaking his head and mouthing a silent 'NO' even as the Attorney General was saying "Yes."

The General had a reputation for striving to make his visitors happy, so he would agree without hesitation to whatever they were asking for.

The General thought he had done well.

Finn was wondering whether it would be beneficial for him to review the entire investigation for The General, but he got a clue from Mr. Reese, who interrupted to say, "We can discuss the details in my office later. The General has a meeting to make at 5 p.m."

As it was already 4:35, Finn took the hint. He stood, shook the great man's hand, and headed for the door. But not before Mr. Reese grabbed his arm.

"A word, Finn?"

"Of course," Finn said.

Reese led him into a small office outside of the Attorney General's anteroom. He walked around a desk and sat down with a thump and a sigh.

"You know, the general's always full of good intentions and sometimes speaks beyond the Justice Department's capacity to respond, Finn. We can't give you ten investigators for ten months. We can give you, maybe, one or two investigators for a month to see where it leads. It's a big state with lots of demands on us. So understand that up front."

"Okay," Finn said.

"I'll take what I can get. But I think it would be better for the state if the Justice Department took over the investigation of the criminal aspects of this case or handed what it could to federal authorities. We aren't equipped to conduct that kind of investigation. You have the authority and the skill to do it. And the feds certainly do. I think you should. We simply don't have the manpower to do this. But it has to be done."

Reese sat quietly for a moment, then picked up his phone and asked for the "criminal division" of the state police. He heard a voice answer.

Then Reese said, "Al, Reese here from the general's office. We need to open an investigation of black powder marketing thru northeastern coal mines. It's ending up with radicals in Western

Pennsylvania. It will be yours to handle. Shift as much of it as you can to the feds. They have this new Federal Bureau of Investigation thing. I'm sure they want the work. Contact Ed Finn in the Mining Department for a fill-in and have the feds talk to him, too. His people have found a lot, and they will give you all that they have found."

Reese turned to Finn.

"Okay?" Reese said. Finn nodded.

"That's done. They will call for you when they are ready."

Finn let out a sigh of relief and stood to leave. He thanked Reese and asked him to relay his thanks to The General. Then he headed out the door and into the fresh air and the short walk back to the Commerce Department. He felt like 100 tons of coal had been taken off his back. Now he could get back to finding out how Delaware and Hudson so completely broken the rules that more than 100 miners were dead.

That seemed relatively simple.

He was back in his office in 20 minutes. There was a call from Anders and Valery just after he sat down.

He told them to come home and get to work on the Delaware and Hudson explosion report and their recommendations. They would be contacted by state and federal agents who would be taking over responsibility for the criminal parts of the probe.

One thing, Mr. Finn, she told him. "Mrs. Enders is armed, always, a pistol in her purse. So everyone should be careful."

"Jay-sus," Finn said.

He called Trooper Howard in Johnstown and told him to stand down on the criminal aspects of the case for the time being.

"State and federal agents will be talking to you over the next week or so, I suspect. They will be doing the heavy lifting on this one. We have to get back to mine safety and inspection violations in the Delaware and Hudson case. You've done great work so far, so keep it up, Detective Morgan. Come on back in and get together with Valery and Anders and see what we can say about the Delaware and Hudson explosion. Okay?"

"Yes, sir," Howard said.

"We will meet on this on Monday. Have a good weekend!"

"Thank you, Mr. Finn," Howard said.

Trooper Morgan returned from Western Pennsylvania on Saturday afternoon and sat down to review his notes on what he had found. He was convinced the black powder from Wilkes-Barre was being used to fill stores that had been raided for a variety of bombings across the region, most of them in connection with labor trouble or the "black hand" crimes of Sicilian immigrants.

He identified a series of bombings of buildings, storefronts, and autos that seemed as though they were connected to various kinds of labor trouble, although he did not rule out standard crime as an explanation for some of them.

The bombing at the coal company headquarters was the most obvious. The people who caused that wanted to open a safe that held the monthly payment for more than 400 miners at three relatively busy shafts, well over $250,000. But all they succeeded in doing was wrecking the building the safe was sitting in and destroying all the mine's records. He had visited the site near Cassandra and concluded that the miners knew a little about black powder but not enough to use it to blast the hinges from such a substantial safe. He checked with the Portage constables to see what their investigation had turned up. Basically, people needed money and were hungry, they said, and they were not surprised by anything that happened these days.

Trooper Howard had an additional thought about the incident, one that came from his training. In explosions, always review the extent of damage to see what was destroyed. That could point an arrow toward why an explosion happened. Sometimes, the reason is not obvious. What if it wasn't about the safe and its contents? What if it was about the records? He made a note to talk to Finn about that, knowing that Finn was passionate about using records to determine the causes of all kinds of problems. All the fire boss reports, all the mine air readings, and everything you might want to know about conditions in the mine were all destroyed. They were not kept safely as required by law, not kept in a blast-proof or fireproof containment, so that part was certainly suspicious to Trooper Howard's mind. The Cooper Brothers Mining Corp., which owned the building, the safe, and the records, managed operations at three mines in the area, "Last Chance," which was literally the last chance for old and damaged miners to get some work, Fiddler's Green, a medium-sized mine that was moderately productive, and, of course, the big one, Coalman's, at Portage.

Howard kept one piece of detritus from the blast scene, the cover of a ledger book that was supposed to hold the results of air quality testing in all three mines. The blast had burned the cover and about half of the pages, but there were still some intact pages recording carbon monoxide and dioxide readings. He thought Finn might want those.

He was, of course, uncertain of himself.

The very thought of the meeting made him nervous. Should he just bluster in there and lay out what he found or wait to be questioned? He thought waiting would be the best course. He prepared an extensive set of notes about what he would be saying, almost like a speech. Then he felt as ready as he was ever going to feel. Or so he thought.

Finn and Valery were already in the room when Trooper Morgan and Anders walked in. They all greeted one another. Finn faced Anders and said, "So, literally a baptism of fire!"

"Yes, it was," Anders said. "I can't believe Getner left that much powder unattended in his garage. Anything could have set it off. It would have taken most of the town, I think. I'm glad the mining company was able to collect it and get it out of there."

"You all made the right calls on this up to this point. This meeting is to discuss a couple of things, with an important one being what falls under federal jurisdiction and what remains in our control," Finn said.

"But now we have to talk about what we're going to tell the feds when they come calling, and believe me; they will come calling, maybe as soon as this week. Detective Howard, I want you to be our liaison with the state troopers because you know them and how they work. I will handle the feds with help from Valery. Anders, what will Delaware and Hudson do with all that black powder? You should find out. They can't sell it because they aren't licensed, and they might not be able to use it because they have no idea where it came from. That should keep them tied up for a while, I think."

"Valery, I want you to start working on a summary report of our investigation and what we found at Delaware and Hudson. I also need a good idea, in the form of a report by mid-week, of how we can slice the federal part of this investigation off and give it to them. I also want you to continue working with Mrs. Getner, but carefully. We know her late husband was a criminal and the likelihood is she is, too. So be aggressive but don't let yourself get stuck between her and a wall if you know what I mean. "

"Then he asked Howard what he had found and what he had concluded in his rambles around western Pennsylvania. He reported he was now certain that the black powder from Delaware and Hudson was being used to replace black power siphoned from mine supplies on the scene in western Pennsylvania. He identified two car explosions, a storefront explosion, and the explosion that left only the safe standing as the likely targets for the black powder."

"There's something I need to say here that goes beyond what you asked me to do," the trooper said, now a little shyly. "I'm not certain the safe was the actual target in that Cassandra bombing. It touched on too many other things to be just about that money. The important one is that all the daily records for Last Chance, Fiddlers Green, and Coalman mines were destroyed in the explosion. I'm not sure I know why anyone would want to do that, but that is what was done. I'm not sure why their records were stored there and were not in a safe location, as required. I talked to some local managers. They knew nothing about those other records."

Finn was quiet for a moment while he digested what Detective Howard had just reported. Mine records were at the heart of Finn's business. It would be impossible to act on transgressions if you could not show there were transgressions, after all, and most of those were contained in detailed records of conditions in the mine. Short of that, you might be able to show that methane was the cause of an explosion, but not that it had been ignored over many months of daily testing. That kind of negligence is built into criminal cases. Also, you could hardly order a mining company to improve its air circulation if you had no records of what it was in the first place. The problem with the theory about mining companies destroying their own records was that the fines for violations were a pittance to them. Why blow up an entire headquarters building when the offenses you were covering up might cost you $1,000 over a year? And why were records from unconnected mines being kept at Cassandra? Changing how the state approached those charges had been one of Finn's quiet missions with the governor's office under the argument that the loss of life should not be measured against such a petty collection of fines. Finn wanted to base the fine on the number of miners killed and injured. The governor's office was reluctant, and he could tell that because his proposals kept getting respectfully referred to The General for consideration or action. They would not actually die there because The General never killed anything. But he could certainly stretch an issue beyond recognition by asking the five thousand questions he needed to understand anything. Finn had been through the process once.

He swore at that point he would avoid it.

He had to decide if he would make an exception for this case, which was so revealing in so many ways. It not only shined bright lights on how coal companies worked, but it also illuminated the dark corners of state government, where people may or may not have been doing their jobs without supervision, certainly without any kind of backup.

179

But he interrupted his thoughts to make an announcement.

He reached into his leather bag and pulled out a blue and gold cardboard box with the State Police insignia on it.

"Today, the idea of Trooper Howard Morgan moves into history," he said. Holding out the badge, he said, "Detective Howard Morgan, we are delighted to present this new shield to you. The governor sends his regards."

Everyone clapped, and not just one or two times. They didn't give Detective Howard a standing ovation, but it came close.

He opened the box revealing a state police detective's badge, silver with gold trim, and the seal of the commonwealth in the center. It sat in a brown leather wallet with Howard's name on it.

There was no cake.

Chapter 13: Lucille Getner

Lucille Getner was polite when she got the call the next morning from Valery, who asked if she would mind another visit for a little more conversation about Mr. Getner and his businesses. "Of course, you are welcome. Just don't bring any more black powder," she joked. Valery was surprised Mrs. Getner could make jokes about the powder store her husband kept in the garage, it being so dangerous and so volatile. But she never ceased being amazed by the people she ran into in investigations. From good to bad, she touched all the bases. She was wondering, even as she talked, where Lucille Getner would fit on that scale. She got one of the state cars the next morning and prepared for the long drive to Avoca. She was wondering whether she should be armed. Avoca was a tough place full of coal miners who drank a lot and were not at all subtle in their approaches. Maybe Lucille used the gun to wave them off. Valery decided she would leave her father's old pistol at home.

The other important questions were still forming in her head. She wanted to know what Emil Getner did with his money, whether he put it in the bank or hid it at home. She didn't think Lucille would tell her, but how she refused to tell her might hold a clue about the money.

She also wanted to know what Lucille knew about his accomplices, and he clearly had some in western Pennsylvania. The National Miners Union was passionate about its own causes, and she wanted to know whether Mr. Getner, who, after all, was management, had any connection at all to those sentiments. She couldn't imagine it, but that was because she was working on the premise that all of Mr. Getner's Western connections were about money.

Maybe his wife could cast a light on that question.

She took along a half quart of bourbon, but she didn't know whether she should use it. She didn't want to make Mrs. Getner any more of an alcoholic than she already was, and she was also a little shy about the value of information collected under those conditions. The minute she got into the car, she knew it was a mistake. But she was still thinking about it. Mrs. Getner became almost gabby with a few drinks in her, kind of like one of those "girl talk" sessions where women griped about their husbands or boyfriends.

She arrived at Getner's house just after noon and decided to leave the bourbon in the car. If Mrs. Getner needed a drink, Valery thought, she surely knew where she would find one.

She knocked on the door, which was answered by a man in a nice suit wearing a white shirt and tie. He introduced himself as Edward Finch and said he had become Mrs. Getner's attorney in the wake of her husband's death.

He invited Valery in and led her to the living room, where Mrs. Getner was sitting comfortably in an overstuffed chair next to a fireplace. Finch took a chair from the dining room and sat beside her. "Edward is the family attorney," she said. "I thought it would be best for him to advise me on answering any questions about my late husband's business or connections in Western Pennsylvania."

"First," said Finch, "I need to know the purpose of this visit. What are you investigating, and why do you want to talk to Mrs. Getner?"

"I am the deputy director of the Mining Division in the State Department of Commerce, and I am here in connection with an explosion that killed more than 200 miners at Delaware and Hudson's Baltimore Shaft two weeks ago. Our mission is to examine the causes of the accident to determine whether there were safety violations, prosecute those violations and recommend regulations to prevent a repeat. But these kinds of investigations frequently uncover conditions and circumstances that go beyond the incident, but may help explain it."

"And have you found such circumstances and conditions in this case? How do they relate to my client?"

Valery wanted to avoid any conflict at this point in her questioning, so she kept it simple.

"Your client's husband was running a business as part of his supervisory position at Delaware and Hudson, which is not illegal, and had a storehouse of roughly 600 pounds of black powder in his garage, which is." She said the department had no immediate criminal interest in Mrs. Getner, was interested only in her husband at this point, and would appreciate any information Mrs. Getner could provide that would help explain what Mr. Getner was up to."

"So you are here in a law enforcement capacity?" he asked.

"I am," she said.

"But I want to stress that Mrs. Getner is not a target of this investigation. We are focused now only on her late husband and his connections in Western Pennsylvania. We do have a warrant for a search based on a previous visit that located 600 pounds of black powder."

"What kind of connections?"

Valery saw a red flag on the horizon at this point.

"I'm not prepared to present much detail in connection with that question," Valery said. "This is an ongoing investigation, and we have to be cautious in how we pursue it."

"It's the Communists, isn't it?" he asked.

"Not in a position to reveal that," Valery said.

"I want to make an offer," he said.

"Mrs. Getner is willing to share everything she knows in connection with her husband's business in Western Pennsylvania in exchange for a guarantee of use immunity so the information cannot be turned against her later."

"I can't make that deal," Valery said. "I have to discuss your proposal with our legal counsel and the director of the office."

183

"Please do," he said.

"And then let us know."

"Indeed," Valery said. She got up and headed for the door.

"By tomorrow if at all possible," the attorney said.

"I will do what I can."

She took his card and headed for the car.

She drove straight to the William Penn, booked a room for the night, had a good stiff drink, and sat down to call Finn for advice.

He answered his own phone.

"Ah, Valery, from lovely Avoca!"

"Lovely it is, especially the way the sun sets behind the boney piles in the evening!"

"What did you get from Mrs. Getner?" he asked.

"An offer," she said.

"She will tell us everything she knows in exchange for use immunity. She had her lawyer with her. I hope he explained the details of use immunity to her because I don't feel confident as an investigator going into any detail."

"We can grant that. It just prevents us from using her testimony against her, and she is not the target of this probe."

"Okay, I'll call him and tell him. Should I talk to her?"

"Nope. Once immunity is on the table, it all gets very formal. We have to interview her before a court reporter and build a record of what she says. You'll like that because someone else gets to take the notes!"

"Lovely. I'm calling her lawyer now."

Finch's phone rang four times before he answered.

184

"We'll take the deal," Valery told him.

"Mrs. Getner gets use immunity. What she tells us cannot be used against her. But she should understand, as I am sure you do, that we can still use other witnesses to investigate her."

"Deal?"

There was a pause. Then...

"Deal," he said.

Then he hung up.

She was surprised that it went so smoothly. Then she thought again. This was not yet over.

Her phone rang again.

It was Mrs. Getner.

"Buy you a drink?" she asked.

"Sure," Valery said. "Downstairs in the bar."

They met in the William Penn Bar a few minutes later. Mrs. Getner said she was glad she would not face any more investigations. Valery said nothing because that was not likely the case. She had no idea what Mrs. Getner's testimony about western Pennsylvania would tell them or where it would lead.

"Lucille, there's nothing you should tell me now and nothing I can tell you. Everything we say to one another from now onward has to be before a court reporter so there can be a transcript. That's to avoid any chance of misunderstanding. So, have your drink, and let's talk about something that's not about Delaware and Hudson."

"That guy you are with, that Anders guy," she said. "Is he your boyfriend?

"No," Valery said.

"We are good friends and colleagues, but there is nothing romantic between us."

Valery knew that was a lie, of course, but it was a lie she didn't mind telling and one she would have to live out in the office, too. She did have feelings for him, feelings unlike she had for anyone else. But for the moment, that was no one else's business. Especially not Lucille Getner's.

What do I do now? Mrs. Getner asked.

"We'll be in touch," Valery said. She was going to ask her about her pistol, then decided to cut the conversation off.

"Well, I'm tired," she told Lucille. "I'm going to bed. See you down the road in a bit."

Back in her room, she called Finn.

"We need to make arrangements to get her testimony before she causes more trouble," Valery said. "This woman is a one-person wrecking crew. I think we should squeeze her and then get her out of our hair."

"Okay. Come back tomorrow, and we will make arrangements. I'll call the Commonwealth Court in the morning and see if we can get a transcriber and an office for our interview. She needs to come here for that, and she can bring her lawyer, too. We need to sit down with Anders and Detective Morgan and see where we want to go with her. We don't know because we don't know what she will say, but I'm sure it will have some weight, or she would not have gone for the immunity package. See you tomorrow."

"Right," she said.

The drive back to Harrisburg was pleasant. She had stopped noticing the boney piles near the mines, the vast collection of mining junk that was rusting away at every mine site. Instead, she focused on the forest, on the trees, on the beauty of the Endless Mountains. She could see why people might want to live here. Then she remembered that it was June and that the place would not seem so

186

friendly in January when it was covered in a thick layer of snow with ice an inch thick on top.

It was one of those places in Pennsylvania where you had a remarkably clear sense of descent, that you were coming down from the mountaintop and heading for the rivers and plains down below. Up and down, it made your ears pop. Everything changed during this descent. The trees were a mix of hardwood and soft pines that seemed to billow in the wind. You had a sense of driving in the foothills toward the bottom of the mountain, then it all leveled out into a big valley with the broad Susquehanna running through it. Beautiful in the summer, with red-winged blackbirds squawking and robins chirping all along the highway. Valery was a cautious driver but also one of those people who noticed everything. She had to be careful not to be distracted and drift into an oncoming lane.

She found herself thinking about Lucille Getner again.

Didn't she notice that there was more money around, more ability to do things, because of the cash he was picking up at the mine? How could she not have known about the black powder in the garage? She was a smoker, and if she had been incautious with a cigarette or a match, she could have destroyed much of the town, herself, her husband, and everyone in the neighborhood.

"She simply had to know," Valery thought.

"It would be like living beside a bomb. She had to know about it. And the money, too. She had lots of nice clothing. A new car. Enough cash to go out for drinks and food any time she wanted to. She carried herself like a person of substance, too, not haughty, but comfortable, alert, and always ready to respond. No, it was not yet over for Lucille Getner, Valery thought. She had more to do with this than they knew, and one of her objectives would be to find out what that was."

Valery met Finn in the hallway that led to their offices. He told her he had made arrangements with Commonwealth Court for a hearing room for Mrs. Getner's interview and for a court transcriber to get all of her comments on the record. That would be in about ten days. She was to call Lucille Getner and attorney Finch and get them on board as soon as she had a day and time for the interviews.

"This can all wait for the morning," she thought. She walked down the hallway to see if Anders was still at work. He was. She asked him if he wanted to go out to dinner. He said sure, but nothing fancy.

The New Cumberland Inn was not an inn at all but just a bar built on the foundation of an inn that had burned down off a busy street near the center of the town. She had not been there often, so it was unlikely anyone would know who she was, and no one would recognize Anders, she was certain. The cab driver knew the place. It was a $4 ride. Anders gave the man $5, and they got out of the cab. The first thing he noticed was the smell, the scent of broiled fish, and something else. That turned out to be a crab. The specialty of the house was a flounder stuffed with crab meat and broiled. It all came fresh from the Chesapeake Bay. They were seated near a window that looked out onto the parking lot. It was not romantic. But it was comfortable and spotlessly clean. The waiter said the flounder was excellent, and the crab was fresh. He brought a small loaf of sweetened bread and butter. It passed Anders' bread test, and he ate two pieces before the food arrived. He had Yuengling's Beer, and she had a martini.

"I think Mrs. Getner has a lot to tell us now that we have got a grant of use immunity," she said.

"That doesn't mean we can't investigate. It just means we can't use her testimony against her. We can pursue other witnesses to testify about her. But the immunity means she will have no reason to keep quiet about anything she might have been doing. We can get her to open up, I think."

She told him her thoughts about Lucille and the money Getner was making, and the fact that she had a huge bomb out in the garage. "She just had to know about that. It would be way too dangerous to just let it sit out there and assume she wouldn't stumble over it. I mean…ka-boom!

"I think she had some role in the distribution of that powder. As best I could tell, she never went to western Pennsylvania with her husband. Maybe she delivered it. I don't know. But we have to find out her connection to that part of her husband's business. And what about his boyfriend out west? What did she think about that? Was it okay that he was making love to a man? Or was that part of the arrangement? We have a lot to talk to her about."

Anders stayed quiet and let her talk. He liked the way she thought out loud, laying the groundwork for interrogation as clearly as though she were planning the planting of a garden.

"We should have asked Detective Howard to come to dinner with us," Anders said. "He might have more to say about her and what she was up to. Do you have a number for him?" She opened her purse and took out a small black book, flipped some pages, and gave Anders Howard's number.

"Let me call him. Maybe he can get here."

He went to the pay phone and returned in a few minutes. "Howard is on his way. He said it should take about a half hour. He's using a state police car, so he can move pretty quickly."

Valery ate some bread and sipped at her drink.

"Do you think Mrs. Getner is dangerous, Anders?"

"I don't know her that well. How do you mean dangerous?"

"There's a gun in her purse."

"Yes then, she is most certainly dangerous. The question is how she might use it. I don't know."

"Do you think we should be armed, too?" she asked.

189

"I haven't thought about that. We do have the authority to ask questions and demand answers. I thought that would be enough. But I didn't realize we would be moving so quickly into a criminal world."

"I don't know," Anders said.

"I just don't like the thought of you being out there with a woman who is armed and dangerous."

"I'm tickled you are worried about me," Valery said. "But I'm not, so you shouldn't be either. I'm not going to take any risks or chances that would lead to that kind of trouble. I'm asking questions, after all, not waving a pistol and trying to intimidate someone. I've seen people do that kind of work, and it's too easy for something to go wrong. I think that's why Finn doesn't want anyone carrying weapons on field investigations. You know you end up out in a bar with a bunch of drunk coal miners some night, and who knows what might happen. We have the authority to arrest people, and that should be enough."

"Agreed," Anders said.

"Even in Transylvania, when there was trouble, the investigators had guns but rarely used them. If they wanted to take you in or question you, they would just sit you in the back seat of a car and then put their hands on your knees. That's how you knew it was serious when they put their hands on you. It was like they were saying, 'I am the state, and now you are my prisoner. My suspect. My witness.'

"I don't know if that would work here," Valery said. "First, I'm not comfortable putting my hands on someone, and second, it would be very easy for someone to misread that kind of action and misunderstand why I am touching them."

"You mean hanky panky?" Anders said. "That kind of misunderstanding?"

"Well, yes," she said.

"Men always misunderstand just about everything."

Anders added that to his growing list of mental notes.

Trooper Howard came in just 35 minutes after Anders called him. He was wearing a dark blue suit, white shirt, and tie.

"It's new," he said. "It's my official detective suit. It's going to take a while for me to get used to it, especially the shoes." They were black, and the detective had spit-shined them, so they were like dark mirrors.

"It all looks great on you, Howard," Valery said.

"It sure does," Anders agreed.

He looked like a g-man from the movies.

He pulled his jacket front to the side to reveal his pistol in a shoulder holster made of dark brown leather. That had also been spit-shined.

That opened the door to a conversation.

"What were you talking about before I came?" he asked.

"Hanky-panky," Valery said.

"Transylvanian police," Anders said at the same time, rolling his eyes and adding, "Valery!"

"Okay, which was it?"

"We were talking about Lucille Getner and the questions we needed to ask her, then we got into a conversation about police methods, and that's how hanky-panky came up," she said.

"My point was that men generally misunderstand everything, that they would not understand if I put my hand on their knee in the back seat of a police car. They might think it was a romantic gesture. Anders said that was common in Transylvania, a sign that you were under the control of the authorities. It's why they didn't have to use their guns very often; people knew they had that kind of authority."

191

"So, Howard, do you think we should carry guns on investigations?" Valery asked.

Howard paused for an instant, then looked right into her steel gray eyes.

"Could you kill someone?" Howard responded.

"That's the first question you had to answer correctly at the academy because, for a policeman, that is what a gun is for. It's not something to use to scare someone into answering a question. It's for killing people who are threatening your life or the life of someone else. As for questions in investigations, your presence, your authority, should do that in itself. The weapon is only for taking and saving lives. That's how I see it."

The topic shifted to the interrogation of Mrs. Getner. Valery wanted to know if Howard ran across any sign that she had traveled to western Pennsylvania with her husband or maybe delivered powder or picked up the money.

"No one seemed to know anything about her," Howard said.

"They knew Getner well, that he had a boyfriend he met at a motel outside Johnstown, but nothing about her, at least not that I could see. As best I could tell, he usually delivered the powder to the Miners Union people, and then it found its way into the hands of criminals for all kinds of uses. I didn't get to pursue much of that once Finn said we were handing off a lot of the investigation to the federal authorities."

"Did you interview the boyfriend," Anders asked.

"AHHH….Angel Corder…Couldn't get near him. I knew where he would go to hang out and drink and where he lived, but I could never figure out a clear path to him that would not reveal what we were up to. I suppose that doesn't even matter now that Emil Getner is dead."

"He is dead, isn't he?"

There was a pause at the table.

"That was our assumption based on what the people at Delaware and Hudson told us. But we don't know for sure. We didn't check the county coroner's office to make sure. Do you think we should ask Mrs. Getner if she is certain her husband is dead? That's kind of off-putting, don't you think?"

Anders and Howard stared at Valery for just a few seconds.

"If he is still alive," Anders said, "We have to find that out and find him, too. He is at the center of all of this, and it would be good to catch him at something so we can "squeeze" him, as you people say about witnesses."

"Why would you want everyone to think you were dead?" Howard said.

"Maybe it's not everyone. Maybe it's just Lucille; he wants to think he is dead."

"Why?"

"I think we really need to get this boyfriend and talk to him."

"Yeah," Valery and Howard said at exactly the same time. They were both thinking the same thing. Whatever happened had more to do with Emil and Lucille than with anything else. Angel Cordner.

They laid out the plan they would use to present the case to Finn the next morning. Howard would talk about Angel Cordner and why he was important. Anders would talk about Delaware and Hudson and its records, and Valery would talk about Lucille Getner.

But that could wait until morning.

Howard offered to haul everyone home in his patrol car, but Valery said it would be simpler just to get a cab and pay the $5. Anders went to the pay phone to call the cab.

"So," Howard asked when Anders had left, "Is there something going on between you and Anders? Clearly, you get along very well."

"Mind your own business," she said, but she was smiling.

Finn was eager to get his meeting underway, so he avoided useless chatter.

"Anders, tell us what you know about Lucille Getner," he said.

"Well," Anders said, "the first and probably most important thing is that we don't know for certain that she is a widow. We don't have a county coroner's report confirming Emil's death, and it would appear no one has put together a formal list of victims. That's not so surprising in a case this big, but it's an important question for us. Lucille Getner is playing the widow's role well, at least until she gets a few drinks into her. She knows he had a boyfriend in western Pennsylvania, and it didn't seem to bother her, so we wanted to talk to her about that. We know she has plenty of cash on hand, a healthy bank account, and was sitting right outside of a gigantic black powder bomb, apparently comfortably. Did she know it was there or not? What role did she play in the collection and distributing it out west? Those are the avenues we should travel in talking to her. But first, we need to find out about Emil Getner's remains, assuming there were remains, and whether they have been buried or whether he is out rambling. That's what I think at this point."

"Great, Anders," Finn said. "When this meeting is over, get on the phone with the county coroner and find out if the man is actually dead. He might have been blasted into tiny pieces, but that would still mean he is dead. Also, make arrangements for Mrs. Getner to be here two weeks from today at 10 a.m. in Commonwealth Court hearing room 400. There will be a court reporter there. I will meet her in the room. I want you to decide among yourselves who needs to be part of this. Too many people will spook her, so think about it. My own preference would be for Valery and Howard to question her, with Valery in her 'gentlewoman, so sorry for your loss mode.'"

Howard and Valery glanced at one another and nodded.

"Anything else," Finn asked.

"Well, yes," Valery said.

"We think we should be carrying firearms. We are law enforcement people, after all, and this case has shown pretty clearly that we can be in jeopardy on occasion.

"I can see that, but you all would have to be trained before the state would issue a firearm. Who is going to do that?"

"I can," Howard said.

"I was a firearms training officer at the state police academy. I could do that for us, too, I am certain."

Finn said he wanted to think about it. True, sometimes they were dealing with lying felons, but they weren't armed lying felons in most cases.

Chapter 14: "Dead or alive"

Back at his office, Anders looked up the phone number for the coroner of Luzerne County. He had no idea what he would find.

The telephone in Wilkes-Barre rang 11 times before a woman answered.

Anders introduced himself and said he wanted to talk to the Luzerne County coroner, a man named Loverly. There was a delay, and then a man picked up the phone, "Loverly here, how can I help you."

"I'm wondering whether your office has assembled a complete list of victims from the explosion at Baltimore Shaft a couple of weeks ago. I know there were more than 100 victims, and the scene was a nightmare, but I thought by this time you might have put a list together."

"Sure, we have a list. You looking for any particular name?"

Anders took a deep breath.

"Emil Getner."

There was a pause while the coroner went down his list. He found no Emil Getner or any name that even looked vaguely like it.

"Nope. Not here."

"Many of the bodies were destroyed in the explosion, so there may have been no remains to work with. What do you do in that situation?"

"Generally, we depend on the companies to provide information about who is missing after this kind of a disaster. It doesn't always work the same way. People lost in floods you have to wait for because, generally, they fill up with gas and then pop up downstream. But explosions are something different for sure."

"Is it possible Emil Getner was not killed in that explosion?"

"Well, I can tell you if he was on the man trip going down in the mine, he was killed. But I don't have any way of telling whether he was on the man trip. If he wasn't on the trip, he might not even have been underground when the powder blew up."

The coroner said there would be no reason for the mining company to forget his name. He was a supervisor, after all, and well-known in the company.

"I think you need to assume he is out there someplace in one piece," the coroner said.

"You might want to ask the company if it paid death benefits to the man's widow. That's what usually happens after these things."

"Thank you," Anders said.

He went straight to Finn after the call.

"I think Getner may still be alive. The company provided a list of all the dead people on the mantrip, and his name was not there. So where is he?"

Finn paused for a few seconds.

"Get ahold of the company again and ask if they have updated their lists of victims or whether they have approved payouts for survivors. Then ask about Getner. Someone is going to tell us about what happened to him, maybe Lucille, maybe Delaware, and Hudson. I don't know, but someone does. Even in that violent an explosion, people may be blasted to bits, but they don't completely disappear. I can't believe the coroner just takes the word of the company on something like this. We're talking about building the official record of who died for chrissakes!

"Well, Mr. Finn, you know how it was down that shaft after the blast, burning piles of dead miners, body parts all over. Maybe the fire department wasn't able to find all of them."

"That's what we have to look at, Anders," Finn said. "That chief was pretty helpful. You might want to talk to him about it. The department is right down the road from the mine. Take one of the cars and go back up there."

"Yes, sir," Anders said. He told Valery where he was going and what he was doing, then got the state car and headed north. It would take a couple of hours.

The Luzerne County Volunteer Fire Department was headquartered in an expanded two-story garage made out of cinder blocks. It was the first garage in the county that had a big automatic door. You just hit the button, and up it went, clearing the way for the trucks. The garage had room for two fire trucks. The second floor was set up as a dormitory in the days when Chief Dzerzhinsky had ambitions to take the force full-time and add some paid firefighters. One of the trucks was a green Dodge with a heavy-duty winch on the front and a water tank with a nozzle for chasing down grass fires and solving problems along the road. Despite its age and utilitarian design, it was spotless. The other was a new American LaFrance pumper with an extension ladder fixed to the top that could reach up a couple of stories or pump water from a big nozzle. It was the pride of the locals, a truck bought with money raised in raffles and bake sales and at special fire department barbecues, where half chickens and baked potatoes were the favorites. You would get a healthy scoop of sour cream with each potato. The truck cost $15,000 brand new, which was a king's ransom for such a small department. They had an option for buying a used pumper for half that price, but it had none of the spunk of the new one and was rusting, to boot, along the bottom of the tank. So, they went for new. Volunteers washed and waxed it each weekend or after it was used.

Chief Thomash Dzerzhinksy was in the office doing the books. He was the department's only full-time paid staff member, and he took the job, $900 a year, so seriously that he rarely went home. He had a comfortable day bed in his office and could spend nights there in the fall and winter, with a warming fire in the franklin stove, when house fires were more common. Part of his job was to drive the new truck, which he loved unconditionally.

198

In the summer, Dzerzhinsky planted a vegetable garden beside the firehouse and grew prize tomatoes, peppers and onions. The produce was used for the department's late summer festival. Chief made tomato sauce with hot peppers in it ("Firey! he called it, as in "Put some Firey on that brat!)

That also became the base for the barbecue served at the dinner. It cost $5 to attend the dinner, and sometimes people would double up on the fee just to contribute to the volunteers. Everyone appreciated the Luzerne Volunteers because they were, as it said on each of their helmets and under the Luzerne County seal on the doors of the trucks, "The Dependables." Many a barn was saved, and many a house in the dead of winter, by volunteers who scrambled from all over to respond to the firehouse siren, big and loud enough to call in people from great distances.

They were well led by a chief they loved, and he loved all of them back in a manly, fatherly way. He would tolerate no shenanigans around his equipment or during firefighting. Beer was allowed at the festivals, but never to excess and never for minors. The chief had his standards.

Anders parked to the side of the front of the station in case anyone needed to bring either of the trucks out. He walked in through a side door and saw Dzershinsky sitting at his desk.

"Chief," Anders said, knocking on the door, "My name is Anders Apostle, from the Mining Department in Harrisburg...."

"I remember you!" the chief said, turning from his desk to shake his hand, "You were one of the first of the inspectors to go down Bethlehem Shaft after the explosion. That took some balls, Mr. Apostole, and we all recognized it. How can I help you...."

"Thank you," Anders said, puzzling at the tribute because, in his experience, all men had balls.

"I'm sorry about the losses you all suffered at the mine, and I know that was a very difficult time for all of you. I'm wondering how you identified the remains when you were bringing the bodies out."

"Well, each man had a copper token on a pin in his jacket. Usually, they would hang those on the wall when they got to the bottom of the pit to show they were at work. But this time, they served us well. We lined up the numbers with the numbers Delaware and Hudson had issued, and we found the tokens for all of the miners who were missing. We found 150 of them in all. So that meant just a couple of dozen were totally gone."

"I'm looking for one name," Anders said.

"Emil Getner. Do you have a list?"

The chief pulled out his records of the blast and opened a book of names of the dead. He said he found no token that would identify Emil Getner."

"He was a supervisor," Anders said.

"That explains it. The company only gave those tokens to miners who were digging coal. It was how they knew what to pay at the end of the week. But supervisors never wore them. They were just listed in the company record as "company men" who worked above ground. You have to go to the company and ask them to show you work records for the day of the blast. That will tell you if your man was on board the trip.

"What about death benefits? Any records on those?"

Same story, the chief said. They would be on record at Delaware and Hudson. He thanked Dzershinsky, who said he could always move to Wilkes-Barre and become a volunteer because companies always needed men like him. Anders thanked him.

It took an hour to drive to the Delaware and Hudson headquarters down the road, and the people in charge were at lunch. He accepted a cup of coffee and sat on the steps of the main office, awaiting their return.

He was happy to see them back and sober after an hour of sitting on the steps.

"Hello," he said. "I'm Inspector Apostle from Mining in Harrisburg, and I need to talk to you about the fatality list from the Baltimore Shaft explosion.

"Rita is in charge of that. We will introduce you to her."

Rita was a schoolmistress-looking woman in a gray dress with her hair pulled back in a bun and glasses so thick you could barely discern her eyes, which were a foggy blue.

"I'm looking for the fatalities list from the Baltimore Shaft explosion. Could you let me see it?" Anders asked.

"Why?" she asked.

"We're looking for someone who might or might not be dead. His name was Emil Getner, and he was the shift supervisor."

She looked into a file marked "Baltimore Shaft" and then, peering at him through her glasses, said, "He's not on this list. He was a supervisor, so why would he be going down into the mine?"

"Thank you," Anders said.

He gave her a little salute and turned, and headed out of the office. On the steps, two men in miner's coveralls approached him. "You're the inspector from Harrisburg. So, what have you found out about the explosion?" one of them asked.

"Well, we're not finished yet," Anders said. "We're looking for the man who was the shift supervisor."

"Getner?"

"I sure hope he is dead. What a thief that man was. He would charge you for sunlight and air. No damn good to anyone, I heard."

"Are you sure he was killed?"

"Well, no, we aren't. He might have run off with his boyfriend; that's what we heard. Imagine that, a boyfriend!"

Anders gave him one of his new business cards, white with a Gold seal of Pennsylvania on it and the title "Mining Department, the investigator," with a phone number in Harrisburg.

"Why don't you just talk around and see if anybody has seen him since the explosion? Let me know. I would really appreciate it."

"Sure."

He was certain he was unlikely to hear from them but figured he would keep an open mind and an open door for them. No telling what they might know about the place.

After he left the mining company, he headed to Avoca to see if he could get anything from Lucille Getner, any sign she knew what happened to her husband. It was after lunch, and Mrs. Getner had been drinking. He walked up on the porch and knocked on her door.

"Mrs. Getner…It's Anders from Harrisburg. I'm just here to make sure you know when to come to see us for your testimony."

"Come in," she said.

As soon as he was in the living room, she embraced him and kissed him hard on the mouth. He tasted alcohol and cigarettes and a breath mint. She persisted.

"Anders Apostle," she said.

"That's such a lovely name for such a lovely man."

"Mrs. Getner," he said. "I really need to stay focused on our investigation, and I'm not interested in hanky panky with you. (He didn't know what else to call it.)."

She began laughing hysterically, so hard she spilled her drink on the sofa and plopped back on top of its pillows.

"Hanky panky?" she said.

"What is this, high school? Let me be a little more blunt about it. Do you want to fuck me or not?"

Anders realized he had just a few moments to regain his composure and drag the conversation back to the topic at hand, the whereabouts of Mr. Getner.

"No," Mrs. Getner said. "I don't. And I'm sorry."

"We need to find your husband as soon as we can," he said. That is all I am interested in."

She kept on laughing, mocking him with questions about why he didn't find her attractive. "Mr. Getner didn't either, but he liked men more than women. Are you that way, too? Do you like men more than women?"

"No, Mrs. Getner. I'm just here to work."

She began to quiet herself after that when Anders made it clear he had some questions to ask. "I'm not trying to offend you, Mrs. Getner. I need to know whether your husband was killed in the explosion. Do you know? Have you heard from him? Did you get any benefits from the company or an explanation that would indicate they think he's dead?"

"I have nothing to say to you about that," she said.

"You can leave now unless you really want to stay if you know what I mean," she said.

At that point, he gave her a letter from Finn laying out the hearing times and noting the state would cover her stay in the Hilton Hotel downtown, thanked her for her time, and headed to his car.

Detective Howard was in his office when Anders returned, so he thought he would tell him what he found.

"Each of the bodies from the explosion had a metal tag the coroner used to identify those who were killed. That's why they were able to be certain even about partial remains. As for Mr. Getner, he was viewed as management, so he wore no tag. No one could say for certain whether his remains were found in the carnage after the explosion. The fire chief told me he believed if Getner was on the man trip, then he was most certainly killed, but he didn't know whether he was on the trip. The woman at the mining company office who assembled their list said Getner was management, so he would not have been on the trip going down into the mine. She clearly didn't know but had no record of his death. Outside the place, a couple of miners said he was not liked by the men and had a "boyfriend" someplace, so there's that. Mrs. Getner attacked me and stuck her tongue halfway down my throat. I pushed her away and tried to calm her down. She said maybe I just liked men more than women, just like her husband. But she had been drinking, so I don't know what to say about her. You'll have lots of questions for her when she gets into the interview."

"You pushed her away?" the detective asked, "after she stuck her tongue down your throat? What's wrong with you?"

"Not interested in her, I guess," Anders said. He did not tell Howard how intense his feelings had become for Valery. Best to keep all that quiet.

"Well, you are a better man than me," Howard said. "She's a good-looking woman, even if she is a souse, and it would be hard for me to pull away from that."

Anders said something about differences and let it drop. Then he went looking for Finn or Valery.

He told the whole story once again to Valery and then sat back in his chair and waited to hear what she had to say.

"People who drink too much often do things that even they don't understand, so I wouldn't read too much into it. I don't think you are particularly vulnerable, and you know I have feelings for you. But that's personal, you know? You're a pleasant-looking man, and you seem very kind, and a lot of women respond to that, even when they are not drinking. We can talk about it at some point but not here in the office."

"Pretty clear at this point we have more work to do on Mr. Getner before we interview her. Let's see what Howard thinks. He has been closest to the situation out west, so he might have some ideas."

They walked down the hallway to the detective's office and found Howard reading a book about mining, the same one she was using to teach Anders.

"Hey, Howard. What do you think we should do next in the attempt to locate Emil Getner? Do you think we would have a chance with Angel Cordner in Johnstown? You seemed to think it would be hard to approach him where he drinks or hangs out. What if we just go to his apartment and see if we can find him?"

"Sure," Howard said, "But who? I'm afraid I would scare him, and I don't know whether Anders is ready yet to ask the kinds of questions we need to get answers to. We don't know a lot about homosexuals in Johnstown. But that's the community we have to start searching in. Valery suggested she might be ideal to approach Cordner, not threatening or friendly, and the question of sex would be off the table, of course."

"Okay," Howard said. "Let's make a plan and take it to Finn."

They agreed they would drive to Johnstown, set up in a local motel, and use it as a base in the search for Getner. It would also be where Valery would set up her meeting with Cordner, should she find him.

"Do we need a subpoena?" she asked Howard.

"No," he said, "We're not searching his place; we are just going to ask some questions. If we find we need to search, we can get a subpoena approved in Ebensburg at the County Prosecutors' office."

They said it as directly as they could. They believed Angel Cordner was central to finding Emil Getner, who was central to the explosion at Delaware and Hudson's Baltimore shaft, with its attendant deaths and mayhem.

Finn asked how long it would take.

"We don't know. We don't know that community and how it functions, who it supports, you know, the questions you would ask in an investigation. We won't actually be using Valery undercover, but she will play that kind of a role, not saying much at all about what we are after other than finding Getner. We don't think there are a lot of risks attached to this investigation. Detective Morgan will be on hand with his firearm if he is needed."

"Okay," Finn said.

Remember, the objective here is not Johnstown homosexuals. They can do what they want. It's black powder theft and marketing. Keep that in front of your heads. Be careful, and most of all, please don't kill anyone.

They all chuckled at that, but they also knew that Finn wasn't kidding. He hated putting his mine inspectors in danger as it was, and adding these kinds of investigations only made it riskier.

"We'll be careful," Valery said.

She walked out and was joined by Anders, an alliance everyone in the room noted.

The three would leave for Johnstown first thing in the morning. It was a six-hour drive, even speeding in an unmarked trooper's car. They agreed to meet at 7 a.m. for breakfast near the office, pick up the car, and hit the road by 8:30.

Valery quietly asked Anders if he wanted to get dinner, and he readily agreed. He enjoyed her company and admired her skills as an investigator. The fact that she was so pleasant to look at didn't hurt, either.

They went to a steak house just outside of town, a place with a reputation for good, juicy meat, strong drinks, and privacy in booths that had high backs. Valery walked in first and asked for a table for two. The greeter sat them near a fireplace at the end of the dining room and gave them menus big enough to hide behind. They couldn't have asked for a more private spot. It was dim, so no one would see them. Valery wasn't sure why she wanted to be so private about Anders. It would become apparent to everyone before long that they had become a couple. Still, she didn't want to wave the flag. She was always eager to control information about herself, basically because she only wanted people to know what she wanted people to know about her.

Anders remained oblivious to all of this, delighting in the company and developing stronger and stronger feelings for Valery. He didn't know whether that was appropriate, but he didn't know what to do about it either. "The heart wants what the heart wants," he told himself.

The dinner ended without interruption, and Valery and Anders went their separate ways.

Valery went to her mother's house in New Cumberland to talk with her sisters about Anders. They rarely shared discussions about boyfriends, but they were both eager to hear about this new man in Valery's life. She didn't reveal much, only that he was Transylvanian, not a vampire, very smart and quite engaging and handsome. The conversation, of course, settled on the vampire aspect of the relationship. They had all seen the movie by this time.

"So, what does he say about the vampires?" one of her sisters asked. "He says they don't exist, not today and not anywhere in the history of Romania. It's just one of those old tales that somehow got out of control, then became a book and then a movie, and there you are! Suddenly, a nation full of vampires."

They all laughed at that, and then Valery went off to her room to go to bed to think about Johnstown.

No one who wasn't a part of it had any idea about the size of the homosexual community in that determinedly Catholic and German town.

"Lots to do," she thought.

Valery, Howard, and Anders met at 6:45 the next morning at a downtown diner famous for its omelets. Because they were so close to moving into a case, no one spent much time eating. Instead, they talked on and on about how to break into the homosexual community in Johnstown to find out about Angel Cordner. They also still were not convinced Getner had been killed in the Baltimore Shaft explosion, so they hoped his visit could put an end to that part of the mystery. They agreed they were not going to Johnstown to investigate homosexuality. But they did have to find Getner and his boyfriend, and the community was one way to do it.

It was a tedious drive from Harrisburg to Johnstown, although the parts of it that cut through the Allegheny Mountains were lovely. It was exactly the time of year to make this drive, spring had passed, and the trees were green and loaded with chirping birds. Along the highway, hawks sat on farm fences and searched for prey. The corn was waist-high. It all looked lush and prosperous; hard to tell the nation was struggling through depression.

They entered Johnstown on a highway called "the easy grade," which was not actually a grade but a huge, long hill that worked its way down the side of a mountain and carried cars into a city that had been built at the confluence of a collection of rivers and streams. Johnstown flooded frequently and sometimes disastrously. The city's many industries needed the water, but it was a devil's bargain whenever the skies opened up and sent floods cascading down into the valley.

Valery, sitting in the back seat with Anders, was wondering where she would find the door that would lead her into the homosexual community in Johnstown. She knew how that worked in Harrisburg, which had evolved an interesting collection of sexual speakeasies for lonely men far from home and the withering gazes of their wives and friends. Maybe Johnstown had the same kind of thing. They stopped downtown for coffee, which is where she got the idea of asking a waiter for advice on where she could find a homosexual hideout. "For women?" he asked.

"I wouldn't know at all. For men, there are some bars just off the end of the Easy Grade where you might find that kind of thing. If I were you, I would look into a place called "San Souci" and talk to any of the men there.

"I want to go to this Sans Souci Bar with one of you. But we can't make it look like we're a couple. You have to pretend you are interested in finding men for sex. That's why I don't want to go alone. It just wouldn't work for me. Can you do that?"

Anders and Howard both agreed that the argument made sense. But Anders was uncertain about how to handle the role. Howard was not. They planned an evening at the bar. Valery would pretend to be drunk so the men could try to dump her and take her up with their own kind. It would take some imagination and acting, but they thought they could handle it.

Chapter 15: "Sans Souci"

It was a very quiet, very out-of-the-way bar that might hold 40 people if it was packed, clean, and tastefully decorated. There were fake trees at one end with coconuts and fake pineapples hanging from them. Valery gave them a glance and concluded the people who decorated the place knew nothing about coconuts or pineapples but did not let that deter them. She ordered a dry martini to get her in the right mood. Anders asked for a beer and Howard for a whiskey on ice. They knew they were creating a scene and immediately drew some attention.

A man in a blue jacket and white pants walked over to them at the bar. He said he had not seen them at Sans Souci before. He said he hoped they would enjoy themselves and then ordered a Manhattan and asked whether he could sit with them.

"Sure," Howard said. "I'm John Howard, and this is my friend Valery and her friend Anders." The men stared at the bar as though their eyes were welded to it. Clearly uncomfortable, which worked well for their purposes.

"Just enjoy yourselves," the man, who said his name was Clay, said. "Make sure of that. It's a safe place. We always have plenty of guests on these kinds of evenings. Relax."

Perhaps emboldened by her drink, Valery decided she would step in to ask a question because her bar mates were clearly uncomfortable and had no idea what to say.

"I have a friend who comes here, I think, named Angel Cordner. Do you know him?"

"Plenty of Angels come in here, sweetheart, but I'm not familiar with him. I can ask around if that would help."

"I would appreciate that, Clay. Let me buy you a drink."

He ordered a chablis and then sat quietly at the bar while it was served up. Valery broke one of her own rules and told Clay where she was staying, what room, and the phone number, and said, "If you see Angel here at all, please, please call me, okay?"

"Most certainly," he said. "But I don't know that he will want to get in touch with a woman, however beautiful if you know what I mean."

"I do know," Valery said. "But this is about business, not at all a boy-girl thing, you know?"

"Okay," Clay said.

Then she moved down the bar toward Anders and Howard and told them what she did. "Kind of a trap." Clay is dying to know what's up, and I am certain if Angel comes in here, Clay will spot him in a second and relay the message. So let's drink and not stick out too much!"

Which is exactly what they did.

The bartender was so friendly he and Howard got involved in a long conversation about the Pittsburgh Pirates and the fortunes of the National League, sports talk Anders could neither understand nor take much of a part in. Valery just sat and looked increasingly hammered as the evening moved on. They left early, at 10 p.m., and headed back to their hotel.

They were in Valery's room gabbing when the phone rang. It was Clay. Angel Cordner was with him. She said she would be right back to Sans Souci as soon as she put her face on. "Wasted makeup in a place like this," Clay said to her. "I know, but I do it for myself."

In 40 minutes, she and Howard, and Anders were back at Sans Souci, which by 11 p.m. was hopping. There was a quartet doing a great imitation of New Orleans jazz; the bar was lined by young, well-dressed men drinking and talking. A few couples were even dancing.

Anders was uncomfortable about that.

211

Howard was not.

"They aren't bad," he said. "Not bad at all."

The band shifted into an upbeat blues piece, and Howard asked Anders if he wanted to dance. "You know, for the image," he said.

Anders said he had no idea how to dance. So, Howard asked Valery how she felt about it.

"I love dancing," she said.

"If they could pick up the tempo a bit, maybe we could do a little jitterbug.

"Grand," said Howard. He walked over to the band and asked the trumpet player if they could handle a little up-tempo, maybe something you could jitterbug to.

"You betcha," said the Trumpeter.

He chatted for an instant with the drummer and clarinet player, leaned back, and blasted his way into a very well-rehearsed version of "Gut Bucket Blues" and then segued, flawlessly, into "Muskrat Ramble."

It wasn't like Louis Armstrong had moved to Johnstown, but it was a very well-done imitation. They pushed the tempo a little to speed things up.

"Let's go, Valery," Howard said.

What played out left Anders speechless and the rest of the bar in silent admiration. Howard was a fantastic dancer, strong and right on the beat. People hardly even noticed his revolver flopping around as he danced. Valery rode him like a racehorse and even let him toss her, first off his hip and then between his legs. She moved her butt like a pro, fluid and completely comfortable. The harder they danced, the more solid the band played. They were all leaning deeply into it by the time the tune ended. Howard took Valery's right hand, turned to the assembled men watching, and they both bowed deeply from the waist. There was a strong, sincere applause from the watchers. Even the band clapped. It lasted a good 20 seconds or so.

"Howard, where the hell did you learn to dance like that?" Valery whispered to him.

"Where all the good Catholic boys learned to dance from my three sisters. What about you?

"Same thing from my sisters. That was great fun. Thank you!"

Beaming and laughing, they went to their table and sat down for more drinks.

"Howard, that's the smartest thing I have ever seen a cop do in my whole life, and I've seen some cops," Valery said. Anders just stared at her and at Howard, too.

"That was just wonderful," he said.

"Howard, you move like a movie dancer. And Valery, so graceful!"

"Everyone wants to feel comfortable in here," Howard said. "Remember, many of these men are hiding. Anything you can do to take their minds off of that will warm up the room."

Men started gravitating to their table, offering drinks and sitting to talk. Most of them were drawn to Detective Morgan, now a little sweaty in his fantastic blue suit. Two men sat to talk to Anders, who said he was sorry he could not dance and always wanted to.

"We could teach you," they said in unison.

"Well, maybe," Anders said.

Valery was approached by a tall man in a well-fitted suit who reached out his hand,

"Angel Cordner. And may I say you are a fantastic dancer?" Cordner said.

"Thank you. It's a comfortable place for that," she said.

Valery found herself trying to calm her breathing and thinking very carefully through the next thing she would say to Cordner. She took a sip from her martini and then took a cigarette from her purse, lit it, and leaned forward.

"Angel, I need you to tell me about Emil Getner. Do you know him? Do you know where he is?"

"Are you cops?" he asked.

"Well, actually, no," Valery said.

"We're Mining Department investigators, and we're working on a case related to Mr. Getner. We need to find him.

"Okay, this stays at this table," Angel said.

"Valery said "yes" with her eyes but reminded herself she never actually said "yes" in case that became an issue later.

"I haven't seen him in weeks or heard from him, not even a phone call. That bastard. We have some business together, and I need to talk to him too. If you find him, will you tell him Angel is looking for him?"

"Sure," she said.

"But I thought you two were together."

"How do you mean together?" Angel asked.

"Stop fucking with me! You know what I mean," Valery said, raising her eyebrows and putting an edge in her tone.

"No, we haven't been lovers in quite a while now, but we were in the beginning. I'm beginning to think he was just using me. That's how it feels now, anyhow."

"Using you for what?"

"Selling stuff to make money."

"What kind of stuff?" Valery asked.

"Un…uh," Angel said.

"I'm not going to talk about that. It could get me killed."

"Was that about the powder," Valery asked. At that point, Angel seemed to freeze in his chair.

"You know about that?"

"Sure do," she said.

"My friends and I have been following that powder ever since it started disappearing from the Delaware and Hudson Mining Co. stores months ago, she lied. That's where Emil worked, you know?"

"Yes, I do know."

"So where is he? Do you have any way of contacting him?"

"He was a very private man. We had some good times, even right here, but after a while, he became very shy about being queer, so shy he would disappear for weeks at a time. Then he would come sailing back in with money and humor and lots of interest. Then he would disappear again. I assume he went to Pittsburgh.

"Why Pittsburgh?"

"Because it's the only safe place for people like us," he gestured around the bar, "to go. There's nowhere else in Johnstown, and the further you get from town, the more dangerous the place becomes. You know about Cambria County and the Klan, don't you? Not much time for Queers in the Klan. So, Pittsburgh, that would be my guess. Look for a bar there called "Cave of the Fallen Angel" and ask there. That's where we would go when I visited him in Pittsburgh."

"Did he have an apartment, a place to stay there?" Valery asked.

"Never got there," said Cordner.

"Like I said, he was a very private man and working in what had to be a very private business. So, I don't know."

Valery wrote "Cv Fn Angls" on a matchbook and put it in her purse.

As soon as Clay left, Howard and Anders were back at the table, asking Valery what she had learned. "I learned that these poor men are always half frightened to death. I also learned we need to take a trip to Pittsburgh. I'll talk to Finn in the morning. Howard, want to dance again?"

"You bet," Howard said.

They closed the place down three hours later, sweaty and half drunk; they walked to the car and tried to decide who was safest to drive back up the Easy Grade to the motel they were using. Anders won that contest, fortunately.

"You know," Valery said in the car on the way back to the motel, "I haven't met nicer people in all my bar hopping back in Harrisburg. They also seem to be pretty honest about their lives and how they have to live them. I would hate that, being so secretive about everything. But they treated each other well and treated us well, too, so what's not to like?"

"People don't get to choose who they are; they only get to adjust to the realities of it," Howard said.

"Not everyone can handle that, and some of those people we were just drinking with are living terrible lives. But some of the people we were drinking with in Harrisburg live terrible lives, too. It's not about what kind of sex they are, what they do with it. They are just terrible people. But most of them are not. I am certain of that."

For Anders, that was about all the philosophy he could stand in one evening. He had no problem with homosexuals when he went into Sans Souci, and he has no problems with them now. He just wished he could dance better.

Back at the motel, they agreed to meet at 8:30 a.m. and talk about what to tell Finn when they called him.

In Harrisburg, Finn had spent the day juggling federal agents who were looking for Anders and Valery to get a report on what they had found. He wanted them back in town as soon as possible. He was eager to unload as much of the Delaware and Hudson mess on the feds as he could. It was a dirty business that stretched well beyond mining and safety. That's what he wanted his people to pay attention to.

The search for Emil Getner would have to wait.

***

Valery was the first person to wake up after the night at the Sans Souci, and she had a terrible headache as punishment for it. She took two aspirin and walked early to the restaurant to get a lot of black coffee, which always solved her morning after problems. She was surprised to see Detective Howard and Anders already in the dining room. They were eating eggs and toast and drinking coffee, and laughing hard at something Howard had said.

"What did I miss?" Valery asked.

"Howard was just saying the state police had fantastic dance courses at the academy if you didn't mind dancing with other men."

"That, of course, just isn't true. But it's a funny thought, a couple of hundred troopers jitterbugging in a homosexual bar. I'm going to have to keep that image in my head for a while."

"Well, my head is throbbing, and I have to call Finn in about 45 minutes, so what do we think I should say?"

"Anders and I were just talking about that. It might be very good for us to crash the homosexual scene in Pittsburgh, but then again, we're basically cops, so we have to get on with what we have to get on with."

"Exactly," said Valery. "We really need to find Emil Getner quickly and find out where he is selling that powder."

"Or," Howard said, "We could let that all up to the feds. What we need to know is what role, if any did, Getner play in the explosion at Baltimore Shaft? As I understand it, that's the Mining Department's interest in this case. But there's so much stuff here that pulls us in other directions. It's easy to lose sight of that. I think we need to hear what Finn has to say."

"Okay," Valery said.

"I'll call as soon as we are finished eating. I am NOT eating pancakes this morning. I just want a bunch of scrambled eggs and dry black toast. I need to calm my insides down. Martinis are not my best friend.

"But you looked really *good* last night," Anders said. "Like dancing was your real business."

"Thanks, pal, but this is my business… And Yours, too!"

That ended the conversation about dancing. She ordered her eggs, asked the waitress to keep pouring black coffee, and gathered her thoughts for her call to Finn.

She was very disappointed that they still had not found Emil Getner, thinking about where he might be. At that point, Angel Cordner and Emil Getner walked up to the table.

"I'm Emil," Getner said, extending his hand.

"How can I help you? I understand you are all looking for me."

"I should fucking arrest you right now," Howard said, with more of an edge in his voice than Valery and Anders had ever heard. He got a steely look from Valery, and so he backed off a bit.

"We need to go somewhere and have a talk."

The restaurant had an anteroom with chairs and a table. Valery led Angel Cordner and Emil Getner to the room. Howard stood by the door.

218

"Mr. Getner, how long had you been stealing black powder from Delaware and Hudson Coal, and exactly where were you selling it."

"Now, wait a minute! That was Lucille's business," Getner said. "I would take it from the company supplies and give it to her. What she did with it, I just don't know. I did that for the past six years or so."

"Were you driving it out west to deliver it? How did it get from Wilkes-Barre to Johnstown? There are a lot of important questions here. And why did you leave Baltimore Shaft the morning of the explosion? You had to know we would be looking for you."

"I was scared, and I didn't want to be blamed for the explosion. I knew it would only be a matter of time before the investigators learned about my business and about the opened barrels on the mantrip. That was my fault. I should not have done it. I am sorry."

"Mr. Getner, our investigators found more than 600 pounds of black powder in your garage, all in barrels and ready to ship. Are you still saying you knew nothing about that?"

"Well....I....I...Lucille ran that whole business. She had the contacts, and she moved the powder. I just got it for her."

"Why would you do that?'

"She paid me and paid me well. I was out of her life by that time and out here when I could be with Angel but still running my businesses, and she became an important part of the black powder sales, to the point at which I simply delivered the product, and she handled all the arrangements. And by that, I mean ALL the arrangements. She would move the product once or twice a month. A refrigerator truck would come by and pick it up. It belonged to some food chain in Pittsburgh. She thought that would be the safest way to move it."

"What food chain?" Valery asked.

"You have to ask Lucille. I just don't know. I stayed away from that part of it."

At that point, Howard spoke up, putting his hand on Getner's on the table near Valery's. Anders observed it from a fourth chair. "Emil Getner, I am arresting you for theft of black powder from Delaware and Hudson, and I am charging you with the sale of that powder without a license. And more charges will be coming later."

He took the handcuffs off his belt and snapped them on Getner's wrists. It all happened in one swift motion, like a prisoner's waltz.

Anders and Valery were impressed.

"If you have a lawyer, you best call him now."

Getner asked whether he could use a house phone. Howard located one and brought it to the table. He dialed just one number and said, "I have been arrested. I am in Johnstown. I need your help."

Then he provided an address and put the phone back on the receiver. "He is coming straight away," Getner said.

Howard then used the phone to call Johnstown Police to see whether they had a free cell for Getner. He explained what had happened, why Getner was charged, and where they were.

"Wow," the desk sergeant said. "You have had a busy morning. Sure, we can take him."

"Okay, we'll bring him over in a couple of hours. His lawyer is coming here to talk with us. We'll touch base with the DA and see what he wants to do," Howard said.

Howard hung up, and Valery immediately picked up the phone to make a call to Finn.

It took 20 minutes for her to tell Finn all about what had happened, how Howard had arrested Getner at the perfect point in the interview, how everyone was in good shape and how they wanted to head back to Harrisburg as soon as they could.

"We know what happened and how," she said. "We will be having a very interesting interview with Lucille Getner next week. I can't wait to talk to her about all this stuff. Emil says she was behind it all."

"Sure," Finn said.

"But remember, most of the criminal stuff we will be handing over to the feds, so keep good notes and get ready to talk all about it."

"Okay,, Mr. Finn," she said.

Valery reported back to Howard and Anders and said they should head back to Harrisburg to prepare for meeting the federal authorities about the case.

"That's going to be very interesting," Howard said. "The Bureau of Investigation is a new thing in the federal Justice Department, and I don't know how prepared they are to pick up our investigation. But Finn clearly wants to get us out of stuff the feds should be doing, so we'll see how that happens."

"It's all so complicated," Anders said.

"We have Constitutional protections here, Anders," Valery said.

"People's rights don't disappear simply because we have arrested them. The assumption here is just the opposite...."

It was a timely moment for attorney Amos Davis to walk into the little room. He was a florid-faced man with thinning black hair that was slicked straight back. His eyes were as brown as his suit. He smiled freely and had a solid handshake. Getner said hello, and Davis returned the greeting.

"What's the charges?" Davis asked.

"I'm arresting him for stealing black powder from the Delaware and Hudson Mining Company and selling it without a license to people we don't yet know out here," Howard said. "We found 600 pounds of the powder in his garage at home. He said it was all his wife's fault, and we're still investigating on that part."

"Sounds federal to me," Davis said.

"Have you contacted the U.S. Attorney in Pittsburgh?"

Howard paused for a second and said he and the team would be meeting with federal agents and prosecutors in Harrisburg next week.

"That's not going to do my man any good at all," the lawyer said.

"We could turn him over to the feds today, and you can work with them, or you can work with us now. Either way, we don't want him skipping off."

The attorney said he would be asking for bail, and Howard said he would be opposing that because it took so long for them to find Getner. Still, he noted, Getner offered no resistance and gave himself up without argument. So there was that.

But Howard was still concerned about flight.

"Can you wait a couple of hours so I can get a judge to give me a bail setting?" Davis asked.

Howard looked to Valery and Anders, who both said "sure" on that question.

"Where can we get a good lunch?" Howard asked.

"Cambria Diner right down the street. Looks like an old railroad dining car. You can't miss it. I'll catch up with you there as soon as I can corner a judge on bail."

Attorney Davis was right about the lunch. Good corned beef sandwiches on rye bread with German mustard, beer, and coffee, and pound cake for dessert. Howard was ready for a nap when Davis strolled into the restaurant and sat down with them in the booth.

"Judge said $2,500 should hold him, and he needed only 10 percent of that to spring him. So even as we speak, Emil Getner is a free man facing charges. I don't think he will flee."

"Better not," Howard said.

It was a long drive back to Harrisburg, but Howard drove like there were no police to catch him, confident his detective's badge could deter anyone who tried.

Valery wondered where all this was actually going to lead. Getner and Lucille, Angel, Clay, they were all wrapped up in it somehow, but it was going to take more than a mining inspector to figure that one out. She was eager to talk to Finn about his view of the case, from the explosion onward, to see if he had ever seen anything like it.

By the time they got back to Harrisburg, it was late. Finn had gone home, and there was nothing to do but head down to see if Nick had any Chili left. Anders, Howard, and Valery made an interesting trio in the dank old bar. Still, in his new suit, Howard looked like a million dollars. Valery was always lovely, even when she was worn down, and Anders looked like a character from film noir, short, dark, and mysterious.

The chili was just as good at 11 p.m. at Nickie's Last Stop as it was at midday. Everyone wondered how Nick did that. He would never say, other than to note it was "constantly and perpetually revived."

On the walk to the car, Valery wanted a kiss, but not in front of Howard. Anders needed a kiss, too, but he had no idea what to do about that. With Howard striding ahead, Valery grabbed Anders by his tie and pulled him into a doorway, and planted her lips on his.

It was a great kiss, Anders thought.

"We need to be talking about this soon," she said.

"Yes," Anders replied.

Everyone went home, and no one slept. It was going to be a busy day.

Edward Finn was eager to gather his troops back in from the field and see what they had to say, but not so eager that he would avoid the coffee stand with its fresh donuts and premier java. Barry and Emma seemed to be faring well, with his coughing all but gone for the moment and her worries suspended, at least for a little while.

"So Finn, where's the troops today?" Barry asked as he gave Finn a hot cup of coffee and a cake donut."

"They are back in today, and I hope their adventure is over for a while. I've got lots of people in the field, but I admit, I like these three an awful lot. And, of course, I need Valery's help almost every day because she types like lightning and never makes mistakes at anything. It's going to be a big day for them. I'll pay you now for their coffee and donuts when they arrive. Tell them it was a gift from an admiring stranger."

They all laughed, and Finn went on his way. It was 8:30 a.m., and the feds would be dropping in at about 11:30 to talk with Valery, Anders, and Howard. Finn wanted to be ready for that. Just in case, he called Dorrance to see if he had any ideas on how to handle it.

"Well," the governor's aide said, "You could call The General and ask, but that would take two days, and you wouldn't know what he meant at the end of it. I think you should just ride on your instincts and do what seems right. Remember, they are coming to you for help, so they will owe you. Did Howard like his badge?"

"Damn," Finn thought.

"It always IS a transaction with him."

"Tickled with it. Wears it on his belt."

He sipped his coffee and ate his donut, and perused the local paper for crime news. He didn't know why because he lived across

224

the river, but he was always interested in who was doing what to whom in the city. There was one murder connected to a traveling craps game, one big burglary in one of the mansions along the river, and two thefts of fancy cars owned by a local businessman.

"About par," Finn thought.

The murder was apparently part of a love triangle that blew up when one of the men found out the woman was two-timing both of them. He pulled a pistol, she told the police and shot the other man square in the forehead. It left only a little red dot and killed him instantly. Finn checked the names and was relieved he neither employed nor knew any of them.

So, it was just another murder.

"Thank God for that kind of shit doesn't play out in coal mines."

He was lost in pondering that thought when Valery and Howard walked in with a bright good morning and a thanks for the coffee and donuts. Anders was going to be a little late because he was picking up a new suit, a new dark suit with a white shirt and blue tie.

Howard told him the only way to buy a suit was to think of it as something he would be buried in. It had to fit so well that it would seem like he was born to wear it. It would, after all, spend eternity with him.

Anders was beginning to like Howard a lot, not only as a colleague but as a guy, too. He was cool-headed at all times, endlessly funny, and now was defined by the memory of his jitterbug dance with Valery at Sans Souci in Johnstown, so fine no one would ever believe it who had not seen it. He was a rare combination of a great guy and a great cop.

He also admired the firmness he displayed in arresting Emil Getner, just a hand over his hand and a few very clear words. Not a hint of force or fight in it. It was all about Howard's authority as a detective, and Anders appreciated that because he had seen it work so well back in Romania. There's nothing quite like respect for authority, he thought, particularly when authority was on the right side.

No one was watching Lucille Getner and her husband, Emil, was out of jail in Johnstown on bond. They had a lot of ground to cover in the interview with her.

Finn told Anders to call Lucille and make sure she would be available in Harrisburg the next day. He told Anders to offer a ride if she needed it. That was unusual, but Finn was particularly interested in hearing from Lucille and didn't want logistics to get in the way of her coming to testify.

The interview would be divided into three parts. The first would cover what she could say about Emil's role. The second would be about her role. The third would be about what she could tell them about the operation in western Pennsylvania.

It was decided that Valery would be the first questioner about Emil, Howard would question Lucille about her role, and Anders and Finn would ask questions about the western operation and how it functioned.

"We're all going to have to be flexible with this," Finn said. "At any point, the focus could shift, so keep your eyes on her and what she is saying."

Anders called Lucille from his office. She answered right away, and after she said hello, he said she should plan to be in Harrisburg the next morning for interviews that would begin at about 10:30 a.m.

"Can you make it by that time?"

"I don't know," she said.

"Do you want me to come to pick you up?"

"Sure. You can come tonight. Okay?

"Let me see. Plan to be ready to leave at about 730 a.m., okay?"

"Sure," she said.

Anders immediately called Valery.

"I have to go collect Lucille in the morning. Can you ride up there with me tonight? I don't want to be near that woman alone. We can stay in Wilkes-Barre and just go over to Avoca first thing in the morning.

"Okay," Valery said. "When do you want to leave."

"After work. I'll call the Penn Harris and get us rooms."

"She's going to think you are my boyfriend," Valery said.

"Fine by me," Anders said and meant every word of it.

Anders met Valery at her office and picked up the state car. He drove her home to New Cumberland so she could get some clothes, then they headed to Avoca, planning to pick up Lucille first thing the next morning and return her to Harrisburg for the first day of her questioning. It was a long drive up through the mountains, but the weather was clear, the car was fast, and Anders, relatively new to America, drove like a champion. He liked Fords. He liked where he was sitting.

The hotel was beginning to view The Mining Department as a regular customer, so it set up two big rooms next to one another and offered a complimentary dinner, which Anders eagerly accepted. They headed for the dining room just after they checked in.

In his new meat and potatoes mode, Anders got a small steak and baked potato and a side order of apple sauce. Valery had a salad and white wine. The dinner was calm, the room was almost empty, and it was a good time to talk about Lucille Getner.

"We have to be on the watch for surprises," Valery said.

227

"The woman is smart, and I think she knows she is in trouble, so we have to give her room to move so we can hear what she has to say."

All of that made sense to Anders, but he had no idea how to accomplish it. Valery, without lecturing him, said he could back off and watch because she knew how to draw people out. Anders concluded that would be a most interesting thing to witness, two very smart women in a dance that was all about criminal behavior.

They knew that Lucille was fully aware of her husband's connections in Western Pennsylvania, so their questioning would be aimed at finding out how much of that was hers and how much of that was his.

"Don't be surprised if she tries to shift it all over to him," Valery said. "We've already seen Getner try to shift it all over to her. If the answer is someplace in the middle, then we're looking at a team in a criminal conspiracy. I don't know how that fits with the explosion, but somehow, I am certain that it does. We need to pick away at her to find out what she knows."

"Agreed."

They got into the elevator to head to the third floor for their rooms. Valery leaned over and kissed Anders on the cheek, and said, "We have to behave now. It's business time."

The next challenge, he knew, would be Lucille and what she could tell them about black powder, communists in labor unions, the explosion at Baltimore shaft, and exactly what Emil Getner was up to.

They called her from the hotel. She answered on the second ring and told them she would be ready at 7 a.m. for the trip to Harrisburg. "What are you doing tonight? I could make dinner," she said.

"I think Deputy Valery and I will eat here. We will be getting up early, after all."

"Valery is there, too?"

"You are important to us," Anders said. "We wanted some authority to be present for the trip. After all, she runs the agency under Finn."

"Okay. See you in the morning," she said.

Chapter 16: The Love Story

He was relieved when the call ended. He met Valery in the hotel bar, where they had a very light dinner and some wine for her and beer for him. Then they decided to take a walk on the river.

She told him all about it.

In the air above them, there were swallows at first, then bats chasing insects. They sat on one of the benches to talk.

"The scientists say those bats eat 100 times their weight in insects every year," she said. "It's buggy here now, but I can't imagine what it would be like without them."

They talked about the Romanian culture and where vampires fit. Anders said it was all modern mythology, that there would be no benefits to drinking someone's blood, vampire or not.

"Human gravy," Valery said with a chuckle.

"But for what meat? Leg of man, man burgers…."

They played with the theme for ten full minutes before Anders, feeling bold with her sitting next to him, told Valery she was exactly the kind of woman he might want to marry.

"That's such a sweet thought," Valery said.

"But I don't want to talk about marriage until I have moved well into my career. "

"So you are saying 'no' to me before I have even asked?"

"I know it might feel that way, but I am not. I'm just telling you I have a loose plan for the future. That doesn't mean I can't be married eventually. It also doesn't mean we couldn't be a couple, you know? I really enjoy your company. You are smart and well educated and thoughtful, not bad looking, if a little short, but a true gentleman in a world where I can think of just a few others, one being my departed father, the other being Finn."

"Just don't run off with Detective Howard," Anders joked. Personally, he was upset at the description "short." Back in the mines, he said, everyone thought that was ideal. He didn't have to squat a lot. Out in the fresh air, it meant he was looking at a lot of shoulders when he talked to people.

"There's only one solution for that. You are going to have to learn how to dance. My sisters and I can teach you. After that, Anders., even short, you will be just perfect! Don't get fat. Besides, Howard already has a girlfriend."

It was a night for staring at the ceiling and wondering what was going to happen.

Not about the case.

That they could work out. About themselves.

Valery knew from their first moments together that Anders would be a fine partner, full of thought and experience, and humor. What else could there be in the governor's office for her? Some kind of a liaison person? Maybe an overseer or inspector general type of executive? She didn't want to get involved in the dinginess of re-election politics. The bureaucratic side of it was soul-sucking and crushing at the same time. What a mess to get lost in!

As for Anders, he was one of the sweetest men she had ever met. Did she love him? She didn't know. She didn't want to lose him, probably ever, but she didn't want him to be like an anchor around her neck.

"That one I am going to have to manage."

It was stormy the next morning when Anders and Valery headed off to pick up Lucille for the trip to Harrisburg. That should take no more than a couple of hours so they could get her into her hotel and prep for her testimony on the next morning, Wednesday. There was flooding near the road to Avoca, and some trees were down after a storm moved through. They had to pick their way down the road that led to the Getner house, watching all the time for downed power lines and loose limbs. They got there at 8:10 a.m. and found Mrs. Getner drinking coffee in her kitchen. She invited them in, but they said it would be better to get on the road and head down the mountain into Harrisburg. They left at 8:45, with Mrs. Getner carrying her handbag and a suitcase.

In the house, before they left, Valery told Lucille she would be searched at the capitol and that if she was carrying any kind of a weapon, it would be best to leave it locked up at home. She took a small black automatic from her purse and, after arguing she should keep it, was convinced to leave it at home. It was a good pistol, a Browning, and Valery told her that it would probably be stolen by the capitol police if they took it from her before she testified. It was not the same pistol Valery had found in her purse earlier. So she had at least two guns.

"They would do that?"

"Yes, they would," Valery answered, knowing full well it was not true. But it worked, which was more important. They got into the car and headed for the capitol.

Lucille wanted to know what kind of questions she would be asked so she could prepare.

"If you just answer them truthfully, you won't need to prepare anything. You know what we want to talk to you about, so don't worry. You'll handle it well, I am certain."

That seemed to quiet Lucille for a while.

"Did you interview my husband yet," she asked.

"No," Valery lied once again.

When they arrived at the Commonwealth Court office, Finn was already waiting, with Morgan at his side and a thick pile of folders on the table. The woman who would transcribe the interview

232

was in place, along with the Commonwealth Attorney required for all such legal proceedings.

Lucille Getner sat on one side of the table beside her attorney, and Finn, Howard, Anders, and Valery on the other.

"Let the record show this is the transcript of a formal interview with Lucille Getner on this 23rd day of August in the year 1934 at the Commonwealth Court of Pennsylvania. Present are myself, Edward Finn, director of Coal Mine Safety and Practice in the Department of Commerce; Valery Miller, deputy director of mining and safety, Detective Howard of the Department of Mining and investigator Anders Apostle. We are discussing the explosion at the Baltimore Shaft of the Delaware and Hudson Coal Co. in Wilkes-Barre on June 19th at 7:30 a.m. and circumstances that were discovered in the investigation that followed that incident. We are questioning Lucille Getner, present under a grant of use immunity, about her knowledge of the actions of her husband, Emil Getner, a company supervisor for underground miners at Baltimore Shaft.

"Director Finn will be the first questioner, followed by Assistant Director Miller, then Detective Howard and investigator Apostle. The witness may consult with counsel before answering any questions."

"Q. How long had Mr. Getner worked at the Delaware and Hudson Co.?"

"A. About ten years, I guess. We never talked much about it, so I didn't pay much attention."

"Q. How much money did Mr. Getner make in his position?"

"A. I have no idea."

"Q. Were you aware that he had business beyond his mining company job at the shaft?"

"A. I'm not sure what you are referring to."

"Q. Were you aware he was selling various items to miners as they loaded on the man trip in the morning?"

"A. Oh, that. Yes, I knew he was doing that. He was always running around to food stores to stock up for his sales in the morning. He'd fill the back of the car."

"Q. How much money did he make at that business?"

"A. I have no idea; I guess whatever he needed to buy what he bought to take to the mines. It all came out to maybe $100 a week in profits. The miners were happy to get the food, I think, at any price."

"Q. Did he share the money with you?"

"A. (laughter) No! Never. He kept that for himself."

"Q. Mrs. Getner, I'm going to show you a statement from the Avoca Bank, an account under your names, over a few months. Do you see the deposits made very regularly in that account?"

"A. Yeah. Sure."

"Q. How much did they come out to, reading from the bank record?"

"A. Looks like about $4,000 to $5,000 a month, and on top of that, his salary was put in there, too, so maybe $7,000 a month."

"Q. So Mr. Getner's business at the mine was creating something like $5,000 in profits each month, right?"

"A. Yes."

"Q. That was a lot more than he made in salary, wasn't it?"

"A. Yes. You could not live on the salary they were paying him."

"Q. So he found other ways, right?"

"A. Yes, he did."

"Q. So where do you live?"

"A. In a company house in Avoca."

"Q. Nice house?"

"A. We think so. It has four bedrooms, two bathrooms, a modern kitchen, and a living room, and a garage."

"Q. Did you have a car?"

"A. Of course."

"Q. What kind of car?"

"A. It was a Ford. He loves Fords."

"Q. Where did you get that car?"

"A. It belonged to the company."

"Q. Did you both use that same car?"

"A. No. I had my own."

"Q. Your own car?"

"A. Yes."

"Q. Was that a Ford, too?"

"A. Yes."

"Q. Buy it in Avoca at the Ford dealership?"

"A. Yes."

"Q. How much did that cost?"

"A. I think it was $3,500. New."

"Q. Who paid for that one?"

"A. I did."

"Q. Did you have a job, too?"

"A. No."

"Q. Where did you get that money?"

"A. I'm not sure I understand your question."

"Q. That money. Where did it come from?"

"A. Avoca Bank."

"Q. I don't see it in the banking record. Are you sure it was from Avoca Bank?"

"A. Mr. Getner told me that's where it came from."

"Q. Did you pay cash for that car?"

"A. I did."

"Q. Mr. Getner gave you that cash?"

"A. He did."

"Q. And where did he get it?"

"A. From his business at the shaft."

"Q. Was he selling enough groceries at the shaft to make the $3,500 it cost for that car?"

"A. I guess."

"Q. What about his own car?"

"A. That was from the company. Because he had to be there early in the morning and late at night, the mining company let him use that car."

"Q. So it wasn't your car, was it?"

"A. I had my own."

"Q. What did you do with your car?"

"A. I went here and there with it, you know?"

"Q. No, I don't."

"Q. Where is here and there?"

"A. Just around."

"Q. Did you ever drive it to Johnstown?"

"A. Why are you asking that?"

"Q. Mrs. Getner, we will ask the questions. You just answer them, okay?"

"A. Sure."

"Q. So, Johnstown?"

"A. Yes, I went to Johnstown."

"Q. Who did you go to see in Johnstown?"

"A. Friends. Mr. Getner had friends in Johnstown."

"Q. At this point, I'm going to ask Miss Valery Miller, the deputy director, to continue the questioning."

"Q. Hello Lucille. I need to ask some questions about you and your husband and your contacts in Johnstown. Are you aware of a man named Angel Cordner?"

"A. Oh yes, Angel. Sweet man. He's from that bar; what's it called 'Sans Souci?'"

"Q. Correct, Sans Souci. What was your relationship with Angel Cordner?"

"A. I believe he was my husband's boyfriend."

"Q. Your husband's boyfriend?"

"A. Yes, he was queer, at least queer for a while."

"Q. And by queer, you mean..."

"A. He liked men more than he liked women. Mr. Getner and I had an understanding about this. He would keep that life away from me, and I would make no effort to pull him away from it. We didn't want each other anymore."

"Q. That must have been hard on you."

"A. Not at all. We had our arrangement."

"Q. So, did you split the money from his business at the shaft?"

"A. No. We worked it out so that I would be compensated in supplies for my own business."

"Q. And what was that business?"

"A. I'd rather not say."

"Q. Now, Mrs. Getner, you are testifying here under immunity. Nothing you say can be used against you. So what was that business? Did it involve explosives? Did it involve black powder your husband stole from his employer?"

"A. I don't know where you got that idea. I was just an independent businesswoman trying to get by. And I know you can't use my testimony against me, but there are other people, violent people, who could."

"Q. Lucille, we can put you in jail if you refuse to cooperate at this point. Tell us about that black powder. You had 600 pounds of it in your garage, remember? I certainly do. What was going to happen to that powder?"

"A. I had a market for every ounce of it. I had a network of buyers who were very interested in it and would pay top dollar for it. It cost me nothing, and I had to make a living from it. It was a good product for me."

"Q. Even if it was used for violent purposes? Was it still a good product for you if it was used in attacks on union offices, on people's cars, in pipe bombs, and on their homes? Was it still a good product for those purposes?"

238

"A. How it was used was not my business or my problem. I got it. I sold it. That's it."

"Q. On the morning of the explosion, Aug. 23, where was your husband? Did he go to the mine as usual? Did he take the provisions he would sell to the miners?"

"A. I don't know. I was not up early that morning. Usually, he would have left by 7 a.m., so I just don't know. He was gone by the time I got up."

"Q. Do you know whether he went to the mine or someplace else?"

"A. I would have no idea."

"Q. Did you deliver the powder you sold to people in Western Pennsylvania?"

"A. Sometimes."

"Q. How?"

"A. I made arrangements for them to come and pick it up. They would park a truck, it was a refrigerator truck, outside the garage, load the powder and leave. I would find a brown envelope in my mailbox with cash in it for the powder."

"Q. Generally, how much cash?"

"A. Several hundred dollars."

"Q. But not a thousand dollars or more?"

"A. No. Hundreds."

"Q. How often did they come to pick up powder?"

"A. Generally every two weeks or so. It was a regular trip for them."

"Q. Did the truck have a name on it?"

"A. It was a store name, an Italian grocery store. Bagnotti's or something like that."

"Q. What color was the truck?"

"A. It was dark green. The letters were yellow."

"Q. Did you ever talk to the drivers?"

"A. Never. I would leave the key to the garage in the mailbox. It would all happen pretty quickly."

"Q. Lucille, when we visited you at your house after the explosion, you had, what, 600 pounds of black powder in your garage in individual barrels. Who loaded them?"

"A. My husband did that at the mine, then brought them to the garage when he came home at night."

"Q. Did he make the arrangements for the pickups, or did you make the arrangements for the pickups?"

"A. Always him. I just collected the money."

"Q. So, if we asked you to name some of the people who were buying the powder, you could do that?"

"A. I didn't know them."

"Q. Are you sure?"

"A. Yes."

"Q. Could Angel Cordner name them?"

"A. He was Emil's contact out west. Maybe."

"Q. Was Angel buying powder from you?"

"A. He was Emil's contact. I barely knew him."

"Q. But was he buying powder?"

"A. Yes."

"Q. Was he working with you or for someone else?"

"A. You would have to ask Angel about that."

"Q. What is your relationship with Mr. Cordner?"

"A. I don't have one."

"Q. When was the last time you talked to him?"

"A. Months ago, in Johnstown."

"Q. And why were you in Johnstown?"

"A. Business."

"Q. What kind of business?"

"A. My business."

"Q. Over the past year, how much money has Angel Cordner paid you for powder?"

"A. For powder? Nothing."

"Q. For anything else?"

"A. Like what?"

"Q. Lucille, remember, we're asking the questions here."

"A. Sorry."

"Q. So how much money in 6 months?"

"A. I think about $10,000, maybe a little less."

"Q. That's a lot of money."

"A. He bought a lot of powder."

"Q. You said just a minute ago he wasn't buying powder. Now you say he did. Which is it?"

"A. Okay, so he was buying powder."

"Q. Did Angel work with anyone else you know of?"

"A. A bunch of political types, Red union members, and the like."

"Q. Was he supplying powder for them?"

"A. You would have to ask him."

It was clear to Valery by this point that Lucille was going to do nothing but load the problem on the shoulders of her husband and cast as little light on their business as she could. No matter what direction she took, she thought, the answer would be the same. If it involved Angel, she concluded, it involved Emil, and if it involved Emil, then it involved Lucille.

She asked for a break.

"Finn, do you have some time?"

"Sure," Finn said.

They went out front, nominally for a cigarette but, more importantly, for a little talk about where the questioning was leading.

"She's smart," Valery said. "She has told us enough, just enough, to convince us she knew what her husband was up to, but she continues to protect herself. I don't know if we want to try to crack that wall because she has immunity. But I can think of some avenues to pursue based on what she told us, with the key one being Angel Cordner and his associates."

"Yes," Finn said.

"But I'm intrigued by what she said about the union involvement and the communists. I think there's more there than we can know at this point, but we have to find someone in the National Miners Union who is angry enough to want to tell us what is going on. How are we going to do that?"

"Maybe Lucille can lead us to the right person," Valery said. "We can ask her some more questions about Cordner and the union, but Howard should be out trying to find the National Miners right now to find out what the hell they were up to."

"Right," Finn said.

"I think Howard and I should go back to Sans Souci and find out what we can about the Reds and the National Miners. A lot of it is right there, I think."

"Okay, we can end this for now and pick it up later."

They went back into the hearing room, where Lucille was drinking a glass of water at the table. Valery told her she was finished asking questions for now, and Finn told her she could leave but could be called back at any point for more.

Lucille smiled and said, "Thanks," and turned to her lawyer.

"How much more of this do I have to put up with," she asked.

"Until they are satisfied," the attorney said. "You're getting immunity from this cooperation."

She picked up her bag and left the hearing. Valery said she would call her at the hotel later in the day. Finn thanked her and left the room with Howard. They went across the street to The Forum for a talk about what was coming next.

"Howard, pretty clearly, her role is to load this all on her husband and play the loyal wife, at least as far as she can push that role. We already have one charge pending against Emil for selling powder without a license. Should we try to build a case on her, too?"

"Seems to me she is giving us the case as she testifies about all of this. She has already admitted to playing a role in distributing the powder. We just need to find out who was getting it. I think you should get to Johnstown and lean on Cordner a bit to see what he can tell us."

"Also, remember we've got the feds coming in tomorrow to collect what we know, so prepare yourself for that. Okay?"

"Okay, I'll go to Johnstown after we talk to the feds tomorrow, Valery and me, if that's okay with you. I'm not sure where this is heading at this point, but maybe a little talk with Cordner will help with that. Anyhow, I'm going back to my office to prepare for the feds."

The feds, Agents Joshua Logan and Michael McCarthy, brand new members of the Federal investigations bureau, came early. Both men were attorneys in the district before signing up for federal jobs. They seemed enthusiastic and eager to help Finn and his mine investigators with the explosives investigation. They wanted to spend about an hour talking about it with Finn, Valery, Anders, and Howard. Howard noted he needed to drive to Johnstown later in the day, so it would help if they could get their briefing over as soon as possible.

"Fine," the agents answered, like twins, in unison.

They used the meeting room outside of Finn's office.

Valery spoke first.

"What we have is evidence of a conspiracy that runs from Wilkes-Barre to Cambria County that involves the unlicensed sale of black powder stolen from Delaware and Hudson Mining Corp. and transported to Western Pennsylvania for a variety of purposes. We think it's making its way to black hand organizations and then is used for homicide, intimidation, and general threats. Detective Howard has already identified five incidents of black powder explosions in the region. One of them killed a man in his car. He was a National Miners Union official but of no importance. Our interest in this is finding out whether the various conspirators had anything to do with the black powder explosion that killed so many men at the Baltimore Shaft of Delaware and Hudson Coal on June 19th. We know that the day supervisor for the underground miners, a man named Emil Getner, was selling black powder from the company to NMU people and criminals in Cambria County. But we don't know who. We will give you all of our files and all of our contacts, but we would ask that you share with us what you collect. We are primarily interested in making coal mining safer, but this has now fallen into our area of responsibility, and we need help with it. How do you feel about that?"

"It's fine," one of the agents said.

"One of our witnesses, Mrs. Lucille Getner, is cooperating with us under a grant of use immunity, and we are continuing to talk with her."

"That kind of state immunity won't apply to us," Agent Logan said. "We don't know yet what kinds of laws may have been broken, but we will be proceeding on a set of assumptions based on those laws. Federal authorities are not required to observe immunity grants at the state level."

"Sure," Valery said.

"But we would like you to keep quiet about that because she is cooperating, and we don't want her to shut down."

"Fine," said Agent McCarthy.

The long ride to Johnstown gave Valery and Howard a chance to talk through how they were going to proceed with Lucille Getner. They gave her a Greyhound ticket back to Avoca and sent her off. Howard would be going to Avoca bank in a week to review her financial records, which the mining department put under subpoena as a part of a search of her home.

"I think if we follow some of the money, it will lead us where we need to be in this case," Howard said. "At least, that's how it seems to me at this point. We know she was getting those envelopes regularly when the people came to pick up the powder. How much is another question? Even as contraband, black powder has limited value in the marketplace unless you are so dangerous and desperate that you were willing to die to get your hands on it. That might be what we are dealing with here."

245

"That's why we need to find the unhappy NMU member who knows what is going on and wants to talk. Once we get a little piece of that, I think it will come rolling along like an avalanche, but not until we get that first little piece. How do you want to pursue this since you're basically the cop on hand?"

"How determined is Finn to get to the bottom of this?" Howard asked.

"What do you mean? He has a couple of hundred dead bodies to explain and wants to know if he can prevent that the in the future, so it's a pretty compelling case."

"Do you think it's compelling enough for him to look the other way while we get...ummmmm.... let's call it "creative" in our investigating?"

"How creative, Howard?"

She was getting nervous about the conversation.

"Let me break into the National Miners Union local headquarters and rifle their files and look for the paper to tell us what these people are actually up to. I know it's illegal and dangerous, but no one knows like a cop how to break the law, and I've always been drawn to those dramatic solutions to things."

"We shouldn't be talking about these kinds of things," Valery said.

"I'm a state official. I can't ask you to break the law. I won't ask you to break the law. Now, if you want to go out there on your own and find what you can find, that is your business. But remember, we can't use any of it at trial. It has to be just for us, for us to know where to go next to find out what has happened. But it's dangerous, and as far as anyone else is concerned, we haven't talked about it at all, okay?"

"Sure. That's not a problem for me. My thought about this kind of stuff is that someone is breaking the law, so that means we are always on the side of the angels as long as we're looking for the truth. Do you see what I mean?"

"Yes, I do, and I strongly disagree, but we're not talking about this at all. I will say a little prayer, not a big prayer, that you don't get caught."

"Fine."

"So, we lean on Cordner for what we can find and then go see if any of it is on paper anyplace? Okay?"

"Howard, you keep wanting me to agree with you, and I keep trying to build a wall of deniability between us so we don't have to talk about this again until it yields something undeniably bad that we need. Is that clear?"

"Yes, ma'am," Howard said. He was smiling.

Chapter 17: Howard the Thief

The National Miners Union existed hardly anywhere but in a budget file buried in Moscow. It had a nominal headquarters and mailing address just outside of Ebensburg, the Cambria County Seat, in an old building that had once belonged to a German-American dancing and drinking club.

It was a castle-like cement building in serious need of attention, sitting at the end of a road that turned off another road that turned off yet another road. It was not easily found, which was one of the reasons why it was in such a god-forsaken location.

The NMU, as it was called in labor circles, had roughly 230 members in a part of the country where just about every other citizen worked in a coal mine. But it could never get enough of a purchase going to draw a lot of members. The United Mine Workers were viewed as its existential enemy. People knew the NMU was pink, if not Red, and the nation was up in arms already about Eastern Europeans and Hunkies and a host of other outsiders who came in to work in the mines. There was almost no sympathy for Soviet Communism, Godless and hostile to everyone but its own (and sometimes to some of them, too.) For decades, the Russians had been trying to create influence in organized labor by pushing socialism and progressive thought, trying to corrupt the process from the inside. But that's not what miners were actually interested in. Admittedly, there was a core group of intellectuals who considered themselves radicals and socialists in the mining community, but they were not from the same backgrounds as the typical men who struggled each day to chop a living out of a coal face.

They almost all cast their lot with the United Mine Workers, from hard to soft coal; it was the dominant union. It was fiercely patriotic, essentially Catholic, and as anti-Soviet as any American labor institution could be. The Russians tried to infiltrate the UMWA a number of times but could not pull it off. That's why they decided to build their own union, the NMU, outside the traditional union channels. From its earliest days, it was clear it could not succeed. Miners were about survival. Dig enough coal to feed the family, and then get the hell out of there. Political arguments did not sell well with them. Economic arguments, which is what the UMW was all about, did.

Moscow pumped tens of thousands of dollars into organizing attempts and was able to chop off little corners of the body of union membership, but not enough to make NMU a force to be reckoned with. All of its loyalists were paid for their presence. At best, it was an irritant under the UMW saddle. When there were strikes, the NMU would show up for a while to provide some benefits, food, and the like for hungry families. But it was never at the table when the disagreements were being hammered out.

It was simply too radical.

It showed up where it could, then generally got pushed out.

Delaware and Hudson Mining Co. in Wilkes-Barre was one of the places it showed up, but not to any successful end. At best, it could disrupt the daily workflow, disrupt coal on its way to the market, and disrupt finances, but not much else.

Angel Cordner was one of the hidden members of the NMU in Cambria County, a character everyone knew but no one trusted. He always had a supply of cash for whatever anyone wanted, rental of a hall for a big party, beer wagons for the summer festivals the miners would sponsor through their churches.

But he could never get them to commit to his union. Catholics and Communists didn't mix, and most of the miners' Angel Cordner approached were Catholic to the core. The fact that he was a homosexual never really entered the conversation because Angel Cordner never got close enough to share that with the rank and file in the county. He was something of a mystery, showing up uninvited at places like Wilkes-Barre.

Howard had learned much of this on his way to talking to Cordner late one night at Sans Souci in Johnstown. People may not have been close to the National Miners Union organizers, but everyone knew about them and simply could not say enough bad things about them. A few days of visiting miners' bars (not Sans Souci!) and an investigator could fill a desk with notes on Angel Cordner and the kinds of things he did. If you were on strike and needed a firearm, Angel was your man. If you needed a couple of pounds of black power, untraceable, to make your point, Angel was your man.

If you were a man and needed a man, Angel was also your man.

The more he heard, the more focused he became on Angel Cordner and what he was up to.

He wanted to talk to working miners about the attempts to organize them, so he went to what might seem an unlikely place, the first mass of the morning at St. John's Catholic, a church far up on the side of a hill overlooking the newly completed Pennsylvania Turnpike. The problem with the turnpike was that it just slashed through whatever was in its way, and one of the things in its way was the hill that led up to St. John's, which had a great view of the valley in front of it following a terrible climb of 435 steps. The state, to keep people becalmed, had installed a long, long set of cement steps with a pipe railing that went from the berm of the Turnpike all the way up to the church, with one stop in the middle for a rest. It was at the 200-step point.

Howard parked his car, with its state license placed, alongside the Turnpike and began the long climb to the church to attend the 6:45 a.m. mass. He did not know what he would find. Apparently, everyone walked to church in Myerstown, the little village at the top of the hill. It was easy for them to get down the hill to St. John's., and easier still for them to get to any of a number of bituminous mines around the town.

The priest was just beginning the Apostle's creed when he walked in. "Credo In Unum Deum," he chanted, and the church, as though it were a choir, droned along in their profession of faith. The sun was just beginning to rest on the side of the church, sending courses of colored light across the gathered congregation. They were not fancy windows, Howard noted because this was not a favored church. They were just colored panes of glass mounted in a frame. But it worked in a very effective way when the sun came bursting through.

Truth be known, Howard loved going to Mass at least once a week just to bask in the best intentions of the believers. He knew, of course, they were all sinners, but for a couple of hours on a Sunday morning, they seemed to regret that and tried their best to be worthy. It was why being a priest had been so attractive to him, back before he began to understand the mysteries of women.

He was happy to see there would be a "coffee hour" after mass, which meant he could mix and mingle with lots of people, and there were a lot of people in that church, at least 250, which Howard thought was a good attendance for Sunday morning in a town where most of the men toiled from sunrise to sunset in the dark.

After what seemed like a small eternity, complete with a sermon on goodness instead of badness; the priest finally chanted, "Ite, misse est," and the congregation joined in to sing "Deo Gratias," signaling the mass was at its end. He blessed everyone, and then they all headed to the back of the church for donuts and not a bad cup of coffee at all.

Breaking the ice in a place like this was never easy.

He could not say, "State Police," because that would be of no value with this crowd on a Sunday morning. It might also spook the miners who were also brewing their own alcohol, which had become a good side business during Prohibition. So, he told them he was from the bureau of mines and was looking into safety issues for underground miners. The women took their coffee cups and donuts and children and headed toward a corner of the church to gossip. The men, once they realized Howard was a mine safety investigator, gravitated to him. It worked just as he had intended. They started to tell him about their concerns. He had to ask just a few questions in this setting. People seemed to be delivering evidence on a plate, just like a donut. "They are supposed to, but they don't always take the gas readings before we go into the mines. Sometimes they come around with their lamps hours after we start working," one man, obviously a veteran miner, said. "We're complaining about that all the time." More men approached with comments about conditions in the mine, the use of black powder where that was forbidden, bad wiring, and lack of safety devices. It went on and on. Then Howard asked if they had taken the issues up with their union.

"It might as well not even exist here," one of them said.

"The National Miners Union is a big waste of time, much more interested in politics than in mining. And they chased the United Mine Workers out of the county a year ago when the UMW was at its weakest point."

"So, who was organizing for them?" Howard asked.

"Angel Cordner from Johnstown," one of the miners answered. "Not a bad guy at all. But he also was one of those people who talked about a good union game but never got anything accomplished. He would bring his buddies to the union meetings, and they would all end up arguing about how to overthrow the government. They were communists, we knew that, but it was our only option at the time. These guys were tough, too, not shy about shooting or beatings with sticks. Whatever it took. They threw good parties, but that was about it. They also didn't seem to have anyone on board who actually worked in a mine. You didn't get that with the United Mine Workers. But these guys, they might as well have worked in an office someplace. People joined up because it didn't cost anything. Someone else was paying all the dues."

"I think they were a lot more interested in what was happening in the anthracite mines up in the northeast," another one said. "That's where that union wanted to plant itself; I think, so it could be close to the people who ran it in New York. That's what they were looking for."

"So," Howard said, "Were they bitter about the United Mine Workers, or did they just ignore them?"

"Bitter doesn't describe it. I think they wanted them all dead, and if you ask me, they were evil enough to try to find a way to do that. Mining is an easy place to kill people, you know because the accident and death rate is so high anyhow! Nothing these people would do on either side would surprise me. It was all about building a powerful base and then making it bigger and bigger. But the United Mine Workers had the advantage at that, particularly up in the northeast."

"This is a nice old church," Howard said, changing the subject because he didn't want to give anyone clues about what he was actually pursuing. "It looks like it was locally built..."

"That's because we built it," one of the miners said.

"We took the plans for an old barn, and the Amish came in and put up the frame, and we finished it out as a church. We saved a lot of money that way, and it became a place we came to because we wanted to, not just because we had to."

"Basement?" Howard asked.

"Yep," one of them said. "Let us show you."

They went to the back of the church and walked down a double-wide set of steps and into what seemed to be a cavernous hall underneath the church. There was a brick support wall up front beneath where the altar would be upstairs, then a couple of side rooms that smelled like candles and starch, which was where the Ladies Auxiliary did its cleaning and ironing.

The place was spotless.

"Wow," Howard said, "You folks know how to keep a place clean. You could eat off the floor in here. I've never seen big city churches this well-kept."

253

He was just about to leave the basement and make the long climb back down to his car when he was approached by the parish priest, Father Daley, who said he needed to speak to him in confidence.

"I can't tell you where this comes from, but you can probably guess," he said.

"I think you need to look closely at Angel Cordner's connection to that explosion at Baltimore shaft in Wilkes Barre in August. There is not much I can say about any of this, but there is an involvement with the NMU and that explosion that I think you should examine it. If you make reference to this conversation, please refer to me not as a priest but as a well-intentioned source here."

"So," Howard said, "It came in a confession?"

"I can't say. That's a sacred place. I just can't say."

"Well, thank you, father, and thanks for your effort here in this little church. It's a beautiful building, and the people clearly love it."

"Yes, they do," he said.

"Remember what I said, 'A source.'"

"Thanks and bye," Howard said. He pondered the long descent back to his car. "If a person tripped on these stairs, he would roll all the way into the next county," he thought. He made his way slowly to the bottom. By the time he got there, his calves had ached."

He headed on down the Turnpike to an exit that signaled "Altoona-Johnstown" and turned off. He found himself driving through rolling farmland with knee-high corn, grazing milk cows, and the occasional farmhouse with chickens and dogs in the yard and, in one case, a dozen goats grazing.

He was still 20 miles from Johnstown when he drove by a motel he decided to use as a headquarters for this visit. It sat on the ridge of a hill and had a long, sweeping view of a valley that rolled to the horizon beneath it. A half dozen farms filled the valley, each with a big barn, a house, some outbuildings, and an array of fields where silage and corn had been planted.

Howard parked in front of the motel and then walked in to get a room for the night, or perhaps two nights, depending on what he could find. There were no phones in the rooms, so he used a pay phone on the corner of the building to report in to Finn and Valery.

"I'm finding something that might be very bad here," he told Finn. "There are some signs, not yet very clear, that the Baltimore shaft explosion might not have been an accident at all. I'm going to lean hard on Cordner about this. I think he and Emil Gartner might have had a central role in that explosion. How and why, I don't know, but I'm going to be looking hard here."

Then he called Valery Miller to tell her what he was thinking.

"I suspect the NMU was behind the blast at Baltimore Shaft, which means we're looking at a murder case here at the very least. We promised to keep the feds informed, so I think you should tell agents Logan and McCarthy that we're on to something big and ugly."

"Okay," she said.

"Be careful if you are planning anything fancy I don't want to know anything about, you know?"

"Exactly," Howard said. "Very, very careful, not that I'm planning anything."

He went searching that afternoon in the Ebensburg area for the headquarters of the National Miners Union and found it, after a lot of turning and reversing and map checking, just at the end of the road where he suspected it would be located.

There was an old sign about a mile from the building that announced "German Friendship Society" in English but nothing else to explain what the place might involve. He drove up to the entrance and found a building that was intact but just barely. Some of the windows were broken, and there were signs that there had been a fire at some point, but not recently. He had been concerned about how he would get in, but that, it seemed, would be no problem. The front door was opened and hanging on its hinges. That meant he did not actually break and enter. There had been a lock, but it had been drilled out, maybe by the fire department or by thieves of some kind later. Cautiously, he stepped on the porch and walked toward the door, ever watchful for rotted wood or loose floorboards. It was all very creaky, but he made it inside. It was damp and moldy in there, with rugs and rotting overstuffed furniture. He could not imagine that it had been used for any serious purpose for years. There was a phone, but its line was dead. There was no power in the building, either. He was standing in what appeared to be an old ballroom.

There were signs on the wall for weekly dances, German lessons, translation services, and local German history studies, like a small school on German culture. It had once been a very robust club, Howard thought.

There was a door marked "office" in the back, broken open by someone else. He walked in. There was a big, heavy desk in front of a fireplace, some chairs, and an old safe so dinged up that Howard assumed it had been looted some time ago.

There was also an old wooden filing cabinet with six drawers. That intrigued him.

He opened the first door and found alphabetical files back to the letter "L," a filing system that continued in the second drawer. There were lots of files and papers in the drawer, but the light was failing. Instead of trying to squint through them with his flashlight, he just decided to steal them, all of them, from the drawers and read them back at the motel. He carried five loads from the office to the trunk of his car, carefully stacked them there, and weighted them down with the tire-changing equipment.

Then he decided to search the rest of the building, just to see what it held. In the basement, he found an array of gaming machines, from slots to poker-playing machines, all of them illegal in

Pennsylvania. That he would leave alone, he found cabinets full of alcohol, obviously for parties that had never been held. He found a refrigerator which, when opened, pumped out such a foul smell he almost wretched.

And he found a gun cabinet full of rifles. Not old rifles, relatively new rifles. There were 10 Springfield M1A1 rifles in 30.06 calibers, as many Krag rifles in the same caliber, and a case of ammunition with the right size rounds for those guns. It seemed someone was getting ready to arm a big force of people with the same kinds of firearms modern armies were using. None of the guns was rusty, so someone was maintaining them. They seemed to be in waiting, for what, he did not know.

There was nothing of any interest in any of the other rooms in the building. Lots of old portraits of officials long dead, some awards, and membership photos. He took the last of those photos, one that showed about 120 people lined up at an event celebrating a German holiday. Everyone had a big glass stein full of beer with a thick head. He did not know what the party was, but he thought the picture might be of some use somehow.

Then, retracing his steps, he walked carefully back to his car. He made one stop on the way, pulling the center drawer open on the desk in the office. There were two pistols in the drawer, loaded but rusty. One was a Browning .32 Caliber, and the other appeared to be a Russian pistol, a Makarov, in 9MM. He took both of them with him. They were too rusty to fire, but he wanted to take them apart to see what identifying numbers they carried.

It was starting to get dark, so he made a quick search outside the building.

There was nothing more of any interest to him.

He got back into his car and drove to the motel. He was eager to read the documents he had stolen to see whether they might cast any light on what was going on. He stopped at a roadside stand and picked up a pork sandwich and a soft drink for his dinner, then headed back to the motel. By the time he arrived, it was too late to get Finn to work. So he called Valery at her mother's house.

"Well, I'm safe, and I'm here to say no one has used that building as a headquarters for anything in a long, long time. I found two pistols in a desk drawer, and I took them both so we could check them out. I also took about 50 pounds of documents from a cabinet I found in an old office. I'm going to read them tonight. I have to go see Cordner in the morning, so I want to see if anything in there relates to him at all. The people at the church knew him as an organizer for the National Miners, but they didn't seem to like him and certainly didn't trust him. I need to talk to him about his role with that group and its long-running battle with United Mine Workers."

Valery listened to Howard's report and then said, "I think you need to read those documents and then get rid of them. Take notes on what seems important or relevant, but don't drive around with them in the trunk of your state car. Do you know about the concept of the fruit of the poisoned tree? Well, that's what you have in your motel room, the benefits of an illegal search and seizure. You don't want to get caught up in that."

"I'll dump them as soon as I am finished with them," he said. "Don't worry about it."

"About what," she said. "I don't know what you are talking about." Howard laughed. Valery did not. Then he put the phone back on its receiver and went on reading.

Most of what was in the files were mundane, membership lists, applications, and receipts. Howard pushed on through it, diligently enough but not with much fascination. There was an exchange of letters about the dangers of food poisoning and the need for better refrigeration for the club. He was about to fall asleep when he ran into a set of files under the heading: "Outreach." He thought it might be interesting, but he could not understand the files. There were a lot of them, at least 70 pages, and they were in Russian.

Shit, he said quietly.

Then he took a shower, put on clean underwear and turned off the light, and went to sleep. It rained, and the sound of the water on the roof was soothing for him. He slept a just sleep, worn out from his snooping and reading records.

The first thing the next morning, he called Valery.

"Is Anders around," he asked.

"I think he is down the hall with Finn. Wait a minute; I will get him."

"No, don't bother him. But there are some records here I can use his help with. I think they are in Russian. They look like letters to Moscow to me and lots of return correspondence. But I have no way of understanding them, and I don't want to look around Johnstown for someone I can trust who can translate. Besides, I have an hour to get there to meet Cordner. What do you think I should do with these documents?"

"Keep your notes and keep them separate from the rest of them. Dump the other stuff and get the Russian ones back here. We can meet, I think, at Anders's place tomorrow and see what they tell us. I'll set that up."

With that, Howard hung up and headed off to find Angel Cordner. He called the bartender at Sans Souci and asked if Cordner had been in. "It's early," the man replied. "If you see him, tell him Howard is looking for him, okay?"

"Sure."

He decided to drive into Johnstown and see what he could find there. He knew where Cordner lived, but he didn't want to approach him at home. Sans Souci would be a better spot a little later in the day.

He drove down the easy grade, and past Sans Souci at its base, then turned right into town and headed for what appeared to be the town square. Lunch would be grand just about now, he told himself.

There was one restaurant on the square, Von Linden's, that looked just fine. He parked out front and walked in.

It was a busy place, which he took as a good sign. He sat at the counter, and a woman with the name "Mary" on a tag came to serve him. She was very pretty, tall, and with lovely hands that had long fingers. He asked her what was good, and she gave the traditional optimistic restaurant response, "Everything!" with a laugh.

Then, she leaned over and, in mock confidence, said, "I would avoid the ground beef suggestions. They are, of course, very good, but they are also no longer young, if you know what I mean. She winked at him, which he appreciated. "Pork chop then with a side of apple sauce," he said.

"Great choice," she said.

It came with wheat rolls, which was standard for the German restaurants he had visited in his time, and mashed potatoes with a dollop of sauerkraut on top. The pork was great, marbled with fat, fast fried on the surfaces, and then rolled on the sides, so the whole chop was crispy on the edges. He knew when it arrived; he had made the right choice.

Mary offered him a glass of water and coffee. He asked how long she had worked at Von Linden's, and she said, "I've been a Von Linden girl forever," which he took as a joke. It was not. She was an actual Von Linden girl, the third daughter of the owner.

She was training to manage the place; she said because that's what you got to do in Johnstown if you were a young girl whose family owned a restaurant.

"I'll marry someone and have a dozen children, and we'll live happily ever after, just the way it's supposed to be," she said. "We'll have a house high on a hill above the flood plain. Even the basement will be dry!"

They both laughed.

Howard loved her sassiness, which fit the place perfectly. He could become a regular if he lived in Johnstown.

He guessed she was about 27 and, from the look of her, had taken good care of herself her whole life. She had teeth that were ivory, white and perfect, and when she smiled, she put them on display like fine china. A thoroughly engaging woman, Howard concluded.

"Ever go to Sans Souci?" he asked.

"Not in this lifetime," she said.

"I'm a church-going Catholic girl, and we don't hang out with men who are with other men if you get my drift. I don't drink hootch, and I never kiss on first dates!"

"So, if I asked you to go there with me tonight, you would say no?" She put his chop in front of him.

"Hit that chop, trooper."

"Why do you call me trooper?"

"Well, the gun is a little clue. You're either a cop or a criminal, and I know all the local cops, and you are too clean looking to be a criminal. Not many men wear a gun that big under their arm to lunch, you know, and you have state police stamped all over you like a badge of honor. No belly yet. Broad shoulders. Sitting up straight. You look like you were cut from stone for that.

"How long have you been on the job?"

"Not long at all," he said. Then he decided he had told her enough and would sit with the rejection and a piece of banana cream pie and more coffee.

"Now, I might go to Sans Souci with you if you can dance. I hear they have a great jazz quartet there, and we don't get much of that in the bars here, and I don't have much reason to hang out in a gay place. It would be a good chance for me to stretch out and build up a little sweat. Waitresses don't get to do much of that."

"I need to warn you that I am here for work," Howard said, "so I might have to break away for a while at Sans Souci. But I won't just leave you there, I promise."

"As long as it's not a love interest, I don't mind."

She said she had to work until 8 p.m. but could change quickly and be ready to go at 8:15.

"Where are you staying?" she asked.

"Motel up on the hill. Where do you live?

"Parents. Don't make any romantic plans, you know? And I have to be home before midnight."

"Not a problem at all," Howard said, hiding his disappointment so well she did not know it was there, but of course, it was. He paid for his lunch and then went to the booth to use the phone.

The man who answered at Sans Souci said Angel Cordner had been in and would probably be hanging out all afternoon. Howard said thanks and hung up. He walked toward his car, then turned around and went back into the Von Linden. "Mary still here?" he said to one of the women waiting on the counters. "She'll be back. She had to run home for something."

He was disappointed. He had no purpose in returning to the restaurant other than to get one more look at Mary. She was that good-looking. He knew he was acting like a teenager, but he admired that about himself. All of his training made him into a hard man, a man who could make life and death-decisions in an instant, and he could still be swayed by a pretty woman in an engaging manner. He thought he should work on that vulnerability, then thought again.

He drove to the base of the Easy Grade and turned on the street where Sans Souci sat in the shade like it was hiding. He parked the car and walked in the door. Same smell as before, he noted right away. Same fake trees. Same South Pacific theme. There was a man sitting at the bar drinking something creamy and green. It was Angel Cordner, nursing a grasshopper.

Howard walked over to the bar and sat beside him. "How are you, Angel?" he said.

"Howard! Hello! It's too early to dance. Want a drink?" Howard took a coffee, which he sipped at between sentences.

"Angel, we need to stop pretending. I know you are an organizer for the National Miner's Union. What can you tell me about what happens between here and Wilkes-Barre, the National Miners Union stuff?"

"Nothing," Cordner said.

"That doesn't mean nothing is happening. That means there is nothing I can tell you."

"Why would that be?"

"Because some of it is pretty dicey, dangerous."

"I'm a cop Angel. I'm not worried about danger when I know what direction it's coming from."

"Well, that would be the problem here. Even I don't know what direction it's coming from. What I can say is that something happened in the past month that shut almost everything down between Johnstown and Wilkes-Barre. I was surprised about that because I thought the NMU was making some good advances up in UMW territory in Luzerne County. The UMW is collapsing in the anthracite region, and we saw an opportunity. I don't know why I am telling this to you because you're a cop. But I like you."

"Everyone does," Howard said.

"But that's not the point. Have you ever been to the NMU headquarters outside of town, the one down the one road and then down the other road and then down the other road?"

"Sure have; used to be monthly meetings of the particulars there. But that hasn't happened in a while. What a pit that place was! I can't imagine people going in there to party and dance, but they say

263

that's what the German club was for not so long ago. They should had paid more attention to the roof."

"Did Emil ever talk to you about the Baltimore Shaft and the people who worked there?"

"Just about the pretty little business he had set up. That gave him enough profit to move his stuff here and set up a household. But I'm not one to talk about Emil these days, that sonofabitch. Broke my heart."

"Understood," Howard said.

"What about black powder?'

"Out of bounds, Howard. I'm not talking about any of that."

Howard thought, "Pay dirt!"

"Why not?"

"Because I don't want to be killed. It's that simple. And that complicated."

"What if I subpoena you and drag you in front of a grand jury? Will you talk then?"

"That's a nice try, Howard, but I would be dead before I got up the courthouse steps. I'm not talking about it, but I know these people, and they know what they are doing. I think they even have contacts in the police department and sheriff's office, so it would be very hard to hide something like that from them.

"So, you are telling me you know something about the Baltimore Shaft explosion, but you aren't going to tell me? That's going to make trouble for you, Angel, a huge amount of trouble. This is likely a murder investigation now, not just a coal mining disaster investigation. What you know about Baltimore Shaft, you ought to say to me before the whole process gets a whole lot tougher and a whole lot more formal. Do you hear what I am saying about this?"

"Can you protect me? Can you keep them away from me? Can you help me go away somewhere?"

"I need to hear what you have to say first, Angel. I need to know it's worth it to give you that kind of cover. I'm not a fool. There is a reason why we're looking where we are looking."

"I'm coming back to Sans Souci tonight with a date, maybe to do a little more dancing, I don't know. But I want to hear from you sometime this evening. We need to talk about all of this. You've already told me enough to be in trouble. How much trouble is going to be up to you, depending on what you tell me."

"The Baltimore Shaft explosion was no accident," Angel said.

Then he put his head down and stopped talking. Howard looked straight ahead and, in a firm investigator's voice, said, "You are going to have to tell me all about this, Angel. Take some time to think about it, but I have to know everything."

He thought briefly about calling Mary Von Linden's house and canceling the evening, but he rethought that, realizing it would be best for him to stay in character, not only to impress the local boys but to impress Angel Cordner, too.

Besides, he wanted to see how well the Von Linden woman danced.

He picked her up at Von Lindens just after 8:15 so she would have time to change. It was quite the transformation, from the common waitress blouse with an apron and pockets for pencils and an order pad to a blue dress that looked like it was painted on and moved with her at every point. Not much makeup but very red lips that seemed to emphasize the natural blush in her cheeks. Howard was surprised at how much he noticed about this woman, who was, after all, a stranger except for the lunch she delivered.

"Mary, you look wonderful!" he said, fully aware that, in his clean and well-pressed blue suit, he, too, looked wonderful.

"You too, trooper," she said.

265

"Mary, a favor. You can call me trooper all you want in private, but when we're at Sans Souci, let's keep it to Howard. I suspect they already know I'm a cop, but there's no point in broadcasting it, you know. It can really dampen the conversation."

"Roger, trooper," she said with an eye roll and a laugh.

They walked into Sans Souci at 9:05 p.m., and you could have heard a pin drop. Men with women guests were a rarity at Sans Souci. But the bartender immediately recognized Howard and asked where his other girlfriend, the dancing one, was.

"That was not my girlfriend," Howard said. "That was my boss, Valery. This is not my girlfriend either, not yet (he glanced at her and winked, and she winked back). This is my dancing partner for tonight. Mary, this is my friend Clay, who knows an awful lot about the Pittsburgh Pirates."

"Plenty of guys in here were looking to dance with you last time, Howard," Clay said.

"It's the suit," Howard joked.

"No, it's not. It's you."

"Fine," Howard said.

"So good to be wanted. Mary, what would you like to drink?"

She got an Iron City beer. That pleased Howard. She would most likely be on a fun and cheap date, drinking a local beer. They sat at one of the tables and listened to music. The quartet was just getting into the mood for the evening. The drummer waved hello to Howard, and then the other band members recognized him, too.

"You're going to dance, aren't you?"

"With you guys playing, how could I not dance?"

Mary watched him. He was glowing at the attention the band was paying to him. They kept it up, and he played along.

266

What struck Mary about Howard was the sense that he was always comfortable, no matter the circumstances. She decided she would ask him about that later. For now, it was time to dance.

The band launched into "King of the Zulus," not an easy piece to dance to. They decided to listen and wait it out. "Oriental Strut" came next. Howard looked at Mary, and she nodded, "yes." Off they went.

She was as light on her feet as a bird, eager to imitate him; hips, shoulders, it was all there. Howard thought this was just about the perfect match when she put her hand on his neck and pulled him in close for a kiss.

He kept dancing but could not hide his smile. They both appreciated that. The music shifted time three times, and she and Howard moved flawlessly into the new beat. It was not a pure jitterbug. In fact, he searched the memory his sisters built into his dancing and could not find a name for it. He settled on rug cutting.

"I can't give you anything but love, baby," came next. It was a dangerous song because too many band leaders tried to imitate Armstrong's singing, which could not be effectively done by anyone but...Armstrong. They moved in close and slowly danced. Howard felt Mary radiating heat, or was it just him? It didn't matter. It was so delightful he wanted it to last all night.

"You are one great dancer," he whispered. "Why thank you, trooper....whoops...Howard." Then she followed that with a little chuckle.

"Adorable," Howard thought.

When they were done, the same thing happened as happened when he danced with Valery. The men lined up and leaned back on the bar and applauded and cheered. He kissed her on the cheek, and they sat down to their beers. "Man, I haven't danced like that in a good long while. Thanks for bringing me, Howard."

He was warming to talking with her when Angel Cordner came to the table and sat down.

"I need to talk to you," he said to Howard.

"Mary, can you excuse me for a little while? I need to talk to this man."

"Certainly, Howard."

They walked to a small room just off the dance floor and sat down on a bench.

"I can talk to you about the Baltimore Shaft explosion under one condition," Angel said. "I need immunity from prosecution."

"You been talking to Lucille?" Howard asked.

"What do you mean," Angel responded.

"Just a guess on my part. Talk to me, and let me talk to my people and see what can happen."

"Can I trust you if I say that you will work out an immunity agreement?"

"Of course, you can," Howard said.

That, of course, was a lie.

This was no longer just a search for mining violations. More than 200 men were dead, some of their remains so damaged they would never be adequately identified for their families. No one involved was going to walk away from this. But sometimes, you had to lie to move things along, and Howard was not shy about that because moving the investigation along was his key objective.

"The union set off that explosion," Angel said. "It was set up here at National Miners Union headquarters about a month before it happened. We knew we could get access to the man trip with the powder on board. All we had to do was plant our powder at a point at which it would also set off what was on the man trip, about 600 pounds there."

"How did you do that?"

"Delayed fuse about 100 yards into the mine on the right side going down. It was well hidden because there was nothing over there but the gob. We planned it pretty well. You couldn't see anything after we planted the wires and placed the powder. We only needed a few pounds to set off that haul on the man trip. It worked perfectly."

"Who placed it, and who planned it."

"Emil did all that," Angel said.

"Killed the men who had worked with him for years?"

"That's right, but it was for the greater good. The UMW was giving away everything. We thought we could build a strong organization there because everyone knew that. He didn't go down in the hole that morning. He stayed behind and flipped a switch, and it all blew up. A perfect crime."

"Really?" Howard said.

"Yes," Angel replied.

Howard said he had to go talk to Mary for a minute and would be back. He went to the table and told Mary to get a cab back home, and he would call her. "Something's about to happen here that could get ugly, and I don't want you to see it," he said.

"What's going to happen?"

"Trooper business. Just please get home, and I will tell you all about it when I get back to you. Promise."

"Okay."

He watched her go to the pay phone and hoped at the same time he had not wrecked the beginning of a relationship. On the other hand, he had a man in another room who was complicit in mass murder, and he wanted to arrest him right away.

Which was what he did.

"Angel," Howard said when he returned, "I have my pistol on my lap under the table here, and I am arresting you on suspicion of

269

murder. Don't try to escape, or I will shoot you dead right here. I'm not kidding. Stand up and walk in front of me." He cuffed his left arm and put the other cuff on his right. Angel would not be able to go anywhere. Howard kept his pistol tucked in his pants, his belt holding it in place. He could see it, and so could Angel. He patted Angel down and found a small revolver in his front left pocket. He took it, cracked it open and dumped the rounds, and put it in his coat pocket.

"You said you would try to get me an immunity agreement," Angel said.

"And so, I will. But I can't guarantee anything. That's up to the Luzerne County prosecutor. You just put yourself at the center of a murder conspiracy. Neither of us can walk away from that, so let's go."

He checked around the bar as they walked to the door. Mary had left.

"Where are you taking me?

"Where we always go when we arrest someone in Johnstown, the city jail. We have an arrangement."

He put Angel in the back seat of the Ford and locked the door. It could not be opened from the inside. Then he walked around the front and got in to drive to the city jail.

At the jail, Howard said hello to the same sergeant he had met when he took Emil Gartner to the jail.

"Another one," the sergeant said, mock surprise in his voice. "Will it never end? What's the charge?"

"Let's call it a conspiracy to commit murder, okay?"

"Going to need some details on this one," the sergeant said. Angel said he needed to use the phone, and the sergeant got up from his desk and let Howard sit. He called Finn.

"Finn, Howard. I have just arrested Angel Cordner on a charge of conspiracy to commit murder. He told me the NMU set up the explosion at Baltimore Shaft, how and why they did it, and fingered Emil Gartner as the bomber. We're holding him at the Johnstown Jail for now. He's going to get a lawyer, and I think we need to argue against bail. He's a flight risk, for sure. How do you want me to proceed?"

"First, good work. Second, make sure he's lawyered up. We don't want this one tossed for a technicality, you know? Valery told me you have some records you got someplace that are in Russian. When you get back here, Anders can translate them and see what they say. I'm going to come out there by train tonight. We both need to spend some time with Angel to find out what else he knows about all of this.

"He wants to go for a plea if we can help him out. But I don't know, you know, it's a murder case with a lot of innocent victims. He wants us to try for immunity in exchange for cooperation, but I don't think we should. I haven't had to lay a hand on him so far to find out all we needed to charge him with conspiracy for murder. Maybe we can get further just talking to him and holding out the promise of some kind of juicy deal, even if we can't get one. Or I can pound the piss out of him because I dislike him that much."

"Howard, no piss pounding. That's not how we work."

"I know, I was just kidding…Well, no, I wasn't, but I understand you don't want that to happen, so it's fine."

"I can get a train to Johnstown at 10 p.m. out of Harrisburg, but it's not going to get in until morning. Can you get me a hotel room where you are staying?"

"I'm way up on the hill, Finn. Let me just get you a room downtown. We can talk about it in the morning. Okay?"

"Sure…Howard?"

"Yes."

271

"Don't touch him."

"Okay."

Howard gave the desk back to the sergeant and said he and Director Finn would be in the next morning to talk to Cordner. He said he needed a few words with Cordner before he left.

"A few words?"

"Just words."

He walked back into the cell area and looked at Cordner, sitting on a bench.

"Get a lawyer tonight," he said.

Then he left to see where Mary was. It was 11 p.m., so he thought he should call first.

"It's Mary," she said.

"Howard...did you get home okay?"

"Sure. Tell me what happened?"

"Well, I think the man I was talking to confessed to being an accessory to a huge murder, so I had to arrest him, and I didn't know how that would go, so I thought it would be best for you to leave. I am very sorry. I loved dancing and being with you."

"Same to you," Mary said. "I know you were working. You warned me. Trooper, are you as good a man as you seem, or is that all a cop act?"

"Well, I'm just me. Always and everywhere. Why are you asking?"

"Because I don't want to be in love with someone I don't really know."

That took his breath away. It's exactly what he wanted to hear.

"You can be in love with me any time and under any circumstances. It will not be hard to love you right back. I'm going to be here for a couple of days, I think. My boss is coming in the morning. So, can I see you again?"

"Of course. But I'm working until 8 p.m. every night this week. You can come to Von Linden's, and I'll feed you. It will be on the house! Pick a night. Bring the boss if you want to."

"Are you sure you are allowed to do that?"

"My father's going to disown me for free meals for cops?

"I don't see that happening."

"Mary, small favor. Don't think of me as a cop. I'm a mine disaster investigator now, although I still have a gun and a detective's badge, and of course, a police car. You should just think of me as anything you want but a cop."

"Okay!"

"Trooper. It is."

Once again, he found himself laughing with her. A good sign, he thought to himself.

***

Finn arrived late the next morning on a train that was delayed three times on its way west for equipment failures. He made a note to himself to contact the Transportation Department and get them to take a look at the Pennsylvania Railroad's passenger services.

Howard picked him up at the station, and they stopped for coffee and a discussion about how to handle Angel Cordner, now charged and presumably awaiting bail. Howard had strong feelings about this one, that Angel was at the heart of something awful and should be watched very closely while he was in jail.

"I think we need to get him on the record talking to us about Lucille and what she was up to. I don't think his interest stopped at

Emil. He might be able to tell us some stuff we can use to charge her as a co-conspirator."

"As long as it's not based on her own testimony, we should be okay on that."

They finished their coffee and headed for the Johnstown City Jail. A different sergeant was at the desk. He was pleasant but very formal.

"We need to get what we need to get for handling this guy," the sergeant said. "That's going to be about $30 a day for food and jail services. You can have the state treasurer cut us a check. But we don't want to hold this guy for too long. He's facing a big charge, and he should be in state prison."

"We'll get him back to Harrisburg as soon as we can," Finn said. "We have a little more work to do on him here first."

"What do you mean by work?" the sergeant asked.

"Just that. Questions. You know. No rough stuff."

The sergeant led them back to Cordner's cell. He talked to them through the bars. They sat on office chairs they borrowed from the desk area.

"I'm Edward Finn, head of mining safety in the Department of Mines. I'm here as an investigator on the Baltimore Shaft Explosion from a few months back. I understand there's information you can share with us."

"Yeah, but I need to get immunity before I say anything else," Cordner said.

"May be too late for that now, Angel," Finn said. "It looks to us like you are up to your eyes in this, and we aren't going to let you walk away from conspiracy to commit murder in exchange for some evidence."

"What if I can deliver the whole bunch of them, all the National Miners Union guys who were involved in the Baltimore Shaft explosion? Then what could I get."

"Angel, every time you open your mouth, you walk deeper into the hole," Howard said. "We're already charging you with conspiracy to commit murder, and that won't be the end of it. We have more investigating to do. Then there's the powder stuff. We could charge you and Emil in a conspiracy to sell that stuff and in the crimes it was used to commit.

"I don't have to tell you that you are fucked, Angel. Completely fucked. The best thing we can do is argue with the prosecutor for mercy based on the cooperation you offer from here on out, so I surely would give us the names of the NMU people involved in the Baltimore Shaft explosion and everything else you know. I don't want to diminish the seriousness of your situation, Angel; you could be toasted for this."

"You mean the chair?"

"Exactly."

He began weeping.

"OH! Jesus. Oh Jesus, Jesus, Jesus."

"I have to be honest with you, Angel," Finn said.

"Look at your situation. You will go on trial in Luzerne County, where most of the victims of this disaster worked. You aren't going to have much of a chance with a jury up there. Maybe you ought to talk to your lawyer about pleading guilty."

"Jesus, Jesus, Jesus, they are going to kill me for sure now. I can't win in this thing. Jesus, Jesus, Jesus."

Finn and Howard looked at one another, and Finn told Angel the conversation was over. He was going to have to dump everything he knew about the Baltimore Shaft explosion, and even then, he would be facing at least life in prison.

"We'll help you if we can, but there is nothing we can promise in this. You are in way too deep."

"They are going to kill me," Angel said.

"No," Howard interrupted.

"We are going to kill you, as in "we" the state of Pennsylvania. See what you have to say tomorrow morning. That's the last chance.

And with that, they left him to his fate.

Finn talked to the sergeant out front.

"Keep a close eye on Mr. Cordner," he said. "He is in a desperate situation, and I don't want him killing himself in your jail here, right?". We'll make arrangements to take him to Harrisburg right away. We'll be back to pick him up in the morning. Put him in chains for us, if you will. 8 a.m."

Finn went to his hotel room, and Howard popped into Von Linden's for a coffee and a few words with Mary if she was working.

She was.

"Well, I will bring my boss in here tonight, and he will almost certainly order up a big steak. I would, given what we've been through this afternoon. He's on the state's tab, so we'll pay for it, of course. How much can I tell him about you and me?"

"How much do you want to tell him about you and me?" Mary asked.

"That you dance very well and That I want to marry you so we can start having all those children you want, but I haven't asked you yet; we don't really know each other well enough for that, and I don't know what you will say."

"That's just fine with me. You know I can't leave Johnstown, that my family is counting on me," Mary said. "But I do believe I am in love with you, even with the little bit I know, and we can find a way to make it work. That's what you can tell your Finn. I'm not saying yes just yet because you haven't met my parents and the rest of my family, and you don't really know me. But you can think of me as Mrs. Trooper except for that formality. If they hate you, we will have to do something else, make some other arrangement."

"But I would be happy being with you. You like having sex, don't you? I do, and I can't marry anyone who doesn't."

"Hmmm. I think I could tolerate it."

At that, they both laughed, and Howard left to reconnect with Finn.

"I would like to walk down to Von Linden's for dinner if you don't mind. It's not fancy, but it's good, and it's just down the street. There's someone I want you to meet there."

"Okay, Finn said.

"Let me just make some calls to Harrisburg to find a place to stick, Mr. Cordner. We may have to take him back with us."

Howard arranged to return at 6:15 p.m., and Finn returned to his business. He knew the local state prison would have room for Angel Cordner, but he wanted to make certain because he didn't want him in the Harrisburg jail. The place was out of control, and a man with Angel's tastes might find it a little risky there. He dialed the warden's office, and the phone was answered by a woman named Nancy, who Finn knew as a neighbor.

"Warden Lincoln is not in right now, Finn. What do you need?"

"I have a felony charge I need to house for a while. I don't think he's dangerous, but I do think he needs some close watching for potential suicide. Can you handle that for us for a couple of days?"

"Sure, Finn. Call before you get here so we can make the arrangements."

"I don't think I want him out on bond, so he's going to have to stay there," Finn said.

"Okay."

There was a knock on his door. It was Howard, talking much too fast.

"Finn, I want you to go with me to Von Linden's to meet Mary because I think I am going to marry her. I'm not asking for your approval. I just want you to have a look to make sure I'm not just nuts."

"Fine," Finn said.

They took a brisk walk to Von Linden's and went in. They sat at the counter and were greeted by Mary.

"Mary Von Linden, this is my boss, Edward Finn," Howard said. She shook his hand and welcomed him.

"Anything you want, we can make for you, so just ask."

"I think a New York strip steak, medium, with mashed potatoes and apple sauce on the side and a cup of coffee and all the refills you can muster," Finn said. She wrote it all down and added Howard's hamburger with cheddar cheese and fries and a Coke. She turned away to give the order to the cook.

"You are not nuts, Howard. She is one fine-looking woman," Finn whispered. "But are you sure you aren't rushing this? I mean, you don't even know her much."

"Yes, of course, I am rushing it. I'm a cop. I don't have time to wait. I've had plenty of girlfriends, but none of them could touch her. I don't know why. I just know."

"Well, it's your life, Howard," Finn said.

"I felt like I had been struck by lightning when I first met my wife, and no one could understand that at all, so I guess I know what you're talking about. When are you going to ask her?"

"When the Baltimore shaft stuff is done, I think that would be a good time, don't you? Thank you, Mr. Finn," Howard said.

278

"I want to take Angel back to Harrisburg with us," Finn said.

"I don't see him as dangerous. You can sit in the back seat with him. Maybe he'll tell us something on the drive we can use. Anyhow, I would feel better with him in a state prison near us than in a place out here where anything can happen. As soon as the radicals understand we have him, they are going to be trying to kill him, too, so we have to be careful about it."

"Understood," Howard said.

Then Mary brought the food, and they ate their dinner, all the time watching her as she moved back and forth behind the counter. Finn thought it was somehow strange he was watching her as closely as Howard. But he liked Howard and wanted to make sure he had made the right choice. It appeared to him that he certainly had.

They had pie for dessert, chocolate cream with toasted meringue on top, and coffee. Mary hung around and sparked with Howard, leaving Finn to watch from the sidelines.

"Is he going to care if I just keep calling you Trooper," she said. "I really like that nickname, like the one you would give to a brave dog who loved you. Know what I mean, Finn?"

"Surely I do," Finn said.

"You can call him anything you agree on, Mary. Just call him a lot, you know?"

They finished and paid, and Finn left a healthy tip, although it was clear Mary did not need the money. They walked back to Finn's hotel, where Howard said goodnight and arranged to pick him up at 7:30 for the trip to the jail to get Angel.

It was a dark morning in Johnstown, and Howard left his motel up on the ridge a little early to make sure he could pick Finn up on time. At 7:30 a.m., he was in front of the hotel in his police car. Finn walked calmly down the steps, his suitcase in hand. Howard noted he was wearing a shoulder holster and pistol under his jacket, the

279

first time he had seen Finn arm himself. He hoped there was no need for it.

"Morning, Howard," Finn said. "Let's go to jail and get our man!"

Howard was surprised by Finn's perky demeanor. They were going to go pick up a man who, at the very least, would be facing a lifetime in prison or perhaps a short, violent ride to eternity in the electric chair.

"Why are you so happy, Finn?" Howard asked.

"I know it doesn't seem appropriate, but we have all but solved this case. We need Anders to translate your Russian stuff for us, but we have a confessed murderer in hand who is going to tell us all about it, I would suggest. We may be able to save him from the chair, but he's out of the game either way. That's the reason for us to be happy. We're about to get justice for a bunch of guys who went to work thinking it would be like every other day and then were blown into small pieces, partially because of this man. I think that's an accomplishment for us. A big accomplishment. And I owe lots of that to you, Howard."

Howard blushed and said what happened was the result of work by a team headed by Valery, which Finn acknowledged.

"You people did great work on this. I know that. As will the governor and everyone who watches us. Can't tell you how important this is. Let's go get this guy and put him in the can. For good."

***

Angel Cordner was no happier that rainy morning than he had been the night before when he realized he was facing execution for what, to him, seemed a valiant political move aimed at breaking a corrupt union. That had been Getner's argument all along, that the United Mine Workers were flawed unionists who had only their own interests at heart. He sold the whole plan based on the argument that John L. Lewis, the United Mine Workers head, was more management than worker-oriented and just wanted to keep a corrupt system operating. That fact that he and Getner were lovers had been left far behind them once they started conspiring for the attack at Baltimore Shaft. Sitting in the back seat of the police car with Howard nearby, he was overwhelmed by how foolish he had been, how swept up he felt by the National Miners Union campaign.

"Goddamn Communists," he muttered. "That's all they were. Goddamn Communists."

"What?" Howard said.

Angel then began talking about his history with the NMU, how Emil had recruited him as an organizer, how he approached the disgruntled miners in the bituminous fields and how that stretched all the way to Wilkes-Barre as the plot at Baltimore Shaft deepened. He delivered six names to Howard in that conversation, NMU officials from the east coast who played a role, either by providing money or opening doors for fundraisers that were used to finance the Baltimore Shaft attack.

"I don't think any of them had any idea about what we were doing. These were just a collection of pinks who believed Lenin had found the perfect way and wanted to bring that all home to the coalfields."

From the instant of the explosion, he said, he knew he had done the wrong thing in so many ways that, in his remaining days, he would spend his hours reviewing all his regrets.

"I'm going to burn in hell for eternity for his," he said.

Howard fought his inclination to say, "But you are going to burn here first, Angel."

He talked all the way to Harrisburg. At one point, he eyed Howard's pistol in his brown shoulder harness. "Don't even think it, Angel. I resolved to kill you once if you did the wrong thing, and

I can keep that thought in my head if you try something stupid now. You will be dead before you know it."

Finn didn't like hearing that from Howard, not that he wanted him to go easy. It would have been enough to just say, "Don't think about it." But then, he appreciated Howard's almost complete transparency. You could read what he was thinking on his face. Even in the rearview mirror, he knew he was not toying with Angel Cordner, that he would shoot him dead if he tried to get the gun. That was so unlikely, given the chains Cordner had been locked into, that it wasn't worth much of a thought. Still, it was a thought.

Howard had decided Angel deserved killing, whether it was at the hands of the state or at the hands of him.

It was that simple.

They arrived in Harrisburg without incident, and Finn told Howard to drive across the river to the state prison at Camp Hill. He had made arrangements with warden Lincoln to take Cordner into custody. He didn't want him in jail in Luzerne County because he was convinced someone up there would kill him once they knew he was behind the Baltimore Shaft explosion.

"Okay, Angel," Finn said as he handed him over at the warden's office. "Luzerne County will be in touch before you know it, I suspect. Pick a lawyer now, so you have at least some protection. You might not be comfortable here, but I have been assured you will be safe. They are going to put you in solitary confinement so no one can get to you. I hope I never see you again. Bye."

Then Finn walked out.

Howard was on his heels.

"Let's get downtown and get these Russian records looked at," he said. Anders will be in the office today, so that would be no problem.

"We're going to have a little catch-up meeting with Valery just so she knows what's going on, then you and Anders can sit down with those documents. You're good company, Howard, and thanks for that."

Howard met Anders and Valery in his office at 1 p.m. Valery noted that his suit still looked like the day he bought it, and he said, "When you have something this nice, you want to take care, you know?"

"I do know," she said. Anders asked if he had a chance to do any more dancing at Sans Souci.

"I did. Lots. It's where I arrested Cordner, but not until I had danced for a while with the woman I intend to marry. You will be invited, of course. Her name is Mary Von Linden, and her family owns a restaurant downtown. Sweet, sweet woman, very smart, and, with all respect to you, Valery, a great dancer. I don't know much about her. I just know I want to marry her, and she did not run away when I suggested it. I have to meet the family and everything before we can move on with it, but I'm not letting anything get in the way of this one."

"That's great news, Howard," Anders said, and Valery joined in that she thought it would be grand for him if she turned out to be as good a woman as he seemed to think she was.

"Well," Howard said, "I'm going to be finding out, I guess."

Then they turned to the business at hand.

Howard removed a thick stack of papers from his briefcase and sat them in front of Anders. Anders looked at the address on the first letter and knew immediately Howard had found an important set of papers.

"It's from the Committee on State Security," Anders said. "The NKVD, the Soviet secret police." He read on in the first letter, which had been addressed to Emil Gartner at the National Miners' Union headquarters.

"It refers to a campaign to set up a Moscow-funded miner's union to compete with the United Mine Workers."

Anders shuffled through the papers. "They are all about that, about setting up this competing union."

"It says the Soviet government will deny any role in the effort and, beyond providing the seed money, will play no role in determining what the new union actually does. The objective is to develop influence in American organized labor, this first letter says."

He flipped through the pages and read on. Angel Cordner was described as the central contact for the NKVD in the American labor movement, that he had associates working with him, and he was very influential in the National Miners Union and could help expand Soviet influences in American labor politics.

Anders found no copies of letters Angel may have written to Moscow and guessed they would have been destroyed, at the very least, and not copied because they would prove he was acting as an agent of foreign influence.

"Jaysus," Howard said.

"The feds will be fascinated with this guy. It's pretty rare to actually catch someone who is in their net. Angel clearly had a future with the Russians if he could build a union network in the coal fields."

Finn told Anders to read on, but later, because he wanted to have a conversation right away about Angel Cordner, and Lucille and how they would handle their relationship with the Russians.

"Look, we've got Angel in prison on a capital murder charge, so he could get the chair, and we are going to get Emil Gartner on something a little less than that. Lucille, at the very least, for selling explosives without a license and probably in conspiracy with Emil and Angel to commit murder. All of this stretches us pretty far beyond our role in monitoring mine safety issues and compliance. I'm not worried about that. Crime is where you find it, you know? I'm saying we keep this contained until we deliver it to the Luzerne prosecutors; keep the feds at bay because the minute they see the Russian influence, they are going to want to grab the case.

"I want them tried on murder charges. I don't want them traded to the Russians or set up with another identity. They need to face up to what they did and feel the hand of justice on their shoulders. They killed 120 miners, a handful of them just children. I don't want them to walk away from that."

"How can we go ahead then without telling the feds?" Anders asked.

"Keep thinking of those piles of bodies in Baltimore Shaft," Finn told Anders. "That is what is important to us, getting a measure of justice for them. If it upsets the feds, that's fine. I can handle that."

"Besides, the question here is not if," Howard said.

"It's when."

"Anders should just diligently translate the entire file, quite thoroughly, as we process the murder stuff in Luzerne County, and then we will give the whole file to the feds as soon as the locals up there file their murder charges," Valery said.

"That's a good plan. That's exactly what I want us to do. Valery, you are going to be in charge of this whole package, starting with getting the Luzerne people moving on murder charges. Just let us know when you are satisfied that it is moving along well, and then we can decide when we want to tell the feds about the Russian connection. Is everyone okay with that?"

Finn, Valery, and Anders all answered at once.

"Yes."

Valery said she would start moving first thing in the morning.

"Just one question," she said.

"What are we going to do about Lucille?"

Chapter 18: Lucille's Last Drink

Lucille Getner had felt the walls closing in on her from the day Valery and Anders found her garage full of black powder. She knew it was only a matter of time before one of the mining people found out about a Russian connection to Angel and Emil, too. That would be the end of it for her. She had some money and still had her contacts in Western Pennsylvania, and maybe they could help her. But she doubted it. She also had no way to contact them without traveling, and that would be out of the question with Valery and Anders watching her so closely.

She could still flee but to where?

Her situation, to her mind, had become hopeless. She went to her bathroom and opened the medicine cabinet. She had a small bottle of barbiturates, not enough to kill yourself, but enough to help get you really disabled if you took them with alcohol. She put the bottle in her jacket pocket and then went to the kitchen to collect a pint of bourbon, her "traveling friend," she called it.

She put that in her purse.

Then she left the house, the front door wide open, and got into her Ford. She checked to see if no one was watching, then took four of the pills and washed them down with a mouthful of bourbon. It took a while for the chemicals to react with one another. She drove from her house and turned left on the state highway just after taking another drink from her traveling friend.

She was starting to feel a little drunk, not too drunk to drive, but too drunk to walk around.

That feeling only got worse or better, depending on how you looked at it. She wanted to go faster, and the Ford was up to it.

So she did what she wanted.

The Avoca police were called at 10:15 a.m. and informed a car had slammed into a tree and was burning just outside of town. When they arrived, their report later said, the auto was "fully engaged," and they could see what remained of the driver sitting in the front seat. The fire department extinguished the blaze, and the county coroner pronounced her dead. There was not much left to look at. The inventory noted a .32 caliber pistol in her purse, a few remaining pills in the container, and an empty pint of bourbon. It wasn't hard to identify her. A search of her home located letters from the Luzerne County Court and the Department of Mines in Harrisburg. They all noted she was being charged with unlicensed sales of black powder to "unknown persons." There was a notice that she was to be questioned by the Mining Department investigators, and so on, that she was out on bail.

Lucille took her role in the crime with her into that maple tree alongside the road.

One of the Avoca policemen called Finn's office to report the accident.

"She was burned so badly you couldn't tell it was a woman," he told Finn. "Pills and alcohol. There was no note or anything, so no one wants to call it suicide, but my bet would be that's what it was. Just a drunk woman who slammed into a tree. That's about all we can say."

"Thank you," Finn said.

He felt free of any need to understand what Lucille was actually up to. Maybe she was just a sad woman abandoned by a homosexual husband who got herself deep into trouble, or maybe she was a master criminal involved in an international struggle between mining unions.

Or maybe she was just a pretty woman who drank too much and slammed her fast Ford into a tree one morning.

It didn't matter to Finn.

He had everything he needed to wrap up the Baltimore Mine explosion. Emil and Angel would pay the price for it, and whatever Lucille did, she paid, too, but out of her own pocket, not the estate's.

Even as he was settling his thoughts on it, Valery and Anders walked into his office. They reported the Luzerne County Prosecutor was filing first-degree murder charges against Emil and Angel. They had planned to charge Lucille as an accessory, but the crash on the highway closed that avenue. The prosecutor planned to present the evidence Anders and Valery had provided that very afternoon to a grand jury. Finn knew that meant there would be an indictment by the end of the day. No grand jury ever turns down a county prosecutor looking for a murder charge.

It was almost a rule.

"Your people will be called," he said.

The county would move quickly on the case, Finn knew because it involved their own people as victims of the crime. The only question would be whether to use one victim or all of them to make the case.

The prosecutor, no fool, chose the youngest child victim, a blameless 13-year-old Polish boy named Janesh Placksky, to build the case.

He was a spragger, running alongside the coal cars to slow them down, either with a handbrake or a hickory stick he would jam in the spokes of the wheels. It was hard, dangerous work that he did very well, even as a child. Everyone liked him, and he gave his pay each week to his mother. He had two brothers who worked with him in the mine. But they were off on the day of the blast.

His father was not and was riding down to the coal face on the man trip when the explosion hit.

Nothing was ever found of him, not even a piece of his old boot, and Finn was led to believe his mother would grieve forever. Of that, he had no doubt.

288

"We need to have a talk about how we're going to close this case," Finn said to Valery and Anders. "Let's get Howard in here this afternoon and finish it up."

They agreed and walked out to tell Howard about the meeting.

The meeting room was flooded by blessed afternoon sunlight when Finn sat with Valery and Howard, and Anders to discuss the Baltimore Shaft case.

"We uncovered quite the back story on this one, and I can't tell you how much I appreciate the work you did on it. Howard, you're a great detective! But you all did great work, and I'm glad to have you here. What does all of this tell us about mine safety?"

"We don't want to get into any of the back stories for the Mining Department report. We need to rake Delaware and Hudson over the coals for the many safety violations we found, in addition to their abysmal record-keeping skills. I'm going to recommend a $250,000 fine along with prosecution of the relevant executives for violating state mining laws. The fact that they had children working is unforgivable. They are going to pay a high price for that and should probably be charged. Valery, I need you to draft this report, and I want it to be signed by you and Anders. It will be Anders's first signature on an investigation, and I want everyone to know forever that you all did a great job. Okay? Valery, can you get that done by the middle of next week?"

"Sure," she said.

"But what about the Russian files and the feds?"

"I'm going to handle that first thing in the morning in a phone call to the Federal Inve…what do we call them now? Oh, yes, it's now the Federal Bureau of Investigation as of yesterday. That will make it easy to remember the name, the FBI."

" I hope those guys are still there; I liked them."

The next morning, Finn called the local office of the new FBI and asked for Agents Logan or McCarthy. McCarthy picked up the phone.

"Hello, Agent McCarthy; it's Finn from Mining. I wanted you to know that we have wrapped up the case in the Baltimore Shaft explosion. The prosecutor in Luzerne County is charging two of the guys we arrested with murder in the first degree. Another of the suspects, Lucille Getner, apparently killed herself yesterday. We stumbled over something in this case that you should know. We believe the Russians were involved in the Baltimore Shaft explosion, indirectly as part of their effort to infiltrate organized labor in the coal fields."

"Yes," said Agent McCarthy.

"We know about that. We were going to tell you at the right time, but now that you know, that point has passed. Good work on the murder investigations. If we can be of help in the future, just let us know."

"Sure," Finn said. Then he put the phone back on the receiver and shook his head.

"Son of a bitch!"

He told the team about the feds and that the case was now closed. Valery continued on her report. Anders kept the Russian documents he had translated, which were fascinating to him but more of a picture of the plodding dullness of Russian bureaucracy than anything else. Howard breathed easy because at least no one but Valery would know he had stolen evidence from the old union headquarters near Ebensburg.

It wasn't tied up with a neat, clean bow, but Finn felt the Mining Department had done what it could. He closed his Baltimore Shaft file, put it in his center desk drawer, then got up and walked down the hallway to see if there was any fresh coffee.

He could feel the weight lift from his shoulders as he walked. Barry and Emma could read Finn like a book. He was not quite smiling. But he did not have the look of determination that he carried into the building most days.

"Work out good, Finn?" Barry asked.

"Good as it could, given what we were working with. Thanks for asking Barry. You well?"

"I am today!"

He got coffee for Finn and gave him a donut as a gift, just because. Emma smiled and said he looked well for a man who worked so hard. For some reason, he could not understand, which brought an image to his head of his own wife digging in her garden, glistening with sweat at midday and pleased with the way it was all going.

Sometimes, Finn thought, you need to have a good image to replace the bad ones. He took his coffee and walked back to his office, now in a much better mood.

Valery was waiting for him.

"Finn, I need to talk to you about the governor's office. I suspect they are interested in me, and I know you have recommended me, but I need to get a sense of what I can do there that is better than what I am already doing here.

"This whole Baltimore Shaft investigation has opened my eyes about what we do and how we do it. I love this work, and I know that, ultimately, it leads to more safety for miners, which is what we are all about, you know?"

"I do know," Finn said.

"I will remind you of how frustrating it can be when you can't get anything working when you can't get the change you know needs to happen. I would be delighted to just have you stay here. I couldn't have a better deputy, I know that, and I want you to know that, too. You know how the salary structure works here, you can only make what you can make, and you aren't allowed to do outside work to

291

earn more. But I might be able to work a deal with The General to get too attached to the Justice Department as an investigator. You could work for both of us. There is always a bundle of interesting crimes to dig into over there, and I might be able to get you a little more money since you would be doing double service. That way, you could pursue your career without leaving us here because, frankly, I don't know what I would do without you, and I could never find anyone as good to replace you.

"What would you say to all that?"

Because Valery did not allow herself to tear up under any condition, she did not tear up. But she had a very warm feeling toward Finn and her co-workers and was happy she wouldn't be moving.

"That would be perfect for me, Mr. Finn."

"Just Finn, Valery. You don't have to call me to mister anymore. Just Finn would be just fine."

"Anders will be very happy to hear you won't be leaving us, I am certain. And that will be good for you, too."

"Thanks, Finn," she said.

She walked down the hallway to visit Anders in his office.

"Well, I'm not leaving," she said. "Finn suggested I make myself available to the Justice Department as an investigator. That would add some money and keep me busy, so that's what I am going to do."

"Sweet Valery. Very sweet. I have a question. What do you think I should do with these Russian documents? I have translated them all now. It's a lot of bureaucracy, but it does point to how interested the Russians were in infiltrating American labor organizations. I don't think they succeeded at all anywhere."

"I think our FBI friends would be interested, or at least would know what to do with them," she said. "We have to keep the sourcing on them quiet. Howard broke into the National Miners Union's old office in Ebensburg and copped the files. That's how he got them."

"Is that legal," Anders asked.

"No, it's not. I have forgotten about it now, so I don't have to carry it around with me or report it. Howard is an excellent investigator and, on top of that, now a good friend and a fine dancer. So, I think you should just ship our translations to the feds along with a note that just says we discovered these files along the way in the Baltimore Shaft investigation. Just say you don't know where they came from if they ask."

"You mean lie?"

"Anders, please…

"Okay."

Then he suggested dinner later at the steak house, once again. She accepted, and they agreed to meet there at 7 p.m. She was looking forward to the crackers and cheddar cheese on the table, some nice beer or wine, and a good chance to talk to the man she had chosen to fall in love with.

It was a sweet dinner, with perfect steaks, a great salad with blue cheese chopped up in it, and a shared piece of very dark German chocolate cake with toasted coconut icing. Valery drank Merlot and Anders, beer, a Yuenglings.

"I want to talk about us," Valery said to Anders.

"I think we work very well together as mining investigators, and I don't want to lose that, but I'm thinking we might be moving toward the point at which you ask me to marry you. My inclination, I will tell you right now, will be to hop up and down and say "yes" when that time comes. I know I don't act that way in the office, but I have tried to make my feelings about you clear to you without broadcasting them to everyone else.

"So, stop worrying about us. It's resolved in my head.

"I surely hope you like sleeping with me because I want us to do a lot of that right away. I had a foreboding sense during the Baltimore Shaft investigation that I could lose you at any moment, and the thought of that just broke my heart. That's how much I love you."

Anders sat calmly in the reflection from the candle. He had wanted Valery from the very first moment she welcomed him to the Mining Department but had no idea how to go about it. Now, as she did with everything, she made it clear and easy for him. There would be no long engagement, no difficult distances. They would be together forever.

Just as soon as he met her mother and sisters, she concluded in her head. It's not that they had approval, but she loved all of them deeply and didn't want them to feel on the outside of any of it.

"Come to my house for dinner on Sunday in a couple of weeks, and we'll tell everyone. I can invite Finn and his wife, too, because they are very nice and have always been kind to me. I kind of want to turn it into a celebration. Would that be okay with you? How do you feel about Howard coming, too? It would be like a party. Maybe he can get his new girlfriend, Mary here from Johnstown.

Silence for almost a whole minute.

"Of course," Anders said, smiling broadly.

"All of that would make me very, very happy."

It would take a month; she said, for the arrangements to be made. She would take care of the invitations. All he had to do was come up with a marriage proposal that was unforgettable, and everything would work out just fine.

"No pressure," she said.

It took most of the next week for Valery to wrap up her report on the Baltimore Shaft explosion, and there was no doubt about what happened, from the first sentences to the close 25 pages later. "On June 19th, 1937, a black powder explosion on a man trip killed 147 workers at the Baltimore Shaft of Delaware and Hudson Coal Co. Thirty-five of those victims were under the age of 16 and should not have been working in the mine under Pennsylvania law. An investigation by the staff of the Department of Mining showed the explosion was not an accident, that it was set off as part of a struggle between the National Miners Union and the United Mine Workers, who had been decertified at the mine at the time of the blast. The Department recommended and got the arrest of two NMU functionaries on First Degree Murder charges in Luzerne County. Another suspect, the wife of one of the functionaries, died in a car wreck on the eve of her impending arrest...."

But Valery went on to write that the investigation disclosed an array of violations of state law and common mining practices on the part of the company and recommended a fine of $250,000 as a penalty for those offenses. The Department, she said, would also cooperate with county prosecutors as they pursued a variety of criminal charges against company officials. "Of particular note to the Department," she said, "Were the deaths of minor children who were working illegally in the mine in a variety of tasks. The exact number cannot be known because of the violence of the explosion and the fact that some of their fathers also died in the incident. It was impossible for coroners to identify the remains in many cases. These children were employed less than a month after the state enacted a ban on child labor inside of anthracite and bituminous mines, and because of that, the state's conclusion was the violation was intentional and egregious. The state also notes that company officials were not forthcoming in their response to questions about the incident, fabricated gas and safety readings as common practice, and, in some cases, presented fabrications about details in the mine that amounted to perjuries.

The rest of her report cited chapter and verse of violations, from poor record keeping to the failure of regular air testing for explosive gases, even though those infractions were not the cause of the explosion. The itemized list of mining violations filled four full pages of her report and would later be used verbatim in indictments brought against company officials.

Finn got the report the evening she finished it, closed his door, and turned on his desk lamp. He could not stop reading. Valery may have been viewed as an ice queen by many of the inspectors who worked with her, but her passion for this case was undeniable and most compelling. Finn recognized her work on the case had been brilliant and was eager to tell her so.

He got his chance first thing the next morning when she walked into his office and gave him an invitation to dinner at her mother's house in New Cumberland in three weeks. "You and your wife have to come," she said. "You simply must."

"I'll ask and let you know," Finn said. "I'm sure she will be happy to join me. I'm glad your mother is very well."

Then he did something rare for him. He gushed about the quality of her report for 20 minutes. "I was there, and you saw things I didn't see. That was brilliant, Valery Miller. I am proud to know you and even prouder to have you working for me."

At that, she blushed and walked happily down to the coffee stand for cups of coffee and cake donuts. Anders joined them after a few minutes. He, too, was beaming. Finn had sent him a note telling him how proud he was of his work. A copy went to the governor's office.

"We do hard work, Valery," Finn said to her. "It never hurts to break away for some celebration whenever you can."

Later in the day, Howard burst into Ander's office with his invitation in hand. "Does this mean what I think it means?" he asked.

"Can't say because I don't know what you think it means," Anders replied with a chuckle.

"You guys getting married?"

"Can't say," Anders said.

"You have to come to dinner at Valery's mom's place and bring this Mary person you are so excited about. Can you get her here?"

"If she can come, I will go pick her up. That would be just grand, Mary and you and me and Valery and Finn. What a party that will be!"

"Okay, let me know," Anders said.

"Let's talk business. We have the approval to get sidearms. Want to go look for some? We can go after lunch. You can pick the lunch place. I will pick the gun's place."

"Fine," Anders said.

He said he would come by in an hour.

Howard and Anders drove across the river for lunch at a bar, Findlay's, that had a good reputation for hamburgers.

To be sure, they were thick, juicy, well broiled, and served up with a quarter of a pound or so of freshly made French fries. The bun was made at Findley's with whole wheat, so it was a light brown color, and very unlike the blanched white breads Anders had come to hate.

He had a beer with his, and Howard had a coke. They wolfed down their lunches like they had not eaten in days (it was actually hours).

The waiter was intrigued by the man in the spectacular suit with a pistol under his arm and the calm foreigner with him. He asked where he was from.

"I'm from Vulcan in Transylvania."

"Let me ask you a question, is it true…."

Anders cut him off.

"There have never been vampires, ever, in any part of Romania."

And that was that.

***

Valery Miller's mother lived in a big Victorian house her husband had bought with her in mind. They were a thriving couple in many ways, not the least of which was in the delivery of three daughters within seven years. Valery was first but neither the prettiest nor the most talented. June Miller was taller and thinner and natural on her feet, the dancer in the family. Sally Miller was perhaps the sweetest person on the west shore, always kind to everyone and helpful to her mother, who never had to clean and, truth be known, never had to cook either. Sally took care of all of that for her. She was an elementary school teacher. June was a registered nurse and worked at a home for children with mental health problems in New Cumberland.

The house had been paid for by the United Mine Workers in the wake of the slaying of Mr. Miller in Cambria County. The president of the union at that time sat with the family and promised, his eyes full of tears, they would never have to worry about anything financial again. "We all loved how your father did his job, so honest and straight about it," he said.

The family would be indebted to the UMW forever for that gesture. In truth, it was one of the reasons Valery was so serious about the Baltimore Shaft explosion and its connection to the National Miners Union.

Anders had met the sisters several months before the big dinner in a visit to the house during which they committed to teaching him how to dance, used a Sears catalog to select the proper tie to go with the proper shirt, and tried to talk him into buying a hat, which Anders simply would not do.

"I work inside most of the time. Of what use...." When they suggested he would look more stylish in a hat, he just chuckled and said looking more stylish would be useless for him.

"Just thought we could make you a little more polished," Sally said.

"Yes, a little more 'hot to trot,'" said Jane.

"You would be a little more sophisticated if you smoked, too," Jane suggested. "You can't just have Valery smoking by herself."

"Don't want to," Anders said.

"Polished? Hot to trot? To what end?" he said. ("Hot to trot?' Again, another phrase to add to his collection.) They suggested it would make him more attractive to women. "I am already attractive to Valery. What other woman could I possibly need?"

They had to agree he was right about that. It was the first point at which they realized how serious Anders was about Valery, always viewed as the senior sister and hence, a decision-maker for the trio.

They talked about it for weeks and planned a Transylvanian-themed engagement in secret, complete with vampires hanging from the roof of a big tent.

As the day for the big dinner approached, they became more involved in the planning. It was Sally's idea to rent the circus tent with the dance floor and hire the five-piece jazz band to play after dinner. Valery just shook her head and said, "Why not just invite a priest and have the wedding that afternoon?"

"Valery, you are so practical. But this is not work. This is life, and a party is called for. When one of the sisters goes, the others get to have a party!" She also hired a fire eater, two professional jugglers, and a rent-a-pony man.

"No one is going to forget this one," she said.

Valery bought into it, but mainly because she so loved her sisters. The fact that money was not an issue for them helped with the decision. The nation was trapped in a deep depression, but the Miller family was well-financed and out of debt.

Mrs. Miller watched all of this with the delight of a mother who remembered her own engagement party to Mr. Miller so many years ago. There was beer in a wash tub full of ice, Chesapeake Bay crabs for everyone, and a singer who played guitar and sang old cowboy songs. She thought that was as fancy a thing as she would ever have in her life. Now she listened to her daughters building this layer cake of an engagement dinner and could only imagine what they would do with a wedding.

Anders did what all good men did in such situations. He stayed out of the way and took Valery on lots of long walks down the Susquehanna, looking at the bright lights of Harrisburg across the river and yielding, occasionally, to the siren call of Nick's Last Chance for chili after work. Nick, a criminal for sure but not a hardened man, could see their relationship growing, especially during the Baltimore Shaft investigation, when they would nurse their chilis and beers and talk for hours about how this aspect or that aspect of the disaster might have played out.

He hoped, watching them, that they never investigated him.

*****

The guest list was completed two whole weeks before the event. Howard said it took Mary just two seconds to say "Yes" and accept the ride from him. She would stay at Valery's mother's house during the visit. Mr. and Mrs. Finn were delighted to come, as were Barry and Emma. "Let me make cakes and coffee," Barry said. "I'll bring the big coffee maker."

Jim Dorrance from the governor's office and his latest wife planned to come and bring along a surprise in the form of the governor and his wife, who, despite the office, were common people and very much enjoyed a good time. The General was said to be considering it but having a hard time deciding, of course, because he had passed on one wedding a year earlier and didn't want that couple to be offended if he went to this one. His loyal aide explained it would not be a problem in the least, and he agreed.

The Governor would give him a ride. He insisted there was to be no fuss.

Surprisingly, it did not rain on the big day. July was a problematic month in central Pennsylvania. There could be rumbling thunderstorms and the occasional tornado. That didn't happen.

The tent, which was white and had flags flying from its poles, looked like something from a 16th Century festival. It took 20 men who came in a big truck two hours just to get the roof elevated. The dance floor looked like it was lifted right from a basketball court.

The Miller sisters made the Vampires from black fabric and wood frames, and, to be sure; they were scary but not too scary. They asked Anders as he was checking out the tent whether they looked authentic, and he said, "There are no vampires in Romania. I do not know." Then he laughed and said they were just perfect.

By the time they were done, the Miller girls had invited everyone they could think of who knew Valery, their own boyfriends, their mother's best friends, two local priests from the Children's home, and an array of doctors who just didn't want to miss it. They invited their father's friends from the UMW, and all the mining inspectors they could find, too. State troopers from all over Central Pennsylvania flooded in, some in police cars. One, a sergeant, rode in on a spectacular brown thoroughbred from the police academy all the way over in Hershey. In all, the girls would be feeding 200 people in connection with the Apostole-Miller Engagement.

Nick set up the catering.

He did not use his criminal buddies. Instead, he hired the chef from a resort just south of New Cumberland to organize the meal for 200. It was perfect, chicken, Chesapeake crabs, baked potatoes with sour cream, champagne contributed by the Liquor Control

Board (which was scandalous enough that Valery and Anders would have suggested an investigation, but the governor announced to them privately that he had paid for it. They only looked like a part of Little Nick's criminal empire.)

The dinner began with a toast from Anders.

"I had absolutely no idea what would be happening to me when I got on Leviathan for the long journey to America, but I can tell you now that it was the smartest move I have ever made and, at this instant, the most delightful. Before we have this drink, I need to ask Valery to marry me as soon as possible in any way her sisters think would be appropriate."

Then he gave her a modest ring, and the band played "On the Sunny Side of the Street." To rounds of cheering.

The sisters, of course, wept in unison. Mrs. Miller brushed away one tear but then beamed the entire afternoon. Just after the toast, sirens screamed out as two state police cars, and a white Ford Limo rolled onto the lawn. The governor and his wife had arrived, along with The General, who seemed to be welded to his wife's side but smiling just the same.

"Thank you, Anders," Valery whispered to him. "You are quite the best man I have ever met, and that includes a lot of good men." He just smiled at her and gave her a kiss.

The band started playing just after dinner, and Howard unleashed himself from his buddies, grabbed Mary, and they swept onto the floor like Fred Astaire and Ginger Rogers. They jitterbugged everyone into a frenzy. Even troopers who knew Valery and Howard were dancing with whomever they could find, their pistols slapping their hips and their campaign hats bouncing. June and Sally joined in with their boyfriends. Finn asked his wife, but she smiled and said, "No, I wouldn't want anyone to be hurt, particularly me."

Anders gave it a try but needed guidance form the sisterly trio just to get through some simple steps. He resolved to work on it with them. Each of them gave him a big, red kiss on the cheek. The Miller girls were indeed something, he thought to himself.

The game really picked up when The General and the governor and his wife said good night and motored away with their trooper escorts. Having him was a nice touch, Anders thought. But it had definitely dampened the mood. "I don't want to work up there," Valery thought, resolving to stick with Finn and the mining inspectors. Dorrance and his wife necked off in the corner. They thought no one saw them, but everyone did.

The partiers made a racket until about 12:30 a.m. the next day. Mrs. Miller was worried about the noise, but as one of the troopers said, "What are they going to do, call the cops?"

By dawn on Monday, the tent was coming down; the lawn was cleaned up, and the leftover food, lots of it, was donated to the Salvation Army shelter down in Harrisburg and delivered in the state police cars. Anders and Valery were wrapped around each other in the living room on the sofa; both were sound asleep.

"I guess we have to go to work," Anders said.

"Yes, I have stuff to do," Valery said. "But I could just stay here wrapped up in your arms for the rest of my life. Still, work is work."

Finn and his wife had left at a decent hour, so he would be at work early. Barry and Emma, who had a great time at the party and made even more friends to sell coffee and donuts to, made certain they got out, too, because the government runs on coffee, and that's what they did so well. The troopers, the mine inspectors, even the horse, they were all gone. It was quiet as the sun rose over the river. Mockingbirds were juggling their songs, along with the Robins. Anders and Valery drifted off to sleep for a little while, then got up and prepared to go to work. The tent and the men who put it up and the truck that delivered it were all gone.

Howard found a way to slip out of the room Mary was using, giving her a big, long kiss before he left. The last thing he heard going out was: "Love you Howard."

303

He felt exactly the same about her.

***

Finn was praying for a slow Monday. He was quite good at partying when he was younger, but he was feeling all of his 57 years this particular Monday morning. He loved the time he spent with his wife at the Anders-Miller event, as it was becoming known. Valery brought a whole pack of notes to work that had the date "Sept. 1", the Miller-Apostole wedding printed on them. She had talked that over with her sisters. She wanted a small, quiet ceremony in a Catholic church with only close friends and family. In the wake of the engagement blowout, they thought that was a great idea. They would accept no gifts and suggested people contribute to the Salvation Army downtown.

Anders and Valery came in to work together, beaming like children on a sunny morning and eager to get coffee and donuts and then get the day underway. Valery had no idea what she would be doing, having completed the Baltimore Shaft Explosion report at the end of last week. Now her desk was clean. Anders still had the Russian files on his desk but was in something of a daze.

"Can life actually be this easy?"

He realized that Valery had made almost every decision that led to their engagement. Other than an ongoing conversation about life together, Anders could not remember whether he even asked Valery formally to marry him. He was drifting deep into thought about it when Howard walked in.

"Now THAT was an engagement party!" he said, louder than he should have but with no sense of embarrassment. "I thought my butt was going to fall off with that much dancing."

"You continued to amaze me, Howard. How many women did you dance with?"

"All of them," he said, including Valery and both of her sisters, and I would have danced with her mother, too, but she was too shy."

"Mary looked great, Howard. I was pleased to meet her and talk with her for a bit. She seems to be pretty well arranged in the head if you know what I mean. She thinks the world of you, I can tell you."

"I think I feel the same way about her," Howard said.

"I would marry her as quickly as I could, but I have to get the know the family, and they have to get to know me before I ask, I think. I mean, that's the polite way to do it."

"In this country, yes, it is," Ander said.

"Howard, are you going to be offended if I ask Finn to be my best man instead of you? I would have both of you, but it's not like with bridesmaids, you know?"

"It's not a problem. I would like to remind you that it is the tradition in America for men to take the groom out to dine and drink the night before, so don't plan anything. I have a whole array of troopers who went to the wedding who want to give you that send-off, okay?"

"Whatever you need," Anders said.

Then he returned to the Russian translations on his desk. None of them added much detail to the Baltimore Shaft explosion investigation, but they were certainly case studies of how old-fashioned bureaucracies worked in Russia. The sentences ran on and on and leaned on the very limited collection of nouns and verbs available to bureaucrats. "No wonder they can't get anything done," Anders thought. "It would take days just to understand what they were talking about."

On the 45th page of the documents, he found something he needed to report to Finn right away so it could be relayed to the feds. It was a suggestion to expand infiltration efforts into almost all aspects of the American Federation of Labor. Anders picked up the document and walked to Finn's office.

"Hello, Mr. Finn, and thank you for coming and bringing your wife yesterday," Anders said. "We loved having you there.

"I found some business in these Russian letters you should know about. It appears they wanted to infiltrate about all of the AFL they could, and however, they could. There are no details. But your federal friends might appreciate the heads up."

"I'm certain they will say they already knew about whatever it was we tell them. I think that's how they avoid having to return favors, by pretending they already know everything. Still, it's the right thing to do. Could you type up a translation of just that section for me so I can tell them?"

"Sure. And one more thing, if I might. Would you please be my best man for the wedding? Valery and I can't think of anyone we would want more."

"I would be honored," Finn said.

He wrote "Sept. 1, Valery and Anders wedding" on his calendar, then went back to reading accident files from his many field people.

He completed the pile that had been left for him and was about to head for a coffee when the phone rang.

"Chief Madden from Portage Finn. There has been an explosion at Coalman, and we have at least 110 men trapped in the mine. We're working on the rescue with the mining team, and we can use any help you can muster."

Chapter 19: Coalman Mine

Finn told Madden said he would be sending a team of investigators headed by Valery Miller along with her associate, Anders Apostle. "He's fluent in almost any language you might run into in a mine in Portage, Tom, so I think he will be of great help to you. Are you okay? Are your men okay?"

Madden paused at that and thought for a minute.

"Yes, we're all fine, but this is a bad one, Finn. We're going to need a lot of help. We are going to use the firehouse as a makeshift mortuary. I've called in coroners from five counties to help us with the dead."

"We're all on the way, Tom."

Finn knew Madden well. His father had been the local law for many years, then burgess for the town. Tom had run the fire department for 20 years after he left Miller Shaft and knew what he was doing down in a mine. He had started working when he was 12 years old and had done everything from spragging coal cars to running rooms dug into the bituminous. He also had a good collection of volunteers who were eager to help with rescues. Like Tom, many of them had worked at Coalman and knew the layout of the place and the challenges they would be facing.

Finn walked to Valery's office and got Anders to join him on the way.

"What I was worried about for a long time has happened. Gas explosion at Coalman Mine at Portage. There was a small fire, but not enough air to support it, I suspect. We have over 100 men trapped in that mine. I need you to get there right away, Valery, and run the investigation until I can get there. Make sure the records are sealed in the office, the ventilation is up and running, and get all the inspectors we can to the mine. Don't let the bosses push you around.

307

They are pretty aggressive. I know you can handle it, but you have to show them right off that you know exactly what you are doing.

"Everyone needs to be careful in that mine. It's gassy and has had a lot of roof falls. It also has running water, like rivers in some areas, so you have to watch for that. Make sure you have complete kits with you, cameras, and all when you leave here. Don't go down there without your harnesses. Use tethers, and don't go off on your own. See Chief Madden when you get there. You will recognize him right away, short with gray hair and solid as a rock. It will take a good six hours to get there by car. Now. Go."

They left at that instant and went to the state garage to get one of the department's cars. They checked the trunk to make certain there were two disaster kits, flares, cameras, and all the equipment associated with them. Valery grabbed a highway map. The best route, she concluded, would be to head straight west on the two-lane state highway instead of going south to hook up to the turnpike. She scoped out a course that would get them to Duncansville and then Southeast to Portage. She said she would drive. They headed out of town along the Susquehanna and then went straight west at Duncannon on Rte. 220. It was a well-kept road, with not too many trucks at this time of day. They started heading into the foothills of the Alleghenies at Huntingdon, then drove up the mountains. At Duncansville, they stopped for coffee and sandwiches on the grounds they would have no idea when they would be eating again, got the restaurant to pack them two lunches, and drove up the mountain toward Portage.

It would have been a stunning trip on a nice day with no pressure. Now it was just a nightmare. The road from Duncansville to Portage twisted and turned as it climbed up the side of the mountain. It had been paved but not well maintained and also torn up by coal trucks. One hairpin turn, locally known as "Devil's Elbow," nearly led to a skid off the road. But Valery glued her eyes to the road, kept the Ford under control, and had little to say. They reached a high point on the road, an intersection with farms all around, then turned right at a sign that said Portage was just 10 miles away. But it was like driving into a different world in a different century. Coal mines, working and abandoned, dotted the hillsides and defined the towns along the road. "Last Chance Inn" was a bar near the Last Chance Mine, the last place a working miner could get a job no matter his condition.

They passed a dozen mines before they reached Portage, each of them marked by a big boney pile that seemed to tumble from the sides of the mountain. Decades of mine waste made these hills. Some of them were still burning. It gave the hills a scent of rotten eggs and seemed to paint a gray glaze over everything. The company houses, long away now from the point at which they were well kept, seemed to be collapsing into the ground at some point, their porches sagging, and front steps were broken. Old appliances rusted in the yards, along with old cars. It was as depressing a scene as Valery had ever witnessed. They drove into Portage from the top of a hill where the highway split off. A funeral home sat on one side of the road. By the time Valery was halfway down the hill, she could see the commotion building at the other end of town. Cars, ambulances, fire trucks, company trucks, they all lined the streets down to the end of town, where the road turned off at a simple sign that said "Coalman."

It was raining, and hundreds of people lined up on the hillsides and coal banks above the mine to wait for word about the men trapped inside. Valery parked in front of the mine office, left the car, and immediately went in to seal the records.

The day boss was in the office and was reluctant to allow a woman in to seal records.

"Get out of my way, or I will have you arrested right now," she said. "Stay the fuck out of this room.

"I need to see the fire bosses and their superiors in this room at 9 a.m."

She went to the long filing drawers where records were kept and put a bright green "Commonwealth of Pennsylvania, Department of Mining" seal on each drawer.

She asked Anders to look for Chief Madden to get a report on what they had found so far. Five other mine inspectors from the region waited at the company office.

She posted two of them inside.

"No one is to touch anything," she said. "We need these records for our investigation. You have my authority to arrest anyone who gives you trouble."

She knew it was important to establish herself as early as possible in the investigation. She did that by acting very much, not like a woman.

There was no time for formalities. Madden told Valery, as best as anyone could tell, there was a gas explosion deep in the mine, probably caused by an electrical fault. He and his crew of volunteers had recovered a dozen bodies from the pathways inside the mine, but there were still many more missing. Although there was a small fire, the chief said, most of the bodies had not been burned.

"They suffocated," he said.

"Do you have a map of the mine? Is it up to date?" Anders asked.

"Yes," the chief answered. He took them inside to a room used for meetings. A collection of volunteers was at the table, drinking coffee and talking quietly about what had happened. The map was big and drawn in great detail. It showed a slice of the mine about 300 feet underground. It looked like the map of a city, with entry avenues running front to back and hundreds of rooms cut into the coal. They were created, some of them many years ago, by miners working in teams. They would work their way down the main corridors, which were used to haul out coal. Each team of two miners would cut a "room" in the wall, create space for an undercutting machine to come in, then harvest the coal from the room. The undercutter would come in and clear a space in the coal face about two feet wide and as much as ten feet deep. The firing teams would set their charges along the tops of these cuts, then set them off, creating a pile of bituminous to shovel away. It was a very effective way to harvest coal in the vein, part of a vast stretch of bituminous that ran all the way from the New York border to an area south of Portage when the field headed west and ended up in Illinois. It was the world's largest deposit of bituminous coal, and it had kept Portage prosperous since it was first tapped in 1880.

The longer they mined, the deeper they cut into the mountain.

Valery set the map on a north-to-south axis and asked Chief Madden where the explosion was in the mine. He walked all the way around the table and put his stretched hands over the far southeast corner of the deepest segment of the mine. It was more than 3 miles from the entrance. There was a back entrance used for ventilation, but the explosion led to a massive roof fall in that part of the mine. It was unlikely anyone could get through.

Valery and Anders asked everyone but the mine inspectors to leave the room. Then she set out her plan, leaving no doubt about who was in charge.

They would use the front entrance of the mine, then work their way down the main corridor, front to back, and check each of the intersecting corridors that crossed the main path. They were all to wear breathing apparatus and keep an eye on gas and air levels as they moved into the mine. "Don't take any chances here," Valery told the inspectors. "There has been enough death here today."

"What we need to do in our first pass is look for any signs of survivors, but also take notes of where bodies are found along the way. Take notes, also about where you see the damage and what kind of damage you see. Everyone is to wear breathing apparatus and a line, and all the teams should be individually attached. We don't want anyone slipping away, either in water or under a roof fall. We will be carrying horns, and we will blast them at half-hour intervals. Three blasts in a row will mean someone is in trouble. We know there's a lot of running water at some points way back in the mine, so we have to be careful. No one goes in without a safety lamp, and keep an eye on gas readings while you are going into the mine. The explosion,

Chief Madden says, initiated in the far southwest corner of the mine, so we need to get there first and lay out a zone of damage, so we know how far it reached. Keep an eye on the roof! In fact, each team should have its own fire boss checking roof and gas levels. We can stay as teams in the mine for no more than ninety minutes. So, you have to get in and get out in that time frame. Come back here and report on what you have found and then we can update the map and extend the plan. Make clear notes about whatever victims you find because, after the first pass, Madden and his firemen want to come in to retrieve bodies. There is no power in the mine right now, so the wiring won't be a worry. But there is also no ventilation yet, so watch for gas. We're going to try to get the fans running aboveground right away to get some air in there. See you in a while."

Valery and Anders, and two other inspectors made up the first team and entered the timbered opening that led down into the mine. Their headlamps reflected against the dust that had been sprayed on the walls of the mine to lessen the chance of an explosion. It absorbed dampness. It had a scent, a moldy scent that saturated the still air. There were no signs of life in this part of the mine, but it was perhaps three miles from the point of the explosion that trapped the men.

The pathway in was steep and, at about a quarter mile, led to the man trip that the miners rode to get down to the mule barns and the coal face. It was strangely silent, walking into the mine that morning. Valery and Anders were kept 30 feet apart, tied together with a safety line. All the other inspectors were connected that way, too. They were behind them using slats of wood and canvas to construct an airway, so fresh air could move through the mine again. The explosion had ruined many of the brattices that had been built to control airflow in the mine. Those structures had to be replaced so fresh air could be controlled when the big fans were turned on again. That could be coming at any minute.

The roof parts of some of the rooms at the coal face were working, creaking, and groaning. Occasionally, a slab of rock would break away and slam to the ground.

Valery turned toward Anders and shouted, "How is your head?" She was checking for headaches, the first sign that the carbon dioxide level was rising to unsafe levels.

"I'm okay for now," he said. He checked his safety lamp, which continued to burn, signaling enough air for now.

They found the first bodies some 400 feet into the mine. The concussion and carbon monoxide, black damp, of the explosion had apparently killed them. Their bodies were not burned or bruised. They looked like they were sleeping. There were three of them in the same area. Anders made a note on his map. He looked for their ID tags and wrote down the numbers.

Their lamps were showing an increase in carbon monoxide, and after that reached a certain level, they would have to leave. Then he and Valery moved on, deeper into the mine. Valery was reading the map kept in the main office, so she knew in one sense where she was going. She could see a pathway that led all way back to that southwest corner where the explosion occurred. They walked carefully. Anders checked each of the stations the fire bosses would use in their morning walks into the mine. There were no records.

At each station, the fire boss, and every shift was supposed to have three of them, kept his own log of gas and air readings and conditions and entered those into a central set ¬of records in the office.

They followed the tracks down into the mine but avoided the gob side, where the wiring was overhead, and the toilet was underfoot. They stopped every 100 feet or so and listened to the earth, which was moving all over the mine and creating an array of squeaks, cracks, and bangs.

They sat down, and Anders took air readings. It was still safe. They would wait there for 15 minutes, then move ahead another 100 yards and repeat the process. There were fire boss stations every couple of hundred feet. Anders noted their presence and checked two of the spaces, really not much more than rectangular holes chopped into the rock and coal. There were no books or notes in these stations. Anders couldn't help but think about anyone who was trapped in the mine. He was keeping his eye on his lamp, too, to make certain they still had enough air to live. The men who were still alive would be hearing those noises, too, and wondering what they meant. They could be an early warning of an impending roof fall, or they might be nothing, or they might just be the noise the mine made. No one noticed it when the machinery was running because it blotted out all other sounds. But now that it was quiet, everything that shifted made a noise, generally a crack or a squeal, or a bang.

Two miles ahead of them, deep into the mine, a collection of miners and their foreman had worked their way after the explosion into a 20-foot by thirty-foot room with a ceiling of coal 8 feet overhead. It was a safety room, a place to escape to in the event of a disaster. There were 35 of them in the room, and they were struggling for air after they had been in the room for the first few hours.

They were unable to complete building a brattice that would have kept the bad air out and left enough inside for them to live on. Black damp, that fatal mixture of gasses sometimes created by explosions, got into the safety room through the back and eventually killed all of them.

Valery and Anders, and the others continued building their airway and cautiously working their way down the shaft until they came to the partially bratticed room. Anders was first in. He counted 34 dead miners, many of them down on the floor where the air would have been better. It took all of them hours to die. He thought about how it must have seemed, watching your friends die one by one, like candles burning out. Some of them were gathered into groups.

Valery was next in the room. "Shit," she said.

"All dead. Every single one of them. Look at them, peaceful as angels but dead as the rocks they are sitting on. They watched each other die."

314

She and Anders went around the ghastly room, collecting the numbers from the brass discs each miner wore up on his collar.

They had still not reached the site of the explosion, which was another 300 feet down into the mine. Their headlamps jumped along the rock of the walls, the lumps of coal on the floor. Off in the distance, Anders saw a form. It was a man sitting with his lunch bucket on his lap. Rolling out his safety line, he walked up to the man, who looked as though he could sit up and tell everyone what had happened.

Dead. "That one was killed by the gas," Anders said to himself. He took down his number.

The foreman was in the room, and investigators found later he had made a list of all the men who were with him and a list of where other men had been working at the time of the blast.

Anders could see how it was.

The time for shouting for help had ended quite some time ago. No one was coming. Some of the men had already fallen asleep. No one was injured in the room, yet everyone was dying.

The last hours of the victims of the disaster would play out in this dark room, the stale air disappearing and the men growing quiet and then falling into their last sleep. They hugged the floor to find what air was left. Some of them wrote their wills on the tops of their metal lunch buckets. One wrote a letter to his wife, scratched into a flat rock. They knew they were dying and that there was nothing anyone could do to help them, so they suffered in silence or uttered a few last words before falling asleep. There was no light and not so much as a breeze to provide relief. This is the way, so many miners died.

"I'm sorry," one of them wrote on the bottom of his lunch bucket. He never had the chance to say for what or to whom. It was just one man's legacy as everyone around him was dying.

"I think we need to get out of here now and let the crews do their work collecting the bodies," Valery said. They turned and started the long, sad walk back up from the bottom of the mine. Every 50 yards or so, they passed miners and other inspectors coming in to help remove bodies or create the schematic of what had happened. Valery wanted to talk to survivors above ground, but the day was fading, and families still waiting for word were gathered around the mouth of the mine.

It took an hour and a half to get out of the mine, much of the time used to make certain they were still in safe areas. At some points, gas levels were still high. But as ungainly as the kits were, the inspectors and Valery were wearing breathing apparatus that allowed them to proceed.

No one saw what was happening, but everyone in the string of mine inspectors knew.

With a series of cracks, at first just pops and then louder, a slab of rock broke from the roof of the mine and landed on Anders Apostle, smashing him to the floor, crushing his breathing equipment, and breaking one of his legs.

He was trapped within sight of the opening to the mine. Valery and the other inspectors rushed to him and struggled to move the slab of rock that had pinned him to the floor. They could not budge it. One of the other inspectors grabbed a timber that had broken from the roof and used it to try to wedge the rock off Anders while another man worked with a hand pick to try to break the rock. Three other inspectors joined in. They were able to get the slab off his leg and drag him to the pathway out of the mine. But he was in bad shape, bleeding and drifting in and out of consciousness. Valery took his hand as the other inspectors hauled him out.

"Ambulance and medical help!" one of the men shouted at the mine entrance. Madden and a collection of his volunteers rushed over and took Anders from the other inspectors. They laid him on a stretcher and put him into a waiting ambulance. Valery could not leave the site. Finn had not yet arrived. She sent one of the inspectors along to take Anders to the hospital. She looked at him as he was being put into an ambulance. "Hold on, Anders, hold on. I'll come to you as soon as I can."

Its red light flashing against the hillsides in the night, the ambulance sped away. Valery turned to the other inspectors and, with the same diligence that had defined her from her first day on the job, said, "Let's get inside and look at this map and start talking to survivors."

But inside of her, she was weeping.

Somehow, that anxiety melted away when she walked into 's meeting room and saw Howard waiting for her.

"Anders was hit by a rock fall just before we got to the opening. He's seriously injured, Howard. I think he will survive, but I don't know. I need a favor from you. Could you find out what hospital they took him to so I can call later?"

"I'm sorry, Valery; of course, I can."

Somewhere inside her, a switch flipped, and she stopped worrying about her fiancé. Howard would be looking for him, and no one was better at that than Howard.

Then she turned to the room and began her work.

"Anyone gets anything from the survivors?"

One of the inspectors from Pittsburgh said he had talked to a man who described seeing a bright light, like a fire, down the shaft in the corner where the explosion occurred. "He said he thought the motor on the trip was on fire, then the concussion of the explosion hit him, and he was knocked out. I think he was looking at a gas explosion set off by the trip."

Valery spread the map of the mine out on the table.

"Do you know where he was when this happened?" she asked.

"Yes, he was about 150 feet or so from the intersection of the crossway that goes over the main track. He pointed to the map,

317

"right here." One side was a mined-out section that was awaiting a brattice. The other side was a set of working rooms. The trip was pulling nine cars up the shaft at that point, and it had just moved through a switch and was heading upward."

"Did he say anything about the air?" she asked.

"He did. He said it had reversed and then stopped at that point, that there was no air moving through the mine just then."

"Had any of you reached that area before you had to come out?" she said. Another man said he had. He reported that the mined-out section looked like it had collapsed, with lots of rock and splinted wood, and a very high gas reading in the area, even this many hours after the explosion.

"They knew they had trouble there," he said. "The area was dangered off with boards and not accessible. One of the signs said 'Do Not Enter,' and the other just said, "Danger." No one was working in that room and had not in quite some time, I would guess. There was damage on the roof, too, like minor falls. It was not a stable roof."

"And the gas readings at that point?"

"My Davy lamp flame was high, so it was very gassy even then," he said. "In fact, I thought I should get out of there until we got some air moving in that area again, and that's exactly what I did."

"Okay," she said. "Let's start the tab on who was killed or injured, then mark the schematic on where the bodies were located." She spread the big blueprint out on the tabletop, excused herself to go to the bathroom, and got a coffee from the Red Cross. She had a cigarette on the porch and then went back into the room. There were a dozen men around the table comparing their notes. She had Anders's collection of tab numbers from the dead he had found and the bodies in the room.

By the time they were done tabulating, they had 63 dead miners had spread across a limited area down in the corner of the mine. In a dash to safety that was later labeled nothing short of a miracle, a dozen men crawled with their faces as close to the floor as they could get and worked their way to a passage that led to fresh air and an exit from the mine. They had walked out of the mine to the cheers of the hundreds of people waiting for word about their kin. Many of them had already talked to the mining inspectors.

Edward Finn walked into the mine office at 9:30 p.m. after his long drive from Harrisburg. He shook Valery's hand and asked everyone to join him so he could get an initial sense of what was going on. Howard walked into the room just after him and approached Valery.

"He's at St. Joseph's in Johnstown, and there is a team of surgeons working on his leg. He's going to be okay, but it's going to take a long time; that's what they told me. He told them to tell you not to worry."

"Thank you, Howard," Valery said. She didn't hug him or kiss him because she was surrounded by miners. It had been hard enough to win their respect over the five years she had been their supervisor, and she didn't want to lose it in what might appear to some to be a moment of weakness.

The locations of the bodies were marked on the schematic, which would serve as part of the official record of the incident. The men presented their findings while Valery and Finn took notes. It was getting late, and everyone was exhausted.

"I need to go to see Tom Madden at the firehouse. You might want to come along," he said to Valery. "He will already have the first version of what the hell happened."

Madden was on the second floor of the firehouse when Finn and Valery arrived. It was a sturdy brick building with tall windows on the second floor that looked out onto Main Street. They could see it was busy, but nothing prepared them for what they found.

Madden was bathing and shaving; all the miners and barbers were cutting their hair.

"Hello, Finn, Miss Miller," he said. "I'm sorry to have to see you again under these circumstances."

"What are you doing, Tom?"

"We're bathing them and preparing them for their families to come up and say farewell," he said. "It's important that they get to see them the way they looked before." Madden had even collected clean clothing. Some of the men were in suits with white shirts and ties. Some of them were in coveralls. Except for the men who had been burned, they all seemed peaceful, somehow at rest.

The chief said the plan was for the families to identify their loved ones, even though their tags had been collected. Then they would be released to individual funeral homes across the region for embalming. The families would make their own funeral and burial arrangements.

"We're going to have a Mass up at the church day after tomorrow, a memorial," Tom said. "Of course, you and your people would be welcome."

"Thanks, Tom. I don't know how long they are going to be here. We have 43 inspectors here, and you know the kind of work they have to do. I'll come back to see you tomorrow, and thanks for your work on this. I'm sorry you lost your friends and some of your crew."

The chief nodded but, typical of a man who had seen death so many times, displayed no emotion.

Finn asked Valery to join him in a quiet office on the first floor of the mine headquarters. "We're going to have to start on the records tomorrow, and I know you are worried about Anders, but we need to nail down the cause of this one as quickly as we can. I would like you to pay close attention tomorrow morning to the fire boss reports and summaries of conditions in the mine. From what I have heard, one of the ceilings in a mined-out area collapsed and released a huge volume of methane gas that killed most of those men who were together in that room. The trip set off the explosion, either with its roof guide or with sparks from the engine down below. We need to see what kind of maintenance records the mine had on that trip if any. We also need to know about gas in that part of the mine over time. One of the inspectors told me his Davy Lamp flame was burning very high even when they got to the area, and that was hours after the explosion. They were worried enough about it to get out of there until ventilation could be restored. I think we should leave Howard in Johnstown with Anders and then start reviewing the records and asking some questions about this. Is that okay with you?"

"Of course, Finn. Do you mind if I go to Mass the day after tomorrow? Chief Madden said it's going to be the main memorial service, and I want to pay my respects first and just talk with people and see what they heard about the mine."

"Sure, I would expect nothing less," Finn said.

"The people are already talking about needing to get the mine reopened as soon as possible. You know how those people are. It's all money lost to them. But we don't want that to happen until your inspectors have had a good bit of time to work through that blast area and let us know what actually happened.

"Okay, Finn."

"And Valery, I don't want you to worry about Anders. Howard is one of the best men we have, and I have already talked to the hospital administrator and told him how important Anders is to us. We'll have him covered from lots of directions."

"Thanks, Finn," she said. Then she turned away and walked back outside for some air. "The people who had gathered at the mine had received their sad news, and we were on our way home. It was dark. The rain had stopped, and the stars were shining over the Alleghenies. It was a beautiful thing to see," Valery thought to herself. "I just wish I wasn't seeing it alone."

Finn made arrangements for a meeting of all the state inspectors in the main office the next day. They all needed to hear what had been found, what they had learned, and what they needed to pursue. It would take a lot of control to make that meeting work right, so Finn decided he would handle it himself and let Valery continue her search of company mining records, which was equally important at this stage.

There were 35 inspectors in the room when Finn opened the meeting the next morning. They had all been in the mine since the explosion. Some of them had talked to company executives. Some of them had talked to families. All of them had some first impressions of the level of safety in the mine before the blast.

"They weren't dusting and keeping the place clean of coal dust," one of them said. There was enough explosive dust in there to make the mountain disappear. There's no sign of comprehensive rock dusting on the walls.

"I don't like the look of the wiring," said another. They have 440-volt lines hanging so low I'm surprised they haven't lost more miners from electrocution." But another of the inspectors noted that at least the overhead lines were on the gob side of the tunnel, which was used for all kinds of garbage, including human waste. No one would be tramping around in that stuff.

The complaints went on and on, which might be expected once experienced mine inspectors are unleashed on an accident site. It wasn't that they wanted to draw attention to themselves, but they tended to pay attention to everything they saw, sensed, touched, and somehow made contact with in the dark, damp mine.

This kind of venting was important, Finn knew, because all of his men were touched by the losses in and felt for the families. They had to have a chance to vent about what they had witnessed before Finn directed them into a more purposeful review of what they had found.

"Did any of you do lamp readings?" Finn asked.

The Davy Lamp had been a fixture in coal mining since its invention more than a century earlier. It was a reliable source of safe light; first, that would not set off a gas explosion because of its design, and second, the length of the flame in the lamp was a dependable measure of how much explosive methane was in the air. Some of the more recent lamps had glass globes in them with black lines to measure the flame height.

Seven of the men said they took regular readings as they were moving into the mine. Gas levels were very high at some points, in particular near mined-out areas where the air currents carried leaking gas into the main passageways. They didn't get sick because they were wearing breathing apparatuses in most cases. But that kind of gas was such a common problem that it was viewed as a violation of state mining law and required an immediate repair, usually with bratticing to redirect the flow of fresh air. Methane, Carbon Dioxide, and Carbon Monoxide all played a role in the sad legacy of mine disasters of the time, and the inspectors were always measuring volumes of those gases wherever they could. Usually, they used a device that had a vacuum in it that took air samples that were checked at a lab later. But for immediate reference, nothing was better than the Davy Lamp, an early 18th-century device invented in England that saved the industry and countless lives in the mines by detecting different kinds of gases. The men who reported were finding methane all over the mine. But that problem disappeared in most areas as soon as the huge fans that sent air into the mine were put back into service a few hours after the explosion. That left only pockets of gas in isolated areas. They were dangerous and marked off by the inspectors as they moved through the damages in the mine, looking for victims.

"I'm surprised, so few of the men had fire injuries, except for those closest to the explosion," one of the inspectors said. "I found two dead mules that had extensive burns on their heads and bodies, but they were pulling cars right in front of the area where the explosion hit."

"Any thoughts about the cause?" Finn asked.

One of the veteran inspectors from the western part of the state spoke up.

323

"Methane unleashed by a roof fall, I would bet, carried into the main air current in huge volumes and then set off by one of the trip motors. Seen that before. It's all too common in these older mines."

He said, "some of the survivors had talked about hearing rumbling above the ceiling near the explosion point. That may have been a warning that the ceiling was on the verge of collapse."

There was a pause. Everyone in the room knew what they had heard about.

Then Finn asked a tough question.

"Who wants to volunteer to go back to the area where that man trip was sitting and check all the adjacent rooms and passageways for gas, roof falls, and air circulation? Wear breathing equipment and keep your lamps burning."

In a response that did not surprise him at all, 12 men said they would do that.

"Sort it out among yourselves," Finn said. "No fewer than six. Wear tethers and keep in sight of each other. I need the equivalent of a fire boss report on the areas around the explosion. Careful, please."

"Yep," one of the men said.

They headed outside to smoke and set up a team. Finn went to get coffee for himself and Valery, who had locked herself into the central office space and was pouring over mine records."

"You finding anything?" he asked as he delivered the coffee to Valery.

"Quite a bit," she said.

"It's another one of those situations where it looks to me like they would sit down once a month and make sure all the spaces were filled in on the forms. The gas readings are too consistent with being collected from the results. You can tell because all the ink is the same on those entries from the fire bosses. We have to talk to the fire bosses about how they did this if they did it at all."

Finn nodded and cast a glance at the mountain of documents Valery had already reviewed. "You hear from Howard about Anders?"

"Other than that, he is in good hands, no," she said.

"Maybe we can run down there tomorrow and see him," Finn said.

"I would like that," she said. The prospect of a visit gave her a little more energy for the tedious work she was doing. The coffee helped, too. Page after page, she reviewed the fire boss reports and mine conditions. On most mornings, they reported the mine was safe to use. Specific areas had been "dangered off" at certain points when gas readings were high, but those incidents rarely spread past two days.

Curiously, some days were missing. Some whole pages of entries had been cut from the record.

Why?

That would be a question for the mine operators and the people who controlled these books. She made a note to ask Finn about all of that and about when they could assemble the fire bosses.

Then she closed the books, gathered up her things, and walked out on the front porch. It was evening, cool, clear. The smell of the disaster was gone, along with all of the emergency equipment that sat at the mine opening when it was thought some workers might have survived.

She was in a lonely, sad place and feeling it. She had a cigarette and walked to the Red Cross wagon to see if there was any coffee left. She had one cup, then headed to her state car and drove to the hotel in Cresson where she and Anders had planned to stay. It was a classy old place constructed when that part of Cambria County was a magnet for big money looking for fresh air and good hunting. It was called The Grant Hotel because Ulysses S. Grant, riding on what was then the new Portage incline railroad, stopped over on his way to begin school at West Point. Lots of woodwork, lots of open windows, and big porches on the first and second floor. Even in the decline of the depression, it remained a delight to visit. She decided she would settle in and go rock on a rocker on the second floor. She wasn't hungry and never drank by herself. She just sat, rocked, and looked out over the Alleghenies at the rising moon and a few fluffy white clouds in a deep blue sky.

She could not stop thinking about Anders and would not sleep a wink that night, waiting for Finn to come for breakfast and then for the drive to St. Joseph's Hospital in Johnstown.

Finn met her in the restaurant at 8 a.m. They talked about the mine and the problems identified so far, and also about the problem in law that limited most individual fines to about $100. "I think we have to start working on that as soon as we get back to Harrisburg. We need to have fines that are based on the true damages of an incident. Prison sentences in some cases, too. Now it doesn't even seem like we're slapping them on the wrist.

Valery toyed with her oatmeal, digging little pits and filling them with brown sugar and milk. She mixed it all up and ate it very slowly, with bites of toast between the spoonsful of oatmeal. It tasted good, just like at home, and with the coffee, left her full and ready to face her lover's injuries in the hospital.

"I know you are worried, Valery," Finn said, "But Anders is a very strong young man, full of energy, and he will get over this before you know it. Maybe he'll have a limp when it's raining…I don't know. I just hope he's not in a lot of pain."

Finn finished his breakfast, and they headed to the car for the trip to Johnstown, a 45-minute ride. They went down the Easy Grade, and she pointed out Sans Souci, the gay club, for Finn. "Howard and I danced up such a storm in there I thought they were going to adopt us. For a big boy, that Howard has some moves that just won't quit."

326

"I'll bet he does," Finn said. "The wife danced with him five times during your engagement dinner and would probably have run off with him, except he had that Mary woman with him. She's quite the looker, too."

"That she is," Valery said.

Finn turned into the hospital parking lot, and Valery felt her heart begin to throb. She had no idea how Anders would look or what condition he would be in. They went to the desk, and the receptionist sent them to the third floor. They rode up in an elevator that smelled of disinfectant. They got off, turned left, and walked three doors down and into the room where Anders was lying quietly on the bed. Howard was sitting in the chair next to the bed, reading True Detective. "Ahhhhhh!" He said.

"Valery, Finn, here's your man Anders." He had made enough noise that he awakened Anders from his sleep.

"Valery, I am so happy to see you!" She leaned over and kissed his lips, and squeezed his hand. He didn't look bad, but she could see that his left leg was in a heavy cast that ran all the way up to his hip.

"That slab that hit me broke it in four places. It's all wired together and bolted with screws and metal. The doctor says it will be okay in a couple of months if I do my physical therapy and keep moving. No damage to the hip joint. I told him I was getting married in September, and he said I should be good to go for that."

"You do still want to marry me, don't you?"

"More than ever," Valery said.

At that, Finn blushed, and Howard suggested they go out for coffee and a smoke. Finn agreed.

"I'm really happy they are together," Howard said. "Anders is one of the most solid people I have ever met, and Valery is perfect for him, just the right mix of proper behavior and...and...and...

327

"Passion," Finn said, finishing Howard's thought.

"Don't be shy; we have all seen it in her."

Howard asked Finn what he thought had happened at the mine, whether there was wrongdoing or just indifference and sloppy management.

"Can't tell yet," Finn said. "It was a dirty mine for sure, and gassy, but that's not a reason for 63 deaths. Valery's going through the fire boss's records to see what she can find. She's also checking the management staff to make sure the place was run right. So…we'll see. We want to get as many of the fire bosses as we can find in one place and talk to them. Maybe they have something to tell us about all of this."

"If you need anything, just ask," Howard said.

"Thanks," Finn replied.

"So, Mary?"

"I'm going to see her later tonight after I am sure Anders is set for the day and everything is okay. She's some great girl Finn; I have to tell you. Great dancer. Great cook. And sweet."

"Hmm," Finn said. "Do I smell another wedding boiling away?"

"Soon enough, I think. I have to pass muster with her family first."

The Von Lindens were a solid lot, with Mary surrounded by three brothers and her widow mother running the restaurant, which was the most successful eating place in all of Cambria County. They were generally in total agreement on everything, from how the restaurant should be run to how late Mary should be allowed to be out at night. That alignment happened after the father, George, died. They had only each other and came to depend on that. Watching over Mary seemed like a natural thing. They didn't circle her like eagles, but they were always at a distance, watching.

They liked what they saw in Howard.

He was not afraid of anything but a real gentleman around Mary and, they had heard, quite the dancer. As a state police detective, he carried a reputation into the house that was like a gold standard, well beyond a common trooper, which would have been enough for any of them. His detective status gave him a swagger that he had never used.

It was just there.

The bond was forged during deer season when Howard killed a buck at 300 yards with a 30-caliber Springfield with a shot so clean the animal just dropped down and died on the spot. The rifle had no scope. The brothers marveled, but Howard was shy about it. "Rifle like that shoots relatively flat for the first 1,000 yards," he said. "All you have to do is a bead in where the heart should be and squeeze."

Later, over beers, the brothers told Howard they could barely even see that far. "I couldn't either," Howard said. "But I know where the heart is on a deer, so it's just a matter of taking the bulk into consideration and making everything kind of level out." They had no idea what he was talking about, but he talked about it so well that it did not matter.

They had the deer butchered and split the meat four ways. Howard told them he would be up for bear if he could get the time off in the late fall. That would have to be further north in the state, up in the mountains, probably at the beginning of winter. Bear was always a big challenge because of where you had to go to find it. Howard told the brothers there was only one rule if they were going to hunt with him, no alcohol on hunting day until the game was hanging and the day was over. Not even a beer. After the hunt, that was the time for drinking.

They talked about him among themselves for days and concluded he and Mary should be wed, but they didn't know how to raise it, Howard being the one who was expected to ask. So, they went to Mary to talk about it. She told Howard about that later.

"I couldn't believe what I was hearing," she said.

"It was like the hero of the deep woods had taken them and shown them how it really was! And that shot, they talked about that shot for more than an hour. Then they asked me if I thought it would be okay if they suggested to Howard that he ask me to marry him. Well, I said, let me think about that. I let it sit for one day and a half, then said, "I think it would be good to marry him. I played it very cool. So you have to ask me to marry you, or the boys will be angry, but first, you have to let them ask you to ask me to marry you."

"Jaysus, is everything going to be this complicated," he asked.

"I sure hope so," she replied.

Arrangements were made with the boys at dinner that very night. "I think you have to ask him to ask me, but I wouldn't waste any time on this one. Do it right away. He's staying in a motel up on the ridge, so he is not hard to find. Just look for the state police car."

The boys left after dinner and headed to the ridge at the top of the easy grade. Sure enough, there was a state police car sitting in front of one of the motel rooms. They went and knocked on the door. A beautiful woman answered, which shocked them until they realized it was Valery. Then they approached Howard.

"Sorry, Miss Miller, but we need to ask Howard to marry our sister Mary. It's certainly okay with mom and all of us if he just asks her right away. Howard, are you okay with that?"

Howard smiled and said sure he was, with one proviso, the wedding would have to occur at the same time Valery marries Anders on September 1. That would give them six months to set it all up.

"Okay," the brothers said in unison and left like characters in a Broadway comedy. "Drive carefully," Howard said. "Of course," they answered, again almost in unison. And off they went.

Mary was delighted with their report.

"That's grand, particularly since he asked me already the day before yesterday, and I said 'Yes," she said, smiling at her brothers. "You could have told us," one of them said.

"And spoil the fun? Not me!"

***

Finn had called the office the day before and asked them to assemble all of the fire bosses for an interview as soon as possible. They said they could get them all in two days. Finn said he would like it sooner, but if that was the best they could do, then okay.

"I just have a couple of questions about the process," Finn told the people. "But I need them all there at once to ask them."

He did not tell the mining people why, but he did not want the fire bosses to have the time to conspire and build uniform answers. He would rather have them surprised and disagreeable than have them answer in unison like a Kindergarten class.

He and Valery met beforehand at Von Lunen's to plot out the course of questions. Valery would ask most of them. "Be tough about it," Finn said. That was wasted breath on Valery, who knew exactly how tough she had to be to keep the fire bosses in line. "I guess it would be inappropriate to put my gun on the table," she said. "That's not what it's for!" Finn said. He gave her a very stern look for three seconds, then broke into a laugh.

"You know how to handle this. Just don't let them slip away from you."

The fire bosses, all eight of them, had been told to show up on time for the meeting, which was scheduled for 9 a.m. Valery made sure there was a big pot of coffee and cups and donuts so they could at least feel respected, if not comfortable. She gave them ten minutes to settle down, then went to her seat at the head of the table, where her notebooks and some records were stacked up.

"I need to know what procedure you used for logging the results of your morning air and safety tests," she said. "Anyone can answer."

"We rarely did them," one of the men answered.

"What?" she said.

"We would generally wait until the end of the week then fill out the documents based on notes."

"What notes?"

"Notes we took on-site."

"Let me see them."

There was silence around the table. One of the men presented a black cardboard notebook with scribblings on the pages. Valery asked him to read the first page.

"Ummmm…I can't remember what I wrote here."

"And you used this at the end of the week to fill out the fire boss reports?"

"Ummmm…sure."

"I've read what fire boss documents I could find in the company records, and they all report conditions in the mine were safe. Were they accurate?"

She waited for a full moment, staring at the wall in the back of the office. Then she shifted her steel gray eyes, so they moved all around the table as she talked.

"This is an important moment," she said very slowly. "You have your chance right now to tell me what was going on and be free of any criminal charge in connection with the falsification of records. Or you can keep on going like this and find yourself charged with perjury before the board of a state agency. That's money and jail time, I would add. I'm going to give you a little time to talk about this, and then I'll come back. But I want a clear answer then. Make certain you all agree on it. If I don't hear what I need to hear, I'm going straight to the District Attorney and recommending charges against each one of you."

"I've got them," she thought to herself as she left the room.

She was right about that.

"Who the fuck does she think she is?" one of the men said after she left the room. "I'm not going to be talked to like by that a woman. I say we say nothing. Fuck them if they want to know what happened. That bitch."

"I don't know," said another of the men.

"She seemed pretty specific about what she wanted to know. Remember, they're here trying to find out why so many of our friends died that way. I think we should just open up and tell them.

"We all know that the people told us not to take any of that too seriously, that gas-reading stuff. Hell, half the davy lamps we used didn't work at all. They just wanted to keep the mine going best they could so no one would lose any money. Can't blame them for that. But we shouldn't be the ones to blame for that kind of stuff. It was bad management, and you all know that...."

"Yeah, but I still don't like the way that Harrisburg woman talked to us. No respect, nothing, looking down her nose at us. She comes in here with a bunch of inspectors, good guys for the most part who have done the work, who know what they are doing, and ask questions of us?"

"Who does she think she is?"

That answer became apparent 15 minutes later when Valery walked into the room with Detective Howard, his badge and pistol showing, and Finn at her side.

She introduced them both as being representatives of the Bureau of Mines in the Pennsylvania Commerce Department and added Howard was a State Police detective working with the bureau.

333

She offered a very brief summary of what transpired and then asked the men if they had agreed on what to say about their role as fire bosses.

"We have," said one of the men.

"I know it's going to sound bad for us, but we never did much of anything about anything we found in the mine. We had to walk the site two times a day by law, but there were no regulations about writing things down or keeping records over time, and the mining company people said that was just all state bullshit; pardon me, ma'am, so why bother. Hell, most of the records got blown up over in Cessna a couple of weeks ago when those guys tried to explode that safe."

"Who moved the records from here to Cessna," Valery asked, her gray eyes settling again on the men around the table."

"Management," one of them answered. "We don't know why. Didn't bother us because we were not using them anyhow…."

"At that, she softened her tone and told the men to have some more coffee and donuts. The tense mood in the room lifted, and the men all went to get their coffee and donuts. Finn and Valery, and Howard stayed to talk with them for a bit. That was where Finn learned the mining company people had no interest in anything that slowed the process down. Every shovel of bituminous was like a shovel full of dimes for them. They didn't want anything to get in the way of that.

Finn had seen this so many times over the years that it ceased surprising him. Miners, their bosses, and their bosses' bosses were in it to make a dollar, and they didn't care a bit about how that happened as long as coal kept moving. Even now, the officers were asking how soon the Coalman mine could reopen. Finn was still shaking at one of the answers from one of the executives, a man who was supposed to walk through the mine each morning with an anemometer to make certain the air was flowing.